CROSSING THE LINE

CAITLYN ARMISTEAD

Flashover Press

FLASHOVER PRESS

This Flashover Press paperback edition March 2016

Cover art by DanSun

ISBN: 978-1311459497 (ebook)
ISBN: 978-0692619919 (paperback)

DEDICATION

To listening ears and comfortable silence,
To warm, fresh wind that wrinkles the tree's leaves,
To good food and friends' laughter and a hand to hold
in the darkness.
But mostly to you.
May you have all those things.
And if you have lost them, may you find them once more.

CONTENTS

Chapter One

EMS Station 1 was the largest station in the Barrington County system. Nestled under the Sacred Heart Hospital parking garage, it boasted a duty room with lightly stained recliners and a break room with a working microwave. The business office windows displayed the hospital's new cancer wing, and the lockers in the locker room closed most of the time.

Megan leaned against the locker room wall. "Where's Emily?"

"Doctor put her on bed rest," Richard said, pinning the month's schedule to the bulletin board.

Megan straightened. "Is she okay? She's not due until June!"

"Seems to be," he said. "Her blood pressure spiked. If she comes back, they'll put her on light duty behind a desk. She won't be on the ambulances again until after she delivers the baby."

Megan folded her arms warily, and Richard avoided her eyes. Emily's absence begged the question. "Who's subbing for her?"

Richard opened his locker. "There's no sub." He shrugged on his jacket. "We've made a five-month personnel change to cover her maternity leave."

Megan caught the locker door as he tried to close it. "Who's my partner?"

"Nathan Thompson."

"That soldier guy with one leg?" she sputtered. "Are you kidding me?"

Richard held up his hand. "Don't start, Megan." He slammed his locker and walked into the hallway.

She grabbed her jacket and strode after him. "Why do I always get the newbie?"

"He has combat experience, and he's been here three months," Richard said. "He's not a newbie."

Megan rolled her eyes. "But he was a mercy hire. The last thing I need is for something to go down on scene and I get left holding the bag because some poster boy for disabled vets can't handle his end of the stretcher!"

Richard turned the corner and stopped short. Megan swung around. Her eyes locked with a tall man, stern and silent. His broad shoulders filled his red Barrington EMS polo shirt, and his chest tapered to a trim waist. He braced his hands on his hips. A muscle twitched in his jaw.

"Nathan," Richard said with a simpering smile. "We were just talking about you."

Nathan glared. "I heard."

Embarrassment crept into her cheeks.

"Yes. I—Well," Richard stammered. "This is your

partner, Megan Henderson."

Nathan offered his hand, and Megan shook it. His grip was firm. His brown eyes betrayed no emotion.

She looked away. "Nice to meet you," she muttered.

"Charmed."

Nathan brushed past and continued down the hallway. Megan turned to stare at his back and sighed as the awkwardness abated.

Richard sucked a tooth. "You two should have fun today."

She scowled. "Seriously, you can't find me anyone else?"

"No."

"Where are we posted?" she said, shoving her hands into her pockets.

"Station 6, like usual. Stay safe."

Megan nodded and walked away. "That'd be easier if you had my back," she grumbled, slamming her palm onto the door and entering the ambulance bay.

Nathan slung his backpack into the ambulance.

"We need to check supplies," Megan said, resigned to her fate.

A thrill-a-minute chore with Wonder Boy.

"Already did."

Megan raised an eyebrow. "You did?"

"I'm not an idiot. We only need a backboard." He walked toward the supply room.

Hoping to underscore her authority, Megan climbed into the driver's seat. She cranked the engine and charted the mileage. The singer on the radio crooned about his honky-tonk lady until Megan slapped the knob. A flash in the side view mirror caught her attention, and she stared at Nathan's muscular arms as he carried the backboard to the truck. She leaned on the door for a better look.

At least he's hot. He looks like a swimmer.

Squinting her eyes, she detected a slight limp, a small favoring of his left side.

Megan climbed out of the cab and felt a twinge of remorse for her comments. "I'm sorry I said what I did."

"No, you're not." He shoved the backboard into the side compartment.

Megan's anger flared. "You're right. I'm just sorry you heard."

"That's the truth." He slammed the cargo door and folded his arms. "I know what people say about me. I saw you staring in the mirror, and I don't give a damn what you or anyone else thinks. I can out run, out climb, and out work anyone in this service, including you."

"I have to be able to depend on you," Megan said. "I have to know that when I need you, you aren't going to trip over your own—" She cut her words short but saw the challenge on his face. "Trip over your own feet."

"Foot. I only have one." Nathan pulled up his left pant leg and revealed the metal pylon that extended from his boot to the socket that fit just below his knee. "Take a good, long look, Megan. Let's get this over with. It's hard to hear about how I'm such a big liability from a…" he stepped back and considered her, his eyes roving down her figure, "21-year-old, five-foot-three, 130-pound female."

Megan glowered. "120."

Their radios screeched a loud tone.

"You're not 120 pounds," he chuckled.

His laugh crushed her last nerve. "I'm 23!" she said. "You're being—"

The dispatcher's voice spoke from the radio. "Med 3, be en route to Harrison and Monroe, Harrison and

Monroe, signal 4."

Megan tipped her head to her mic. "10-4."

Nathan smirked. "What were you saying?"

"Get in. I'm driving."

With Megan at the wheel, they drove code 3—lights and sirens—through town. Traffic moved to the side to allow them to reach the signal 4, a car wreck. To avoid talking, she pretended the drive required all of her focus. To her relief, he accommodated her silence.

At least he's not a pest.

Fire trucks and police cars clogged the intersection ahead. Megan scanned the area and pulled to the side of the road.

"The driver of the ambulance," she said, carefully avoiding the derogatory term 'ambulance driver,' "assists the person who rides in the passenger seat, so I'll assist you. I'll be watching your technique and therapeutic rapport. Follow protocol, and show me what you've got."

He smiled as he put on his gloves, further rankling her.

Megan slid the stretcher from the back of the ambulance and set the backboard on top as Nathan pulled the jump kit over his shoulder and walked toward the smashed cars. She wheeled to the scene.

"Martin!" she called to a firefighter. "There's only one patient?"

A man in bunker gear and a red helmet grinned and strutted over to her. His black eyes sparkled mischievously. "Hey, Doll! Yeah, just one. Head hit the windshield. It's not bad, just bloody. Where's Emily?"

Megan scowled. "She's on bed rest now."

"Sorry to hear that."

"Yeah, I was, too," she said, missing her friend and long-time partner more than ever. "Now I'm stuck with

Nathan Thompson."

"Is that so bad?" Martin said. "He's been around a while. Seems competent."

"Don't remind me. I want to be angry."

He winked. "You're beautiful when you're angry."

"Still married, Martin," she said, smiling in spite of herself. "I'm still married."

He wiggled his black mustache. "You just let me know when that changes, Doll, and I'll be first in line. Is that a new ponytail holder you're wearing?"

"Go away, Martin," she laughed.

Megan rolled the stretcher to the mangled car where Nathan knelt next to the driver's side. The woman's head and torso were covered in congealing blood and little glass squares from the side window. A glass spiderweb rippled across the windshield where her head had impacted. A firefighter, who had curled himself into the backseat, held the woman's neck still.

Nathan wrapped a collar around the woman's neck. "We're going to move you to a backboard now."

Megan watched him work, searching for mistakes and admitting he had made none. He was thorough and attentive. His motions were firm but gentle. She felt her resolve melting. He seemed to be the well-trained paramedic everyone said he was.

Megan moved to help, and they inched the woman onto the board and slid her into place, securing the straps. The board wobbled, and the woman flung her arm out, smearing blood and glass crumbles onto Megan's shirt.

First call, and I already need a clean shirt.

Nathan strapped the board to the stretcher as Megan stepped away to brush glass from her stomach and chest.

"Here, let me help you," Martin said eagerly.

She jumped away. "Touch me, and I'll slap you with battery charges so fast your lawyer will have to fly a Concorde to keep you out of jail."

His black eyes twinkled. "I love it when you talk dirty to me, Doll."

With a smile, Megan shook her head and followed Nathan to the ambulance. She slammed the doors after him and climbed into the cab, waiting for his signal and then easing into traffic.

So, he's not an idiot.

Megan released a bit of her hostility, reassuring herself that she did not have to like him, only work with him. But she tucked away a generous portion of her reservations. The shift was still young.

At the hospital, Nathan reported to the receiving nurse and washed his hands.

"Go ahead and restock the truck," Megan directed. "I need to clean up."

"Sure. Should I call 10-8 and let dispatch know we're ready?"

"Yeah, I won't be long."

Megan walked through the sliding doors of the Sacred Heart Emergency Room, jumped down off the ambulance dock, and walked down the hill to Station 1. Grabbing an extra shirt from her locker, she went into the bathroom, careful to lock the door and test the knob twice. She pulled the soiled shirt over her head and stood before the mirror in her bra. Turning slowly from side to side, she stared at the purple, green, and yellow bruises on her chest.

MILE MARKER 6, HIGHWAY 42
APRIL 12, 2013. 10:30 PM

Nathan squinted in the flash of red and blue lights as he climbed out of the ambulance. He scanned the scene: traffic stop, medical assist.

Probably a drunk. No big deal.

He threw the jump bag strap over his head and across his chest and snapped gloves on. Megan walked next to him. He had heard much about her in his few months with Barrington County EMS. Supervisors had described her as a 'dependable presence' on scene; others had said she was nice to work with; a few had called her bitchy. Most had commented, more or less colorfully, on her figure. But all had spoken with respect and mentioned her compassion. She helped cover others' shifts when hardship hit. She would buy groceries for shut-in patients and spend extra time at assisted living facilities, talking with the residents. She was known to return insult with kindness and a smile.

He chuckled at that.

They had each dished out fair return to the other throughout the day, but even so, he suspected there was more to Megan Henderson than the gruffness he had seen. Already, she had dialed back the strut in her step and the bite of her words.

They walked toward a group of police officers that stood talking by the side of the highway.

"About time you showed up," a blond police officer called. Nathan didn't like his tone, and when the cop flipped his hair like a surfer at the beach, it set Nathan's teeth on edge.

"What do you want, Todd?" Megan said.

"Girl, you know what I want," Todd said. Nathan

expected snickers from the other officers, but they only watched as Todd and Megan continued to the patrol car.

Nathan trailed after them, watching Megan's long, brown ponytail bob back and forth. The advanced reports of her good looks were not exaggerations. She was easy on the eyes.

Megan and Todd stopped by the car. Nathan's gaze slid to the escaped curls at the nape of her neck, continued along her shoulder, and then dropped to her hips. Her cargo pants were too baggy to form to her legs, but her smooth waist was highlighted by the regulation black web belt. She put her hands on her hips, and he easily noticed her curves. Were she unwed, she would be on his radar.

Todd cleared his throat.

Nathan looked up to Todd's angry disapproval.

What the fuck? Why does he care if I check her out?

Nathan glared back, undaunted.

"Guy I arrested says he's having chest pain," Todd said.

"And you left him in your car?" Megan said.

"He's faking."

Megan frowned. "Let me decide that. Next time, you keep an eye on him." She stepped to the car.

"I'll keep an eye on you," Todd said and smacked Megan's ass. She jumped, and Nathan blinked with surprise. He waited for her explosion.

"Don't," she said.

Todd laughed and caught her waist, pulling her toward him as if for a kiss.

Megan ducked. "Stop it!"

Nathan shouldered his way between them. "Cut it out. She doesn't want you to do that."

"She doesn't want you to do that!" Todd mocked.

Nathan stepped closer. Had Todd been two inches

taller, they would have been nose to nose. "Leave her alone," Nathan growled.

Todd sneered. "You need to mind your own business."

"Can I just see my patient, please?" Megan asked.

Nathan held Todd's gaze, willing himself not to blink. Todd looked away, and Nathan stepped back.

That's right, punk. Do your job.

Todd opened the back door, hefted out a middle-aged man, and leaned him on the side of the car. The man's hands were cuffed behind his back. His skin was pale, his eyes wide, and his face sweaty. Nathan realized the man was very ill.

"How do you feel, sir?" Megan asked.

"My chest. It hurts," he wheezed. "I have heart problems."

"How long has this been going on?"

He coughed. "Two hours or so."

"We'll get the stretcher," Megan said to Todd. "I want to hook him up to the monitor."

Todd jerked the man forward. "You heard the lady. Let's go." He strode to the truck as the man hobbled at his side.

"I said we'd get the stretcher!" she called after them.

"Hey!" Nathan shouted.

"Too late," Megan said. "They're in now."

Nathan touched Megan's elbow. "Are you going to be okay with that cop in the back of the ambulance?"

She tossed her head. "Psh. I'll be fine. Why?"

"He's a jerk."

Megan laughed. "Tell me how you really feel." She walked to the ambulance.

Nathan caught up with her. "I'm not kidding. I'll take the patient if you want me to."

"You just want the cardiac."

"I don't care about the cardiac," he said. "That jerk cop was getting fresh with you."

She grabbed the door handle and looked back at him. "That jerk cop is my husband."

Thunderstruck, Nathan raised his eyebrows as she climbed into the truck. He put his sound foot on the back step and lifted the other up next to it, trying to make the movement as smooth as possible.

Todd connected the handcuffs between the patient's wrist and himself and plopped onto the bench alongside. Megan climbed over him, ignoring his grope of her leg, and moved around the stretcher. As she interviewed the patient and placed the pulse oximeter on the patient's finger, Nathan wrapped the blood pressure cuff around the patient's arm. The machine whirred as the cuff inflated. He attached the 12-lead heart monitor.

Megan opened a nasal cannula and attached the tubing to the wall. "Sir, I'm going to give you some oxygen to help you breathe," she said, slipping it over his ears.

Nathan pointed to the bags of intravenous solution. "You want Lactated Ringer's or saline?"

"Saline," she said. "Sir, my partner's going to start an IV line."

Nathan pointed to the IV supplies by the jerk cop. "Give me that bucket."

Todd huffed and handed it to him. Nathan peeled open an IV pack and unrolled the tourniquet.

Megan handed the patient some pills. "Chew these, sir. It's aspirin."

She studied the blipping green line on the screen. "Heart rate 40," she murmured as she withdrew her keys from her pocket and unlocked the med box. "90 over 60," she said when the blood pressure cuff hissed. She put her stethoscope in her ears and listened to his breath sounds.

"You've got a line," Nathan said as blood flashed into the IV tube.

"Just enough fluid to keep it open, please," she said, looping her stethoscope back around her neck. He allowed the fluids to drip, and she moved beside him holding a medication syringe. "Sir, I'm going to give you some medicine for your heart." She met Nathan's eyes. "Pushing atropine. Let's move."

Nathan jumped out the back of the ambulance and jogged around to the driver's seat. Buckling his seatbelt, he opened the small window between the cab and the box. He eased the truck out onto the highway, listening to the conversation in the back in case he needed to upgrade to lights and sirens.

"So you're stuck with Peg Leg for five months," said Todd's voice.

"Don't call him that! Be quiet now. I have to work."

FIRE STATION 6
APRIL 13, 2013. 2:30 AM

Fire Station 6 was dark when Nathan backed the ambulance into the bay. He killed the engine and rubbed his face, his eyes stinging from fatigue. His first day on C shift had been one call after another.

"I'm exhausted," Megan groaned. "Have you stationed here before? Do you know where everything is?"

He grabbed his bag. "Yeah, I'm good."

The EMS room was separated from the fire station by the truck bay. Megan unlocked the door and stepped into the darkness. Nathan leaned on the doorframe. The air smelled of CaviCide disinfectant and stale Chinese food. Her keys jangled against a table as she fumbled with the lamp, and he wondered why she didn't flip on the overhead light.

When the lamp finally clicked on, he followed her into the room. It was small, especially compared to the fire department side of the station. A table with three chairs sat near the window that looked out to the truck bay. Two recliners had been crammed into the corner in front of a television, and a bunk bed lined the wall. Megan retreated into the bathroom.

Nathan stood in the center of the room. It was awkward being alone with a new partner. He was unfamiliar with her habits and levels of neatness and modesty, or the lack thereof. Dropping his bag, he sank into a recliner and raised the footrest as he listened to her brush her teeth. He flipped on ESPN and watched the recap of the Braves vs. Washington Nationals baseball game he had missed.

Megan left the bathroom, and Nathan kept his eyes trained on the TV. It was her turn to stand disconcertedly in the middle of the room.

"Um?" she mumbled.

He turned his head to her. Her hair fell freely down her back, and she held her boots.

"I usually sleep on the bottom bunk, but if you need it …" Her voice trailed away, and she lifted her shoulders.

Nathan kicked the recliner's footrest so that the chair popped back into an upright position. Striding to the bunk bed, he launched himself to the top bunk.

"Listen," he said, swinging his legs over the side and leaning his elbows on his knees. "If—"

"I was just trying to be nice!" she interrupted.

"That wasn't nice. That was patronizing." He leaped down next to her. "I want you to assume my ability. Assume I can do anything you can. Isn't that what you want from them?" he said, pointing toward the fire department side of the station.

She nodded.

"Do that for me," he said. "I'll let you know if I can't handle something, but I've been with this service for three months and Retton County for six, and I have yet to find anything I have a problem with."

Megan sat on the bottom bunk and dropped her boots. "You work for Retton County? Do you like it?" She pulled off her socks.

Nathan noticed her pink toe nail polish before she tucked her feet underneath her. "They're good people."

"Are they hiring?"

"Yeah. Why? Are you looking for something else?"

"I'm not leaving here. I just want a second job."

He turned off the TV. "You ready for lights out?"

"Yeah. Thanks."

In the dark, Nathan shuffled to the bed and climbed onto the top bunk. "Why do you want a second job?" Lying on top of the covers, he rested his arms behind his head.

The bed frame shook as Megan slid under her blanket. "Have you ever noticed how there are so few older paramedics? I mean, sure, there's Jerry—I think his first ambulance was drawn by horses—and Mark and Patty are fantastic medics, but most are just younger?"

"Yeah."

"This isn't a forever job. Not without a degree. I've got to think ahead, you know? I want to go back to college, and I need money for that."

Her voice was soothing. He stared at the ceiling and

pictured her in his mind. "What will you study?"

"I don't know."

"Fair enough."

He waited for her response, but it never came. The room was quiet; only cricket song broke the silence. He found it difficult to sleep in his prosthetic, but he always kept it on while on duty. He hated when people saw his residual limb. Other soldiers in his rehab program had seemed confident, almost proud, of their limb loss. They had worn shirts with sayings like, 'Go, go, gadget leg,' or 'You should have seen the shark,' or 'You've got me stumped.' But Nathan, in his Army unit t-shirt, had kept to himself, only sharing his difficulties with a counselor and his civilian buddy, Sam.

Megan's breathing was slow and even. Nathan carefully rolled to his side, trying not to shake the bed and wake her. The darkness pressed around him, making visions of the past sharper and clearer.

Chapter Two

TWO YEARS EARLIER
NANGALAM, PECH DISTRICT, KUNAR PROVINCE,
AFGHANISTAN
12 APRIL 2011. 0650 ZULU

Sergeant Nathan Thompson sat at a plywood table in the barracks and examined his rifle's star chamber.

Still dirty.

He stretched his back and took up the cotton swab once more.

Specialist Lowell walked in and dropped to his cot. "It's clean, Doc."

"You can tell from over there?" Thompson said and puffed air into the chamber.

"You're wasting your time."

Thompson turned around and held up the blackened swabs. "There's carbon in it."

"Still wasting your time," Lowell said, with a sly smile. He lay back on the blanket, rested an arm behind his head, and propped his boot on his knee. He fanned his face with a piece of paper. Thompson turned back to his rifle.

"You're wasting time you could be using to read this letter," said Lowell.

Thompson's head snapped up. "A letter?"

"It's got girly writing on it. Heather Shipley, 97 Primrose Court—"

Grinning, Thompson pushed away from the table and vaulted across the room. "Give me that!"

Lowell jumped up laughing and hurdled over the cots. "I bet there's naked pictures in there!" He held up the envelope to the bare light bulb. "You gonna share if there's pictures?"

"Fuck, no!" Thompson yelled and lunged for the letter.

Lowell hooted and punched him. "It's probably—"

"Mine!" Thompson tackled him and seized the letter. Lowell punched him once more before leaving the room, his laughter echoing through the hall.

Thompson tucked the letter safely into his pocket and put his rifle back together. Sitting on his cot with his back against the wall, he crossed one boot over the other. He felt a little silly, like a kid away at camp. He studied his name, the APO, and her return address, all written in bubbly handwriting. Warmth filled his chest.

Paper instead of e-mail. Nice touch.

He slit the envelope.

Dear Nathan,
This is really hard to write. You've been gone a long time. I've changed, and I just don't feel the same way about you anymore. I've met someone really nice. You're a good man, and I know you'd want me to be happy. When you get back,

maybe I'll see you around.
Thanks for the good times,
Heather

Shock pounded his heart. Thompson read the letter twice more and scrambled for his phone.

"Hey, this is Heather! Leave me a message."

Words caught in his throat, and he pressed the end button.

Text, just text.

NATHAN THOMPSON: I got your letter. Do you really mean that?

He tossed his phone on the bed and ran his hands over his head, the stubble of his high and tight rough against his palms. His phone vibrated.

If she was there for the text, why didn't she take my damn call?

HEATHER SHIPLY: yes i mean it
NATHAN THOMPSON: Let's talk about this. I'll call you. We can talk now.
NATHAN THOMPSON: Please.
HEATHER SHIPLEY: no. plz dont call any mor

This isn't happening. This can't be happening.

He read the letter again, wiping his nose on the back of his hand.

Thompson crushed the letter and stormed from the barracks. The smell of burning shit turned his stomach. An Afghan National Army soldier monitored the burning of the day's waste, wielding a stirring stick and kindling paper. Thompson threw the letter into the flames and stalked away from the miasmic smoke. He looked up at the mountains, one jagged ridge after another, after another. As if God had raked His fingers through the rock. And turned His back.

Lowell fastened his helmet for patrol. "You okay?"

Thompson lifted his body armor over his head and rested it on his shoulders. "Heather left me."

"What? That sucks, man."

"She sent a fucking letter," Thompson said, pulling on a strap. "Didn't even call to tell me with her own voice."

Lowell scowled. "What a bitch."

Thompson bristled at Heather being called a bitch, but he reminded himself she was not his girl anymore. His heart sank lower. "All I want is a girl who's loyal. I guess that's too much to ask."

Lowell shook his head. "When I get back, all I want is a girl. I don't care what kind. And lots of beer. Loyalty later." He slapped his hand on Thompson's shoulder. "Forget her, man."

"Yeah." Thompson secured his helmet and sighed.

Sgt. Thompson and Spc. Lowell joined up with six other American soldiers, an interpreter, two Afghan National Army soldiers, and one Fucking New Guy. Thompson tried to pay attention during the briefing, but it was the same old information. He kept seeing Heather's smile, her strawberry blond hair, the dimple he had loved to kiss.

They left the wire. Thompson followed Lowell down the road, rifle at low ready across his chest and resting on his gear. It had rained the day before, and the mud sucked at his boots. The road needed grading again.

A wall separated the road from a field of knee-high corn. Field followed field, merging into a green smudge in the distance. At the valley's edge, the fields terraced into the mountain, creating stripes up the summit where mist swirled around the peak.

A motorcycle with a coughing engine zoomed by. Lowell waved, but the rider ignored him. The locals never acknowledged the soldiers. Women passed with lowered eyes. Men walked in stony silence, their faces as drawn and grizzled as the mountains. Thompson stared at their henna-dyed beards, wondering how Kool-Aid red could be seen as dignifying.

A boy with a long, thin stick in his hand shooed cows down the road near the wall. He ran to the FNG. "*Sharana! Sharana!*"

"Uh, yeah," he nodded. "Cow. Moo."

The boy held out his palm and shook it. "*Sharana!*"

The interpreter laughed. "He wants candy."

"I got some. I got some," Lowell said, digging in his gear. He tossed the kid two butterscotches and a Tootsie Pop. The boy grinned and raced after his cows.

The team walked past mud huts stacked one on top of the other. Constructed of formed blocks and rocks from the countryside, the huts clung to the mountain, defying gravity and anything else that would attempt to tear them down, a mirror of the people who lived within them.

The soldiers reached the wall's end and trekked across a small field toward the river. A snake raced away, parting the new grass. Thompson made a mental note to put up more plastic in the barracks. If the snakes were out, then it wouldn't be long before they attempted to hunt the mice under his cot.

The bank was strewn with boulders. Trees cast deep

shadows, raised the humidity, and dropped the temperature a few degrees. Though the mercury only hovered at 70, the 60 pounds of heavy gear Thompson carried as a combat medic pulled enough sweat to soak his shirt. His legs ached. His shoulders hurt. Listening to the rush of the water, he checked for snakes and then rested on a boulder.

He had met her at a party. Mesmerized by the gleam in her eyes and the swing of her hips, he had danced with her until early morning. After that first night, they had been inseparable. They had shared a love for the outdoors and spent hours kayaking, canoeing, and geocaching together. But hiking had been their passion. They had bought matching gear and hiked every trail they could find: flat lands, piney woods, grassland, mountains, camping along the way. He was saving money for a through-hike of the Appalachian Trail upon his return stateside.

They had shared their hopes and dreams. Planned their future. He had met her family, taken her little brother fishing, shaken hands with her dad. She had blushed when she first saw him in uniform and had kissed him tearfully when he left.

What am I doing here?

"Come on, Doc," Lowell called. "Snap out of it."

Thompson shrugged but made no move to stand. "I was gonna buy a ring when I got stateside."

"You've got more life to live before you tie the knot, man." Lowell spat on a rock.

Thompson watched the spittle ooze down the rockface.

The group moved on, picking their way up the bank and toward another road. This one had better drainage than the first. The sand and gravel were dry and dusty, and his boots crunched as he walked.

A rooster crowed in the village ahead and was echoed by two others.

Lowell laughed ruefully. "They lied to me."

"Who lied to you?" Thompson asked.

"Everyone. My entire life I thought roosters only crowed when it was time to get up. But they crow all the fucking time. If I never hear another damned rooster, it'll be too soon."

Thompson kicked a rock. "I should have Skyped more. I should have called."

"Naw, man, you've been busy. We're fighting a fucking war here. A chick like that would have left you anyway. It's just the way some are."

"We're not fighting a war," said Thompson. "We're humping gear up a mountain or giving out candy or cleaning weapons. Nothing ever happens."

"Shut up, man. Don't say that."

"I'm tired of waiting. Just let me fucking do something."

"Yeah," Lowell said. "It's the quiet that messes with your head."

She sat on the wall, the Afghan girl. Her leg dangled over the side, her loose shalwar trousers pulled up just enough to reveal her bare ankle and the curve of her calf. She was too womanly to be a child, too brazen to be married. She met his eyes and smiled, a dimple forming near her mouth. A dimple like Heather's. Her fingers, dusty and graceful, touched the edge of her white hijab.

It had been a long time since he'd kissed a girl.

Lowell brushed past.

Thompson elbowed him and nodded toward her. "Give her some candy."

Lowell smirked. "Why?"

"Hearts and minds."

"And ankles." Lowell dug out more candy and walked to the wall.

Blinding light.

Tangible silence.

Swirling, dusty blue.

On his back, Thompson looked at the sky.

What the fucking hell was that?

The rooster had stopped crowing. The river had stopped running. His boots did not crunch any more. Thompson rolled to his side. Noxious chemicals burned his nostrils. He tasted metal. His eyes burned.

Fucking gear! Where's my rifle?

A squealing buzz filled his ears. He shook his head, but it continued. Lowell lay face down on the dark red road.

The road's red. Shit! The road's red!

Thompson pushed himself up and fell back into the dust. He couldn't run. He couldn't stand.

Lowell!

Forearm over forearm, he dragged himself across the dirt.

His shoulders strained. Propelled him forward. Gravel, rocks, ceramic shards flayed his skin through torn shirtsleeves. Blood, sweat. Smear and soak. He touched a white cloth, now red. Tattered and torn.

A soldier and the FNG ran to him. They moved their mouths as if shouting, but he couldn't hear them over the buzz.

Get me to Lowell!

They understood. He looked down on Lowell's still form.

He's fucked up bad! Where's my tourniquet?

The FNG grabbed the release ring of Thompson's vest.

What the hell are you doing? I need that shit for Lowell!

Thompson punched the FNG.

His gear was gone. The road was gone.

Dust pelted him, and the throb of rotor blades pulsed through his chest.

Only a Chinook feels like that. Lowell needs a Chinook.

Thompson blinked.

Light.

A ceiling this time.

The buzzing had ceased, and disinfectant pricked his nose.

A woman's face hovered over him. "Welcome to Germany."

8735 PETERSON AVENUE, APT. 218
APRIL 13, 2013. 1:30 PM

Nathan backed into his apartment, his arms full of groceries. "Sam, catch the door."

"Hang on. Hudson's at bat." Sam took another handful of popcorn from the bowl next to the couch where he lay.

"What's the score?" Nathan called as he trudged to the kitchen and dumped the bags on the counter.

"Zero all, top of the second, two on base, two outs."

Nathan returned to the living room. "Man, you still didn't close the door!" He pushed it shut.

"My bad. Shallow left! Ugh!" A car commercial flashed across the screen, and Sam sat up.

Nathan eyed Sam's emergency room scrubs and radiology tech badge. "When's your shift? I thought you went in at eleven."

"I go in at three. Jessica's at the imaging conference, so I'm covering for her until eleven, then I'll be back in ER radiology until seven a.m. Nothing says 'weekend' like working a double." He grabbed a fistful of popcorn. "How was your first day of C shift?" he asked through extra butter.

Nathan shrugged. "Your burritos are thawing."

"Ooh!" Sam jumped off the couch and hurried to the kitchen. "Oh, scrumptious sustenance! Worry not that thine wrapper shalt grow moist with condensation!"

Nathan followed him. "Your relationship with your cholesterol logs is getting way too serious."

"Don't listen to him," Sam whispered to his frozen burritos. "He's just jealous." He threw them into the freezer as Nathan washed an apple. "So, really, how did it go? Who's your partner?"

"Megan Henderson."

Sam pursed his lips. "I know guys who'd kill for that."

"She's married."

"I know guys who don't give a damn about that."

Nathan frowned. "Well, I do. A spouse should be loyal. Megan's pretty—"

"She's beautiful," Sam interrupted with unfocused eyes.

"But she's—"

"Gorgeous."

"Would you be quiet and let me talk? She's off limits," Nathan said. "The shift was okay. She needs reeducation on prosthetics, but I think she'll get the message."

Sam dug through the grocery bags, wrinkling his nose at Nathan's protein bars. "You'll like her. She knows her shit. And considering how many kinds of shit there are in this world, that's saying something."

Nathan held his apple in his teeth and slid ground beef and eggs into the fridge. "She's all right. Todd's not."

"Her husband, Todd? I've never heard anything bad about him. The few times I've seen him in the ER he seemed cool enough."

Nathan took another bite. "He's a prick. She takes too much crap off him."

Sam clasped his hands together. "I love how you give marriage advice after knowing someone for twenty-four hours. You should have a talk show."

"I'd make more money doing that than being a paramedic. I'm not much on TV, though. Maybe a radio show."

"And just think of all the interesting crazy people who would call in for your help," Sam said, clapping Nathan on the shoulder.

Nathan shrugged. "So, exactly like being a paramedic, then."

"Yep, but you might score some free Braves tickets out of the deal."

"Where do I sign up?"

CAITLYN ARMISTEAD

Chapter Three

802 WILLOWMERE DRIVE
APRIL 25, 2013. 3:00 PM

Megan bounced into her kitchen and kissed Todd on the cheek. "I got the job in Retton County! They hired me on the spot!"

Todd opened a beer.

"I'll take my drug test in the morning," she continued, "and start work at 6:00 p.m. It might be a close shave sometimes to leave Retton County at 6:00 a.m. and be at Station 1 at 8:00 a.m., but I'll make it work. I can start classes in the fall." Her thoughts careened between new job jitters and programs of study.

He took a swig. "Glad you're happy."

Megan smiled. "Thanks." She was mildly surprised at his support. It pleased her, and she felt her confidence soar.

Todd belched. "And by next week you'll realize how hard it is to bounce two jobs off each other, and you'll give up this stupid idea."

Her spirit fell, and her smile faded. "It's not a stupid idea," she said quietly.

"It's a waste of money when you're just going to flunk out again." He set his beer on the counter and folded his arms.

"I didn't flunk out!" she cried. "I failed one course. And passed the next semester!"

He shrugged. "You can't work two jobs and go to school."

"I can! I can take as many online courses as possible and study during the slow times. I can do this."

Todd got a beer from the fridge and opened it. The spray splattered him, and he wiped his shirt. "You're just gonna blow a lot of money." He pointed at the sink. "Look at those dirty dishes! You already leave a mess around this damn house! With another job and school, you won't get anything done around here. You'll start screwing up at work, and then you'll come crying back to me."

She choked back her emotion and lifted her chin. "Oh, no, I won't. I'm going to be a...a—"

"You don't even know," he said with a smirk.

She faltered. "I want a better job."

"Aw, sure." He rolled his eyes. "No one would possibly want to work in public safety their whole life."

Megan blinked. "I didn't mean it like that."

He stepped closer, into her space. "You never do, do you? But it always comes back to bite you."

She looked away, feeling his breath on her face. "Stop being so negative all the time."

"Don't criticize me!" he shouted.

"You criticize me!" she countered, leveling her gaze with his.

Todd grabbed her forearm, his knuckles white. "Don't you talk to me like that."

Megan inhaled sharply at the pain. "Let go," she said, pulling against him.

He released her with a shove, and his beer splashed on

the floor. They stared at each other.

His eyes softened. Slowly, he brushed a strand of her hair behind her ear. "I wish you didn't make me so angry. I don't want to be like this."

"I know. I'm sorry." Megan looked at the beer in his hand and the one on the counter. "Why do you have two beers open?"

"I don't have—oh."

Megan's brow furrowed. "It's your memory again."

He grunted. "My memory is fine."

"Did you remember to pay the utilities bill?"

"Yes, I paid the damn bill!"

"Did you—"

"Shut up!" Todd raised his arm. Megan flinched. "Get out of here!" he yelled.

She fled to the porch, the screen door smacking behind her. She sat on the swing. A breeze blew across the mint and rosemary she and Todd had planted around the footpath. She breathed the herbal fragrance and kicked her feet off the porch boards, swinging back and forth and listening to the rhythmic squeak of the chain.

Todd had almost hit her again. But he hadn't, and that gave her hope. Maybe he never would again. She chided herself for her childish behavior. Her anger and yelling were only making things worse. She remembered the article she had read in an old *Better Decorating* magazine she had found in the station bathroom. 'It's unfair to expect your husband to change for you.'

I can only change myself, right? I can do better. I can fix this. If I don't make him angry, he won't hit me.

She clung to the moment when he had caressed her ear. She thought back over the years and smiled at the memories of his sweet kiss and gentle hands.

She had been sitting on the same swing, sipping raspberry tea from a mason jar. A police car had pulled into the driveway.

"What are you doing home?" she asked, setting down her drink.

Todd held up an envelope. "I stopped at the post office and got the mail."

Megan snatched the envelope and ripped it open. "I got accepted! I'll start EMT school next week!"

Todd kissed her and held her tightly. "I'm proud of you, Sunshine."

"Do you have to go back to work?" she said into his bulletproof vest.

He nodded and nuzzled her hair. "I've been out of zone too long already, but I wanted to be here when you opened it."

Todd held her hand as they walked to the police car. He kissed the shiny, new wedding band on her finger before sitting in the driver's seat. "I couldn't stop at both the store and the post office, so I picked these instead." He offered a little bouquet of goldenrod.

Megan smiled. "They're pretty. Thank you."

"They don't do you justice. I love you."

She had kissed him. "I love you, too."

2000 BLOCK CARTER ROAD
APRIL 27, 2013. 10:00 AM

Sirens blaring, Megan slowed the truck at the intersection, looking for approaching cars. They were on their way to a call for abdominal pain, and she reviewed a mental checklist of various differential diagnoses and treatments.

"Clear right," Nathan said.

She ran the red light and accelerated up the thoroughfare.

"What's with the turtleneck under your uniform shirt?" Nathan asked. "It's going to be eighty-something degrees today."

Megan's stomach turned. Her arms and chest were covered in new bruises, and she had covered them with the long sleeves. "It's chilly."

"Yeah, at six this morning, maybe. You're going to roast, that's all I'm saying."

"Thank you, Mother," she snapped.

He didn't press the issue, and she slowly relaxed her shoulders.

Megan parked the truck in front of a three-story apartment building. She shook her ponytail, ridding herself of irritation. Nathan grabbed the jump kit, and they stood on the sidewalk, looking up at the top floor.

"Why doesn't anyone ever have abdominal pain on the first floor?" he asked.

Megan grinned. "Studies show a positive correlation between a patient's weight and the height of the building."

The corner of his mouth, usually so serious, curved to a smile. It was brief, but she considered it a victory.

They walked past the fire truck, and Nathan punched the button on the elevator.

Martin leaned over the banister of the third floor. "Doll! Lift's broken!"

"Is there another?" Megan asked.

"Nope," he called. "Better bring a Reeves stretcher."

"Why not the stair chair?"

"Patient keeps passing out."

Megan closed her eyes.

"Go get it," Nathan said. "I'll head on up."

"But can you—" she began. Nathan scowled, and she bit back her words.

"Go," he said.

Megan went back to the truck, dug out the flexible stretcher, and hurried back up the stairs. Her initial concerns over Nathan's ability bubbled back to the surface.

There's no way he can do this. If he drops the patient, I'm gonna get sued.

The shabby room, crowded with firefighters, smelled of garbage and unwashed dishes. Tables and counters were littered with newspapers, cardboard shipping cartons, and pizza boxes. In the center of the room sat a rotund and blustering woman ringed by firefighters as if she were the subject of worship.

"My pills! My pills!" she moaned.

Megan placed the stretcher on the floor as Martin shuffled to her side.

He wiggled his eyebrows. "You look gorgeous, Doll."

"Still married."

Nathan pulled the blood pressure cuff from the patient's arm and looped his stethoscope over his neck. "Ma'am, calm down," he said, in his ever-level tone. "Slow breaths."

"Oh, my! Oh, my!" the woman wailed, fanning herself with her pudgy hands. "I need to go to the hospital! I must get my pills! My pills! I can't breathe! My hands are tingling!"

Megan and Martin exchanged knowing glances.

"Hand Nathan an ammonia inhalant," she said. "She's going to need it."

Martin did so just as the woman's head flopped to the

side and her shoulders slumped. Nathan cracked the vial and wafted it under her nose.

"Oh, my. Oh, dear..." she murmured.

"Let's get her on the stretcher," Nathan said. He heaved the woman to one side while Megan slid the stretcher under her and secured the straps. "Megan, stay on that side. What's your name?" he called to a firefighter.

She stepped forward. "I'm Carrie."

"Carrie, you get the other side. I'll get the feet. Martin at the head and call it."

Martin nodded. He squeezed Megan's shoulder reassuringly and took his place at the patient's head. "On three. One, two, three."

Megan lifted with the others. She could scarcely breathe from the exertion. They hobbled to the door. Megan and Carrie slipped through first, and Nathan and Martin carried the entire load through the doorway. The two women rejoined them, and the four walked together. Megan watched Nathan closely as he approached the stairs. He had not called for a spotter.

Show off.

She analyzed his movements for any sign of faltering. His jaw was clenched; his eyes flicked to hers and away again.

Assume ability.

She glanced at the sharply-descending stairs.

Yeah, right.

As Nathan stepped backward down the stairs, bearing the brunt of the weight, she wet her lips and prepared for the worst.

"Take it slow," Martin said.

She ignored the lurching of her stomach as they rounded the first landing. Their boots shuffled on the dusty floor, and she strained against the stretcher.

"Get the gurney ready!" Martin called in a herniated voice.

Nathan's face showed nothing of his thoughts. He exuded confidence as he controlled the descent of the stretcher. Megan glared at his unshakable demeanor.

One more floor.

Nathan reached the bottom and placed his end of the stretcher on the gurney. Megan and Carrie stepped aside, and as Martin placed the patient down, Megan released the breath she had been holding. Her relief over not falling to her death or dropping the patient or getting sued lessened the blow of her being wrong about Nathan.

She met his eyes as he fastened a strap.

"Assume I'm able," he said in a low voice only she heard. She conceded with a small smile, and when he responded with a half-smile of his own, she felt her cheeks warm and her heart quicken.

"Doll, you look overheated," Martin said. "Or have my strappin' good looks got you all hot and bothered?"

Megan turned away, flustered. "What? Oh," she laughed. "Martin, don't flatter yourself."

Martin rubbed his mustache. "That turtleneck is too much. You're going to pass out."

"It's fine."

"Well, at least pull your sleeves up," he said, reaching for her wrist.

Megan jumped back. "Concorde, Martin."

He held up his hands. "Whatever you say, Doll."

Nathan handled the patient while Megan drove to the hospital. Her stomach crawled at the idea of someone seeing her new bruises, of someone asking questions, of someone knowing.

Everything's fine. No one will find out. It's no big deal.

FIRE STATION 6
APRIL 27, 2013. 1:00 PM

Nathan unlocked the EMS room at Fire Station 6 as Megan closed up the truck. He flipped on the light and searched frantically for the TV remote. The Braves vs. Detroit Tigers game was about to start.

Tones dropped.

With a groan, he turned off the light and relocked the door.

"Med 3, be en route to mile marker 2 Warren Highway, mile marker 2 Warren Highway, signal 4."

"10-4," Megan's voice responded in the radio on his belt. "Nathan!" she called from the truck. "Let's go! This is far!"

Nathan jogged to the ambulance. With a final hop, he jumped into the driver's seat and cranked the engine.

"Geez, this is gonna be a hike," Megan said, hitting the lights and siren. "It's going to take us at least 25 minutes to get there. They'll call out the volunteers, if they haven't already." Traffic clogged the road in front of them. "Move out of the way, people! It's open over there."

"I see it." Nathan threaded through the cars and jammed the accelerator as they turned onto open highway.

The radio crackled. "Med 3, be advised that Warren Volunteers have called a trauma alert times one."

"10-4, trauma alert times one," Megan responded. She grinned. "Nice."

Nathan hit the brakes as they approached a car that refused to pull to the right.

Megan gripped the seat. "Pass him. Keep going."

Nathan pulled into the opposite lane. "I've got this," he said and flew past the car.

"Accelerate out of the curve."

"I know," he said, his irritation growing.

"Go faster at the straightaway."

Nathan tapped his fist on the steering wheel. "Unless you want me to pull over, shut up and let me drive."

Megan withdrew a pair of gloves from the center console. "Let me tell you how a trauma alert works on scene."

"I'm waiting with bated breath."

Let's hear it, Trauma Queen.

"We'll need two medics in the back," she said, "so Richard will respond to the scene, too. As supervisor, he'll decide who will drive. If we're working together well and have a good rhythm going—our rhythm, not the patient's—then he'll let us keep working, and he'll drive. If not, he'll pull one of us to drive. I'm the senior medic. He's not going to pull me."

He nodded slowly. "So, if I want to work the call, we have to work together."

Megan propped the toes of her boots on the dash. "I'm glad you see the dynamics. This all depends on you."

On me?

Nathan was faced with a decision: keep her happy or confront her skewed ideas. He risked a glance at her. Her hair draped over her shoulder, and the adrenaline lightly flushed her cheeks. The afternoon sunlight highlighted her hands as she flipped through a trauma reference app on her phone. It didn't seem wise to anger a beautiful woman, but he couldn't let her pile all the responsibility on his shoulders.

"It depends on me less than you think," he said.

She looked up. "What do you mean?"

"If we're going to be a team, you need to get off your high horse."

"Hey, I'm on your side!" she said, dropping her phone into her lap. "I didn't have to tell you that Richard pulls medics."

"No, and you don't have to tell me how to drive, or about stairs, or the bottom bunk. Now you're assuming we won't have a rhythm, and that I'm going to get pulled unless you tell me the right things to do. You're expecting me to fuck up on scene."

Megan waved her glove. "You are way too sensitive."

"Am I?"

She paused. "Arrogant, at least."

Nathan chuckled. In his peripheral vision, he could see her staring at him. She had fought his words, but he knew she had listened. He understood why men didn't care she was married. She was spunky, could pull her own weight, and didn't mince words. She was willing to help him succeed, even though he neither wanted nor needed her help. Her misguided kindness softened her rough edges.

Nathan blew the air horn and guided the ambulance around another car.

"All right," she said. "I'll give you a shot."

He smirked. "Oh, I'm forever grateful." He looked at her boots. "But I'm not wiping scuff marks off the dash."

"Who asked you to?"

He grinned and slowed the truck. The road ahead was filled with the cars of volunteer firefighters. Nathan slowed the truck and put it in park. "Looks like a family reunion."

"Without the salmonella salad or weird Uncle Phil," Megan said, opening the door.

A car had smashed into a tree. Firefighters swarmed the road such that Nathan could barely see a backboard resting on the asphalt. Megan walked toward the scene.

Nathan retrieved the stretcher and hurried after her. "How many firefighters does it take to—"

"Are they doing compressions?" Megan asked, walking faster.

A firefighter was kneeling beside the board with his arms locked straight, pumping the patient's chest. Another firefighter squeezed a cantaloupe-sized bag, breathing for the patient on the backboard while a third held the mask in place.

Megan knelt next to the firefighter who was bagging. "What have you got?"

"We pulled the guy from his car. He had a pulse like three minutes ago," the volunteer said, panic in his voice. "Now there's no pulse, no breathing."

Nathan dropped beside her and started cutting off the patient's clothes.

"Other injuries?" she asked, running her hands over the patient in a rapid trauma scan.

"I didn't see any. He was leaned over the steering wheel."

Megan pointed at a volunteer. "Henry, bring me the compression system." She pointed to two other firefighters. "You and you," she commanded. "Help us get him to the truck."

Nathan leaned toward her. "Traumatic arrest. We're working it?"

She leveled her gaze. "Witnessed arrest. You got a problem with it?"

"No," he said, measuring his tone. "Just making sure we've got rhythm."

She nodded. "You're on airway."

"Yes, ma'am." He thought it odd that she would not command the call from the airway position.

Nathan took over bagging the patient as Megan and the firefighters lifted the stretcher. Henry arrived with the compression system. Megan set it up, securing the patient's arms, and the machine took over compressions. They rushed to the ambulance and climbed into the back.

Richard walked around the end of the truck. As Megan hooked up monitors, Nathan felt the pressure of being watched. Grabbing the laryngoscope from the roll of intubation supplies, he steeled himself and placed the blade in the patient's mouth, lifting the tongue. He pulled back on the scope, inserted an endotracheal airway, and slipped it between the two white cords. Inflating the tube cuff, he unwound his stethoscope from his neck and stuck the earpieces in his ears to check the tube placement.

No abdominal sounds. Diminished breath sounds on the right. No breath sounds on the left.

He adjusted the tube, yet still did not hear breath sounds on the left. The patient's lung had collapsed.

"Airway in place," he said, attaching the bag. "No breath sounds on the left. Right diminished."

Megan paused the machine and watched the patient's heartbeat on the monitor.

"V. fib," she said. "I'm going to shock on three. One, I'm clear."

Nathan lifted his hands.

"Two, you're clear," she said. "Three."

The patient shrugged with the electrical shock.

Nathan looked at the monitor. The green line moved across the screen with a beat. He reached for the patient's carotid artery. "There's ... actually a pulse."

41

A little smile curved Megan's lips. "Sweet! We need to go, Richard. Now."

Richard nodded. "I'll drive." He jumped down and slammed the doors.

While Megan inserted a large-bore saline IV, Nathan percussed the patient's chest, striking one finger against another. The sound, barely audible with the noise in the truck, was hollow. He grabbed the bag again. It whined with each breath he gave. "Still no breath on the left," he reminded her. "It sounds hyperresonant. He needs decompression."

"Sir," she called to the patient, "I'm putting a tube in your arm. Big stick."

Nathan frowned.

She's crazy. He can't hear her. He's basically dead.

The ambulance turned around, tossing everything back and forth as the tires left the pavement and bumped back on. It rumbled onto the highway.

"Looks like V. fib again," Megan said.

"There's a lot of artifact from driving."

She reached to the patient's neck. "No pulse. Compressions."

Nathan leaned toward the window to the cab and slid it open. "Richard, pull over!"

"All right!" Richard called. "Damn, I didn't even get up to speed!"

As Nathan closed the window, the ambulance wobbled and jostled and slowed to a stop.

Megan stopped the compression machine. "Yep. V. fib," Megan said. She lifted her hands. "Shock on three. We're clear. Two, three." She pressed the button. The patient jerked. "No pulse." She started compressions once more and unlocked the med box. "Tell Richard to drive for a bit. I'm pushing epinephrine."

Resistance increased under Nathan's hands. "Megan, I've checked this tube. No sounds on the left. He's got a fucking tension pneumothorax. He needs decompression."

She pushed the epi. "Tell him to drive."

"Did you hear me?" Nathan asked. "You need to decompress."

She leveled her gaze. "No."

"Didn't they teach you how?"

"Yeah, but that doesn't mean we're actually supposed to do it." She dropped the syringe onto the counter and tied a tourniquet for a second IV.

Nathan was stunned. "Are you here to do emergency medicine, or do you just like wearing the uniform?"

"Advanced EMTs are taught combi-tubes," she said as blood flashed in the needle chamber, "but they never use them here because medics can drop ET tubes. Why should I decompress when the doc with a chest tube is," she glanced out the window, "20 minutes away?"

"Because he needs it now."

Megan popped the tourniquet and ran the fluids wide open. "I'm not decompressing," she said with finality. "Tell Richard to drive."

Nathan pulled his radio from his belt and clicked the knob on top. "Med Control, this is Med 3."

A female voice responded. "Go ahead, Med 3."

Megan's eyes widened.

"Approximately 45-year-old male with blunt force chest trauma from a single-car wreck. Lost pulse on scene under ten minutes ago. While in V. fib., received one shock at 200 joules with return of sinus rhythm. Two large-bore saline IVs on board. Pt. back in V. fib. Received one shock with no return of circulation. One milligram epi given. Breath sounds absent on the left side, diminished on right, with hyperresonance upon percussion. Neck veins distended, and oxygen saturation is falling. We are 20 minutes out. Do you copy?"

"10-4, I copy."

"Requesting permission for bilateral decompression," Nathan said, meeting Megan's eyes. She shot him daggers.

The radio fell silent.

"Med 3, identify yourself!" Medical Control demanded in a new, male voice.

"Paramedic Nathan Thompson, Army medic, retired."

Silence.

Nathan shook his head. "This is Mickey Mouse shit!"

Megan looked up from her reassessment. "No one decompresses. They're trying to figure out who the hell you are to even request that."

The radio crackled. "Med 3 secondary, identify yourself."

"Secondary," Megan muttered. She tipped her head to her mic. "Paramedic Megan Henderson."

"Secondary, do you agree with the findings?"

"10-4," Megan said.

"Secondary, do you support decompression?"

Their eyes locked. She took a deep breath. "10-4."

Nathan watched the oxygen saturation drop lower. He knew the chances of traumatic arrest survival were slim. The red tape decreased the odds every second. "We don't have time for this. In Nangalam, we would have been in and done by now!"

"This isn't Afghanistan!" Megan said, reaching over him to adjust the monitor. "I'm stretching the system to work this trauma at all! And we don't decompress!"

"Permission granted for needle decompression," said

Medical Control.

Nathan shook his head. He didn't want needle decompression; he wanted to be able to finger sweep the lung, to obtain proof of decompression that a needle couldn't give. "Requesting permission for simple thoracostomy over needle decompression."

"Oh, God," Megan breathed.

Nathan chewed the inside of his cheek.

The radio crackled. "Permission granted for bilateral simple thoracostomy, per Dr. Patterson."

"Roger," Nathan said and clipped the radio back onto his belt. "Watch the airway." He held onto the overhead bar while she shifted under him to the captain's chair. He rifled through the cabinet and pulled out a sealed plastic tray.

The window banged open. "What the hell's going on?" Richard bellowed as country music floated in. "Do I need to come back there?"

"No!" Nathan and Megan said together.

"Just get ready to drive. And don't worry," she said, dropping her voice into a calm, relaxed tone. "We've got it all under control." She slammed the window shut. "Buddy, you'd better rock this."

Nathan counted the patient's ribs. "No problem." He stopped compressions.

Megan placed her palm on the patient's forehead. "Sir, my partner's going to help you breathe."

Nathan paused. "You know he's unresponsive. He can't hear you."

"You don't know that," she said. "Wouldn't you want someone to talk to you?"

"I guess."

I'd rather they let me die.

Nathan put down the cleanser and took up the scalpel.

He touched the blade to the skin and cut into the patient's chest. Dropping the scalpel onto the tray, he placed the forceps and pushed his finger between the ribs. The tissue gave way. The trapped air released, and he felt the lung's spongy resistance.

Success.

Nathan restarted compressions and knelt on the stretcher's other side. He counted ribs and glanced at Megan as she bagged. She was leaning forward on the cot's edge, nearly obstructing his vision field.

"You know how to do this?" he asked.

"I read a book and saved a plastic person."

He smothered a laugh. "Want to do a real one?"

Her brows lifted. "Yes."

"Get over here."

As Megan knelt at the patient's side, Nathan stopped compressions and braced himself on the CPR bench. Space was tight. Her boot rested against his sound leg, and her hip bumped his prosthetic. He cringed. Though her closeness exhilarated him, he didn't want her to feel his prosthetic. He tried to shift away, but there was no room to move.

Megan prepared for the thoracostomy. Nathan expected nerves and questions, but she immediately counted ribs and cleaned the area. Her hand was steady as she cut with the scalpel, and she took up the forceps without hesitation. She slid the curved metal into the incision and paused.

"You should be far enough," he said.

She nodded and retracted the forceps. Blood flowed from the incision onto the stretcher and the floor. Nathan grabbed a towel and tossed it onto the growing puddle.

Megan pressed her finger into the site.

"Fat or lung?" he asked. He placed his hand on her shoulder and leaned to check the wound.

"Lung. I think?"

"Judging from the blood, probably so." He palpated the tissue. "Lung. Good job."

Megan looked at his hand, which still rested on her shoulder, and met his eyes. He quickly pulled back. "Sorry," he muttered, clearing his throat.

She looked away. "It's okay. I'll bag." She shifted back to the captain's chair.

Nathan placed his stethoscope on the patient's chest and heard air movement on the left side. The lung was functional again. "Excellent. Bilateral breath sounds, slightly diminished on the left side. Starting compressions." He pulled two packs of Vaseline gauze from the cabinet. Peeling open both packages, he covered the surgical wounds with the sticky packaging, and taped them down on three sides.

"Hold up on compressions," Megan said.

Nathan pushed the button. The green line moved in a ragged fashion.

"V. fib," she said. "Shocking on three. We're clear. One, two, three."

The patient shrugged with the shock, and the green line beat across the screen. Megan slid her fingers to the patient's neck. "A pulse!"

Nathan lifted his brow in surprise. "Really."

Megan hit the wall with her palm and opened the window. "Richard! Let's go!"

"It's about damn time!" he yelled. "You two are the slowest—"

She closed the window.

"Do you have a marker?" Nathan asked.

Megan patted her pants and handed it to him. "Here."

Nathan drew a circle around each incision and marked them with 'EMS.'

Minutes later, the ambulance beeped as it backed into the ER dock. They wheeled the man into the ER where Nathan gave report.

Dr. Patterson gave orders to the nurses and then clasped his hands behind his back. "Nathan, the nurses tell me you were in Afghanistan. I was in Desert Storm." He examined the decompression sites. "You two have done some excellent work here."

"Thank you, sir," Nathan said, feeling a moment of pride as he watched the nurses continue care. The respect on Megan's face didn't hurt either. He winked at her, and she smiled.

SACRED HEART AMBULANCE DOCK
APRIL 27, 2013. 2:00 PM

Megan's stomach growled as she buckled her seatbelt. "I could really go for the soup and salad place—it's pasta e fagioli day—but most guys I ride with prefer something like hamburgers, or whatever."

"Sounds good to me," Nathan said. "I stay away from fast food as much as I can. I want to keep everything I have left healthy."

Nathan parked in front of Stanley's Soupin' Salads. Megan dug in her bag for money and shoved a ten into her pocket. She was going to lunch with a handsome man and getting paid for it.

I love my job.

She slammed the door.

"Got what you need?" Nathan asked.

Brakes squealed. Metal shrieked as two cars hit head-on.

Megan gaped as she stared at the steaming cars. Traffic slowed as cars attempted to maneuver around the wreckage. Some drivers veered dangerously close as they rubber necked to see if anyone was hurt.

Nathan rubbed his chin. "We should do something about that."

"But my soup," she sighed.

He smiled his sympathy. "I'll call dispatch."

Megan stepped into the street, ready to work. "Wait! I don't have gloves. I don't have anything!"

Nathan's voice rumbled over the mic as Megan trotted to the truck and snatched the jump kit and gloves. She was edgy with hunger and arriving on a scene without the mental preparation that driving time usually afforded made her anxious and slightly confused. She forced herself to pause. Automatic recall.

Gloves on. Scene safe.

She scanned the scene, sizing it up. Two cars, each on all four tires. Steam rose from the hoods. Traffic now held itself at bay. Glass covered the asphalt, and ectoplasmic antifreeze oozed a green river across the road and into the gutter. She strode toward the mangled cars.

"Dat bitch!"

Startled, Megan slipped in the slime and landed hard.

A teenager raged around his crashed car. "Dat bitch fucked up my car!"

Strong hands lifted Megan up and set her on her feet. "Easy now," Nathan said, his breath on her ear. Butterflies sprang to life within her.

He strode past and confronted the teen. "Hey! Calm down!"

Megan touched her ear then quickly gathered her thoughts. She went to the other car. A matronly woman sat very still, her eyes blinking, her hands shaking. "I don't really know what happened," she said. "I just don't really know what happened."

Megan knelt beside her. "Is there anyone else in the car?"

"No, it's just me."

"How do you feel?" Megan asked, assessing quickly.

"My chest hurts, and my neck is sore. I just wish I knew what happened."

"You've been in a wreck. I think you should go to the hospital."

The woman nodded.

"Keep your head still. I'm going to put my hands here to help." Megan leaned into the car, placing her hands on the woman's neck.

"Then what?"

Megan smiled. "Then we wait."

Sirens drifted in the distance. Megan took advantage of the time by asking about the woman's medical history, grandchildren, and pets. But her arms soon grew tired of remaining in one position. Her toes prickled with numbness.

Megan heard footsteps behind her, and a sheriff's deputy squatted next to her. "What do you need?" he asked.

"I need my truck over here," she said. "Stretcher, backboard, collar. Nathan, if he's not busy."

"You got it."

"Thanks, Thomas," she said as he walked away. "I'll just … wait here."

I can't feel my knees.

Megan sighed when she heard the familiar rumble of the ambulance's diesel engine and the rattle of the stretcher.

"Let me take C-spine," Nathan said, kneeling. He leaned his shoulder over her arms and covered her hands with his. She smelled his laundry detergent as his shirtsleeve brushed against her cheek. "Got it," he said.

Megan eased around him and stomped her boots on the road to return feeling to her feet. She shaped the flat C-collar into its protective shape and leaned into the car again to fit it onto the woman's neck. Carefully, they placed the patient on a backboard and onto the stretcher.

"Nathan!" Deputy Thomas called.

"I've got this, if you need to talk to him," Megan said.

Nathan nodded. "I'll help you load the stretcher first."

They rolled the stretcher to the back of the ambulance. Megan hooked it on the floor and lifted the wheel carriage as Nathan slid it in.

"Set?" he asked. His intense brown eyes held her gaze. She couldn't find words to say. He nodded again and walked toward the deputy.

Megan blinked a few times and then climbed in. "You doing all right?" she asked the woman.

"I think so."

"I'm going to take your blood pressure."

Megan heard shouting outside.

"—that mudderfucker fucked up my car, and she all up in this amb'lance."

Megan spun to face the rear of the truck as the teenager stormed around the door.

"Stay back!" she shouted.

He mounted the step. "Man, I ain't—"

"Get out of my truck!"

"Dat bitch gone an—" He lunged into the ambulance.

"Get out of my truck!" Megan shouted.

They collided, her elbow striking his chest.

The teen stumbled back. Thomas ran around the door and grabbed the neck of the teen's shirt, yanking him down onto the pavement. Megan leaped to the doors and slammed them. Breathing hard from adrenaline and exertion, she turned around to see Nathan standing in the side door stairwell. He gave her a thumbs-up. She bashfully dipped her chin.

"What's happening?" the woman asked.

Megan looked up at him again. He was still watching her.

What is happening?

"Just closing the doors, ma'am," Megan said. "We're leaving now."

Nathan nodded. "Roger that."

SACRED HEART EMERGENCY ROOM
APRIL 27, 2013. 4:00 PM

In the emergency room, Megan slid her paperwork into the folder on the EMS desk.

"You're covered in antifreeze," Nathan said.

Megan turned herself in a circle, trying to look over her shoulder at her back. "It's fashionable. It's what all the paramedics are wearing now."

"Not all of them."

"Just the good ones," she quipped with a wink.

Megan walked down the hill to the Station 1. She retrieved her spare uniform from her locker and went to the bathroom to change. She peeled her dirty shirts off and froze.

I don't have another turtleneck.

Slowly, she dressed. Nausea settled in her stomach. She tucked in her polo shirt and brushed her hair into another ponytail. Lowering her arms, she stared at the splotches where Todd had bruised her. She had no way to hide the marks. She grabbed the trash bag that held her clothes and popped the lock on the bathroom door.

"You ready?" Nathan asked.

She avoided his eyes. "Sure. Call 10-8."

"No turtleneck? You might get chilled. I mean, it's only 84 outside." He pulled his radio from his belt as she threw the trash bag into her locker.

"Are you all right?" Nathan asked. "You're shaking. A lot."

She held her hands behind her back and tried to keep her shoulders still. "I'm fine. Let's go."

"No, you're hungry. We never ate." He clipped the radio back on his belt without using it. "You're not going 10-8 until you eat."

"I'll grab something from the machine. Richard will want us back on the road."

"You can, but you wanted soup and salad. There are four other available trucks right now, and Richard wouldn't want you to pass out on scene or make a medication miscalculation. Which is it? I promise I won't tell."

Her stomach growled, and her shoulders drooped. "Pasta e fagioli."

STANLEY'S SOUPIN' SALADS
APRIL 27, 2013. 5:00 PM

Megan ladled a steaming bowl of Stanley's pasta e fagioli. Walking carefully to a seat, she inhaled the aroma of thyme, oregano, and just a hint of basil. She began eating, feeling more human by the moment.

Nathan stood awkwardly next to the table, holding his tray of soup and salad. "Um, can I sit here?"

Megan lifted an eyebrow. "Yes? Why wouldn't you?"

"No, I mean, can I sit where you're sitting. Do you mind moving? I don't sit with my back to the door."

"Oh. Okay." Megan slid her tray across the table and went to the other side. She glanced over her shoulder toward the door, suddenly uneasy.

"The soup smells good. Great idea to come here," he said.

Megan blinked at the two huge mounds of salad and three bowls of soup on his tray. "That's a ton of food."

"I have a hollow leg."

She choked on her sweet tea.

Nathan grinned. "I swam yesterday, so I have to make up the calories."

Bingo. I knew he was a swimmer!

"What kind of swimming do you do?" she asked. "Are you competitive?"

His fork stopped on the way to his mouth. "Do you know about swimming?"

"Of course, I do," she said. "I watched the Olympics."

Nathan chuckled. "Name one swimmer other than Michael Phelps."

"Um." Megan tipped her head. "Well, see, he was why I was watching the Olympics." She lifted her chin. "Just like every decent, red-blooded, American woman."

"No judgment here," he laughed. "For all my watching, I can't name a single beach volleyball player." He wiped his mouth on his napkin. "I'm not competitive. I just go to the gym, swim my laps, and go home."

"And eat your weight in food."

"Yeah," he said.

Megan's stomach was warm with soup. She called 10-8 and pushed away her bowl. She felt sociable and wanted to talk to Nathan and learn more about him, but he was eating ravenously. She didn't want to interrupt.

Instead, she studied him, averting her eyes to the restaurant often enough, she hoped, that he would not feel watched. He had taken the time to place his napkin in his lap, salt his food carefully, and put hot sauce in his soup. She watched his hands and wondered what it would feel like if he touched her with a purpose other than patient care. Her cheeks grew warm.

Todd would kill me if he knew what I was thinking.

"That was a ridiculous run," she said, escaping her thoughts. "Abbott and Costello couldn't have done it better."

Nathan smiled. "Next time, let's just walk away and have them call it in. 'Sorry, folks! You have to do this right and call 911.'" He chopped the lettuce on his plate. "So, how'd you get the bruises?"

Ice flooded her veins. She dropped her hands into her lap, out of sight. "I fell in the antifreeze."

He lowered his fork. "That doesn't seem right," he said, frowning. "Have you had your blood levels checked?"

"Not recently." She picked at her napkin.

"Maybe we should have gotten you a steak or something. Get your iron up."

"I'm fine," she muttered.

He drank his water. "How do you like Retton County?"

"It's going well," she said, jumping on the new subject. "You were right. They're great people."

"Who'd they put you with?"

55

"Kristen."

He nodded. "That's good."

Megan ate a few bites of her salad and thought about the calls Nathan and she had run. For two people who had clashed so much in the beginning, they were developing into an effective team. She bit a roll and chewed her pride. "I guess I owe you an apology."

"Probably."

"I sh—wait, what?"

Nathan put down his cup. "Kidding. Keep going. What'd you do?"

"I assumed you would trip over your own ... foot, but I'm the one who busted on scene."

He shrugged. "I took your statement as a metaphor."

"It was, but the literal makes it all the more difficult to ignore. I'm sorry." She met his eyes. "You're a really good medic."

Nathan considered her. "Thanks."

Megan gathered her courage. "So, how did you lose it? If you don't mind my asking."

"IED."

He had spoken casually, as if discussing the weather. She clamored for appropriate words. "That sucks."

"Could've been worse. My buddy stepped on it." He abruptly set his napkin on his plate. "It killed him."

"I'm sorry to hear that."

Nathan frowned and pushed away from the table. "Are you finished eating? I think we need to get back to the station."

"Sure. Of course," Megan said, certain his attempted nonchalance had been a poor act.

EMS STATION 1
MAY 15, 2013. 7:55 AM

Nathan hung an extra uniform in his locker as the locker room door swung open.

"You ready?" Megan's voice asked behind him.

"Yes, I'm coming," he said, digging in his locker for an ink pen.

Must be here somewhere.

He heard shuffling feet as someone else entered the room.

"Whoa!" Richard's voice said. "What happened to your chin?"

Nathan leaned around the door of his locker. He could see Richard, but Megan had turned her back to him.

"It's nothing," she said. "Bad call in Retton County over the weekend."

Richard folded his arms. "Well, be careful."

"I will," she muttered. Nathan watched her ponytail swing as she walked out. Richard let the door fall shut behind her.

They exchanged glances.

"Completely off the record," Richard said, "I worry about her. She's a magnet for all kinds of attention, most of it not good."

Nathan looked at the door. "She's a decent medic. I think she delegates too much, and she tends to—"

"You're right. She's a decent medic," Richard conceded. "But she pays a price. She feels too much, so life beats her down sometimes."

Nathan sensed genuine concern and knit his brow. "What do you mean?"

Richard sighed. "I don't know. I don't know what I

mean." He shrugged and opened his locker. "She tries to act tough and crusty, but she's not like … I don't think …" He shook his head.

Nathan chuckled. "Take my word for it. She has plenty of natural arrogance, just like the rest of us. She's—"

"No, that's not what I mean. It didn't come out right. I know she's tough, and she can be bitchy enough, but she's one of the few who still gives a shit about patients. Even the drunks, even the gomers, even the frequent flyers. You'll never hear her complain about a non-emergency transport or overtime. Hell, she visits people on her days off. When the bums at the park call us, they'll ask for her because they know she cares. But something's off. I've known her a long time, and something's not right with her. I've never been able to figure it out." He shrugged. "I don't know." He shrugged a second time. "Get to work."

Nathan slung his bag over his shoulder and walked to the truck, thinking about Richard's words. He climbed into the back where Megan rifled through supplies. She failed to acknowledge him, which gave him a moment to observe her. A purple lump marred her jaw line.

"You, of all people, shouldn't stare," she said, her voice tinged with venom.

He sat on the jump bench. "I didn't hear about a bad call in Retton County, and I was there last night."

Her hand paused over the extra oxygen tubing. "It was just a drunk. I doubt people'd gossip about it."

Tones blared.

"Med 3, be en route to 849 Oak Street, 849 Oak Street. Possible overdose."

He pulled his radio from his belt. "10-4. I'll drive."

Nathan climbed into the cab as Megan snapped her seatbelt. "An overdose on Oak Street?" he said. "At eight in the morning?"

She flipped through her reference app. "Meth. Bath salts. Heroin. GHB."

The radio interrupted, "Sheriff advises caution."

"10-4," Megan said. "Yep. Something like that."

Nathan drove through a quiet residential neighborhood to the scene.

"Pull up to the fire trucks, but don't go past," she said.

Nathan stopped the truck on the side of the avenue. Megan withdrew a pair of binoculars from under the seat and perched between the open door and the A-post.

"What do you see?" he asked, scanning the ranch house with white shutters.

"A bunch of firefighters huddled on the ground."

"Not a good sign."

She tossed the binoculars back to the floor. "Nope."

Nathan retrieved the stretcher and jump kit as Megan pulled supplies from the shelves. She unlocked the med box and slipped two pre-filled syringes into her pocket. "Toss a backboard on there," she said.

Nathan got the board and wheeled the stretcher behind her. She reached back and took the end, pulling with him. It was a small motion, but he realized the significance: they were moving as a team. Together, they rattled up the driveway.

He heard the screaming before he saw the patient.

A naked teenager thrashed between azalea bushes on the manicured lawn. He wailed and moaned. Flecks of spittle sprayed into the air. A deputy held one arm, and three firefighters restrained his other limbs.

The patient flung the men around as if he had super-human strength. "Blue ghosts! Blue ghosts!" he shrieked over and over. Nathan was the secondary medic, so he stood by the stretcher and watched, following Megan's lead.

Megan folded her arms, unfazed by the brawl. "Martin, what are you doing?"

"Hey, Doll! Quite—a match—isn't—it!"

"What happened?" Megan asked.

"Pretty much what—you—see. Kid—flew at us. Started punching Thomas."

Megan leaned to the side. "Thomas, you okay?"

"Yep!" he called. "I have—abs of Kevlar."

She grinned. "Martin, can you see his pupils?"

Martin grunted. "Doll, I don't see—anything wrong with his pupils. He needs—10 milligrams—of chill out."

With a roar, the patient threw off all of the men except Martin, who was flung from side to side. The firefighters and deputy scrambled to lay their bodies across the teen. As Megan spoke with medical control, Nathan dropped beside them and grabbed the patient's thigh. He pushed it to the ground and was amazed at the teen's strength.

"You got it?" Thomas asked, with too much suspicion in his voice for Nathan's comfort.

"Yeah," he said, trying to look savvy.

Megan withdrew a syringe from her pocket. "If I'm going to get in there with a needle, you guys need to keep him down."

The patient bucked beneath Nathan's hands, and he pressed harder as he watched her peel off the bar code sticker. She gave no sign of fear, but he felt a twinge of concern for her. He regretted his position on the patient. Had he been at the shoulder, he could have made certain she was out of harm's way.

Megan stuck the sticker to her shirt and, squatting, removed the needle cap with her teeth. "I'm beside you,

Thomas." She jabbed the needle into the teenager's arm. A high scream surged from his throat, causing Nathan's ears to ring.

Megan sat back on her heels and slid the needle into the little jump kit sharps box. "Get him on the stretcher," she called over the screams. "I have an order for soft restraints."

Martin laughed. "Doll, you're asking—a lot."

"You know you love it when I tell you what I want," she said as she threaded the soft restraints through the loops, readying them for the patient's wrists. She pulled the stretcher closer and dropped it to the ground.

"All right, on three," Nathan said. "One, two, three!"

With grunts and groans, the men lifted the patient onto the stretcher, triggering a new bout of writhing.

"Has he thrown up?" Megan asked.

Martin grunted and pushed the teenager back down. "No, I don't think he has."

"I want him supine," she directed, sliding around Martin's arms and fitting the restraint over the patient's wrist. Megan's and Martin's faces nearly touched.

"You look beautiful today, Doll," Martin said as she tied the strap to the backboard.

Nathan narrowed his eyes and wished Martin would be quiet.

"Still married," Megan said and walked around the stretcher.

Megan squeezed between Nathan and Thomas. Her ponytail covered Nathan's face, but he couldn't release the patient to brush it away. He didn't mind. Her hair smelled like peaches.

The patient moaned and extended the sound as if he were an engine revving up. The pitch grew until the shrieks and screams exploded into thrashing. Despite arm restraints, the teen flung off Nathan and the firefighters. He kicked Megan squarely in the chest, propelling her backward. She hit the ground with a grunt.

Nathan scrambled to stand. Megan was gasping air back into her lungs.

Nathan's anger flared. He leaped onto the stretcher with renewed energy, the firefighters joining him. Despite the weight of six bodies, the gurney continued to bounce across the ground with the force of the patient's erratic motions. Megan shouldered her way into the fray and wrapped a strap around the teenager's ankle, first one, then the other.

They all moved back, yet the stretcher continued to rock.

Megan panted. "Time—of restraint—8:53."

"You okay, Doll?" Martin asked.

Nathan, too, looked her up and down, assessing for injuries, and reminding himself that he was concerned for her only because she was his partner.

Megan stuck a second barcode to her shirt. "I'm fine." She jabbed the other needle into the boy's opposite arm. "Are we rappelling Monday?" she asked Martin.

Nathan looked back at him. Martin was the captain of Barrington County's high-angle rescue team. The team members were trained to perform rescues on steep slopes and the sides of tall buildings. Nathan had not realized Megan was on the team.

The patient twisted his neck back and forth like a snake, his eyes rolling in his head. "Blue! Ghosts. Blue … Ghosts … "

"That's the plan," Martin said.

Megan nodded. "I'll be there." She looked at the team.

"Get the kid to the truck and cover him up."

CAITLYN ARMISTEAD

Chapter Four

BARRINGTON COUNTY FIRE TRAINING CENTER
MAY 20, 2013. 1:55 PM

Nathan harnessed up at his personal truck and walked toward the fire tower where Megan sat on a low wall next to Carrie. Both were in rescue harnesses as well, and both chattered away about some nonsensical subject.

High-angle rescue with gabbing girls. Grand.

Nathan walked over to Martin and Thomas, who were organizing gear.

"Hey, Thompson," Deputy Thomas said. "You here to watch?"

Nathan glanced down at his own harness and back to Thomas. "I'm here to practice."

"Nathan's on the team now," Martin said, fiddling with his clipboard.

"When were you going to tell me? I'm your second-in-command!" Thomas said.

Martin continued to flip papers around on his clipboard. Thomas grunted and returned to preparing ropes. Nathan steeled himself; Thomas was going to be a problem. Despite working side by side on multiple calls, he had not won the deputy's approval. Nathan shuffled his boots with frustration.

What's it gonna take, man?

Megan's laughter carried to him. It annoyed him that she was goofing off with her friend instead of working.

"Why aren't they checking equipment?" Nathan said, nodding his head toward Megan and Carrie.

Martin tapped his pen on the board. "They're finished. The rest of us are playing catch up."

Nathan looked back over at Megan. She gave a small wave, and he nodded in return. Carrie leaned to Megan and said something he could not hear. Megan laughed again, and both sauntered toward the group.

Thomas walked back with a length of rope. "All right, Thompson. Tie a bowline."

Nathan narrowed his eyes as he took the rope. "Are we back in Boy Scouts?"

"No offense meant," Thomas said, lifting his chin in challenge. "I start every new technician with knots."

"This is because I'm new," Nathan said, looping the rope, "and not because of other issues you may have with me?"

Thomas set his jaw. "You tell me if there are other issues."

Megan and Carrie joined them.

Martin shrugged. "You could probably let him slide. He's a certified cave technician."

"Really?" Megan said. "Maybe he can recommend a class for you, Thomas."

Thomas glared at her, then turned back to Nathan. "I'll be direct. We're practicing pick-offs today, and no one is willing to get on a rope with someone who—" His eyes dipped to Nathan's leg.

Nathan tossed the bowline back to Thomas with more

force than was necessary. "There's your knot." He crossed his arms. "Now what were you saying?"

Thomas faltered. "I don't think anyone will get on a rope with someone who—"

Nathan raised an eyebrow.

"—who isn't proven on this tower."

"I'll go," said Megan.

Nathan and Thomas both turned to her.

"You usually work with Martin," said Thomas.

She shrugged. "And you tell me I need to work with other techs. We can all rotate through until we run out of time. I'll pick-off Martin, Nathan picks-off me, and so on."

"Works for me," said Martin.

Carrie, Thomas, and Martin climbed the tower, leaving Megan at the bottom to wait for a rope and Nathan to wait his turn. They stood in comfortable silence, used to each other's presence. Nathan watched her shield her eyes and look up at the top. Her navy blue station pants and Barrington EMS t-shirt were bunched up under the old black harness she had been assigned, and she and Carrie wore matching pink and yellow helmets with 'Hello Kitty to the Rescue!' stickers stuck on the side.

Must women make everything a fashion statement?

He wondered where her ponytail had gone and stepped back to get a better look. She had braided her hair against her head and tucked it up under itself. The mechanics of it baffled him, but he thought it was pretty.

Nathan did realize she had stuck her neck out for him. He felt a modicum of gratitude, but the larger side of him didn't want a girl to fight his battles. Especially not Megan. Irritated, he remained perfectly content staying out of her sight line.

"Don't judge too quickly," she said without turning

around. "Thomas is a really nice guy."

"The snide remarks accentuate his good qualities."

"I admire your avoidance of sarcasm," she said dryly, catching the rope that swooped down to her. "Thomas just doesn't know what you're capable of, and he's imagining everything that can go wrong because of your leg. That's his job. Not everyone who's skeptical of you is a bad person."

Overhead, Martin leaned back and walked slowly down the wall.

"You could see past it," Nathan said.

The back of her neck turned pink. "I, well, I—" She cleared her throat and snapped her ascender onto the line. "You're certified. I can trust that. And he will, too, after a while. It would help if you weren't so all-fired defensive all the time."

"I'm not defensive!"

She looked back at him over her shoulder, her forehead wrinkled. "Whatever."

"People should assume I can do this stuff," he said.

Megan pulled the foot loop over her boot and glanced back again. "You're different from their normal. They have nothing to compare you with, so they don't know what to expect. Cut them some slack."

Martin pretended to be stuck halfway down the wall. "All right, Doll! I'm in the middle of a rescue, but now I need to be rescued. Pick-off!"

"I don't think he wants too much slack right now," Nathan said.

Megan pulled herself up a length and grinned at him. "Just stay off my rope."

He nodded with a tight-lipped smile.

Megan continued up, sliding her ascender and

stepping on the rope. She ascended to Martin and went to work transferring straps and carabiners over to her line. Martin drilled her on gear, technique, and safety. She responded back with quick answers and the occasional question.

Nathan squinted. Not one sassy comment passed between Martin and Megan. Instead, the two were focused on their shared purpose and completely immersed in their task. Their actions and statements supported each other, strengths balancing weaknesses. He had never watched a team with such close dynamics. Nathan realized Martin's crude harassment and Megan's seemingly misplaced tolerance was a game, the cover of a strong friendship and mutual respect. He wondered if there was more to their relationship and felt a keen dissatisfaction. If he hadn't known better, he would have thought he was jealous.

Megan and Martin descended smoothly to the ground. "Good job," Martin said as they unhooked everything. "Now get running." Megan hurried up the stairs. Martin passed the rope to Nathan. "You ready?" he asked.

"Yeah."

Nathan reached for the rope.

Martin pulled it away and gripped Nathan's arm. "Everything by the book," he said. "You get her down in one piece, or—"

"I will," Nathan interrupted and took the rope.

Megan rappelled down the wall, hopping spryly with each step.

"That girl needs to slow down and pay attention," Martin muttered.

She stopped halfway and crossed her ankles. "I'm stuck!"

Nathan attached his ascender to the line and put his

sound foot into the foot loop. He stepped onto the rope and slid the ascender up, climbing until he was level with her.

"Hi," he said.

"Hello." Her smile reached her brown eyes. It warmed him, and he grinned back, his irritation forgotten.

Nathan attached an ascender to her line. "Are you going to ask me a bunch of questions like Martin did of you?"

"No," she laughed. "You're a cave technician. I'm going to watch and learn."

"Pick-offs like this are the same at every level," he said, ascending a little higher and affixing the pick-off strap. "It's just a matter of practice."

"We don't get enough practice," she said. "Not like the big departments."

"Take advantage of opportunities as they come. You can only do your best with what's given to you. Ready to move off the line?"

"Yep. Don't drop me."

Nathan grasped her rescue eight, a heavy, steel connecting device. He removed it from her line and attached it to his. "All commands for line one will be coming from line two!" he shouted up to Carrie and Thomas.

Megan pulled on the strap. "Why am I so far below you?"

"So when you have a panic attack, you won't get in my way."

"You have such faith in me."

Nathan removed the final ascender. "I saw you take out that thug who barged into your truck. I'm not taking any risks with my safety, so you just stay down there." He enjoyed her laugh as he controlled their slow descent to the ground.

FIRE STATION 6
MAY 22, 2013. 11:15 PM

Cool air washed over Nathan's face as he walked into the EMS room from the humid truck bay. Megan, with brow furrowed, sat at the table with a rope, a carabiner, and a length of Prusik cord.

"What are you doing?" he asked.

"Trying to tie knots and questioning my career choice."

He chuckled. "It can't be that bad."

She dropped the ropes, and the carabiner clattered across the table. "It's pretty bad. I just want to be able to tie a good knot."

"You did fine on Monday," he said, picking up the rope and wrapping it around his hand.

She leaned her chin on her palm. "I didn't have to tie any fancy knots, now did I?"

"Exactly." He finished a stopper knot and dropped it to the table. "You don't need fancy knots. When would you ever use them?"

"What if. What if. What if," she said. "I can think of a million things that could wrong on the side of a mountain."

"That's why there are redundancies. Focus on the basics, and the rest is gravy." He unzipped his backpack. "I brought something for you." He handed her a thick, black book and her eyes lit up.

"A *Complete Reference for Cave Rescue*. Awesome." She opened the book and turned the first few pages. Nathan watched her slender fingers slide down the paper.

The lamplight heightened the contours of her face. He saw an elegance he had never noticed before.

Snap out of it, you fool! She's married!

Nathan turned the TV over to ESPN and sat in the recliner. "I want it back sometime, but you can borrow it, if you like. And we'll work on your knots. Keep a length of Prusik with you, and we can tie them when we're slow."

"Thanks," she said.

"Sure. But not now. I missed my game." He watched the scroll at the bottom of the screen, looking for the score of the Braves vs. Minnesota Twins game.

Megan put away her ropes and curled up in the other chair. She flipped through the book. Nathan leaned back and watched the highlights, his eyelids heavy. Heyward scored … Gattis homered to right … Freeman …

Tones dropped.

Nathan blinked, trying to rid himself of sleep and orient to the room. Megan lifted her head and closed the book.

"Med 3, be en route to 16 Medici Lane, 16 Medici Lane. Unknown medical."

"10-4," she said.

Nathan pushed in the footrest. "What time is it?"

"One fifteen."

He grunted and walked out to the truck. Megan drove them over to the ritzy side of town while he rubbed his face and yawned. They parked in front of a Spanish-style mansion and walked across the crisp, manicured St. Augustine grass to stand on the brightly lit portico. Bass throbbed.

Nathan rang the doorbell. "Nice of them to invite us to the party."

"Do you really think a group of boozed-up high

schoolers is going to hear the doorbell?"

Nathan cast her a wry smile and pounded his fist on the door. "Paramedics!"

An older woman with curly hair and garish makeup opened the door, laughing, a drink in her hand. "Yes? Oh, who is this handsome jar opener?" She fluffed her hair.

Nathan blinked, trying to conceal his disgust. "Paramedics," Nathan said. "Someone called 911? Is someone hurt?"

"I think I need an exam," she said, running her fingers up his arm. She made his skin crawl, and he pushed her hand away.

"Sharon, let the ambulance drivers in," a man called from in the room.

With pouty lips, Sharon stepped back allowing them to enter. Nathan wiped his feet before stepping into the tiled foyer. A fountain flowed in the center, but he couldn't hear the trickle of the water over the booming music. The house smelled of cigarettes and weed.

"This way. This way," the man said, waving them toward him. "I'm Tim."

They followed Tim into a hallway.

Megan caught Nathan's sleeve and stood on the tiptoes of her boots. "I think that woman likes you," she whispered with an impish smile. Nathan rolled his eyes, but he didn't push Megan's hand away.

The music retreated as they entered a bedroom richly furnished with a mission-style suite. Nathan's boots sank into the carpet, making him conscious of changes in his balance. An elderly man with thin, combed-over hair slumped in a wingback chair. His arms draped over the sides.

Nathan glanced at Megan. She was trying to suppress

amusement and wide-eyed recognition of whoever the man was. Nathan caught her eye, but she shook her head slightly.

Tim scowled. "John's drunk. I've told him he's drunk. Sharon's told him he's drunk. But he insists he's sick and needs to go to the hospital."

John lifted a wrinkled arm. "I'm shick."

Nathan nodded. "How much have you had to drink, sir?"

John flopped his head to the side. "I not," he swallowed, "drunk. Drink? Drrr-oonk? Drunk. Not drunk."

"All right, sir," he said. "Do you have any medical problems? Are you diabetic? Do you have sugar problems?"

John inhaled through his teeth and coughed. Nathan stepped back to avoid the spray of droplets.

"I'm heffy," John slurred. "Heffy as a hoooorse."

"There's nothing wrong with him," Tim said.

Megan took John's vital signs. She looked up at Nathan and shrugged.

John struggled to stand. "I wanna gooo to the hoshpital."

"All right, sir," Nathan said, pulling him to his feet. "Can you walk?"

"Listen," Tim said, with a furtive glance to the door. "There are people here that shouldn't see him like this. I pulled him in here before anyone really noticed, but if you walk him back out and someone sees—can you go out the back? Yeah, just go out the back."

Nathan and Megan exchanged glances and shrugged. "Come on, Mr. Marsh," Megan said. "Let's take a walk."

Tim opened the door to the bedroom's private patio, and the three tramped through into the night.

Nathan turned back. "How do we get out of the yard

and back—" The door closed, and the curtain fell. "—to the truck?"

Megan tried the knob. "It's locked."

Nathan pushed on the door. "Damn." He pulled a small flashlight from his pocket and clicked the button on the end. The light refracted on the evening mist and formed a solid beam. He searched the patio and the yard while the ambulance lights bounced off the treetops.

John tipped his head back. "Pretty shtars."

"Let's go this way," Nathan sighed.

He and Megan each took one of John's elbows and struck out toward the fence.

"How much have you had to drink tonight, sir?" Megan asked.

"I didn't," John said, "drink noshing."

She huffed. "I'm getting drunk off your breath. Tell me the truth."

Nathan willed a straight face.

John slurped the saliva that dripped down his chin. "I had a beeer."

"This ain't my first rodeo," Megan laughed. "How many shots?"

"One."

"Nope," she said. "Try again, sir."

"Eight. And one of them fruity blue things."

Nathan drew down the corners of his mouth, impressed the man was still standing.

"And powder? Any cocaine?" she asked.

"I dunnoo. Might have."

Nathan reached the fence. "Here's the gate."

"Let's hope it's unlocked," Megan said.

Nathan rattled the latch, and the gate swung open. "We're almost there, sir."

The three squeezed through the opening in the fence. Nathan let go of John for a moment to close the gate.

"Oooh," John slurred.

"Stop!" Megan said.

Nathan spun around to see John draped over Megan. She was trying to push the man's bony hands off her breasts. Anger boiled in his stomach. He grabbed John's shoulder and gave him a shake. "I have an M4 and a shovel. Keep your dirty hands off my partner."

They stumbled to the street. Nathan begrudgingly helped John into the back of the ambulance. As Nathan climbed up, Megan pulled him back.

"I can't believe you said that to him!" she said.

"For Pete's sake, Megan! Assault isn't part of the job. My first priority is to make sure you live until end of shift, preferably unscathed, and I hope you'll do the same for me. I'm not going to just stand there while some drunk—"

"You don't get it," she said, crossing her arms and shaking her head. "Junk like this happens on the street. You get through it and get on with things."

"You should make a report."

"What the hell, Nathan! A report? That's John Marsh! You just threatened a senator—a senator! You may have gotten us in serious trouble."

"I don't care if he's the fucking president. I look out for my partner."

Megan swung away with a huff.

"Do you understand?" he called.

She stopped.

A moment passed before she turned back.

"You'll make sure I get home," she said, her voice flat. "Where I'm safe. Yeah, I get it."

FIRE STATION 6
MAY 24, 2013. 9:00 AM

Nathan rolled the vacuum cleaner into the EMS room and plugged it in. He ran the vacuum around the furniture, the hum filling the room. Glancing into the bathroom, he saw Megan cleaning the sink. She had stuffed her iPod into her back pocket, and the earbud cord ran alongside her speaker mic cord. Only the left bud was in her ear; the right hung over her shoulder so she would be able to hear the radio tones. Her head bobbed with music he could not hear, and she mouthed the words to the song, a smile hiding at the corners of her mouth. No glitz, no glamour, just the simple happiness that came with good music and a necessary job well done.

Nathan stared at her as he vacuumed. She was beautiful. Hers was the beauty that made men want to do great things. Climb mountains. Vanquish foes. Her beauty made him want to do other things, too.

He vacuumed the lamp cord, and the lamp fell. "Oh, shit!" The bulb flashed and went out.

"What happened?" Megan called.

He turned off the vacuum and picked up the lamp. "Oh, nothing," he said, casually. "Light bulb burned out."

Nathan was wrapping up the vacuum cleaner cord when the tones went off. Megan moved into the doorway, one hand on her hip, the other holding the toilet brush.

"Med 3, be en route to 424 Main Street, 424 Main Street, Golden Acres Nursing Facility, Code 1 transport."

Nathan deposited the vacuum cleaner in the bay as Megan put away the brush and cleaning supplies. "Want me to drive?" he asked as she locked the EMS room door.

Megan flung her ponytail over her shoulder. "Why? So

you don't have to do patient care?"

"I—"

"Get over yourself! I worked non-emergency transport all through paramedic school. The people on NET calls are in just as much need as those we have to scrape off the pavement. They stay cooped up in those nursing homes day after day, and no one ever gives a crap about them. Medics who work NET see deeper, more profound suffering than 911 medics ever will, all with less support and less recognition! Just because there's no adrenaline high with NET doesn't mean it doesn't have value and—"

"Megan."

"—and import—What?"

"I'm only asking if you want me to drive."

Megan blinked. "Oh. Sure."

Nathan parked the ambulance behind the nursing home. Megan dug in her bag and withdrew a little jar of lip gloss. Instead of applying it to her lips, she rubbed it under her nose.

He frowned. "What are you doing?"

"It reeks to high heaven in there. I chose a nice fragrance I could live without and use it to cover up the smell. It works, but I can't stand strawberries anywhere else now." She shrugged. "Not really a big loss when there's chocolate in the world."

Just when I thought she couldn't get any quirkier ...

Nathan pushed the stretcher up the ramp. Megan knocked on the door. An orderly let them in, and as Nathan stepped inside, ammonia fumes smacked him in the face. He cleared his throat and coughed and considered borrowing her lip gloss.

"Who are we getting today?" Megan asked a passing orderly.

"Mrs. Williams in room 19," he said. "Know where that is?"

"Yes, but I need paperwork first."

Nathan wheeled the stretcher down the hallway. It was dark, dreary, and the stock pictures in the frames were dingy and blued out from years of fluorescent lighting exposure. The hallway was lined with carts holding pungent breakfast trays and soiled linen. Residents slumped in wheelchairs, drooling over themselves. He hated to admit Megan was right. He didn't want to do the transport or the patient care. He didn't want to be there and resented the gumming of the system that would necessitate them taking a NET call.

Megan stopped at each chair. She greeted most of them by name and smiled whether they responded or not.

One man gripped her hands. "Bella! I've missed you. Why don't you come to see me any more?"

Megan hugged him. "I have a different job, Mr. Torelli. I go to emergencies now."

"So you do. So you do."

She looked up at Nathan. "Mr. Torelli had his own restaurant for over 50 years."

Nathan nodded but didn't know what to say.

She patted Mr. Torelli's hand again and bade him goodbye. "Mrs. Torelli died last year," she whispered as they walked down the hallway. "He hasn't been the same since."

Megan went to the front desk and asked for the paperwork. Nathan stood awkwardly at her side, trying not to imagine his own future. He knew how easily he could lose the mobility he had fought so hard to regain. The long-term effects of traumatic brain injury worried him further. But the spectre of loneliness that billowed in his mind terrified him. He stared at Mr. Torelli. The man was alone, with only death for comfort. Death and Megan. Nathan's heart pounded in his ears. His collar felt tight.

Megan touched his arm, and he started.

"You okay?" she asked.

Nathan stared at her soft, brown eyes and the concern written on her forehead. The loneliness lifted. "What?" He cleared his head with a shake. "Yeah, I'm fine."

Megan received the papers and tapped them on the counter. "All right. Room 19."

She led the way and rapped her knuckles on the door of room 19. China dolls filled the shelves, and photographs held by thumb tacks covered the walls. A small, wrinkled, emaciated woman lay curled on the bed.

"Hello, Mrs. Williams, we're here to take you to the hospital," she said.

There was no response.

Megan turned to the orderly who had followed them into the room. "Where's her hair ribbon?"

He shrugged. "Hell if I know."

"Find it," she insisted. "She was a hairdresser, and I'm not taking her out without her ribbon."

The orderly looked for the ribbon while Megan and Nathan carefully transferred Mrs. Williams to the stretcher. Megan lifted the foley catheter bag. The urine inside was green.

"Pseudomonas," Megan muttered. "When was this last changed?" The orderly shrugged, and Megan flipped through the papers. "Three weeks ago. But her symptoms began six days ago. Are you kidding me? She's been symptomatic six days with no catheter change?"

Once more, the orderly shrugged.

"Forget it. Let's go," she said to Nathan. "Oh!" Megan

darted back to the dresser and grabbed a long, violet ribbon. "Here. It's right here," she said, shaking the ribbon at the orderly. She tucked the ends under Mrs. Williams' neck and tied it into a bow on the top of her head.

Nathan pushed the stretcher into the hall. Megan walked at the side, holding Mrs. Williams' hand and speaking softly to her. They left the building, and Nathan leaned back, slowing the descent of the stretcher down the ramp.

"Stop here," Megan said. She walked to the edge of the parking lot. Nathan watched her, confused once more. She picked a gardenia flower and returned to the stretcher.

"Look up, Mrs. Williams. Can you see the sky? It's blue today. The wind is blowing, and it's warm." She placed the flower in Mrs. William's hand. "There's a flower in your hand. You can feel the leaves and the petals."

Megan nodded to him, and Nathan loaded the stretcher. She climbed in and faced him. "I know it takes a while," she said. "And I know it takes us out of service longer. But if it were possibly your last time to be under the sky, would you want someone to take the time to help you see it?"

She held his gaze, her expression neither angry, nor indignant, nor seeking his approval. She only wanted his cooperation, and he nodded. He had never met anyone like her before.

Nathan closed the doors, but his hand lingered on the side as he wondered what made her different. She was a contradiction: strong, and yet weak; smart, yet naive; and beautiful, certainly. She could be bitchy at times, but it wasn't a habit. He had met other women like that, other strong, beautiful, nice women. Her femininity could not explain it all. The other medics had called her compassionate, but as he thought, even that seemed to fall short.

He sat in the driver's seat and listened to her chatter to the catatonic woman.

Mercy.

That was the difference. Megan did not simply pity others; she trusted she had the power to make a difference. She acted as though her words and deeds lasted until the end of time, never doubting their effects, even when others laughed behind their hands.

Megan tapped the window. "We're ready to leave when you are."

"All right," he said, turning the key.

No, he had never met anyone quite like her.

FIRE STATION 6
MAY 24, 2013. 2:30 PM

Nathan had felt pressure building in his residual limb all day. He had ignored it, but now what was left of his leg was bearing all of his weight; he had bottomed out, and the pain was too much to bear. He pulled a chair into the bathroom and locked the door. Simply sitting relieved much of the ache, and he leaned back in the chair, sighing deeply.

Nathan had had his pants altered with a zipper that ran along the inseam of his left leg from the ankle to mid-thigh. He unzipped it and popped the prosthetic lock. He removed the socket and withdrew a ply sock from his pocket. The sock had been white at one time, but Sam had washed it with a red t-shirt, and now it was pink. Nathan had made certain that that was the last time Sam ever washed anything of his.

Nathan pulled the sock over his leg, ensuring it was snug. The hole at the bottom of the sock slid over the metal liner pin. He eased the limb into the socket, and the pin aligned with the hole, click, click, clicking into place. He stood and tested his weight.

Much better.

Nathan walked back into the EMS room. Megan was sitting on the floor with her cargo pants rolled up to her knees. She was painting her toenails.

"Now you're just showing off," he said. "Rub it in, why don't you?"

Megan's jaw dropped. She raised her eyes to meet his as he stood over her. Nathan challenged her with a half smile and enjoyed watching her cheeks blush.

She inhaled slowly, her eyes wide. "I'm so sorry. I didn't even think about your—"

Nathan laughed and dropped into the recliner. "I don't care. But you're going to kill our out-of-chute time. Just what are you going to do if a call—"

Tones blared.

"Now look what you did!" Megan cried. "You jinxed it!" She tossed the polish back into her bag and tottered to her feet. "You drive!" She shouldered her bag, but it fell off as she gathered her boots and socks.

He smirked. "And this is how you steal calls."

"You can still have the call," she said as her bag fell again. "Just drive."

Nathan turned off the lamp and stood in the doorway. "Would you like some help?"

"No—I've—got—it," she said with a final snatch of her sock.

He stepped aside, and she padded barefoot into the truck bay, hugging her boots.

They climbed into the truck, and Nathan called in to dispatch. He flipped the lights and sirens on and pulled out into traffic. Megan put her feet up on the dash as she turned her sock right side out. Nathan was acutely aware that the rolled edges of her pants revealed the curves of her legs. He puffed his cheeks and focused on the road.

Megan groaned. "My toes are all messed up now. I'm going to have to redo them."

"Feet are such a bother. I'm thinking of having the other one removed."

She giggled. "Where are we going?"

"Weren't you paying attention?"

"No. I was hoping you did," she said, zipping her boots.

"I did, but I'm not telling. Call 10-9 and have them repeat it."

"I'm not calling 10-9."

Nathan lifted his foot from the accelerator, the ambulance slowed. "Then we'll stay here."

"Drive!"

"Call it!"

Megan balled up a paper napkin and threw it at him. "10-9 on that location?" she said, tipping her head to her mic.

Nathan accelerated the ambulance again.

"28976 Highway 67. Child with diaper rash," said the dispatcher.

"10-4," Megan said and released the mic. "Happy?"

Nathan grinned. "Ecstatic."

They arrived on scene at a small, lime green house made of cinderblocks. Nathan stood at the steps, listening to a child's muffled wails. He placed his gloved hand on the railing, and years of rust crunched under his grip.

Diaper rash? Are they fucking serious?

He knocked on the door. "Paramedics!"

A black man opened the door. He wore sweatpants and a t-shirt splotched with unidentifiable orange and green globs. "Hi, come in," he said, opening the door wider.

Nathan followed Megan inside. The house was pristine, though the furniture old. In the living room corner, a desk held an open laptop, a lamp, a stapler, and several neat stacks of paper. Even the plastic plants were dusted. He relaxed a bit.

The screaming came from a portable crib. The man lifted out a small child in a clean romper. Her hair had been brushed into two puffs on top of her head. Drool fell in strings from her lips, and tears rolled down her cheeks.

"This is Kaya," the man said. "She turned one last week, and she's got a killer diaper rash. I'm putting the stuff on it, but she keeps screaming. All the time. I think something's wrong."

Nathan resisted rolling his eyes.

I hate bullshit like this.

Nathan nodded at Megan and raised his eyebrows, encouraging her to take over, but she placed her hands behind her back and smiled sweetly as she rocked on her boots. He scowled.

"Well, sir," Nathan said, "a diaper rash can be pretty painful. Did you give her some pain medicine?"

"Yeah, man, as often as I could." The father laid the baby on the couch, unsnapped her romper, and unfastened her diaper as she kicked and squirmed. The baby's skin was angry and raw and slathered with a light yellow cream.

"Does she have a fever?" Nathan asked. The screaming

rang in his ears and irritated his nerves.

"No."

"Is she allergic to anything? Take any medications?"

The man shook his head as he secured the diaper. "Nothing except that cream."

"Any other illnesses or problems?"

"No. I just know something's wrong."

Nathan blinked. "But what makes you say that?"

"I don't know," the man said with a shrug and picked up the baby. He leaned her on his shoulder and patted her back. She cried louder. "I need to change my shirt before we go to the hospital. She got her lunch all over me because she kept pushing it away. Can you hold her?" He held the baby out to Nathan.

"Oh. Well. Um—"

Megan elbowed him, and he took Kaya into his arms. She smelled like cheese. The father walked into a back bedroom, and the moment he was out of sight, Kaya screeched, her voice rising into a sheer scream.

Nathan cringed as his ears throbbed. "Shit calls like this are a waste of resources."

"Don't cuss in front of that baby!" Megan said.

"Don't you think it's a waste?"

She set the jump bag next to the desk.

Nathan squinted. "You disagree."

"I didn't say that," she said.

"You were thinking it."

She folded her arms. "He says there's something wrong."

"But what the hell—"

Megan swatted at him with the clipboard.

Nathan glanced at Kaya and cleared his throat. "What the heck is he basing that on? She's got a diaper rash."

Megan shrugged. "Mother's intuition."

"He's the father."

She grinned. "Caregiver intuition, then."

"What do you think is wrong?" Nathan asked, shifting the baby to his other arm and rubbing his ear.

"You're primary."

"But you're..."

"A woman? How does a second X-chromosome provide pediatric experience?" she asked as the father returned.

"I'm ready now," the man said, pulling a diaper bag over his shoulder and taking the baby back from Nathan.

"Yes, sir," Nathan said. "We need to take her car seat, if we can."

The man looked incredulous. "My wife has the car and the car seat at work. If I had that, I wouldn't need an ambulance."

Megan lifted the jump bag. The strap knocked over the stapler and staples scattered across the carpet. "I'm sorry! I'm forever knocking things over," she said as she picked them up.

"Don't worry about it," the father said. "I've done that twice today already. I'll vacuum it up when I get back."

They walked to the ambulance. Nathan strapped the baby to the stretcher and secured the father on the jump bench. Megan drove to the emergency room where Nathan transferred care to the nurses. He washed his hands and sat at the EMS desk to write his run report while Megan cleaned the stretcher and replaced it in the truck.

Megan returned and sat in the rolling chair beside him. "Almost finished?"

Nathan lifted his fingers from the keyboard. "I just started." He returned to his typing.

'Barrington EMS Med 3 dispatched via 911 for child

with diaper rash...'

Megan withdrew her phone from her pocket. She rolled her chair one way and then another.

'...Patient presented neatly dressed in portable crib. Patient was...'

Megan rolled back and forth.

'...Patient's father reported...'

Back and forth.

"Would you stop it?" Nathan said.

Megan looked up from her phone. "Huh? Stop what?"

"Rolling your chair like that."

"Oh, sorry."

"It's okay."

Nathan found his place again.

'...no known drug allergies...'

Megan snapped the clipboard.

'...patient refused lunch...'

Snap.

Snap.

Nathan ground his teeth.

Snap.

"Megan."

"Hmm?"

"Stop."

'...further examination unremarkable...'

Megan began tapping her fingers on the desk.

Exasperated, Nathan leaned forward and rubbed his temples.

This is what it must feel like to go mad.

Megan's giggle interrupted his thoughts. He looked up to her sassy eyes as she drummed one finger after another, playing the pest. He grinned in spite of himself.

Sam guided the portable x-ray machine as it rumbled

through the hallway.

"Do you know my roommate, Sam?" Nathan asked.

Megan smiled. "Oh, yeah, I know Sam. Funny guy."

"He's a character."

Sam lifted his hand as he walked by. "Hi," he said to Nathan. "Hi, Megan."

"Where are you going?" Nathan asked.

"X-ray on a one year old."

"That's ridiculous," Nathan said as Sam and the machine entered one of the rooms. "Why don't they just go ahead and order a CT? An MRI? Exploratory surgery? It's a diaper rash!"

"The father said something was wrong," Megan said.

Nathan shook his head and returned to his report.

Sam rolled the machine out of the room.

"Well?" Megan said.

Sam pressed the touch screen. "Let me show you." An image of a small belly appeared on the monitor. Three clusters of tiny curls shone in stark contrast with the intestines. "See them?"

Nathan's lips parted in disbelief.

"Staples," Megan said. "Right there." She pointed to the screen. "And there. And there."

Sam nodded. "You got it, kid. That baby ate staples for lunch."

CAITLYN ARMISTEAD

Chapter Five

YMCA
MAY 25, 2013. 7:45 PM

Each stroke propelled Nathan through the water. Nice rhythm; good time. Reaching the wall, he turned around and pushed off with his sound foot and swim/walk prosthetic.

He loved to swim. In the water, he felt whole again. He didn't have to worry about how he was bearing weight, and unless people looked very closely, they wouldn't notice he was different. That was more of a relief than he cared to admit.

His thoughts turned to work. Everyone knew he was an amputee, and there remained an undercurrent of distrust. At least he had earned Megan's respect, both on the trucks and on the ropes. That meant something to him. Again, more than he cared to admit.

He thought about Megan constantly. He looked forward to going to work, knowing she would be there. The prospect of seeing her had pushed him further in the pool, and he had gained three pounds of muscle mass in the month and a half they had been working together.

But he knew he was treading on dangerous ground. He considered himself a gentleman. He had discipline. He had a code. And Megan was over the line. 'Still married, Martin,' he could hear her say. He ached every time she said it.

Perhaps it was time to start looking for someone. He bubbled his breath through the water at the idea. He enjoyed going to the pub with the guys and talking up chicks just like any of his friends, but he always stopped short of pursuing someone. He feared that if his girlfriend found out what living with an amputee was really like—with endless appointments, skin care, and the hassle of crutches and wheelchairs—she would leave, or worse, stay because she pitied him. But dating might push Megan from his mind. He could find someone else to fill the void.

Nathan reached the end of the lane and leaned his elbows on the edge, catching his breath. He heaved himself out of the water. When he had finished his shower, he walked back into the locker room where Sam was shaving at the mirror. Nathan sat on the bench and removed his swim/walk leg.

"The pool room was rowdy last week," Sam said. "I think we should go to the pub tonight."

"Yeah. Sure." Nathan reached into his locker for his everyday prosthetic but couldn't find it. "Have you seen my leg?"

"Dude. You can't just go around losing body parts. Are you molting or something?"

Nathan laughed. "I found it." He dressed and examined himself critically in the mirror. "My shirt's wrinkled. Does it look okay?"

"If you're worried, just wear shorts. Then people will only see your leg."

"And that's a shame because I have great hair."

Sam placed his hand on Nathan's shoulder. "Really, it's

your soft brown eyes that made me fall in love with you."

A man walking behind them hitched his towel a little tighter around his waist.

With a laugh, Nathan shoved Sam away. He glanced back at the mirror and sighed.

Megan has soft brown eyes.

Sam tossed his comb into his bag. "You've gotta cut yourself loose from her, man."

"What do you mean by that?"

"You're not as complex as you think you are. You've been brooding since you started working with her. I get it. Megan's the real deal. It doesn't take genius to figure out you've fallen for her."

"I haven't fallen for her," Nathan said, crossing his arms.

Sam rolled his eyes. "Right. You're playing with fire, man. It won't end well."

"I know. But I keep—And she just—And when she—"

"Good God. She's turned you into a blubbering moron," Sam said, laughing. "Maybe you should just haul off and kiss her. Get it out of your system."

Nathan scowled and picked up his bag. "I don't need sarcasm and stupid ideas."

"Aw, I'm hurt," Sam said, his hand on his chest. "Our friendship was founded on sarcasm and stupid ideas. If we don't have that, we only have antics and blackmail-able offenses. That's no way to live." He pulled the gym bag strap over his shoulder. "Come on. A stout pint and some tail chasing will do you good."

O'MALLEY'S PUB
MAY 25, 2013. 11:30 PM

The dark pub was loud and crowded. The wooden walls shrank the room, while the swag lamps and brass-lined bar lent an old world feel. Nathan and Sam ambled to the bar and ordered pints.

"Commencing recon," Sam said over the pounding music.

Nathan peered over the top of his glass. He watched the couples dancing and the groups of college students and singles mingling around the edge of the dance floor. His eyes roved to a tall, lithe blond with high, angular cheekbones. Her eyes met his, and his heart skipped a beat. He held her gaze, playing the game. She dropped her eyes and then met his again. He abandoned his pint at the bar and strode toward her.

Nathan spoke close to her ear. "What's your name?"

She was near enough that he could see the powder particles on her face and tall enough to look him straight in the eye, a rarity for his height. "I'm Leah," she said with a sultry smile. She ran her hands through her long, shiny hair.

"Nathan. Can I buy you a drink?"

She tipped her head coyly. She checked him out, and he obliged with the smile that had worked so well in the past. "No, but I'd love to dance," she said.

He offered his hand, and she placed her manicured fingers on his palm. Leading the way in her ankle-breaking, four-inch heels, she walked to the dance floor, her hips swaying like a model who owned the runway.

The music drove them into each other's arms. It was clear Leah had had Latin dance training, and Nathan was not complaining. Calvin Harris' song filled his ears, and Leah's body moved under his hands as the beat pounded through his veins. The heat grew with every measure. He was exhilarated. He turned her under his arm and ran his hands over her hips. She pressed against him.

His weight shifted.

Cold sweat broke with the panic. The too familiar fall. His hip, then palms, hit the sticky floor, and his pant leg lifted just enough to show his false foot. Leah gasped, her eyes wide in surprise, and then the change. The Look. The slight curl of the lip, the faint wrinkle of the nose. He'd seen it before.

"Let me help you!" she cried.

He shook his head, his jaw set. "No. Thank you." He climbed to his feet, testing his weight gingerly. "Have a good evening." He strode from the dance floor.

Never again.

Nathan grabbed Sam's shoulder. "Let's go."

"Why?" Sam complained with a pained expression. "I'm making progress here. It's not as easy for us chubby, short guys as it is for you tall, Greek gods."

"I want to leave."

Sam looked at his watch. "Nope, it's only 11:40. I still have twenty minutes until you turn into a pumpkin. Go play."

"Then you'll have to walk. I'm outta here."

EMS STATION 1
JUNE 5, 2013. 8:05 AM

Nathan closed his locker. "Have you seen Megan?"

Richard shook his head. "No, I haven't."

Nathan tapped his fingers on the metal door. He knew

her habits. She always clocked in, went to the locker room, checked her spare uniform, dropped off any extra things she was carrying for the day, and then went to the truck. Always.

Richard looked at his watch. "It's after eight. She hasn't called in, and she's never late. Megan's here somewhere."

Nathan scowled and shouldered the door to the bay. He checked his step when he saw Megan sitting in the driver's seat, writing down the mileage. He crossed the area to stand by her knee. "Why didn't you go to the locker room?"

Megan was leaning on her clipboard. Her hand obscured her face. "I didn't need to. I clocked in and came back out here."

"But that's not what you normally do."

"That's what I did today," she said, flipping on the lights. "Check if these work."

Nathan tipped his head back and peered around the side. "They're fine."

Megan lowered her hand to reach across the cab. A gash cut across her eyebrow. It had been secured with butterfly bandages but still looked painful and swollen.

"What the hell happened to you?" Nathan demanded.

She turned away. "You've seen what bath salts can do to a patient."

"In Retton County? I heard nothing about that."

"Did you work yesterday?" she asked.

"No, but ... Megan, you gotta be more careful."

She scowled. "Thank you once more, Mother Hen, for your sage advice. Let me write it in my journal." She hopped down and pushed past him. Her phone beeped, and she checked it. "Emily's in labor! She's on her way to the hospital!"

want to talk about it but didn't want to
"Yeah. Just … kids." She sat next to him.
get sick, and she's really sick."
and reached for the glove balloon that had
captain's chair. "The question is," he said,
r a rhino with a mohawk?" He offered it to

ugged. "You're not supposed to do that."
Try and make you laugh?"
lloons like that for kids," she said. "It's a
rd."
hed. "Childhood is a choking hazard. I ate
eakfast with a side of marbles. I wore clothes
lastic grocery bags."
reluctantly returned his smile and reached for
ut he pulled it away.
eed to check your ID before I give this to you?"
h one eyebrow raised.
ughed. "There's no way I'm showing you my

lourished the balloon. "Your very own punk
rkey-rhino." As he handed it to her, his arm
hers and sent a thrill through her. "Don't choke
e said. He climbed down the side steps of the
ice.
gan's arm tingled where Nathan had touched her.
ced her hand over the area and listened as he
d a tune and puttered around the truck bay. Simply
g he was there comforted her and soothed her
che.
e's kind. And funny. And handsome. He's amazing.
he had not felt such attraction to anyone in a very
time. It frightened her.

Nathan forced a smile. "That's great. I'll boil water in celebration. Now tell me—"

Tones dropped.

"Med 3, be en route to 24 Longpine Road, 24 Longpine Road. Child with a fever."

"10-4," Megan said. "You drive first. I need to text her back."

Nathan stood by the ambulance and rubbed his chin as Megan climbed in the other side. A good drug story would be rehashed to anyone who would listen, but he hadn't heard about it. Granted, she was right, he hadn't worked yesterday, but even so, one of his buddies would have mentioned it or texted him. He shrugged off his uneasiness and climbed into the truck.

24 LONGPINE ROAD
JUNE 5, 2013. 8:25 AM

Megan climbed the bungalow's porch stairs. She had dodged Nathan's questions, but she felt shaky and drained.

The door swung open, and a woman pulled her inside. "I'm sorry! I didn't know what to do! She's burning up!"

Megan looked back to make certain Nathan was behind her and then followed the mother to the living room. A tiny girl in a pink nightgown lay on the couch. She was lethargic, and her cheeks were a fiery red.

The mother wrung her hands. "She won't eat. I tried to give her juice, but she threw it up."

"How long has this been going on?" Megan asked, kneeling next to the couch and touching the child's foot. She felt a pedal pulse and checked the capillary refill.

Good return.

"Just last night. She woke up crying about ten, just as

the early news came on."

Megan picked up a teddy bear and squeezed its tummy as the girl watched her. "What have you given her?" She palpated the little girl's soft belly. The child barely responded.

"Twice the Tylenol I should have," said the mom, "and twice the Advil. Her fever is so high, I just kept giving her more."

"How high is it?" Megan said, placing her stethoscope bell on the bear.

"104."

"Did you take it under her tongue?"

"No, under her arm."

Megan listened to the girl's breath sounds.

A little junky.

"I think she should go to the hospital," Megan said. The mother nodded vigorously. "Nathan, can you carry her out?"

He stepped closer. "Sure." He reached for the girl, but when his hands touched her head, she screamed. He jerked his hands away and looked back at Megan.

High fever. Neck pain. Vomiting.

Her heart sank. She nodded reassuringly and took the mother's arm. "You can ride with us, but we need to go right now." Nathan picked up the child. Megan knew he was being as gentle as possible, but she screamed again. They hurried to the truck.

Nathan sat in the captain's chair. Megan climbed into the back and sat on the jump bench. The little girl had calmed but still sniffled.

"Hi, my name's Megan. What's your name?"

The girl didn't answer and squinted in the lights. The child's mother climbed into the back.

"Her name

Megan nod
arm, and it's go
long, though."

Nathan hook
blood pressure cu

"22-gauge nee
murmured. "Melar
mustache, can you do

The little girl said
cannula over her face
rubbed her gloved ha
sting," she said, holding
with the needle and fed
the chamber. She remov
into place.

Nathan blew up a glo
smiley face on it and placed
it.

Megan adjusted the IV flo
"Are her immunizations up to
as Nathan slammed the doors.

Tears ran down the mother
divorced. Her father takes her to

The ambulance began to m
lump in her stomach and smiled a
her. It wasn't far to the hospital, an
and transferred care to the nurses.

When the paperwork was finis
the truck. With a slow movement, s
pack into the box. She felt cold and
shake an odd sense of foreboding.

Nathan slid onto the jump bench. "

Megan didn'
be alone either.
"Kids shouldn't

He nodded
fallen under the
"is it a turkey
her.

Megan shr
"Do what
"Make ba
choking haza

He grin
Legos for br
made from

Megan
the glove, l
"Do I
he said wi

She la
license."

He f
rocker t
brushed
on it,"
ambula

Me
She pl
whistle
knowi
hearta

H
S
long

Nathan forced a smile. "That's great. I'll boil water in celebration. Now tell me—"

Tones dropped.

"Med 3, be en route to 24 Longpine Road, 24 Longpine Road. Child with a fever."

"10-4," Megan said. "You drive first. I need to text her back."

Nathan stood by the ambulance and rubbed his chin as Megan climbed in the other side. A good drug story would be rehashed to anyone who would listen, but he hadn't heard about it. Granted, she was right, he hadn't worked yesterday, but even so, one of his buddies would have mentioned it or texted him. He shrugged off his uneasiness and climbed into the truck.

24 LONGPINE ROAD
JUNE 5, 2013. 8:25 AM

Megan climbed the bungalow's porch stairs. She had dodged Nathan's questions, but she felt shaky and drained.

The door swung open, and a woman pulled her inside. "I'm sorry! I didn't know what to do! She's burning up!"

Megan looked back to make certain Nathan was behind her and then followed the mother to the living room. A tiny girl in a pink nightgown lay on the couch. She was lethargic, and her cheeks were a fiery red.

The mother wrung her hands. "She won't eat. I tried to give her juice, but she threw it up."

"How long has this been going on?" Megan asked, kneeling next to the couch and touching the child's foot. She felt a pedal pulse and checked the capillary refill.

Good return.

"Just last night. She woke up crying about ten, just as

the early news came on."

Megan picked up a teddy bear and squeezed its tummy as the girl watched her. "What have you given her?" She palpated the little girl's soft belly. The child barely responded.

"Twice the Tylenol I should have," said the mom, "and twice the Advil. Her fever is so high, I just kept giving her more."

"How high is it?" Megan said, placing her stethoscope bell on the bear.

"104."

"Did you take it under her tongue?"

"No, under her arm."

Megan listened to the girl's breath sounds.

A little junky.

"I think she should go to the hospital," Megan said. The mother nodded vigorously. "Nathan, can you carry her out?"

He stepped closer. "Sure." He reached for the girl, but when his hands touched her head, she screamed. He jerked his hands away and looked back at Megan.

High fever. Neck pain. Vomiting.

Her heart sank. She nodded reassuringly and took the mother's arm. "You can ride with us, but we need to go right now." Nathan picked up the child. Megan knew he was being as gentle as possible, but she screamed again. They hurried to the truck.

Nathan sat in the captain's chair. Megan climbed into the back and sat on the jump bench. The little girl had calmed but still sniffled.

"Hi, my name's Megan. What's your name?"

The girl didn't answer and squinted in the lights. The child's mother climbed into the back.

"Her name's Melanie," the woman said.

Megan nodded. "Melanie, I need to put a tube in your arm, and it's going to feel like a bee sting. It won't hurt long, though."

Nathan hooked up the heart monitor and the pediatric blood pressure cuff. "What do you want?"

"22-gauge needle. Saline. I'll do the stick," she murmured. "Melanie, I want you to wear a funny mustache, can you do that for me?"

The little girl said nothing, and Megan slipped a nasal cannula over her face as Nathan prepared the IV. Megan rubbed her gloved hand over the girl's arm. "Big bee sting," she said, holding the skin taut. She pierced the skin with the needle and fed it into a vein. Blood flashed into the chamber. She removed the needle and taped the IV into place.

Nathan blew up a glove like a balloon. He drew a smiley face on it and placed it on the girl's lap. She ignored it.

Megan adjusted the IV flow. "Let's go," she said to him. "Are her immunizations up to date?" she asked the woman as Nathan slammed the doors.

Tears ran down the mother's face. "I don't know. I'm divorced. Her father takes her to her check ups."

The ambulance began to move. Megan ignored the lump in her stomach and smiled at the mother to reassure her. It wasn't far to the hospital, and they quickly unloaded and transferred care to the nurses.

When the paperwork was finished, Megan restocked the truck. With a slow movement, she dropped a new IV pack into the box. She felt cold and fatigued and couldn't shake an odd sense of foreboding.

Nathan slid onto the jump bench. "You all right?"

Megan didn't want to talk about it but didn't want to be alone either. "Yeah. Just ... kids." She sat next to him. "Kids shouldn't get sick, and she's really sick."

He nodded and reached for the glove balloon that had fallen under the captain's chair. "The question is," he said, "is it a turkey or a rhino with a mohawk?" He offered it to her.

Megan shrugged. "You're not supposed to do that."

"Do what? Try and make you laugh?"

"Make balloons like that for kids," she said. "It's a choking hazard."

He grinned. "Childhood is a choking hazard. I ate Legos for breakfast with a side of marbles. I wore clothes made from plastic grocery bags."

Megan reluctantly returned his smile and reached for the glove, but he pulled it away.

"Do I need to check your ID before I give this to you?" he said with one eyebrow raised.

She laughed. "There's no way I'm showing you my license."

He flourished the balloon. "Your very own punk rocker turkey-rhino." As he handed it to her, his arm brushed hers and sent a thrill through her. "Don't choke on it," he said. He climbed down the side steps of the ambulance.

Megan's arm tingled where Nathan had touched her. She placed her hand over the area and listened as he whistled a tune and puttered around the truck bay. Simply knowing he was there comforted her and soothed her heartache.

He's kind. And funny. And handsome. He's amazing.

She had not felt such attraction to anyone in a very long time. It frightened her.

I'm married. I shouldn't feel this.

The turkey-rhino smiled back at her, and shame over her flirting welled up within her.

That's not for me. I can't ever have that.

She withdrew her ink pen from her pocket and popped the glove balloon. As she brushed her hair away from her face, her fingertips touched the painful wound on her eyebrow. She hissed through her teeth and tossed the glove into the trash.

> BARRINGTON COUNTY FUELING STATION
> JUNE 5, 2013. 10:45 AM

Nathan leaned against the side of the ambulance and watched the fuel pump numbers change. His phone beeped.

KRISTEN: Can you cover my shift tomorrow at 6a?

NATHAN: Working Barrington until 8. Sorry.

KRISTEN: Thnx anyway.

NATHAN: You had a rough drug call the other night?

KRISTEN: ? Not me. Megan in Brton.

NATHAN: We did last month. I'm talking about yesterday.

KRISTEN: ?? you had a bth salts call. She got hurt.

NATHAN: Sorry. Stupid autocorrect. Yeah, we had a drug call.

KRISTEN: Rough huh?

NATHAN: Yeah. Glad Megan is ok.

KRISTEN: Me 2

Someone's lying.

Nathan shoved his phone into his pocket, and the fuel pump clunked. He chewed the inside of his cheek. Kristen would have gained nothing from lying.

He climbed back into the cab, where Megan was filling out paperwork, and gripped the steering wheel as the engine idled. The bruises. The injuries. Her avoidance of questions. Nathan pressed his lips into a thin line.

"Everything all right?" Megan asked.

Ignoring her, he put the truck in gear and drove to the station, mulling over all he had seen.

Maybe she's just clumsy. She fell in the antifreeze.

He stopped at a red light.

You don't fucking lie about being clumsy.

The light changed.

Maybe the bruises are from leukemia or something. She said she hadn't checked her levels.

He switched on the turn signal.

When you hear hoofbeats, think horses not zebras.

He couldn't work his mind around it. He couldn't see any other reasonable explanation. And given what he'd seen of Todd, it made sense.

That shitbag is beating her.

Anger built within him, a rage he recognized. But this time there were no insurgents to take down.

Nathan pulled into the truck bay and killed the engine. "I talked to Kristen. There was no drug call in Retton County."

Megan was silent.

"Kristin said you told her there was one here," he said.

"What did you say?" she asked in a strained voice.

Nathan tilted his head back. "I told her I was mistaken

and that there was, in fact, a drug call here."

Megan closed her eyes and exhaled. "Thank you."

"Don't thank me. I want to know what the fuck's going on."

"There's nothing going on."

He shifted to face her. "That cut on your eye isn't nothing—"

"It's healing!"

"—nor was that bump on your chin a month or so ago. And remember the turtleneck? That wasn't because it was cold. That was to hide marks on your arms."

She shook her head. "It's noth—"

"This isn't nothing, Megan!"

She glared at him. "Mind your own damn business." She climbed out and slammed the door.

With the air conditioner off, the chill slowly subsided, and the air grew stuffy. Despite that, Nathan breathed deeply, bringing his heartbeat into check. When he had mastered himself again, he followed her to the EMS room.

Megan had locked herself in the bathroom. He had expected as much. He searched for the remote, shoving his hands around the recliner cushions until he found it, and sat down. Braves vs. Pittsburgh Pirates. He craved the score, but the commentators were discussing the Boston Red Sox.

Shit. The game hasn't even started yet.

Finally, the bathroom door opened. Megan took her spot in the other recliner. Her face was splotched. Nathan could tell she had been crying, and the idea of that made him tap his fingers on the remote with agitation.

"He beats you," he said.

She curled into a knot, pulling her knees up into the chair and wrapping her arms around them.

103

"Why haven't you gotten help?" he pressed.

"Help?" She lifted her head. "From whom? The cops? Really, Nathan."

"There are secret shelters for battered women—"

"And he knows where all of them are!"

Nathan bounced the remote in his hand. "You've got a job. Two of them. Why don't you just leave?"

She lowered her head again and rested it on her arms. "He's my husband."

"Do you love him?"

"It doesn't matter if I love him. I made a promise. 'For better or worse.'" She laughed ruefully. "This is 'worse.'"

Nathan slammed the recliner footrest down. "Like hell it is! 'Worse' is getting fired. Or the bank foreclosing on your house. Or the plumbing backing up. Or," he flung his hand toward his prosthetic, "losing a leg. Having the crap beat out of you is not 'worse.' That's grounds for a divorce settlement in your favor."

"It wasn't always like this."

"I wouldn't think so. You're too smart to have married someone who was hitting you. How long have you been married?"

She picked at the upholstery. "Almost four years."

"Four years?" he exclaimed. "How old were you? 12?"

"I was 20!" she said indignantly.

He shook his head. "Whatever. When did it start?"

"I don't know. Eight or nine months ago, on my birthday." She sat up. "He got mad and backhanded me. I think it surprised him as much as me. I mean, he was always a little rough around the edges. He's always had a temper. But he had been gentle with me. For the most part." She pushed a stray hair behind her ear, her fingers trembling. "His memory's gone bad, and sometimes I'll see him steady himself, like he lost his balance for a moment."

"Do you think he's into drugs?" Nathan said. "I've heard rumors that some Barrington cops are into cocaine trafficking."

"Not so many any more." She shrugged. "But I've looked. I haven't seen anything."

"Who else knows?"

"Emily. She's the only one."

Nathan rocked the chair. "By law, I have to report this."

Megan's face turned a sickly white. "Please, no ... oh, God, Nathan, no."

Tones.

"Med 3, be en route to 876 Windham Drive, 876 Windham Drive. Chest pain."

Nathan stood and pulled his radio from his belt. He looked down at her tear-stained face. "Why should I cover for him?"

"Because I just need time to get everything sorted out."

"To leave?"

She stood. "To help him."

The radio crackled. "Med 3, do you copy?"

"10-4. We're en route," Nathan said.

Megan walked to the door.

"Do you love him?" he asked.

Her hand rested on the doorknob. A moment passed. He watched her shoulders lift and fall with her breath. "I used to." She shook her head. "No. Not now. But I made —"

"A promise. Yeah, I heard." He walked around her toward the ambulance.

876 WINDHAM DRIVE
JUNE 5, 2013. 11:15 AM

They pulled up in front of a ranch house. The large yard was open and flat, dotted with fruit trees, and ringed with a white picket fence. Nathan slammed the cab door and looked around. There were no cars, no people.

Megan stood by the truck, staring at the house. She nervously cracked her knuckles. Nathan walked to her side.

"Are you going to report him?" she asked.

He frowned. "I'm not talking about this right now."

"Emily didn't tell."

"I'm not Emily," he said, frustrated. "Focus on the scene, please."

The yard was well kept. He heard only far-distant traffic sounds.

"It's quiet," she said.

"Yeah."

They walked up the steps.

"I don't see anyone," he said and pounded on the door. "Paramedics!"

They waited.

He pounded again. "Para—"

The door creaked open by itself. They exchanged glances.

Megan pushed the door further. "Paramedics!" she called, stepping inside.

Nathan caught her arm. "What are you doing?"

"Looking for the patient."

"You're insane. There's no way I'm going in there unarmed. Call PD to clear the house."

She frowned. "I don't want to call PD."

"Why?"

Megan canted her head as if he were stupid to ask.

Nathan glowered. "Because Todd's working today. Look, I'm not risking our lives because you're afraid to follow procedures. If we find something before Todd gets here, we can cancel him, but right now, I need a guy with a gun, and I'm rolling PD."

"Maybe there's someone out back," she said, jogging down the steps to the side yard. Nathan finished talking to dispatch and followed her through the gate, which was weighted to close behind them. They walked around the house and peered into the windows. He saw no signs of life. At the corner of the house, he surveyed the empty yard. The trees whispered softly in the warm breeze.

The growl was low and deep.

Two German Shepherds launched around the house, snapping and barking.

"Shit!"

Nathan and Megan sprinted across the yard. He made it to the fence and with one hand on top, hurdled over and fell to the other side. He jumped up to see Megan take a running leap, grab the lowest limb of an apple tree, and swing herself up. She climbed into the higher branches as the dogs barked and lunged, clawing at the trunk.

His heart hammered. "Megan! Are you okay?"

"I'm fine!" she called. "I think I'll, um, hang out here for a while."

"Hang on tight. I can hear sirens. They've sent Fire, too."

"Animal Control would be nice. I haven't seen them in a while. We could catch up."

"I'll see what I can do."

The fire truck rolled on scene, and the firefighters

climbed out. Nathan shook hands with Martin.

"What's going on?" Martin asked, eyeing the enraged dogs.

"Megan's in that tree."

Martin's mustache twitched mischievously. The firefighters leaned on the fence.

"Doll, you've fulfilled my life's purpose!" Martin called.

"Oh?" she answered. "How's that?"

"I've always wanted to rescue a cat from a tree."

"Well, start rescuing!" she yelled. "I want to get down."

Nathan called to the dogs. The firefighters whistled and patted their legs trying to distract them from Megan. The dogs still growled. One abandoned the tree to bark at the firefighters.

A police cruiser arrived on scene, and Nathan narrowed his eyes as Todd emerged from his car. Raw hatred boiled within him, and he wriggled his fingers to keep from clenching his fists.

"You need me to clear the house?" Todd asked.

"Yeah."

Todd leaned back on his heels. "Yep, you medics always have to wait for the real men to do the dirty work first."

"Real men don't—" Nathan cut himself short. If he revealed his knowledge of Megan's secret, Todd might take it out on her.

Todd stepped closer. "Don't what?"

"Nothing. Clear the house."

"That's what I thought." Todd walked to the porch and turned back. "Where's Meg?"

Nathan considered lying. "She's in that tree."

"What the hell?" Todd stepped toward the fence.

"Hey!" Nathan pointed at the house. "What about my

patient? He could be dying in there."

Todd swung back. "Megan is my wife. Don't ever set your one foot between us." He walked to the yard and laughed. The firefighters sullenly relinquished the fence.

Todd drew his pistol. "I'll take care of this!"

"You can't do that," Nathan warned. "Those dogs are protecting their own property. They're properly confined."

"Don't tell me what to do." Todd raised his arms and assumed a shooting stance.

"Think of the paperwork," Nathan said. "And the SPCA will jump all over you. It'll be a media circus."

Todd lowered his arms. "And you're the freak show." He holstered his weapon.

The radio called, "Med 3."

"Go ahead," Nathan said.

"Call is canceled. Caller advises he is no longer at the property."

"10-4. Is animal control en route?"

"That's affirmative."

Todd's radio crackled. "32, be en route to 64 Lorilee Drive, 64 Lorilee Drive. Possible break in."

Todd tipped his head to his mic. "10-4."

Nathan glared at him.

"I'm warning you, Gimp," Todd said, his jaw jutting forward. "Cross me, and I'll take you down."

Nathan laughed. "The fucking Taliban couldn't kill me. I doubt some two-bit cop could do the job."

Todd puffed his chest. "You leave my wife alone."

Nathan stepped closer. "Treat her right, and it won't matter what I do."

"What do you mean by that?" Todd said, resting his hand on his gun.

Nathan leveled his gaze. "Just what I said."

"I'm warning you."

"I'm not concerned."

Todd scowled and slunked to his car.

The animal control truck cruised up the street. The officer rolled down his window and pushed his thick glasses up the bridge of his nose. "What's the problem?"

"My partner got treed," Nathan said, leaning on the truck door.

"The heck you say."

Nathan grinned. "See for yourself." He pointed back over to the apple tree. Both dogs lay beside the trunk.

The officer grinned. "You just need to get him down?"

"Her, yes."

"All right. Let's try easy things first. I have a dog whistle. I'll go to the other side of the house and blow the whistle and see if the dogs will come to me."

"Sounds good. I'll tell her."

The officer crossed the yard, and Nathan briefed Megan on what he was going to do. He never heard the whistle, but both dogs suddenly bounded from the tree and raced around the house. Megan dropped to the ground and dashed to the fence, where Nathan held the gate open.

Martin pulled on his suspenders. "Doll, you sure do make my life interesting."

Megan laughed.

The animal control officer walked toward them and held up the dog whistle. "Should I leave this with you in case you need it again?"

They laughed, and Megan thanked him before he drove away.

"You look gorgeous, Doll," Martin said.

"Oh!" she said as if Martin hadn't spoken. "Did you

find Jellybean a babysitter for Friday?"

"Jellybean?" Nathan asked. "Is this another dog?"

Martin chuckled. "Jellybean is my daughter. And, yes, Doll, I did. Carrie said she could."

"Oh, okay," she said. "I'm not working Retton that day, so if it falls through, call me."

Martin wiggled his moustache. "So you're asking me to call you."

"To babysit," she said, rolling her eyes. "Just to babysit."

He sighed. "There're always stipulations."

"You ready, Martin?" Carrie called.

"Yeah, I'm coming!" he said. "Have a safe shift, Doll. Or you can come with me, and we'll blow this town."

Megan smiled. "Still married, Martin. I'm still married."

500 BLOCK WHITAKER AVENUE
JUNE 5, 2013. 7:00 PM

Megan sipped her water and put her cup back in the holder. She rubbed the red scratches the apple tree had left on her arms.

"Med 3," the dispatcher called, "standby at Post 4."

"10-4." She sighed. "Is this punishment for some sin I committed in a past life?"

Nathan laughed as he turned the ambulance around. "What do you mean?"

"I hate it when they switch to system status management, letting some computer program anticipate calls and put us in those areas ahead of time. As if the extra calls that tip us into system status aren't enough of a strain, posting from the ambulance instead of a station only makes things more stressful. And I have yet to see a difference in patient care."

"You really should try to form stronger opinions."

"It means I don't have my own bed or my own bathroom. I hate sleeping in the truck." She wrinkled her nose. "And Post 4 is the worst."

"It won't be so bad. You're just grumpy."

"No, I'm not—" She stopped. Anxiety seized her. "Yes, I am." She leaned toward him. "I have to know. Are you going to report Todd?"

"Megan," Nathan groaned. "I don't know, okay?" She dropped back to her seat. "I need time to think. But I'll tell you this." She pricked her ears. "If I report him, you'll know. You'll know first. For now, just let it rest."

As Nathan drove downtown, Megan retreated into her iPod's music. Irritable and worried, she pulled her Prusik cord from her pocket, twisted a loop, and tied a butterfly knot. She straightened the cord and tied it again. The repetitive motions relieved her tension and allowed her thoughts to wander and remember.

Martin had walked into the common room of Station 6. "Hey, Doll, there's a mangy mongrel sniffing around out there for you."

Megan blushed. A police car was parked in the station driveway. Todd leaned against it, a huge bouquet of goldenrod tied with green ribbon in his hands. "There she is," he said. "Barrington's newest and prettiest paramedic." He swept her into his arms and kissed her.

Firefighters hooted behind them.

Megan rounded on them. "Can I help you?"

"We just want to watch," one said. "Keep going."

She rolled her eyes. "Go away!"

"Come on, guys," Martin said. "Leave them alone."

"Don't mind them," Todd said. He held out the bouquet. "These are for you. I had thought about roses, but goldenrod seemed fitting. I love you, Sunshine. I always will."

She had taken the bouquet with a smile.

The Prusik cord slipped from Megan's hands. Her vision blurred, but she blinked the tears away.

Nathan turned the ambulance into a sub shop parking lot. On one side, there was a bar named Rocky's with a cartoon squirrel on the sign. Little shops clustered together.

Nathan backed into a parking space. "Now cheer up. It may be a post instead of a station, but let's make the best of it."

"At least there's good pizza across the street," she conceded, shaking off her melancholy.

"And a little coffee shop over there. Do you want to get some coffee?"

"Sure."

The coffee smell wafted to Megan's nose as they crossed the parking lot. Nathan opened the door and held it for her. His gesture made her feel womanly, and she had the sudden desire to wear something other than boots and cargo pants.

Megan stared at the menu board. "I have no idea what to get."

"Just pick something."

"Too much pressure."

"I've seen you work a code. You thrive under pressure."

She shook her head. "Those are algorithms based on presentation. This is entirely subjective."

Nathan raised an eyebrow. "It's coffee." He approached the counter. "Medium house blend, please."

The barista pushed a button on the cash register. "Cream and sugar?"

"Milk, if you have it."

"And for you?" the barista asked, looking at Megan.

"The same, please," she said.

"With milk as well? Or cream and sugar?"

"Cream and sugar."

"Anything else?"

Megan glanced into the case of baked goods. "Oh! Apple Farm Danish! Have you ever had one of those?" Nathan shook his head. "Two Danishes, please," she said.

The barista wrapped the two Danishes in wax paper and handed them over to Megan and Nathan with their coffees.

"Try it!" Megan said.

Nathan took a bite. "Tastes like," he wafted his fingers near his face, "diabetes. With a side of neuropathy."

"And diabetes never tasted so good."

Tones.

Megan groaned and scarfed down three bites as they gathered their things.

"Med 3, be en route to 76 Industrial Way, 76 Industrial Way. Unknown trauma."

Megan's mouth was full of Danish. She pointed at Nathan.

He flashed a wicked grin. "I don't understand."

Megan glared at him, grabbing her coffee.

"Med 3, do you copy?"

Megan swallowed and chased it with burning hot coffee. "10-4," she choked, dancing on her toes and sputtering as Nathan laughed.

They hurried to the door. "Are you okay?" he asked.

"No thanks to you!" she said, grinning and letting the door slam back on him.

His shoulder hit the frame. "Hey now!" She giggled and trotted across the parking lot, feeling light. His smile energized her and made the world seem right.

Megan jumped into the passenger side and flipped the lights and sirens as Nathan started the engine. "How do you have an unknown trauma?" she asked. "All of a sudden there's blood everywhere, and someone's shouting, 'I just don't know where it all came from'? I mean, surely they know something."

"Maybe the caller hung up before dispatch could ask."

Nathan pulled the ambulance into the parking area outside a steel warehouse. Megan pulled on her gloves and grabbed the jump kit.

A man ran toward her, his shirt covered in blood. "There's so much blood! I don't know how it got everywhere!"

Megan dropped the jump kit and rifled through it for more personal protective equipment. "Okay, sir, tell me what happened." She pulled out a yellow gown and tossed the bag to Nathan before sliding her arms into the sleeves. Once she had her gown tied, Nathan handed the bag back to her and returned to the ambulance for the stretcher. She followed the man inside.

"It's Rodney," the man exclaimed. "He got his arms caught in the cutter. I think it's just his arms, but I can't tell!"

Megan stopped at the door and stared. It looked as if someone had spray painted blood on the walls, floor, and equipment. She wriggled her nose as the metallic smell filled her nostrils. A man lay on the floor in a pool of dark red blood, his arms shredded.

Megan counted fingers as she approached the patient. Her boots crackled in the sticky blood on the floor.

"Rodney!" the man behind her called.

The bloody man gave a thumbs-up.

Megan knelt. "Sir? Can you tell me what happened?"

"My own damn fault. Flipped off the safety. Turned the damn thing back on."

"Why are you lying down?" she asked.

"Dizzy. That's my blood that damn machine sprayed everywhere."

"Yes, sir," she said, looking closer at his hands. All fingers were accounted for and attached. The skin on his hands and forearms had been sliced in multiple places, leaving open wounds of fat and tissue that oozed a trickle of dark red blood. White flashes of bone and ligaments shone through the redness.

"Can you move your fingers?" she asked and was amazed when each one wiggled. She verified a pulse in each hand.

Megan grabbed a stack of 4x4s, divided it between her hands, and covered the wounds, holding pressure. The stretcher rattled into the building.

"Nathan, get some roller bandages."

Nathan found two rolls of gauze and tossed her one. "I've got this side," he said, taking one of Rodney's arms.

Megan rolled the bandage around the 4x4s, anchoring them and adding pressure. She twisted the bandage as she rolled, then tied and tucked it in place. "Sir, can you climb onto my stretcher?"

"Think so," he said, and she helped him up.

In the back of the truck, Megan gave Rodney a nasal cannula and took a blood pressure reading as the ambulance began to move. All seemed stable, and she started an IV above the wounds. When she popped the tourniquet and ran the fluids, Rodney raised his other arm.

"Don't think it's s'posed to do that," he said, pointing to the blood dripping off his arm and pooling on the floor.

Megan grabbed pressure. "No. No, it's not." She leaned over for another roll of gauze but could not reach it. As she traded hands, the ambulance went over a bump. Her boots slid, smearing blood across the floor. She braced herself, her bloody palm on the wall, and wrapped the gauze over the wound again, adding pressure and elevating his arm.

They soon arrived at the emergency room and turned Rodney over to the nurse. He gave Megan another thumbs-up through the bandages.

Megan ripped the thin, disposable gown from around her neck. It was covered in blood. She carefully slid it from her arms, making certain the soiled surfaces stayed to the inside.

Megan walked to the ambulance dock where Nathan stood, with arms folded, staring into the back of the truck. Blood smears marred the jump seat and the cabinets. The floor was covered in bloody footprints and littered with bandage wrappers and other packaging.

"What the hell happened back here?" he asked.

"Unknown trauma."

"It wasn't a mass casualty. It looks like a bomb went off. And I would be one to know."

"It's not just here," she said. "You saw the workshop. His blood was just ... fluffy."

He cast her a glance. "Fluffy."

"Effervescent?" She giggled. "Prolific!"

"The red stuff is supposed to stay inside the patient."

Nathan maintained his straight expression, but she saw his smile in his eyes.

"Well, the bandage that leaked wasn't the one that I tied," she said. He looked down at her, and she lifted her shoulders.

He turned back to the ambulance. "Why is there packaging all over the floor?"

"Where else would it be?"

"We have a trash can. You open the package, and—watch closely—put the package into the trash." He mimed dropping paper into the trash.

"That takes too much time. Look, this is faster." She pretended to drop paper onto the floor. "Besides, I have to clean the truck anyway. Why does it matter?"

"Because it makes a mess. And I have to clean up after you."

Richard walked onto the dock. He looked into the ambulance and creased his brow. "What happened?"

"Unknown trauma," they answered together.

"Why didn't you call a trauma alert?"

Megan rubbed the back of her neck. "It didn't really qualify."

Nathan handed Megan a pair of gloves and a can of disinfectant wipes. "I'll get the mop."

"Before you do that," Richard said, "I wanted to tell you both that Emily had her baby. They're doing fine."

"Awwww," Megan gushed. "We'll have to go visit before we leave."

SACRED HEART EMERGENCY ROOM
JUNE 5, 2013. 9:30 PM

Nathan leaned on the EMS desk while Megan filled out

paperwork.

"Done and done," she said, slapping her hand on her report and shoving it into the file. "Let's go see Emily now."

He frowned. "It's 9:30. Don't you think it's a little late to go visiting?"

"Nah, they're going to be up with the baby all night anyway. Sleep is dead to her now."

He shrugged. "Lead the way."

Megan sailed through the hospital to the maternity ward. "She's in room 248 ... 244, 46, 248." She lifted her hand to knock.

"Hold on," he said, resting his hand on her back. He leaned to the door. "Okay, I hear the TV and voices." He noticed how natural it felt to touch her and that she did not move away.

A baby wailed.

"And crying," Megan laughed, and she knocked. Reluctantly, Nathan put his hands in his pockets.

A man with black hair opened the door. "Oh, hey, Megan, come on in."

"Hi, Matt!" Megan said. "Nathan, you know Matt, right? He's a firefighter at Station 2."

"No, we haven't met," Nathan said and introduced himself, shaking hands.

Megan walked to the bed. "Hey!"

"Hey, you!" Emily said. Sitting up against the pillow, she set her water cup on the bedside table next to a vase that held two red roses. "Come meet Annabelle. She's going to be an opera singer."

Emily held out the crying bundle, and Megan gathered the baby into her arms.

"Ohhh," she sighed. "She's adorable. Look at that little

119

mouth."

Nathan watched Megan croon to Annabelle. Her hair fell over her shoulder, and in the soft glow of the over-bed light, he was reminded of classical oil paintings. Affection welled within him, but he forced his gaze away, deciding to strike up a conversation with Matt about baseball. Or something.

Megan bumped his elbow. "You have to hold her," she declared, lifting the tiny bundle.

"No, I'm good."

She poked out her bottom lip. "Oh, come on."

"What if I drop it?"

"Then pick it up," she giggled.

To make her happy, he took the baby, which to him looked more like a cartoon monkey mummy than a child, but the expression on Megan's face made it worthwhile to him. He smiled and handed Annabelle back to Emily. "Cute kid."

"Thanks," she said.

A knock on the door announced the arrival of the nurse. She pushed a machine into the room. "We need to test Annabelle's hearing."

"Okay, we'll get out of the way," Megan said, hugging Emily. "She's beautiful. Congratulations."

Nathan and Megan walked toward the elevators. "Wasn't that the cutest thing you've ever seen?" she gushed.

Nathan knit his brow. "Oh, yeah, definitely." He stepped into the elevator, and Megan bounced in beside him. It pleased him to see her so buoyant and carefree. The doors closed. "You really like babies, don't you?"

She grinned. "Yeah, I'd love to do neonatal transport."

"You'll have kids yourself, right?"

She deflated and turned away. "That's personal."

"I sleep in the same room with you," he said, kicking himself for ruining her mood.

She pushed the floor button again. "No, I'm not going to have any children," she muttered.

"Why not?"

Megan faced him. "You know why not. He shouldn't be a father." She huffed. "Not that there's any action anymore to make him one. Zero chance of children."

Nathan pushed the mental image aside. "So, you're going to let him steal motherhood from you, too?"

"That's just the way it is."

Her apathy angered him. That she would let a slime ball like Todd ruin her life was more than he could understand.

"Have you enrolled in college yet?" he pressed.

"Damn it, Nathan. Back off."

The doors slid open, and Megan fled the elevator on the wrong floor, catching Nathan off guard.

"Megan!"

He jammed the open button.

That woman!

The doors shuddered and reopened, and he ran into the hall in time to see her enter the stairwell. He jogged to the door and pushed it open.

Nathan could hear her on the stairs several floors below.

She would choose the stairs.

He set his jaw, preparing for discomfort, and began his descent, feeling the heat increase in his prosthetic. He caught up to her in the stairwell outside the emergency room.

Megan had pressed her back to the wall to allow a janitor to carry a large, wooden rocking chair through the door. The chair was used when a child died so the parents could rock their baby one last time. Megan's face was drawn. As the man passed, she held the door. Nathan reached over her head and held the door as well.

Sam stood just inside the emergency room.

"Who passed?" Megan asked.

"A kid named Melanie," Sam said. "Doc thinks it was bacterial meningitis."

Nathan's heart sank. He watched the man carry the chair down the long hallway, past the doctors, nurses, techs, and secretaries. All paid due reverence. He glanced at Megan. She was gone.

He swung around to Sam. "Where did Megan go?"

Sam pointed to the door that led to the ambulance dock.

Nathan palmed the door open. The hospital lights shone into the dark parking lot. The sulfurous floods above the dock hummed, and bugs swooped in clouds around them, clicking as they hit against the plastic covers.

Megan sat on the edge of the dock with her Prusik cord in her hand. She seemed very small, her shoulders bent. The cute ponytail no longer swung with her movements; rather, it draped limply down her back.

Nathan sat down next to her. "You couldn't have done anything else for her."

Megan looked up at the parking garage. "That's just it, isn't it? I can't change anything. Another life lost, another life gained. It's just one big circle, one big cycle that I can't change or stop or slow. There's no purpose to the pain. It just keeps going."

Nathan saw the widening chinks in her armor. The mercy that formed her essence and the confidence upon which it was founded strained against the circumstances.

She was foundering.

He searched for words. "When I was first in rehab, the only thing that marked my day was when they cleaned my wounds. It hurt like hell, but three times a day, no matter what, they came to do it. I could fight, or I could let it happen, but either way, it was coming. I was helpless and soon hopeless. I became depressed.

"They assigned me a counselor, and he'd visit every few days. I refused to talk to him, so he talked to me. He was a bilateral amputee, lost his legs in Iraq. He understood it all. The phantom feelings, the pain, the fear. The guilt I thought no one knew about. But he told me that even though the insurgents had gotten my foot, they didn't own the rest of my life unless I gave it to them. That I was the one in control of that choice, and it was my responsibility. He told me I was—and am—just as much a soldier as I was in Afghanistan. That the fight would continue. I just wasn't in theater anymore.

"Every day was a new battle. If I focused on the pain, I lost the battle that day, but if I focused on the good, even if it was one thing, then I won. One good thing. It was a mantra.

"I started small. A day with less pain. My first time without an IV. One day the only good that came was a cookie with my lunch, but I found the good, and man, that cookie got me through.

"My counselor is the one who told me to get up off my ass and get moving. He's the one who got me into swimming. Swimming gave me the desire to get healthy, to take charge of myself, and do whatever I damn well had to do to keep that good in my life.

He met her eyes. "Your battle's different from mine. But the strategy is the same. You have to find the good.

One good thing. A new baby, soup day, pink toenails." He bumped his shoulder into hers. "Diabetes-inducing Danish." Her smile flickered, but she looked away. "Slowly you move on to bigger things. But taking responsibility for that battle is critical."

She met his eyes. "What do you mean?"

"I'm not going to report Todd."

"You're not? Thank—"

He held up his hand. "No. Listen to me. I'm not going to report him because you need to be the one to get help. No one can rescue you, Megan. You have to rescue yourself."

Silence fell between them.

"I don't know how," she said finally.

"I think you do. Play to your strengths, and the rest will take care of itself."

She shook her head. "You make it sound easy."

"It's the hardest thing you'll ever do." He placed his hand on hers. "But I'll help you however I can." She looked up at him. The yellow floods turned her brown eyes to a burnished bronze that highlighted the weariness that lined her face. He wished he could ease her struggle.

Tones.

"Med 3, be en route to 364 Peachtree Lane, 364 Peachtree Lane. Shortness of breath."

"10-4," he said, carefully climbing to his feet. He offered his hand. For a moment, he thought she would refuse, but finally, she slipped her hand into his, and he helped her to her feet.

Chapter Six

802 WILLOWMERE DRIVE
JUNE 20, 2013. 6:30 AM

Megan awoke to the tearing of Velcro as Todd removed his bulletproof vest. He was in the living room, she in bed, but with the removal of each strap, the sound clawed her ears. She sat up on her elbows and glanced at the clock, hoping for a few more minutes. 6:30. Time to get up, get a shower, and get to work by 7:50. She rubbed her eyes and looked longingly at her pillow.

Climbing out of bed, Megan pulled her hair into a messy bun and padded into the kitchen, still wearing her pink and white knee-length sleep shirt.

Todd, in his boxers and T-shirt, carried his uniform, vest, and duty belt to the bedroom. Neither said a word to the other. It was the way of things, and Megan preferred it over the alternative of yelling and hitting. She yawned and started the coffee maker, wondering if there was enough creamer left. She snapped open a box of Cheerios, and they clattered into a bowl. As she reached for the milk in the fridge, she shook the bottle of creamer.

Eh, I'll make it work.

She poured milk on her cereal and wrote 'creamer' on the grocery list. Hearing her phone buzz in the bedroom, she set her bowl on the counter and went to retrieve it, trying to remember what else she needed from the grocery store.

Megan stopped at the bedroom door. Todd was holding her phone and flicking through the messages. Her stomach dropped. Nathan's messages were in there.

"Give that back," she said.

He continued to scroll. "No."

She crossed the room. "That's mine. Give it back to me." She reached to take the phone, but he snatched it away.

"'Message from Nathan Thompson.' 'Message from Nathan Thompson.' 'Message from Nathan Thompson,'" Todd read.

"He's my partner. I have to talk to him."

"On your days off?" He tapped the screen again. "'What's your one good thing?' Meg, what the hell does that mean?"

The damage done, Megan didn't want to fight. It was too early for loud voices. "It's complicated. Look, I don't have time for this. I've got to get ready for work."

She walked back into the kitchen and picked up her bowl. There was nothing in her phone that needed hiding; she knew she had done nothing wrong. Yet the thought of Todd intruding on Nathan's messages riled her. She wanted to shield Nathan, to hide him, to keep him clean and special and separate from Todd's vindictive rudeness. Her hands shook as she got a spoon from the drawer and went to the living room to check the weather. Her Cheerios were mushy.

Todd stalked in, her phone still in his hand. "You're cheating on me."

"No, Todd. I'm not," she said, looking for the TV

remote. She heard his angry tone, but it was familiar, and she, complacent. She didn't have time for his bellowing.

"You're cheating on me, you fucking whore!" Todd threw the phone at her head. She yelped and ducked as it smashed into the bookshelf behind her. He closed the distance and slapped the bowl from her hands.

Milk sloshed across the carpet.

Megan blocked her face with her arms, but Todd grabbed her wrists.

"Let go!" she said, pulling against him.

They struggled, and Todd shoved her against the wall, pinning her body with his. "I told Gimp I'd kill him." His night shift stubble scratched across her cheek.

Megan turned her face away. "Why would you say that?" she cried and tried to twist from his hands.

Milk beaded up on the carpet.

He shook her, and her head smacked against the wall. "Because you're mine."

"That hurt!" Megan's heart raced. She had seen him violent, but this was different. Darker, stronger. She was scared.

His face contorted. His nostrils flared. "I've seen how he looks at you," he snarled and shoved her again. "The way they all look at you."

Crying, Megan pulled against his grip, frantic to escape him. "You're hurting me!"

He released her hands and grabbed her chin. She froze.

His voice was low. "You're mine."

Todd pawed under her nightshirt and clutched her breasts. He licked her neck, revolting her senses.

Megan understood.

She shrieked and beat her fists on his shoulders.

He grabbed her hair and slung her against the edge of the coffee table. Her rib bent and cracked; her scream died in a gasp of pain. His body slammed onto hers, hurling her head back. Forearm across her throat. She dug her nails into his skin, but he crushed a pressure point at her shoulder. Her strangled cry. Resistance, response, repugnance. Quivering pain and a shortfall in strength. Reality dissolved into a tinge of darkness. Her thoughts flailing, thoughts escaping, thoughts clinging, anywhere, anything. Automatic recall.

Hemorrhage.
Airway, Breathing, Circulation.
Deformities, Contusions, Abrasions.
Punctures, Penetrations, Paradoxical motion.
Burns, Lacerations, Swelling.
Tenderness, Instability, Crepitus.

Hemorrhage.
Airway, Breathing, Circulation.
Deformities, Contusions, Abrasions.
Punctures, Penetrations, Paradoxical motion …

Milk soaked into the carpet. Cheerio dregs abandoned and naked on the floor.

EMS STATION 1
JUNE 20, 2013. 8:45 AM

Megan pulled into a parking space and switched off the car. She glanced at her watch and cringed. 45 minutes late for work, but Med 3 remained in the bay. She felt numb. Her arms weighed tons. She shook with anxiety at the idea of seeing Nathan.

He'll know. He's always getting into my head. He'll know.

Seeing Nathan, though, was better than losing her shift and being sent back home.

Megan willed herself to open the door and step out. Her chest spasmed with the movement. She walked into the station and heard the chatter of dispatch. She listened to Richard and Nathan discussing the Braves and the Mets. Her feet stilled at the normalness of their words. They turned the corner before her.

A shadow fell over Nathan's face. Megan avoided his eyes.

"There you are!" Richard said, frustration in his tone. "Megan, you've never been late. Not once! Now you're almost 45 minutes behind? What's going on? What's your excuse?"

Megan picked at the seam of her pants. "I don't have an excuse. I lost track of time."

"Could you not call? I mean, I've already called Harold. He should be here any minute to take your shift."

Megan withdrew her phone from her pocket. "It's broken. The screen is cracked, and it won't turn on. I'll get it fixed as soon as I can. I'm sorry. Please let me have my shift."

Richard sighed. "If you were anyone else, I'd say no. And I'd probably dock your wages to cover Harold's overtime, if I could. But you've never pulled anything like this before. Promise me it won't happen again, and you can have your shift."

Again.

The word rang through her mind. The thought struck her with panic.

"No," she said, her voice cracking. "Not again."

"Are you all right?" Nathan asked.

Megan stared at a smudge on the wall and nodded.

"It all works out," Richard said. "I need a crew to take a transport to Canton. 48-year-old man is going for heart surgery. He's stable, but it makes for a long day—four hours there and four hours back."

Megan nodded. "I'll move the truck up the hill." She turned around and walked back to the bay.

"Atta girl," Richard called after her.

A transport was perfect. For the next four to five hours she wouldn't have to talk to anyone, and she would not even be in the cab with Nathan. She could rest and think. Megan drove the ambulance up the driveway to the back of the emergency room. She didn't block a space at the dock; rather, she parked next to a ramp the ER shared with Radiology.

Megan opened the back of the truck and pushed the release bar for the stretcher. Pain burned through her chest, leaving her breathless. She pressed her fingers on her lower rib cage, whimpering involuntary, and put her head down on the stretcher.

I can't.

Nathan's familiar, slightly irregular footsteps crunched up the driveway. She squared her shoulders and lifted her chin.

"Megan." His voice cast tremors through her.

She slowly released the breath she had been holding and turned around. "You want to get the stretcher?" She brushed past him without waiting for an answer.

"Megan, talk to me."

She spun around. "About what?" she asked. "What shall we talk about? Let's make it quick. We have a patient to get."

Nathan stared at her, but she couldn't read him. He showed no emotion, no reaction. "I see."

Megan's stomach dropped.

He knows!

She slowly released her breath.

No, that's not possible.

"You see nothing," she hissed and walked up the ramp. "Get the stretcher!"

Megan held the door of the elevator as Nathan rattled the stretcher inside. "Which room?" she asked.

"330."

Elevator awkwardness pressed around them. Finally, the doors opened at the third floor, and they rolled toward the patient's room. Megan thanked heaven for perky nurses. All she had to do was stand aside, and these women did the work of moving the patient onto the stretcher and transferring IVs and heart leads, all with enough winks and smiles and pats on Nathan's arm to keep him distracted.

"I'll drive first," she said as they walked back to the ambulance.

"All right. We can switch halfway. About Laurel City?"

"Sure."

Nathan slid the stretcher into the back of the ambulance and climbed in. Megan slammed the doors behind him.

I'm golden.

Megan climbed into the cab and drove to the end of the driveway. She flipped the blinker on and waited for a break in traffic. When all was clear, she edged forward and turned the steering wheel. Pain ripped through her chest. A cry escaped her lips. The ambulance shuddered as she struggled to pull it into the lane.

"What was that sound?" Nathan called from the back.

"Must be the radio doing something funky. I'll adjust the squelch."

Megan sat at the stop sign, working up the courage to turn the ambulance again. A horn honked behind her. She gritted her teeth and turned into traffic.

Two more until I reach the interstate.

By the time she entered the interstate, she was panting and sweat beaded on her forehead. Exhaling a ragged breath, she shifted in her seat, ready for the long ride.

MILE MARKER 178, INTERSTATE 753
JUNE 20, 2013. 4:00 PM

Restless and agitated, Nathan leaned his elbow on the passenger side door. Something was terribly wrong, but he had no idea what it was. Megan hadn't spoken to him when they had swapped places at Laurel City. She hadn't said a word when they had transferred their patient to the university hospital. At lunch, she wouldn't say what she wanted to eat, only that she wanted a restaurant that was right on the highway. A cloud had hung over the table while they had eaten, and he was sick of her taciturn behavior.

She may as well tell me what I did wrong.

Nathan watched her drive. Her left foot dangled at the side of her seat; she always did that when she drove. She was a supervisor's dream: never overconfident in her driving, never reckless, even while running code 3. Hands always at 10 and 2.

Except today.

Today, Megan pressed her elbow close to her side, the

tips of her fingers resting on the bottom of the steering wheel. Today, she consistently ran 15 to 20 miles over the speed limit. She kept the FM radio so low he couldn't hear the music, and the air conditioner turned up so high that he worried about it freezing up, yet she kept pulling a tissue from her pocket and wiping the sweat from her forehead.

I've had enough of this crap.

"Do you want to switch out now?" he asked. "We're almost to Laurel City."

Her brow creased. "Why?"

"I just want to drive."

"I guess." She moved the ambulance into the outside lane and turned on the blinker for the exit. It was the crossroad of a remote highway, marked only by a gas station and a sign selling baled hay. She pulled into the parking lot, and they switched places.

Nathan got into the driver's seat, his knees nearly bumping his chin. He slid the seat back to fit, and Megan climbed in on the passenger side. Since he was adjusting things, he reached for the FM radio, and as he put out his hand, Megan flinched.

I'm not putting up with this shit.

Nathan pulled out of the parking lot and turned away from the interstate.

"What are you doing?" she demanded as he drove down the highway. "Where are you going? Does this go back to Barrington County?"

"I don't know."

He pulled over and rolled down the windows. Only cotton fields surrounded them. Killing the engine, he pulled the keys from the ignition and threw them out the window onto the grass in front of the truck.

"Nathan!" Megan cried.

"We're going to talk."

"I don't want to talk."

He laughed. "No shit! You've made that crystal clear all day! I've majorly pissed you off, and I want to know what I've done. Now talk."

She met his eyes and said nothing.

"Okay then. I'll talk," he said. "I'll tell you what I see. When I texted you last night, everything was fine between us. So something happened between then and 0800 this morning, and I bet it has to do with your being late for work. Unless it was my last text. In that case, I'm sorry."

She looked out the windshield. "It's not you."

"Then what happened?"

Megan squinted. "Todd found your messages in my phone. He—accused me of having an affair with you. He threw my phone at me. That's why it's broken."

"Fuck. I'm sor—"

"He threw me against the table. I think he broke my rib."

"Megan—"

"He…"

"What?"

She shook her head.

"Damn it, Megan! This is because of me! What'd he do?"

"It's not because of you," she insisted. "Don't worry about it!"

"Did he hit you again?"

"It's nothing I can't handle!"

"Then tell me what happened!"

"No!" she cried.

"Stop shielding him! You think if you don't tell anyone

that everything's fine! Quit kidding yourself!"

"I—"

"I care about y—keeping you safe! Tell me what happened!"

"He raped me! Okay?" she shouted, her chest heaving and her forearm pressed against her shirt. "He raped me."

Nathan was stunned. He closed his eyes. Bile rose in his throat and a searing sensation spread from his core, down his arms, to his fingers, which curled tightly around the steering wheel. He felt a battle lust deeper than any he had ever felt before. His heart pounded, his ears throbbing with his pulse. He dug deep, gripped every ounce of control he had, and focused on slowly releasing his fingers from the steering wheel. He placed his hands loosely on his knees and opened his eyes. The highway stretched before him, empty and barren.

Megan trembled violently in the passenger seat, her breath ragged and shallow. A tear stumbled down her cheek, leaving a moist path that ended near the corner of her mouth.

"We've got to get you to the hospital," he said. "I saw an 'H' sign an exit back—"

"I'm not going to the hospital."

"The evidence—"

"I've already been to the restroom. I've already showered and changed clothes. There is no evidence." She shifted gingerly in the seat to face him.

"You're hurt. You need care. X-rays—"

"I took some ibuprofen."

He unbuckled his seatbelt. "We've got morphine in the back."

"You can't use that. We have to give an account for it."

"I'll call med control. On my cell. So it won't go over

the radio."

"No. I don't want anyone to know. The pain's not that bad. It just hurts to drive the truck, to turn, you know."

"Did he hurt you any, anywhere, um, else?"

"No."

He slid down in his seat. "Okay," he muttered, wetting his lips and measuring his breath. His mind raced through the protocols she refused to follow.

Evidence preservation. Transport. Rape kit. Special Victim report.

He wanted rules, a system. Check the boxes, and everything will be all right.

"When?" he asked. "What time did this happen?"

"A little before seven," she said, her voice flat.

I was asleep. Sound asleep in my own bed while he— I'll break his neck.

Megan's fingers blanched white as she gripped the seat. Her entire body shook. Nathan wanted to hold her, kiss her, and reassure himself that she was alive and whole and safe. But she had flinched. She was skittish. If he acted on impulse, he would destroy her trust.

"You're certain you don't want to go to the hospital?" he said. "Not even to talk to someone? It's confidential—"

"I know the speech. I'm not going."

"Whatever you want. You're in control right now. But, please, Megan, when we get back to town, take the rest of the shift off. Harold will cover for you."

She shook her head. "And go where? I'm not going back in that house."

"You can go to my place." Nathan hesitated, unsure of what exactly he had just offered. Whatever it was, it was said, and he plowed on. "Sam's not there. He has an in-service class today. It'll be quiet, and you can rest."

"What if Todd finds out?"

"I'll drop you off there. Your car will still be at the station. There's no way he can know." He watched her, hoping. He hadn't been able to protect her that morning, but he could start now.

After a moment, she nodded. "Okay."

"Do you have any extra clothes?"

"I have a bug-out bag in my car. A few sets of clothes and things and another uniform."

"I'll call Richard and tell him you're sick. Do you want to ride in the back? You could lie down on the stretcher or the jump bench."

"I want to sit up here," she said. "I don't really want to be alone right now."

"Sure." He looked out the windshield. "But I need to go find the keys. I'll be right back."

Nathan climbed out and slammed the door.

He needs to be dragged into the street and shot.

A car flew by and continued down the highway.

I could arrange that.

As Nathan walked down the shoulder looking for the keys, he dialed Richard on his phone.

"What's up, Nathan?" Richard asked.

"We're just north of Laurel City. Megan's sick. When we get back, she'll need a sub."

"Sick? What's wrong with her?"

Nathan glanced back at the truck. The passenger door was open, and Megan stood by the ditch, leaning over with her hands on her knees. She vomited onto the grass. "She's throwing up," he said.

"Eee. Okay, I'll call Harold in. You've already dropped off the patient, right?"

Nathan saw the shine of brass on the ground. "Yeah.

Transfer went fine. We've gotten something to eat and are heading back." He picked up the keys.

"All right, man. Take care."

Nathan leaned into the truck to get his water cup from the restaurant. He pulled the plastic lid and straw off as he walked to Megan. "Here."

She rinsed her mouth and spat on the ground. "Thanks."

They walked back to the truck, and Nathan helped her into the cab. He noticed purple bruising on her neck and thought he might throw up, too. Instead, he closed the door and kicked the back tire as hard as he could. No risk of a stubbed toe.

Nathan leaned on the side of the ambulance.

I should have reported him! All my talk! One good thing! What did it get her?

His vision blurred, and his face felt hot. He sniffed and blinked and swung his arms as if stretching before a swim. He strengthened his resolve. From now on, nothing was going to hurt her. Nothing.

He grabbed a blanket from the back. "We don't have a pillow," he said, climbing into the cab. "This is the best I can do for you."

"Thanks," she said with a small smile.

"Harold will sub for you when we get back."

She didn't answer. He switched on the truck, pulled a three-point turn, and drove to the interstate.

Nathan merged and accelerated. He knew he was speeding. He didn't care. No cop was going to pull over an ambulance.

"Are you going to press charges?" he asked.

"No."

Nathan glanced over at her, but she stared out at the

interstate.

"He's my husband," she continued. "What kind of wife charges her husband with rape?"

"One who's been raped. A marriage license doesn't prove consent."

"Nothing can prove consent. No one would believe me."

"I do."

"A cop charged with rape," she said. "It would be all over the papers. It wouldn't take long to track its way back to me. People would talk. They don't take me seriously as it is, and with that out there ... no." She shook her head. "I don't want to go through that. I don't want people to look at me differently, and I don't want to be reminded."

"It won't just go away."

"I know that!" she snapped.

Nathan passed another car.

Her shoulders drooped. "I'm sorry. I'm just—"

"It's okay. Act however you need to act. I'd rather you be real with me than polite."

8735 PETERSON AVENUE
JUNE 20, 2013. 6:00 PM

The ambulance turned into the Peterson Apartments. The buildings stood tall and trim, tastefully colored, with neat landscaping. A shimmering blue swimming pool shone beyond a high metal fence.

"These are nice," Megan said, thinking of her own little house and feeling shabby. "I didn't know you lived here."

"Yep. 218."

"Second floor?" She tried not to glance at his leg.

"Yes, and please don't seem so surprised," he said,

with a lopsided grin. "Have I taught you nothing?"

She attempted to return his smile, but it seemed difficult to move the right muscles.

They walked up the stairs on the outside of the building. Nathan carried her backpack, which they had stopped by the station to pick up. He unlocked the door to 218 and pushed it open for her. Megan stepped into the dark and quiet. The air smelled faintly of his laundry detergent. Nathan flipped on the light and closed the door. The open living room was furnished with two lumpy couches and a suede recliner, all facing the television and gaming systems. The back window's vertical blinds were open enough to reveal a small balcony with a café table. Only a worn out pair of running shoes, which lay discarded on the carpet, seemed out of place.

"I swear Sam was raised in a barn," Nathan said, snatching up the shoes and tossing them into the room on the right side of a short hall. He ducked into a room on the other side, and she heard the rattle of a pill bottle.

Megan slid her hands into her pockets and pressed her elbows to her sides.

"So, eat anything you want," he said, walking back. "But I'm not responsible for Sam's reaction if you eat his frozen burritos. There are towels in the bathroom if you want a shower. TV, whatever you want. The Braves game comes on in a little bit."

He held out a small orange pill bottle. "I keep these on hand for the times when I have residual pain. It's just codeine. If anything, it'll help you sleep."

Megan hesitated, then took it. "Thanks."

He nodded. "Sure. Do you need anything else?" She shook her head. "I'll lock the door when I leave."

"Okay."

He smiled and closed the door behind himself. She heard the key turn in the lock.

Megan stepped to the front window and peeked around the curtains. Nathan walked to the ambulance. She heard the diesel engine rev to life and watched him drive away. Letting the curtains fall from her fingers, she turned back to the apartment. The quiet pressed around her. She rubbed her elbow, feeling awkward and out of place and yet strangely at ease. Though she lacked a sense of peace, she knew she did not have to fight any more.

Megan wandered through the living room and into the kitchen. The clock on the wall ticked loudly, and she watched the second hand march around the face of it. She found a glass in one of the cabinets and filled it with water while she studied the codeine bottle. Nathaniel Bryan Thompson, Jr.

I should eat something before taking this.

Megan opened the refrigerator and found good food, but all of it needed to be cooked. She let go of the door and stared as it closed.

Remembering the cereal she had found when looking for a glass, Megan pulled down a box. Corn flakes clattered. And clattered. More and more. Never stopping, growing louder. His grip, his breath.

She flung the bowl away. Shattering in her ears, in her eyes, returning and falling. Slammed back, sliding down. A scream unseen.

Megan sat with her back pressed against the cabinet and her knees bent to her chest. Her breath came in short gasps. Cereal covered the floor. Ceramic pieces lay strewn amidst the crumbles.

Gradually, she slowed her breathing.

It's just the stress. Pull yourself together.

Wiping her wet face with her hands, Megan stood up and found a broom in the pantry. She swept the kitchen, threw away the bowl and cereal, and returned the box to the shelf. Ate an apple from the fruit bowl. Swallowed a white pill.

She went into the bathroom. Dark green and navy blue towels offset a deep brown shower curtain. The counter was littered with razors, toothpaste, men's deodorant, and an out-of-date copy of *Radiology Today*.

Just like any other bachelor pad.

But a chair stood in the corner. Underneath, a spare socket liner draped over the top of a two-liter bottle. Forearm crutches, such as those she had seen used by polio victims, leaned on the wall.

He's not an ordinary bachelor.

She splashed water on her cheeks and buried her face in a towel, intentionally turning her back on the mirror. She couldn't see the marks Todd had left if she never looked.

She returned to the hall. The door on the right stood open and bore a 'Caution: Radiation' sign.

Sam.

Heavy curtains blocked the sunlight, and the glow from a computer screen cast a bluish hue. The fan whirred in the desktop computer. Video cards and cooling fans were piled on the desk and the floor, and a model of a Firefly class spaceship hung on fishing line over a messy double bed. The shoes Nathan had thrown into the room lay on the floor surrounded by scattered papers and dirty clothes, including a t-shirt with a picture of a dancing skeleton that said, 'Keeping the RAD in Rad Tech.'

Megan smiled.

He's almost as messy as I am.

She turned around in the hallway and stared at the door on the opposite side.

Then this must be ...

The door was open a few inches. Sunlight poured around it and into the hall, bathing her boots in light. She bit her lip and pushed on the door, ignoring her conscience.

The same heavy curtains hung at the window, but these were looped back over a hook on the frame, allowing light to fill the room and make it bright and cheery. Everything was neat and tidy and dusted. The queen-sized bed was covered with a dark gray comforter. Megan's cheeks grew warm. She quickly reminded herself that she already slept with him three nights a week.

Not in this bed.

Megan stepped further into the room. The air bore Nathan's scent, not only of his detergent, but his aftershave, his deodorant, and a hint of powder. It was comforting, almost as though he were there, and her shoulders relaxed.

Autographed baseballs, bats, and Braves mementos adorned one wall. Atop a high dresser sat a mason jar of coins, various papers and bills, and another jar, this one full of bullet casings.

Next to the dresser, a wooden case held five rifles. Two reminded her of the old west, and three had a distinct military look.

His voice filled her mind.

'I have an M4 and a shovel.'

A doorstop held the closet door open. Megan brushed her fingertips over the row of sleeves. Red Barrington EMS shirts controlled the center. To the left were the blue Retton County button-ups and still left of that, other red, black, and gray shirts. The right side of the closet held neatly pressed and hung pants, dress shirts, and in the back, an ACU uniform.

Ever the soldier.

A tall bookshelf lined the wall next to the bed. Several heavy textbooks and manuals weighted the bottom. Three tipped to the side as if waiting for a missing shelfmate.

'I want it back sometime, but you can borrow it, if you like.'

One shelf held a framed Army unit photograph. The soldiers stood on dusty ground in front of a shipping container. Megan moved closer. The men wore helmets and body armor and carried rifles, posing in two rows: one row standing, the other kneeling. She scanned the tough faces, and her heart skipped when she saw Nathan. He was kneeling, his left boot forward.

Before.

A display case hung next to the shelf. On the black velvet inside lay army rank patches and several medals and ribbons. Many of them bore a striped pattern of black, red, and green. She didn't know what most of them were for, but she recognized the Purple Heart.

Megan's conscience won her over, convicting her of intrusion. She walked back to the door, but a bedside table caught her attention, and she slowed her steps. Various-sized prescription bottles, skin care ointments, wet and dry powders, and shrinkers sat next to towels and prosthetic socks and sleeves. The difficulties he faced in his everyday life became real. A deep sadness moved her. She pressed her hand over her mouth and sank to the edge of the bed.

How? How could this happen?

It made little sense to her how something so tragic could happen to a man as kind and capable as Nathan. Her anger burned, and she clenched her fists. But she knew the futility of her thoughts. Her hands relaxed, helpless. His limb loss must have changed him. Perhaps—in some ways —made him stronger.

Hardly compensation.

It had certainly changed the course of his life. If not for the IED, he would not have retired and joined Barrington EMS.

And I never would have met him.

Megan picked up a sock and smoothed the knit fabric between her fingers. She wondered why it was pink. Carefully returning the sock to the table, she picked up a prescription bottle and lifted it just high enough from the group to read the drug name. An anti-inflammatory. She lifted another, and another, and stopped. An anti-depressant. Slower, she chose another. Anti-anxiety. She picked up the last one. Anti-psychotic.

PTSD?

He had said he'd been depressed, that swimming had pulled him out. Apparently, there was more to the story than he had let on; she could surmise the rest. No one at the station talked about stress, or depression, or PTSD. When she had been an EMT, Megan had confided to a coworker about a nightmare she had had after a bad call. She had been told to 'Suck it up, Princess,' and she had learned her lessons well. She said nothing when she heard partners moan in their sleep or hastily wipe their eyes and complain about the pollen. She would say nothing about him.

The air conditioner cycled on. The rush of air through the vents returned her to the present. Suddenly aware of her snooping, she shook her head with embarrassment.

A wave of fatigue broke over her. Megan blinked,

feeling the effects of the codeine.
  I need a shower and some normal clothes.

Chapter Seven

EMS STATION 1
JUNE 20, 2013. 7:00 PM

Nathan stared unseeing at the supply shelves. Megan's revelation had completely drained him. All he could see was her small, trembling form in the passenger seat, the pain written in her eyes. It took all of his self-restraint to keep from driving to the police station and tracking Todd down. He wanted to tear him limb from limb.

Richard pulled open the supply room door. "Good to see you back, Nathan. Did you get Megan squared away?"

"Yeah."

Richard creased his brow. "You feeling okay? To use my grandmother's words, 'you're lookin' mighty peaky.'"

"Uh, no, I'm not feeling so great. Now that you mention it," he said, rubbing his forehead.

"Did you and Megan get the same food today?"

Nathan followed Richard's line of thought and chose to pursue it. "Yeah, we did," he lied. "Why?"

"I bet you two have food poisoning. Maybe you should take the rest of the day, too. Evelyn's been bugging me for hours. I can call her in."

"Whatever you think is best."

A half hour later, Nathan pulled his truck into a

parking space at his apartment.

Sam trotted down the stairs and jumped into the passenger seat, slamming the door. "Why is there a beautiful girl sleeping on my couch? Is she for me? Can I keep her? I promise I'll feed her and take her for walks and," he looked up wistfully at the building, "pet her often."

"It's Megan."

"Oh, I know. I recognized her before I tucked my tail and fled."

"Todd raped her."

"Shit."

"Yeah."

Sam sighed. "So, where are we burying his body?"

"Don't joke about this, Sam!"

"Sorry, man. I'm coping."

Nathan leaned on the steering wheel. "You don't know how often I've thought about doing that today. Seriously doing that. There's a spot on top of the bank across from the police station. I could take the M24 up there and— "

"Geez, you have a plan. Okay, let's think down a different pathway, shall we? What do we do now?"

"I have an idea of how you can help, but I want to talk to her first."

"Me? What is it?"

"I want to talk to her. Come on."

Nathan slammed the car door and walked up the stairs with Sam. After a moment's hesitation, Nathan opened the door.

Megan lay on the couch. Nathan's eyes fell to the curve of her hip, and he chided himself for thinking of her sexiness at such a serious time. She blinked and sat up, running her hand through her hair, which was still damp from her shower.

"Hey," he said.

She smiled a little. "Hey. Hi, Sam."

Sam waggled his fingers.

"How're you feeling?" Nathan asked.

Megan glanced warily at Sam. "Fine."

"It's all right," Nathan said, wanting to reassure her. "I told Sam."

"You what?" she whispered, slowly standing.

Nathan had the sinking feeling he had misstepped but wasn't sure what he had done wrong. "I told Sam what happened."

Megan clenched her fists. "I told you not to tell!"

Sam cleared his throat. "I'm, um, just gonna hit the head." He closed himself in the bathroom.

Megan plunged her fingers into her hair. "How could you tell him? Does the whole hospital know now?"

"No, it's Sam." Nathan shrugged. "I mean, he's here. He would find out sometime."

"How?" she cried. "How would he know? Is it written on my forehead? Do I have an indicator light? I trusted you! And here you go blabbing everything to Sam!"

"He—"

"Now I have to trust him! I don't even know him! Confiding in you was so stupid of me!"

Nathan paused and nodded. "You're right. I'm sorry. I shouldn't have told anyone, even Sam, without asking you first."

"You're sorry?" She laughed. "That's it? You're just sorry? Sorry doesn't make it better!" She snatched up the couch pillow and flung it at him.

The pillow hit Nathan's chest and fell to the floor. Slowly, he placed his hands behind his back and interlocked his thumbs.

"Sorry doesn't wipe his memory!" she shouted, bending with the force of her words. "Sorry doesn't make things as they were! Sorry doesn't fix anything!" Tears streamed down her cheeks. Her hair flung about her face. "You think you can just waltz back in here and make whatever decisions you want to. Just because you're bigger and stronger than me doesn't mean you get to control everything! Who are you going to tell next? Richard? Martin? Why don't you go ahead and call the police chief! The newspaper!

"I never would have told you had I known you'd give me away!" she sobbed. "I can handle this myself. I don't need you! I don't want your help! I can manage on my own!" Her voice rose shrilly. "I don't need anyone's help! Just leave me alone and let me handle things!"

She gasped for breath, trembling.

"I'm listening," Nathan said.

"Well, that's a first!" She closed the distance between them. "Why does it take me getting in your face over something for you to hear me? You men are all the same. You never listen. You just do whatever you want and don't give a damn what anyone else says. You just keep going. You and your arrogance and self-assurance!" She shoved him. He rocked back a step but maintained his stance as she shouted, "You're unfeeling! Uncaring! You don't give a rip about me and what I want! You never stop!"

Megan beat her fist on his chest. "You have to listen! I won't let you ignore me and push me aside and take whatever you want. I didn't want it! Do you hear me?" she cried, turning away and bracing her forearm to her ribs.

Nathan remained still.

"I didn't ..." Her voice sank to a whisper. "I didn't

want ..." Dropping down on the couch, she covered her face with her hands and curled down into her lap. Sobs racked through her.

Nathan felt helpless but suspected it was good for her to cry. He released his hands. The room was growing dark. He moved to turn on the overhead light but remembered her preference for lamplight and switched on the end table lamp instead. He sat on the cushion next to her, his elbows on his knees, his hands clasped loosely before him. He wanted to put his arm around her but didn't know if he should, so he did nothing.

Megan sniffed and lifted her head. "I'm sorry. I didn't mean to yell at you."

"You weren't yelling at me."

Nathan watched her, allowed her time to think. The neighbors' door slammed, and he heard them laughing and talking as they walked to the parking lot. Silence fell again, and he studied the carpet and the couch pillow she had thrown. He picked it up and offered it to her. She looked at him, tears clinging to her lashes, and accepted it, pressing it to her chest to splint her ribs.

"I'm never going back," she said.

"No one's going to make you."

"I've thought about it." She wiped her face. "I nannied Jellybean when she was a newborn, so I can probably stay with Emily and help with Annabelle until I can find my own place. Emily has an apartment over her garage. I don't work again until six p.m. tomorrow in Retton, so I can handle it in the morning. And—wait, why aren't you at work?"

"Richard thinks we both have food poisoning."

Megan glanced at him. "Did he say you looked peaky?"

Nathan pursed his lips and nodded.

"He always says that," she said with a small giggle that ended in a ragged breath.

Nathan wrinkled his forehead. "You need to get checked out by a doctor."

"No." She shook her head. "My lung hasn't collapsed or anything. My chest isn't unstable. It's just a cracked rib. Not a big deal."

"I still think it's a good idea. You don't have to do anything you don't want to do, but what if Sam took a chest x-ray?"

"I'm not going to the ER!"

Nathan tipped his head. "I didn't say that."

"But he'll need an order."

"Would he?"

She squinted.

"I haven't talked to him about it yet," he said. "I wanted to talk to you first. Can we just ask him about it?" He waited for her nod. "Sam! Come on out."

The door of the bathroom opened, and Sam walked into the living room.

Nathan gestured to the suede recliner. "Have a seat."

Sam grinned. "In your chair? Really?"

"Don't make a habit of it," Nathan said as Sam plopped into the chair. "I have a favor to ask."

"Oh?" Sam patted the arms of the chair.

"During the course of, um, what I told you about, Megan got hurt on her rib area here," he said, pointing to his left chest. "She doesn't want to see a doctor or go to the ER here or anywhere else, but I was wondering if during your next shift you might be able to snap an x-ray or two of her. Just to make sure there's nothing seriously wrong."

"With no order?"

"No."

"Who's going to read it?"

"You will."

Sam waved his hands. "Dude, I'm not a radiologist. I mean, I know I said that in the pub the other night, but that was just because this redhead—"

"Everyone knows you can read an x-ray. That's why they always ask what you see and you have to say, 'I'm sorry, I'm not allowed to say anything.'"

Sam sighed. "So what do you propose?"

"Megan and I will go the back way into radiology, you take the film and read it, and then we leave."

"The back way?" Megan asked. "You mean, through the morgue?"

"Yeah. Does that bother you?"

She shook her head.

"Will that work?" Nathan said, looking at Sam.

Sam slowly nodded.

"When is your next shift?"

"Tonight."

"You just got here," Nathan said. "You're going back?"

"That was an inservice. Now I have my regular shift. They think my super powers are activated by energy drinks and candy bars."

Nathan nodded. "They may be right."

"Nah," Sam said, flexing his muscles. "I'm super all the time. Without sleep deprivation and nutritional deficiency, the world wouldn't be able to handle me. What time will you be there?"

Nathan shrugged. "When is it slowest?"

"It varies, but usually about four or so."

"Then that's when we'll be there," he said, relief pouring through him. He heard Megan shudder again.

"When was the last time you had pain meds?"

"When you gave it to me this afternoon."

"Then you're an hour late for more. You've got to keep that stuff on board, or you're going to get pneumonia from not breathing deeply enough."

Sam stood. "While y'all discuss drugs, I've got to get ready for work." With another little wave to Megan, he went back to his room.

"Are you hungry?" Nathan asked, standing as well. "I can make you some eggs or something."

"I'd like that."

"Come on in the kitchen. Can I get you something to drink?"

"Yes, please. Just water."

Nathan was relieved to be doing something instead of talking. He filled a glass and handed it to her along with the codeine as she leaned against the counter. It was not lost on him that Megan Henderson was in his kitchen and that her jeans and t-shirt clung to her in all the right places. He suddenly realized what a disservice her uniform did for her figure.

Nathan chose a frying pan from the cabinet. He spun it in his hand as he set it on the stove. "How many eggs?"

"Two."

"Fried, scrambled, sunny-side up—"

"Scrambled." She climbed onto a bar stool.

He lifted an egg carton from the fridge door. "So, after you left today, Harold and I went code 3 on this call—"

Megan shook her head. "No, you didn't."

Nathan grinned. "You know what I'm going to say."

"You can call it code 3. They can dispatch it code 3. You can confirm it code 3. But there isn't anything in Harold's driving that could be even remotely construed as code 3."

"Pedestrians were going faster than we were."

"And the siren!" she said, touching her temples.

Nathan waved the salt. "Phaser. The entire time. I switched it to wail, and he put it back."

Sam walked into the kitchen wearing his scrubs. "Who's this?"

"Harold," Megan said. "So, you're inching along with the same tones that never, ever stop."

"I was hypnotized by the time we got to the call."

"That's what he wants," Megan said. "All the medics hypnotized. It's all his ploy to take over the world."

Sam's hand stopped inches from a plate. He turned back to Nathan with a look of approval. "The Force is strong with this one," he said, nodding his head back toward Megan. Nathan laughed and also took a plate.

Sam dumped the eggs from the frying pan onto his own plate.

"Dude! That's Megan's!" Nathan protested.

Sam pinched Nathan's cheek. "Thank you, huneee. I've got to run." He lifted his hand to Megan. "See ya tonight, kid!" Sam, steaming plate in hand, grabbed a fork from the drawer and walked out the door.

Nathan gaped as the front door closed. He looked back at Megan. A smile flickered on her lips that made his heart melt. "All right," he said. "Let's try this again." He cracked two more eggs.

As he cooked and she watched, they swapped trauma stories. They complained about supervisors and grumpy ER nurses. Nathan slid their plates onto the bar and sat on the stool next to her. Their conversation turned to current events, politics, and movies they had seen. He attempted to think coherent thoughts, but his words tripped over her loveliness. Megan's hair had curled as it had air dried, and it framed her face, highlighting the brown eyes he adored. She wore no makeup, and he thought her beautiful. But as much as he enjoyed her company and conversation, a thought chafed him.

"Do you think Todd will come after you?" He gathered their plates. "Do you think he'll just let you go?"

Megan shrugged. "I don't know. We dated in high school, but I broke it off for a while after graduation and dated," she averted her eyes, " … someone else …" She sipped her water and stared at the glass a moment. "Todd kept trying. Like he never understood I'd left him. Maybe that's what made it so easy to go back. We were able to pick up where we'd left off."

Nathan nodded, curious of her past, but not wanting to pry. "Do you have money? I mean, obviously, you have your own means of support, but what about cash? For an apartment deposit, a utilities deposit, opening a new bank account. Do you have any on hand?"

"Only what's in the joint checking account and maybe $30 in my wallet."

Nathan put the dishes in the dishwasher. "Before we go to the hospital, we should stop at the ATM and withdraw some."

"How much should I get?"

"At least a thousand. Is there enough in the account?"

"Yeah, I can pull that if the ATM will let me. I won't know until I try."

Nathan looked at his watch. "It's almost nine." He hesitated. "I need a shower and a nap."

"I should lie down, too."

Their eyes met, and he felt more awkward than he had the first night they had shared the EMS room. Megan looked away and walked into the living room. He turned to the hallway and heard his chair's footrest open.

Nathan gathered his clothes and locked the bathroom door behind himself. He dropped into the chair and untied his regular boot, setting it against the wall. He stared at his prosthetic. It would be best if he didn't put it back on immediately after his shower.

She'll see my stump. Damn, I hate that word. Stump.

Nathan pressed the release button and removed the leg, propping it next to the sink. His prosthetic gave him equal footing with anyone. It helped people look past his injury; if they didn't know he was an amputee, most of the time, they couldn't tell. Even when he wore shorts, people could still visualize him whole. The brain expected something to be below the knee, and the prosthetic gave it that. But without the prosthetic, people focused on the gaping absence, only seeing the nothing and the crutches, and that produced pity. Shock he could handle. Disgust didn't bother him. Pity churned his stomach and boiled his blood. He pictured the expression Leah had had when he had fallen in the pub. He imagined Megan with The Look. White-hot anger flashed within him.

Fuck this shit. You've worked too damn hard to sit here like a fucking coward. Now get up off your ass and act like a man.

Nathan pushed up on his sound foot and hopped to the sink. He looked himself in the eye.

Hooah.

Nathan showered and dressed in shorts and his army unit t-shirt. He would have to cross the hall to his bedroom to finish his limb care. Clenching his teeth, he turned the doorknob, the crutch clinging to his arm. He crossed the hallway, his ears searching for any sound of her movement in the living room. He heard nothing.

Nathan sat in the chair next to his bed and leaned the crutches against the wall. He squeezed moisturizer onto his hand and rubbed it into the skin of the limb. He reached for a shrinker.

A soft knock.

Nathan's heart hammered. He had left the door half open, and Megan leaned around it.

"I can't sleep," she said. "I slept all afternoon."

He met her eyes. She seemed to ask permission to enter, and he nodded.

Nathan stared at her as she walked closer. He watched her study the crutches, his hands, the shrinker, and finally, his residual limb. She climbed onto the bed across from him and tucked her pink toes under her as she always did. He searched her face and saw sadness and curiosity, but none of the pity he had feared. He relaxed his jaw, the muscles sore from clenching.

"What are you doing?" she asked.

"I have to keep it wrapped to prevent swelling."

She nodded, and he pulled on the shrinker.

"Does it hurt?"

"Sometimes. But the shrinker? No."

"What about phantom pains? Do you ever get those?"

"Yeah, it's like tingling or someone squeezing my foot really hard. Sometimes it's sharper, like the explosion just happened."

Her impish gleam in her eyes, Megan leaned over and put her hand out to where his foot would have been. She squeezed an imaginary foot. "Can you feel that?"

Nathan laughed. "You're not right. And I don't feel phantom pains all the time."

She hugged his pillow in her lap. "So what really

happened?"

Nathan sat back in his chair and ran his tongue along his molars. "We were on patrol. We walked back to the road, and Lowell stepped on it."

"Who's Lowell?"

"Enoch Lowell. A specialist in my unit." He cleared his throat. "He was my friend."

Megan stared at the floor. After a moment, she met his eyes.

He shook his head. "I should have seen that IED. We had patrolled there who knows how many times. I was—" His throat constricted. "I was distracted."

"What distracted you?"

Nathan wet his lips. A feminine hand. A cotton scarf.

"My girlfriend had just broken up with me."

"Oh," Megan said, looking away again.

"Fault lay on both sides. Deployment is hard, and loyalty is rare. She sent me a letter and ended it, right as we went out on patrol. There was this Afghan girl—woman —I don't know. She had a dimple just like Heather's ..."

Nathan rubbed his face and closed his eyes, trying to block the scene that only became more vivid in his mind. When he opened his eyes, Megan was still waiting, her chin resting on the pillow she held. Serene. Gentle and unassuming. Driving his restless compulsion to speak.

"I killed him."

She lifted her head. "You said he stepped on the IED."

"I sent him there. We weren't supposed to talk to the women, but I told him to take candy to her for me. It was stupid ... she's dead, too. They say she was the one who placed the IED."

"You didn't kill him. You couldn't have known—"

"I knew the rules," he said.

"So did he."

A calm silence fell between them.

Megan yawned and lay on her side. "Besides, you were on patrol. You were just doing what you had to do."

"People say that, but I didn't have to be there. It's not like I was drafted. I volunteered. I chose to be there."

"You didn't choose the outcome."

He shrugged. "That's what my counselor says, too."

She smiled. "You should listen to him. He seems wise."

Nathan raised his eyebrow. "You only say that because he agrees with you." He shook his head. "The outcome wasn't the hardest part. The hardest part was not being able to go back."

She frowned. "What do you mean?"

"I wasn't allowed to go back. I couldn't fix what I'd fucked up. I couldn't finish what I'd started. Deployment is different from anything here. The brotherhood, the adrenaline high, sure, but life was simpler there. Stateside, well," he shrugged, "things are complicated here. It's like you hate it while you're there, but you'd give anything to go back."

Megan coughed, and he noticed congestion he had not heard previously. He was glad it was only a few more hours before the x-ray.

"What happened then?" she asked. "After Germany?"

Nathan told her about the Center for the Intrepid that had been built to provide care for soldiers such as he who had lost limbs in Afghanistan and Iraq. He described the therapy pool and the rock wall. When he looked back over at Megan, her eyes were closed and her breathing even. The codeine had finally won.

"Good night, Megan."

8735 PETERSON AVENUE, APARTMENT 218
JUNE 21, 2013. 2:45 AM

Nathan awoke with a start as enemy fire popped around him. He plunged his hand under his cot to get his rifle.

Fuck! Who put this box under my cot?

His phone buzzed again on the end table as he pummeled the couch. Nathan fumbled for the screen and fell back on the cushion. With a grunt, he switched on the lamp.

Picking up his crutches, Nathan went into the hall and stood by his bedroom door. A fleeting vision of a handsome prince kissing the sleeping beauty passed through his mind.

Nope. Too creepy.

He pushed the door ajar. "Megan. Megan!" He heard her stir. "It's time to get up."

Nathan went into the bathroom to brush out his morning breath. When he opened the door, Megan was leaning on the wall. Her forehead was furrowed, and she blinked with sleep. Her hair hung in mussy snarls. As they moved around each other in the small space, she met his eyes and looked away, closing the bathroom door behind her. He went to his room knowing that his pillow had caused those snarls.

Within the hour, they climbed into Nathan's truck.

"This is nice," Megan said, admiring the interior. "It's very clean."

He pointed to a small trash can. "In my truck, all 4x4 wrappers go in there."

"Roger that," she said.

"Are you mocking me?"

"No more than you're mocking me."

"We're even then," he said. "Where's your bank's ATM?"

"There's one over by Station 3 in that little strip mall."

Nathan drove to the ATM, and Megan climbed out to make the withdrawal. He tapped his fingers on the steering wheel as she typed on the number pad and waited. She typed again and propped her hands on her hips. Without getting anything from the machine, she walked back to the truck.

"What's wrong?" he asked as she opened the door.

Megan leaned back in the seat. "I'm trying not to panic. There's no money in the account. $1,984 was withdrawn yesterday afternoon."

"What the—"

"He knew I'd leave and need money. I have $28 to my name, and we don't get paid until next Friday. Oh, God, what am I going to do?"

Nathan watched her a moment. Money complicated everything. But he couldn't leave her destitute. He reached over her knees to the glove compartment and took out the small notebook and pen he used to keep track of his truck's fuel efficiency. Turning to a clean page, he wrote 'Promissory Note.'

"I'll loan you the money," he said, writing out the details in duplicate.

Megan laughed. "I'm not taking your money. I'll ask Emily or—"

"You can't depend on Emily for everything. You still have to ask her for a place to stay. What other real option do you have?"

Megan fell silent.

"That's what I thought," he said.

"Charge me interest."

"I don't care about—"

She turned away. "Then I won't take your money."

"You're not taking it," he said with growing frustration. "You're borrowing it."

"Not without interest, I'm not." She crossed her arms.

Nathan slid his jaw to the side.

Stubborn woman.

"Fine," he said, writing. "I'll lend $1,000 at 4% to be paid off in 6 months."

"Add in the out-of-system bank fees."

"No."

"But—"

"I don't even know how much the fees will be."

"Well—"

He ripped the paper from the notebook. "Your copy." With a small sigh of defeat, she accepted it.

Nathan walked to the ATM and withdrew the $1,000.

This is one hell of an investment.

SACRED HEART PRIMARY CARE
JUNE 21, 2013. 3:45 AM

Because they were supposed to be recuperating from food poisoning, Nathan parked his truck at a nearby doctor's office instead of the hospital parking garage. Megan glanced up at him as they walked along the dimly lit sidewalk. His resting face was stern, but she knew better. She listened to his steps, the slight rhythm of his gait, and relaxed into the familiarity. Normally, the shadows would have made her nervous, but his presence lent her confidence.

Nothing scares him.

They approached an inconspicuous door near the Emergency Room/Radiology parking lot.

"So far, so good," he said, pulling on the door. It didn't budge.

"You have to swipe your card."

Nathan withdrew his wallet and pulled out his EMS ID. He ran it through and pulled the door. It didn't move.

Megan slid in front of him. "Excuse me." She swiped her own ID, and the lock clicked.

"The hell!" Nathan said as she opened the door. "I'm not pretty enough?"

Megan's stomach fluttered at his implied compliment. "You have to have ER clearance, I guess. I'm on the ER sub list."

Nathan held open the door. "Are you ready?"

She hesitated. "I don't think I need this. I mean, what's it going to change?"

"Hopefully nothing. But that cough of yours is getting worse. What do you think?"

"I think you over treat."

He smiled. "Okay. So what are you going to do?"

Megan shrugged and walked through the doorway. A cold hallway stretched before them. The walls, tiled in a sickly green color, were lined with unmarked doors. The chill seeped into her skin and ran through her veins.

Nathan wrinkled his nose. "It smells like body bags down here."

She laughed. "I bought a shower curtain once that was made of the same plastic. I had to take it back. I couldn't tolerate that smell in my house."

A stretcher with high side rails and a thick vinyl cover rested against the wall. A corpse could be placed inside, and when the cover was replaced, the contraption would look like a supply cart. Staff could then wheel the body through the busy hospital, and no one would be the wiser. As Megan and Nathan walked by, Nathan lifted the cover and peaked inside.

"Stop it!" Megan said, looking around for morgue technicians.

"Why? If something's going to come out of that thing after me, I want to know what it is beforehand."

Megan hurried to the elevator, and Nathan followed. Radiology was still and quiet. Most of the lights were turned off. They walked to an office alcove with a light box and rows of large manila files. Sam sat at a desk piled high with more files.

Nathan cleared his throat. "Sam."

"Hey!" Sam moved around his desk. "You ready?"

Megan nodded.

"We'll be right back," he said to Nathan.

Sam led her to the x-ray room. "Take off your shirt and your bra." He turned a deep shade of red as he handed her a hospital gown. She ducked behind the curtain of the changing area.

"Any chance you might be pregnant?" he called from behind the lead partition.

"No."

When Megan was ready, Sam stood her in front of the machine. "Doc Thompson wants you to have a chest x-ray, but I'm going to take a chest series and a rib series, if that's okay."

"Whatever you think is best."

Sam smiled. "I figure what he doesn't know won't hurt him."

He curled her shoulders forward. She felt his knuckle on her upper spine, and he reached past her to tape a metal 'L' onto the surface in front of her.

"When I tell you to, I want you to take a deep breath and hold it."

She nodded, and he stepped into the side room. "Deep breath and hold," he said.

She did as she was told, ignoring the spasms in her chest. The machine beeped. He repositioned her and took several more images.

"All right, kid, you can get dressed." He hurried from the room.

She held her shirt in front of her hospital gown. "Sam!"

Sam stuck his head back in the room. "Yeah?"

"I appreciate—I mean, I know you went out of your way—I really—Thanks."

He smiled. "No problem."

Megan dressed quickly, listening to the low mumble of Nathan's and Sam's voices. She began second guessing the x-ray. If Sam got caught, he might get into trouble. He made it seem like it was no big deal, but it was a big deal to her.

She pulled open the heavy door and walked to the alcove.

Sam touched the computer screen. "All right. Now let's see." He pointed to her sixth rib. "There's a crack there—"

A woman's voice carried through the alcove. "Oh! What have we here?"

The three spun around. A small woman bustled toward them, wearing a white coat and glasses.

"Dr. Nguyen!" Sam said. "We were just, ah, looking over some images for a, um, CEU class I'm taking."

She slid her glasses down her nose. "Excellent. And what do you see?"

"A fracture. Here," he said, pointing.

"And?"

"Um ..."

"Here and here," she said, pointing to two more areas. "Probably from an impact. It looks like this patient was hit by something about this wide." She held her fingers about 3 inches apart. "What else do you see?"

"There's bruising along here," Sam said.

"Yes, slight bruising throughout the area, but no fluid build up. Anything else?"

"Everything else appears normal."

"Very good, Sam. I'll make a radiologist of you yet. On the whole, this patient will do fine. It's not a dangerous injury," she peered over her glasses at Megan, "but a very painful one. Are you two in the class as well? Don't you work with EMS?"

"Yes, ma'am," Nathan said. "We just stopped by to see Sam."

"What good friends to stop by at," she checked her watch, "four thirty in the morning. Well, I'm off to find some coffee." She walked to the hall and turned back. "Sam, you know, I think if that were my patient, I'd recommend lots of rest and lots of pain medication. I'd remind her to breathe deeply. But unless she develops a fever or the cough doesn't clear in a week or so, she should be fine."

"Thank you," Sam said as Dr. Nguyen walked away.

Megan cringed. "Are you in trouble?"

"I don't think so," Sam said. "She's always been pretty cool. I guess what's done is done." He shrugged. "I wouldn't worry about it."

"We'll get out of here and let you work," Nathan said.

"Bye, Sam," Megan said. He waved.

Megan and Nathan rode the elevator back to the morgue.

"I'm going to live, at least," Megan said.

"I'm glad."

Something in his tone caught her attention, but he stared at the light that changed from 1 to B. The doors opened, and they walked into the green hall. Nathan held out his hand and ran it along the side of the covered stretcher. He jerked back. "Damn."

"What?"

"I cut myself on the stretcher," he said, squeezing his index finger. Blood dripped out.

Megan took his hand. "Let me see."

The door at the end of the hallway flung open, and Todd and an officer named Tyler walked in. With a gasp, Megan cast Nathan's hand away from her. "Todd!"

Todd strode toward them. Megan saw only Todd's face, his narrowed eyes, his set jaw. Her mouth went dry, and her knees, weak. Her heart pounded in her chest as she stumbled back and reached to the cold, tiled wall.

Todd clenched his fists. "Why are you dressed like that? I thought you were on the trucks until eight tomorrow."

Megan tried to swallow. There was not enough air in the hall. "I got—the day—off."

"Then what are you doing here? Why are you with him?"

Nathan pulled her away. "She doesn't have to explain anything."

"Get your hand off her!" Todd shouted.

"My hand hasn't hurt her!"

Todd shoved him. Nathan advanced, his boots squeaking on the shiny floor.

"No!" Megan cried, darting between them and pushing

on Nathan's chest.

Tyler grabbed Todd's shoulder and dragged him back. "Todd! Come on! We need to get those body bags and get back in zone."

Todd shook him off and pointed his finger in Megan's face. "I know what's going on. Don't think you can hide from me. I'll talk to you later." He and Tyler walked away.

Megan stared at the corner where Todd had disappeared. She could still hear Todd's voice in her head and feel his breath on her neck.

Nathan withdrew a handkerchief from his pocket and wiped the blood from his hand. "I'm going to get Ebola."

Megan barely registered what he had said. "You—you should get that cleaned out."

Nathan snapped his fingers. "Hey."

She looked at him through her tears.

"It's going to be okay," he said. "You just go to Emily's and lay low for a few days. He'll get the idea you don't want anything to do with him." He checked the wound and covered it once more. "But listen, if we're ever in a situation like that again, stay behind me, all right?"

She nodded.

"You understand? Behind me?"

"Behind you."

Too many thoughts filled her head. She was scared. Hurting. Nathan was fearless and safe. She leaned against his chest, resting her fingertips on his belt, and brushed her cheek on his shirt, his muscles solid underneath. He was warm and comforting. He put his arms around her, and she rested in his strength, grateful for his friendship.

Nathan pulled back and met her eyes. "It's going to be okay," he repeated.

She nodded. She trusted him.

Chapter Eight

EMS STATION 1
JUNE 23, 2013. 7:42 AM

Nathan paced the Station 1 hallway. It had been two days since he had seen Megan, and no amount of swimming had taken the edge off his restlessness. He hadn't eaten much. He hadn't slept well. He had left his work radio on and listened to the calls, just to be sure nothing had happened.

He checked his watch.

0743. Two minutes.

The door opened, and Megan stepped inside. At the swing of her ponytail, a weight fell from his shoulders.

Megan smiled, but her forehead wrinkled. "I don't know what we're going to do," she said in a low voice. "I still can't lift anything."

"We'll figure something out. We may just have to wing it. Ask firefighters or something."

Richard's voice carried from the office. "Nathan! Grab Megan and come in here!"

They exchanged glances.

"Do you think he knows we skipped out of work?" Megan whispered as they walked down the hall.

"You didn't just skip out," he whispered back, arriving

at the doorway.

She pulled him back by his sleeve. "But you didn't have food poisoning. What if Todd told him?"

Nathan paused. He hadn't thought of that, but he didn't think it reasonable that Richard would write him up after his insistence that Nathan looked 'peaky.'

"I can take care of myself," Nathan reassured her. "Don't offer any information. We need to figure out what he knows first."

She nodded and released his sleeve. They moved into the doorway, and Nathan tapped his knuckles on the frame.

Richard sat at his desk, shuffling papers. "You two will have a student riding with you today. Ron Gordon."

Nathan's shoulders drooped.

I'd rather be written up.

"I've heard his name before. EMT or paramedic?" Megan asked.

"Paramedic student."

"I—" she began.

"Now, Megan," Richard interrupted. "I know you don't like the 'newbie' sort of thing, but—"

Megan grinned. "No! It's okay!"

Richard stopped with his mouth open. His brow wrinkled. "What do you mean, 'it's okay'?"

"I'd love a student."

"You're sure?"

"Absolutely," she said. "And thank you for the opportunity."

Richard blinked. "Go on then."

Nathan and Megan hit the door and entered the bay.

"'Thank you for the opportunity?'" Nathan said. "That was a bit much, wasn't it?"

"This is great!" Megan gushed.

"How so?"

"You don't see? Now I don't have to lift the stretcher. I have my own personal flunky to do all my lifting for me!"

A young man in a classic white button-up with the community college patch on the sleeve stood next to the ambulance. His black hair curled over his collar. Nathan judged him sloppy.

Megan held out her hand. "Are you Ron?"

"Yep." He took her hand. "Ron Gordon, paramedic student. I'm an EMT over in Clark County."

Nathan glared as Ron's eyes drifted down Megan's figure.

Megan seemed thrilled to have a student. She gave Ron a tour of the truck and showed him how to check supplies. Nathan waited in the cab with the engine idling. He glowered occasionally at the side view mirror as he flipped through an out-of-date issue of *EMS World* magazine he had found under the seat. He finally climbed back out.

"Megan, we need to go," he said. "Station 6."

"All right," she said.

Nathan pointed at Ron. "You ride in the back." He returned to the driver's seat and slid the window closed. Megan got in on the passenger side.

Nathan turned the truck onto the thoroughfare. "How are you?"

She rubbed her ribs. "The pain is much better. I don't need codeine now, just a handful of ibuprofen every so often. And Emily's letting me rent the apartment over her garage. It'll be really cute once I get some new curtains up."

He stopped at a red light. "Any sign of Todd?"

"No. You were right. I haven't heard anything from him at all. I talked to a lawyer, and she said for now, to try to do without anything that I have at the house. She'll file the paperwork for me to be able to get things without Todd there. Ugh, this is such a mess."

"You're doing really well with it, though."

She smiled. "I couldn't have done it without your help."

He smiled back but felt unsettled.

This seems too easy. He won't just let her go.

At Station 6, Martin directed Nathan's backing the ambulance. As he climbed out, he listened to Megan introduce Ron to Martin. Nathan shouldered his bag and walked around the truck to stand with the others. Ron passed him on his way back to the truck to retrieve his clinical notebook.

Martin grinned. "Doll, you want some spaghetti tonight?"

"Are you cooking?" Megan asked.

"Cooking up something with you!"

Megan's face paled, and her shoulders tensed. Martin waited for her catch phrase. The pause grew. She clasped her hands in front of her, and Nathan realized she was no longer wearing a wedding band. She bit her lip and said nothing.

Martin furrowed his brow. "Yeah, I'm cooking."

"That sounds really good," she said and forced a smile.

"It's settled then." Martin looked at Nathan and then back to Megan. He tried again. "You look beautiful, Doll."

"Thank you," she blurted out and hurried toward the EMS room.

Martin scratched his head. "Does that mean what I think it means?"

"Yes, it does," Nathan said.

"That changes everything."

Nathan nodded. "Yeah." He folded his arms over his chest.

Martin sighed. "I'll see you tonight." He crossed the bay to the common room but then stopped, turned back, and stared at the EMS room door. Concern wrinkled his brow. A moment passed and then another. Still he watched the EMS room door.

Ron slammed the ambulance door, and the sound shook Martin back to life. With a final glance toward the EMS room, he opened the common room door and walked inside. The door closed behind him with a soft thud.

"Hey, Nate!" Ron called.

Nathan slowly turned. "It's Nathan."

"Nathan, whatever. Give me the scoop on Megan. She single?"

Nathan frowned. "It's complicated."

"She'd be worth a little complication. She's smokin' hot."

Nathan stared him down.

A flash of realization passed over Ron's face. "Aw, sorry, man. I didn't mean to cross a brother. You're dating her?"

Nathan hesitated. "No."

"Oh." Ron shrugged. "Then you won't mind if I ask her out."

FIRE STATION 6
JUNE 23, 2013. 9:30 AM

Nathan stared at the TV. The score of the Braves vs. Milwaukee Brewers game had scrolled across the bottom of the screen three times, but every time it went past, his thoughts wandered before he had read anything past the team names.

Ron and Megan were playing cards, and Ron was laying it on thick. Several times, Nathan had rolled his eyes as Ron had hit on her with over-the-top compliments. Yet Megan seemed happy, occasionally giggling and bantering back.

She's free of one asshat only to have another come swooping in after him.

The scores scrolled by again.

What were you thinking, moron? Did you honestly expect her to fall for you? Chicks don't dig a guy with one leg.

Tones.

"Med 3, be en route to Sunset Mountain State Park, Sunset Mountain State Park. Snakebite."

Nathan leaped up and grabbed his bag. "I'm driving." He was out the door before Megan had finished picking up the cards.

"10-4," Megan said over the radio. "Dispatch, is this the front entrance or back access road?"

"Front, southern entrance. At the ranger station."

"10-4."

Nathan turned the engine over. He heard the back doors close after Ron, and Megan climbed in on the passenger side. He flipped on the lights and sirens and pulled into the road without a word to her.

Megan opened the map book. "You're very quiet today."

"I don't have anything to say."

"Do you know where we're going?"

"Vaguely. Out Highway 42. Isn't the entrance about five miles past the train tracks?"

Megan measured the distance and compared it to the key. "Yeah, about that far, at the edge of the county. The park's eastern half is in Clark County. Have you ever been there? It's beautiful! It has some really pretty hiking trails, Buzzard Cliff, Diamond Falls." Her finger traced over the map. "My favorite is the one with white blazes. There's a ledge a few miles up the trail that looks out at Buzzard Cliff. I think it's my favorite place in the entire world—"

"I don't hike. Isn't that obvious?"

Megan closed the book and shoved it back between the seat and the console. "It's not obvious to me," she muttered, withdrawing her Prusik cord and wrapping it around her palm.

Nathan accelerated on the highway. He regretted his harsh words.

She assumes I can do anything. That's what I wanted, right?

They turned into the state park and rumbled up the drive. Megan stuffed her cord into her pocket. A ranger waved his arms, and they pulled to a stop. Nathan rolled down his window.

"Camper got bit by a snake," the ranger said. "He's over there at the third campsite."

"I see them," Nathan said, and he drove to the other side of the campground.

Megan slid open the window to the back. "Ron, this is all you." She pulled on her gloves as she jumped out.

Nathan remained in the driver's seat, slowly putting the truck in park and finding gloves.

Some things only baseball can help. Four hours and counting 'til game time.

He groaned like an old man as he climbed out.

Another ranger knelt next to a man who was grimacing

and sweating and guarding his swollen forearm. The man's friend hovered nearby, holding a shovel.

Ron approached them. "What can we help you with?" Megan traipsed behind him with the jump kit.

She really doesn't need to be that happy.

Nathan stood to the side, his arms folded over his chest.

The man looked up. "I was just picking up a tent peg, and the snake bit me. Big ol' snake."

Ron knelt and examined the wound. "Can you wiggle your fingers?"

"What kind was it?" Megan asked.

"I don't know. It was right over there." He pointed to the edge of the underbrush.

The other man held up his shovel. "I think I killed it."

Nathan scanned the brush line. "I'll go look for it."

"Be careful," Megan said.

He shrugged. "I have half the risk you do." He walked to the edge of the woods, looking for any movement and listening for rattles.

Ron's voice carried back to him. "All right, sir. Let's put a tourniquet on."

"Um, no," Megan said.

"Um, yes," he answered, mimicking her voice. "You have to stop the venom."

"Thank you for your opinion," Megan said, "but you're not doing that."

Nathan paused and listened to her measured tone with the hint of a smile on his lips.

"That's what he needs," Ron said. "That's what we do in Clark County."

"You're in Barrington," she said.

"It's the right—"

"Go get the stretcher," she commanded.

"Is there something wrong?" the patient asked. "Should you be doing something else?"

"No, sir," Megan said. "Everything's fine, and we'll get you to the hospital quickly."

Nathan continued along the edge of the woods. He looked past a green clump of goldenrod and saw a white belly shining on the sandy ground. He poked at the snake with his prosthetic boot. The three-foot snake was dead, its head detached. He kicked the body, and it flopped a few feet. He flung it closer to where Megan was squatting next to the man, marking a circle around the swelling. Nathan kicked the snake one last time. It hit against Megan's boot, and she turned at the bump. With a gasp, she stumbled back and fell over the stretcher.

"Found it," Nathan said.

Megan puffed a stray hair away from her face. "Really."

He helped her up.

The ranger picked up the snake. "Oh! A copperhead. I'll take it. That'll make a nice hat band. Unless you need it."

Nathan shook his head. "The doc just wants to know the size. Doesn't even matter what kind it is. The antivenin treats them all."

Megan assisted the man onto the stretcher and moved aside to allow Nathan and Ron to lift it and put it into the back of the ambulance. Nathan drove back down the mountain to the emergency room. When Megan transferred care to the nurses, the man's arm was grotesquely swollen, and his muscles twitched. Even so, the doctors seemed optimistic as they sent for antivenin.

The three walked back out onto the ambulance dock. Nathan was pleased that Megan's steps fell in synch with his and not Ron's. The doors slid closed behind them, and Megan rounded on Ron, her eyes flashing. "Don't you ever —ever—contradict me on scene like that again!"

Nathan hid his smile.

Popcorn, please.

Ron stepped toward her. "He's probably gonna die because he didn't get a tourniquet! It was obviously envenomated, and you did nothing to stop it. You have to do what's right for the patient!"

"Compartment syndrome is never right for the patient," she said. "Protocol dictates that we transport with IV access and symptomatic support. No tourniquet. No blood or lymph constriction. And you know why? Because that's what the science shows. So unless you've got some brand-new evidence to present to the world, you need to stand down."

"We tie tourniquets in Clark County," Ron said, crossing his arms. "Our protocol is different."

"Then you need to have a discussion with your medical director. And you, as a provider, need to make some serious choices on behalf of your patients."

"I'm a Clark County EMT—"

"You're a guest on my truck, Ron, and on my truck, we follow medical science and Barrington County protocol. Got it?"

"Whatever."

"No, not whatever! If you expect to get back on my truck, you'll agree to follow my rules. Otherwise, you can march yourself down the hill to your car."

Ron leveled his gaze. "All right. I'll follow your damn protocol." He climbed into the back. "Bitch."

FIRE STATION 6
JUNE 23, 2013. 8:00 PM

Megan pulled the truck into the fire station parking lot, grateful to be back. Her chest ached. With every painful breath, her muscles spasmed around her healing ribs. Her stomach yearned for Martin's spaghetti, and her head for her soft, quiet bunk.

"Med 3," dispatch called, "stand by at Post 4."

She sighed. "10-4."

"System status?" Nathan asked. "It's Sunday."

"We must be short a truck. They'll push us into system status if they don't think we have enough regular coverage." She rested her hand on the gear shift to put the truck into reverse.

Nathan placed his hand on hers. "You doing okay?"

She nodded, studying his fingers and feeling the weight of his palm. "I'm sore, but I'll be fine."

"Do you want me to drive?"

She looked at him. "Would you mind?"

"Not for you," he said with a smile.

Her stomach fluttered. "Thank you," she said and quickly unbuckled and climbed out.

He's just being nice. He's a nice person. And thoughtful.

She watched him as he climbed into the driver's seat.

And very good looking.

She shook her head.

Geez! I can't think like that.

She walked around the front of the ambulance. The implications of her new freedom dawned in her mind, and her steps slowed and then stopped. Megan stared at him again as he adjusted the seat to fit his legs.

Maybe I can.

"You coming?" Nathan called.

She hurried around and jumped in the cab. "We're going to Post 4," she called to Ron in the back.

"Where's that?" Ron asked.

"At Rocky's."

"All right! W—"

Nathan slid the window closed.

"He wasn't finished talking," Megan said, still staring at him and imagining possibilities.

Nathan grunted. "I was finished listening."

Their eyes met.

Nathan grinned. "What?"

She looked away. "Nothing." She pulled her Prusik cord from her pocket as he put the truck into reverse.

As Nathan drove across town, past government buildings and the college campus, Megan remained silent. She reorganized her thoughts as she rewove a figure-eight knot in her hands. Eventually, she wandered from Nathan, to the events of the last few days, to Todd. She hadn't seen him or heard from him, and that made her anxious.

"What's wrong?" Nathan asked.

She untied the cord. "I don't want to work Post 4 today."

"I know you hate system status, and Ron's a pain in the ass, but it's not like—"

Megan shook her head, irritated. "I don't mind Ron. He's just a student. And, really, Nathan, system status? I don't care."

"Then what—"

"Todd's working Zone 4 today."

Nathan tipped his head back and flipped on the blinker.

Megan stared at the car in front of them as they waited at the red light. "I just want our other trucks to get their butts in gear and call 10-8 so we can get off system status, and I can post back at Station 6 where I belong." As he pulled the truck into the Rocky's parking lot, she glanced up at the reddening sky and hoped the call volume would fall with the evening.

POST 4
JUNE 23, 2013. 8:15 PM

Nathan turned off the truck and, as Megan climbed out, slid the back window open. "We're getting coffee. If you want to come, grab your stuff." He hoped Megan heard him being so friendly.

The three walked to the coffee shop. Ron opened the door for Megan and followed her in, letting the door swing shut. Nathan caught it just before it hit his shoulder.

"I'll be right back," Megan said.

Ron watched her as she walked to the restroom. He tucked his thumbs into his belt. "I could tap that."

Nathan glared at him. "She's not a badge bunny. And you called her a bitch."

"Personality doesn't matter in a tag and release program. I specialize in the one-night stand."

"Right. Let me know how that works out for you." Nathan walked to the counter, wishing he'd left Ron in the truck. He ordered his coffee and an Apple Farm Danish and sat where he could see the door. Megan returned to the counter and ordered, and Ron stepped in and paid, flashing a smile. Nathan drank his coffee and wanted to retch.

To his satisfaction, Megan sat next to him. Ron sat

directly across from her.

"… so he'd stuck the guy like six times," Ron was saying, "and I said, 'Move over and let me get in there …'"

Nathan slid the Danish over to Megan. A little smile curved her lips. He leaned to her. "Your insulin is in the truck."

"… and I ran over to—are you diabetic?" Ron asked.

Megan laughed. "No, I'm not! He's kidding."

Tones.

Everyone in the shop jumped. Nathan and Megan reached for their radios in unison and turned down the volume.

"Med 3, be en route to 923 Piedmont Trail, 923 Piedmont Trail, unresponsive infant."

"10-4," Nathan said, following Megan as she strode out the door and toward the ambulance.

Nathan caught the driver's door before she climbed in. "It's a pediatric call, do you want it?"

"Yeah."

"I'll drive then."

Megan ran around to the other side while he fired up the truck. "Thank you," she said.

He flipped on the lights and siren. "No problem."

Megan slid open the window. "I want the peds bag and the peds airway kit. Go ahead and put the pediatric BP cuff on the monitor and set the intraosseous case on the bench."

Nathan pulled up at the house and backed into the driveway. Megan leaped out and slammed the door.

A police car, with lights flashing, drove up and parked on the street.

Nathan tensed and watched Megan in the side view mirror as she walked up to the front porch.

Just keep walking, Megan.

Nathan opened the driver's door and heard a woman's screams.

"He's not breathing!" She ran from the house with a bundle in her arms. "Oh, God, he's not breathing!"

Megan took the baby. "What happened?"

"He was asleep! I went to check on him, and he was like this!"

"How long had he been sleeping?" Megan asked.

"Five hours? Six hours? I don't know! Too long!"

Megan began compressions as she held the baby. "Was he sick? Did he have any other problems?"

"No! No! Oh, God, no!"

Megan climbed into the back of the ambulance with Ron as a man ran out of the house and onto the porch.

Nathan rested his hand on the woman's shoulder. "Is this your husband?"

"Yes," she said, sobbing.

"Can you two follow us to the hospital in your own vehicle? We're going to Sacred Heart."

"Yes," the father said. "Yes, we will."

Nathan closed the truck doors and returned to the cab. He put the truck in gear, gladly leaving the police car behind. Merging onto the freeway, he brought the ambulance up to speed with lights and sirens. He strained his ear, trying to hear what was being said in the back.

"You have a patent airway. What does the monitor say?" Megan asked, her voice punctuated with the rhythm of compressions.

A pause.

"Um, asystole," Ron answered.

"What do you do now?"

"Fluids. Push epi."

"Through what?"

"I need a line!"

"Get the intraosseous kit," Megan directed.

"Are you sure?" Ron asked

"Didn't they teach you how to do it?"

"Yeah, but—but I've never done it before. I don't think I should," Ron stammered.

"Are you here to do emergency medicine, or do you just like wearing the uniform?"

A wide grin stretched across Nathan's face.

That's my girl.

He heard the IO case open.

"But it's so small," Ron said. "What if I hurt it?"

"You can't hurt it. This baby is dead. It's not coming back. The intraosseous isn't about this baby. It's about the next baby. It's about you learning what you need to know so that you can save the next baby who actually has life. Now shut up and squeeze the trigger. Insert the needle into the bone until you feel it pop.

Nathan backed the ambulance to the dock and ran around to open the doors. He and Ron pulled the stretcher, and Megan climbed onto the side, compressing the baby's chest with her fingers as they rolled into the emergency room. As Megan moved the baby to a bed, she called out numbers and stats and milliliters to the nurses, who swept into action. She stepped back and pulled off her gloves.

Another night for the rocking chair.

FIRE STATION 6
JUNE 23, 2013. 9:30 PM

Megan and Nathan walked into the Station 6 kitchen.

The smell of spaghetti sauce wafted through the air.

Martin waved a wooden spoon. "Hey, Doll! I thought you'd stood me up!" he said, wiping his fingers on the white apron tied around his middle.

"You know I can't stay away," she said. "You waited for us?"

"Yep. That, and our own calls ran late. You look beautiful, Doll, but you seem tired."

She smiled, feeling as though she could sleep for a week. "It was a long day."

Nathan leaned on the counter and nodded.

Martin handed her a spoon. "Taste this, then."

The sauce had a perfect balance of meat, tomatoes, and Italian spices. "That is amazing," she exclaimed.

"It's just the way you like it."

She winked. "You know how to light my fire."

Megan, Nathan, Martin, and the rest of the Station 6 fire crew sat around the long kitchen table, eating spaghetti. Megan felt the stress of the day roll off her. The loud conversations, antics, and inappropriate humor made her feel at home. Martin sat at her elbow, loading her plate with food, and Nathan sat across the table from her, facing the door.

Martin slipped her yet another slice of garlic bread. "Where's your protégé, Doll?"

"Students can't ride after nine, so he walked down the hill after the last call."

"He was a mighty big talker."

"He was," she agreed. "But his hands sure were shaky in the truck."

"Doll, if I were in the back of a truck with you, my hands would be shaky, too."

"My ambulance, Martin, not the back seat."

"Now you specify."

"Nathan," called Carrie. "Y'all had a snakebite call?"

Nathan nodded. "Yeah, hand envenomation. Swollen and blue."

"Gnarly. Did you find the snake? What kind was it?"

"Copperhead," Nathan said, grinning. "I found it while Megan and the student argued over the patient, and—"

Martin raised an eyebrow. "He was arguing with you?"

"He was about to put a freaking IV tourniquet on it," she said. "I expected him to pull out a pocket knife, slice the wound, and start sucking the venom out. Carrie, you live in Clark County, right?"

"Yeah, why?"

"Do they tie tourniquets there for snakebite?"

Carrie shook her head as she drank her sweet tea. "No. I can't think of any service that does that anymore," she said, raising his voice over the conversation noise. "Nathan, what'd they do with the snake?"

Nathan put down his fork. "The guy's friend had chopped its head off with a shovel. I'm walking along the brush line, and I see this three-foot copperhead, all chopped and bloody, and Megan's over there brawling with the student—"

The firefighters laughed, and Nathan winked at her.

"We weren't brawling!" she said.

"She had him in a headlock. So I kicked the snake—"

Megan pointed down the table. "Carrie, he wouldn't even pick it up."

"I kicked it over—"

"Wouldn't pick it up!" Megan said over the din of two other conversations. She counted on her fingers. "Not with a stick! Not with his knife! Not with that multi-purpose tool thing—"

"I'm not getting snake blood all over my stuff!"

"Admit it!" Megan put her hands flat on the table, a smile flickering. "You were scared!"

"You want scared?" Nathan said, jabbing his thumb toward Megan. "I kick it over to her, and she starts squealing and jumping around."

Megan laughed. "I was not squealing!"

"You sucked all the air out of a three-mile radius," Nathan said and imitated her gasp.

She kicked him under the table.

"I can't feel that," he said.

Carrie yelled over the noisy room. "So where is it? Those are good eatin'."

"Tastes like chicken?" Megan giggled.

"More like fish," Carrie said.

Nathan nodded. "The ranger said he wanted it."

Megan stood and picked up her plate. "Scared," she said to Nathan. His smile appeared, but he said nothing.

Martin reached back to her. "Did you get enough, Doll?"

"Oh, yes, thanks. It was wonderful."

He winked. "Doll, I've always wanted you to say that."

Megan washed her dishes and silverware and set them in the dish rack to dry. The firefighters were still carrying on loudly, and she smiled as she walked to the door. The truck bay was quiet in comparison. The firehouse door was closed; she exited through the side door of the station to the ambulance parked outside.

Traffic noise echoed off the high station walls. The shadow of the firefighters' basketball hoop streaked across the pavement to her. Megan withdrew a mini-flashlight from her pocket and shone it at the truck. Mud from the mountain roadway clung to the tires. It would need to be washed in the morning. She clicked off the light and sat on the bumper, looking up at the sky. Between the pine trees and the lights from the surrounding office buildings, she could see few stars.

Megan inhaled and held it, leaning her head back against the ambulance door. When she released her breath, she realized that, though the rest of her life had fallen apart at the seams, here she was happy. Here she was needed; she knew exactly what was expected of her. As much as the firefighters picked on her and each other, she would willingly go into harm's way for every one of them, and she knew they would do the same for her. She had friends; she was loved—

She thought of Nathan. She saw his quiet strength, his wicked grin. She wondered if she had fallen for him.

It's just a rebound crush. Someone to fill Todd's place.

But Megan knew that wasn't true. Her love for Todd had been chipped away with every harsh word and insult. It had died almost a year earlier, the day he had first hit her. If Nathan was a rebound, he was a year too late.

Am I desperate?

She reminded herself of several medics and firefighters who had crushes on her. There had been motive, means, and opportunity for any number of relationships, formal or casual, but she hadn't pursued them. She knew she wasn't desperate.

Through it all, she had maintained hope of saving her marriage. She still didn't understand what had gone wrong, why Todd had slowly drifted away, why he had responded with violence. There were rumors of Barrington cops being involved in drugs. If he had chosen to get mixed up in that, she knew there was nothing she could have done.

Megan pulled her Prusik cord from her pocket and looped it around her fingers. Her movements slowed, and she rubbed the indentation her wedding ring had left on her finger. She was ready to put Todd behind her.

The side door of the station closed. "Megan?" Nathan called.

"Here," she said.

She heard his boots cross the parking lot.

"You don't have to take a smoke break if you don't smoke," he said.

"Profound. Shall I ponder?"

"Don't hurt yourself."

Nathan leaned on the corner of the truck. Megan could see his shadow on the pavement, but she couldn't see his face. Crickets chirped, and cars drove by. She untied the cord and began a new knot.

"Martin sure knows how to cook," he said.

"I'll never need to eat again."

He cleared his throat. "I saw you talking to Ron after the code. Everything okay?"

"Yeah," she said, with a slight laugh. "He asked me out." She waited for his response, but none came. Nathan's silence was disconcerting. She wondered whether he was jealous or whether he just didn't care either way. "I turned him down."

More silence. Megan wished she could see his face. "I figured between him seeing Caroline in ICU, and Danielle at Station 5, and Lauren, the other Clark County paramedic student, he just wouldn't have time for me."

"You said that?"

"No, I occasionally have good manners. Don't tell anyone, though."

He chuckled.

A new cricket chirped nearby.

Nathan shuffled his foot. "It'd be too soon anyway?"

"Not really."

"No?"

She wrapped another loop. "It just needs to be the right person."

"Like Martin."

Megan dropped the cord to her lap and laughed. "No, not Martin! We talk it up, but it's just good, clean dirtiness, you know? Martin is—we have a history." She shrugged. "It didn't work out. I know it sounds cliché, but he's like a brother to me. We have an agreement, a sort of understanding. If I thought he were serious, I wouldn't play along." She shrugged. "We're friends. Off-color friends. But that's just the way it is."

"So, not Martin."

"No."

"Anyone else?"

The words Megan wanted to say failed, and cricket song pressed around them. She saw his shadow step toward her. Her heart beat faster. He sat next to her and took her hand in his. He aligned his fingers with hers and then interlaced them. His thumb rubbed the back of her hand, and she leaned her head on his shoulder, feeling fluttery and warm.

Tones dropped.

"Med 3, be en route to 847 Blarney Road, 847 Blarney Road, gunshot wound."

Megan jumped up and withdrew the keys from her pocket. "This one's yours."

Nathan jogged to the passenger side as she started the engine and flipped on the lights and sirens. She pulled into traffic and blew the horn at a non-attentive driver.

They flew down the street, and she slowed the truck at a red light.

"Clear," Nathan said, and she brought it back up to speed.

"Med 3, downgrade to code 1, per sheriff."

Megan's shoulders drooped, and she lifted her foot from the accelerator. "Damn." She turned off the lights and sirens.

"What does that mean?"

"It means the sheriff's deputy arrived on scene, and the person is obviously dead. They just need us to confirm it. It's probably a suicide. You'll need the monitor, and that's it."

Two sheriff's cars' lights flashed in front of the house. Megan stopped the ambulance and stood next to the open driver's door while she donned her gloves and prepared her mind for what she might see. Nathan walked next to her up the driveway, the strap of the heart monitor slung over his shoulder.

"Paramedics," Nathan called at the open door. Every light in the house was on, and a wide beam spilled onto the porch.

Deputy Thomas walked into the front hall. "Wife found him. She's at the neighbor's house."

"Suicide?"

"Yeah. Shotgun. It ain't pretty. I just need a heart monitor printout for the paperwork."

"You sure?" Nathan asked. "It's a crime scene, right? Shouldn't we stay out?"

Both Megan and Thomas shook their heads. "Jefferson," they answered together.

Nathan looked incredulous. "Pardon?"

"He's the coroner," said Thomas.

Megan snickered. "He's crazy."

"He wants printouts on everyone," he continued. "I bet he'd want one of a skeleton, if he found one. And he talks to the stiffs. 'What did you see?' and 'I'm going to move you now.'"

Nathan met Megan's eyes. She knew he was thinking of her habit of talking to every patient—even the unresponsive ones. She looked at the floor, sheepishly.

"Come on," Thomas said, leaving the front room. The deputy walked down a narrow hall to a bedroom. "Back here."

They followed. The house was simple and clean. Cat hair clung to the couches, and a few discarded dishes cluttered the end tables. The space seemed comfortable and lived in.

Nathan paused a moment and turned back to Megan. "You have no right to criticize someone who talks to the dead," he said in a low voice.

"My patient's aren't all the way dead." Megan lifted her chin loftily. "No one dies in my truck."

"Uh huh. Sure," he said, with his half smile. She quickly returned it, but then faced the bedroom door and took a deep breath to prepare herself for what she was about to see.

Megan followed Nathan into the room. The bed was made, and a few piles of clothes were scattered about the furniture. A body sat in a chair in the corner, a shotgun on the floor. She could not determine the man's age; part of his head had been blown away. Ragged clumps of pulpy tissue clung to the skin that had peeled away from the skull, the bones, a white, crunchy shell. Blood and brain matter had sprayed across the wall, the dresser, and the mirror, the droplets reflecting and magnifying on the glass.

As Nathan set the monitor on the floor, Megan averted her eyes to the opposite wall. A case displayed army rank patches, some with a familiar pattern of red, green, and black. Nathan had the same ones. Her brow creased, and her stomach clenched. For a fleeting moment, she wanted to dash across the room and hide them and protect him from the connection. But that was foolish—it was against procedure, and he had probably already seen them anyway. She looked at his face, impassive as usual. If he had seen, he didn't let on.

Nathan placed the leads on the body. He verified asystole, printed a strip, and switched off the machine.

A black beret with a blue flash sat on a shelf. A weight settled in Megan's stomach; she felt heavy and numb. She wanted to touch the beret, but as she reached out, Nathan grasped her hand, gripping her fingers firmly. With his eyes devoid of emotion, his expression commanded her silence. She looked back at the soldier in the corner. The lack of urgency, the unnatural stillness unsettled her.

Nathan turned his wrist. "Death confirmed at 2317."

Chapter Nine

EMS STATION 1
JUNE 24, 2013. 8:00 AM

Nathan slid his EMS ID card through the time clock. Megan had already clocked out and walked to the hospital cafeteria for coffee. Dark, puffy patches had encircled her eyes; he had kept her awake all night with his tossing and turning and reliving of the suicide call. The soldier who had lost his battle was throwing another into hell.

Nathan rested his hands on the steering wheel, not remembering walking out of the station or climbing into his truck. His head was in a fog. His mind bounded from one thought to another, returning each time to the blast wound with its splayed star of tissue and bone and blood. He spaced out, staring at the parking garage pillars and listening to the thump-thump of tires bumping around to parking spaces on the level above him.

His neck ached, his body stiff, sore, every muscle tensed at the ready and screaming for release. The demons, familiar. The demons, the same. The hot-flashing cold melted the pressing darkness, a wave rolling into shifting sand. Fingers tapping on the stick shift, shoulders straining, forearms burning as gravel cut skin and flashes streaked through the blue sky outside the wire. His shirt damp, the remains of comfort ebbed away in the grip of fear, seizing, lifting, stealing his strength alongside, concealing it in a jacket pocket with a wary glance over the shoulder.

One good thing. One.

No respite, no end of torment, the future as dark as the past. The press of demon horde, moaning resistance with withering fortitude. To withstand, to fight, to wane, to fall. Not a breath, glimmer, or hint. But nothing.

Her swinging ponytail. Medium coffee, with lid, cream and sugar. Curves hidden by a black web belt and baggy khaki. She walked to her car and set her cup on the roof as she dug for her keys.

He crossed the garage. "Megan."

She turned. He read no surprise.

His hand slid to the small of her back. He pulled her closer, felt her warmth. His palm brushed her cheek; his fingers, her ear. Touching her neck at the nape, he traced the errant curls that had escaped her ponytail. He kissed her, wrapping his arms tightly around her. He immersed himself in sensations that fought the dark figments within.

A moment's lucidity. He released her and cringed from conviction. The clarity lasted only briefly, and shame pushed him once more into the mire. But she rose up on tiptoe and met his lips again. She burned away the fog in his mind. She was real and called him to the present. Returning, he kissed her cheek, her forehead, her hair, and clutched her to his chest as the demons retreated and the gates of hell closed. She, the gatekeeper.

Nathan relaxed his arms.

Megan stepped back and smoothed her hands across his chest. "Your shirt is soaked."

He looked down at his uniform and pulled at his

sweaty collar. "Sometimes …" He fought for words. "It comes back. I dissociate." She looked away. "No, I mean," he continued, faltering, "it's not bad. I'm not unstable or anything. It's just—"

"PTSD," she finished for him.

He met her eyes and saw acceptance.

"I'm sorry," he said and cleared his throat. "I shouldn't have kissed you."

She smiled. "I'm glad you did."

Her phone beeped.

"But there are rules," he said. "It's not professional. It's—"

"A disgrace to the uniform?"

"Yes."

Megan folded her arms. "Kissing me is a disgrace to Barrington County?"

He realized what she had said. "What? No. That's not what I meant. I, well …"

Damn, she makes me a rambling idiot!

Her impish gleam twinkled. "Just what did you mean?" Her phone beeped again. She huffed and checked it, and after tapping the screen, she wrinkled her nose. "I have to go. I told Emily I'd be there right after work so she can go grocery shopping." She tapped the screen again. "But I guess I can tell her—"

"It's okay."

She looked up and laid her hand on his arm. "Will you be all right?"

"Yeah. And what I meant was, with rules about the public display of affection and all, I shouldn't have—"

He stopped. He had just spilled his deepest secret, and she was looking up at him with brown eyes free of judgment.

To hell with rules!

He took her waist and kissed her again, this time with purpose and intention. When he drew back, she was breathless. He grinned. "I'll be fine."

EMS STATION 1
JULY 17, 2013. 8:00 AM

Nathan and Megan walked to the ambulance at the beginning of their shift. "There's no student today," he said. "Are you going to be all right?"

She nodded. "Yeah, I've healed well in the last few weeks. I'll be careful."

"Med 3," dispatch said, "post at Station 4 until further notice."

Nathan glanced to Megan but she had stopped a few paces back, her face pale.

"10-9?" she said into her mic.

"Stand by at Station 4."

Nathan pulled his radio from his belt. "10-4."

"Station 4's zone is completely within police zone 4," she said. "The firefighters are close friends of Todd. They're all certifiable. And the EMS room is a closet with a couch."

Her agitation irritated him, but there was nothing he could do alleviate it. "Don't freak out. Everything will be fine."

Nathan drove to Station 4. He backed into the station parking lot and turned off the engine. "The truck needs a wash. If we do that now, then we don't have to go inside yet. By the time we're finished, we may have a call."

She nodded, but he saw her check the side view mirror before climbing out.

Nathan appreciated washing the truck on such a warm day. The mist from the hose cooled his skin, and he enjoyed watching Megan wash the truck's lower aspects. Sam had been wrong: kissing Megan had not gotten her out of his system at all.

Nathan had stolen another parking-lot kiss, but between their full-time work in Barrington County, their part-time jobs in Retton County, and Megan's nanny work for Emily, there had been no time for each other. PDA rules prevented anything physical from happening at work, and if they were open about their feelings while on the job, they would have to file relationship disclosure paperwork with human resources. Such paperwork could complicate the divorce proceedings.

Nathan climbed into the back and began wiping down surfaces with disinfectant until Megan retrieved a broom from the bay and started sweeping the truck's stairwell. Her ponytail swung with each motion, and he forgot the disinfectant. A slight blush smoothed the contours of her cheek and neck. He lowered his eyes to her breasts and then to her belt, which accentuated her waist. He imagined her curves. He was captivated.

"You're beautiful," he said.

She stopped sweeping, but then began again, a smile flitting at the corner of her mouth. "You sound like Martin."

"Why should he have all the fun?" He pointed at the floor. "You missed a spot," he lied. "Dirt always gets stuck in the corner."

She went back over his imaginary dirt.

"You still missed it," he said, with a mischievous grin.

She raised an eyebrow. "It's fine."

"Gimme that," he said, grabbing the broom. "You

sweep like a girl." She laughed and pulled back on it.

Tones dropped, and she released the broom. Nathan stumbled back amid her giggles.

"Med 3, be en route to 32 Windsor Lane, 32 Windsor. No further information."

Nathan jumped from the back of the truck. "10-4," he said, returning the broom to the bay.

Tones screeched over the intercom.

"Engine 4, Rescue 4, be en route to 32 Windsor Lane, 32 Windsor. No further information."

As firefighters scrambled, Nathan climbed into the driver's seat. Megan was already in and buckled. He hit the lights and sirens. "Where's Windsor?"

"It's out Highway 87 a ways in one of those new neighborhoods."

"Roger," he said, pulling into traffic.

"Med 3," dispatch said, "be advised this is a possible diabetic emergency."

"10-4," Megan said. "Do you think they'll cancel Engine 4 then?"

"Probably not, since they're already rolling."

He ran up to speed on the highway, cruising down the open lanes. He settled back in his seat only to hear an air horn sound repeatedly over the ambulance siren's wail.

Nathan looked in the side view mirror to see Engine 4 dangerously close to the back of the ambulance. "What the hell!"

Engine 4 wove back and forth behind them and then pulled equal on their right-hand side. "What the fuck are they doing?" Nathan shouted.

"Passing us," Megan said as they watched the engine streak past.

"They'll fucking kill themselves!"

"Welcome to Zone 4."

Nathan gripped the wheel. He had written off Megan's concern as understandably paranoid, but if this road rage was any clue of what was to come, he would be on his guard for the worst.

The Engine 4 firefighters were already in the house when Med 3 arrived at 32 Windsor Lane. The lights on Todd's police cruiser flashed.

Megan opened the ambulance door, but Nathan pulled her back.

"You don't have to do this," he said. "I'll take the call for you."

Worry wrinkled her brow. "No. It has to happen sometime."

Nathan brushed his fingers across her forehead and down her cheek, and though she gave him a half-hearted smile first, she turned away. Shouldering the jump kit, she took the clipboard and walked up the driveway toward a house that held her rapist and his cronies. He watched the determination in her step and found her courage more resplendent than her beauty.

Nathan put on his sunglasses. He wouldn't need them; they were purely for intimidation. If they were going to bother Megan, they would have to go through him first. As he strode up the drive, he watched Megan's ponytail disappear through the doorway, which was flanked by two firefighters.

Nathan stepped into a living room decorated with frilly furniture, lacy curtains, and doilies. He assumed a wide stance, his arms crossed over his chest, and with his shades concealing his eyes, he scanned the room without having to interact or acknowledge anyone's presence. Firefighters lined the walls, their turnout gear in sharp contrast with the room's dainty decor. Nathan matched or bested them all in height, but the men were solid and gruff. Even the probationary firefighter next to him was stern.

Megan stood very still in the middle of the room near a woman in a flowered housecoat.

Todd had a portly, middle-aged man by the upper arm. "You're sick. These ambulance drivers will take you to the hospital."

"I know I'm sick! But I'm not going to any hospital!" the man said, breathing hard, his eyes wide and protuberant.

The lady wrung her hands. "He has sugar problems, and he hasn't eaten anything since yesterday morning."

The man mopped his shiny red face. "You don't cook anything I want to eat!"

Todd pulled the man's arm. "Now just come on to the hospital—"

Had the situation not been so tense, Nathan would have laughed at Todd, the cop, trying to take over the medical decision making on scene.

"No!" the man shouted.

Todd turned to the door. "Go get the stretcher," he said to Nathan.

"I don't take orders from you," Nathan said. He nodded his head toward Megan. "She's the primary medic."

Todd released the patient abruptly, and the man wobbled off balance. Megan sprang forward and steadied him.

Todd sauntered toward Nathan until their faces were inches apart. "That's right. Peg Leg and Meg. Joined at the hip."

Nathan remained still, refusing to react. "Act

professional."

"Sir, do you want me to check you over?" Megan said. "I can test your blood sugar." Nathan heard a small quaver in her voice.

The patient leaned on the coffee table. "No. I don't want you to," he gasped.

She stepped closer. "If your blood sugar is at an abnormal level, you can get very ill. If it's not corrected, you could even die. Testing your blood sugar and blood pressure will only take a moment. It doesn't mean you have to come with me."

"No!" he said and waved her away.

She tilted her head. "It seems important to your wife that you get checked out."

"I don't care," he grumbled. "I'm not going to any hospital. I don't want treatment."

Megan tapped her pen on her clipboard. "Do you know what day it is?"

"July seventeenth." He pointed to the calendar dial on his watch. "Three weeks to the day since I last had fried chicken."

She nodded. "Who's the president?"

"No one I voted for," he grumbled.

"What's 36 plus 9?"

"Forty-fucking-five."

Megan turned on her heel. "There's nothing I can do right now."

"Honey, you need to go!" the woman cried.

Todd stepped toward Megan. "It's obvious this man is very sick. He needs to go to the hospital. You will take him there now!"

Megan countered his glare. "No."

The firefighters shuffled on the thick carpeting.

Todd's face contorted with anger. He shouted, "I said —"

"It's not your decision to make," she said. "He hasn't given consent."

Nathan grunted.

We're done here.

He stepped onto the porch. "Dispatch, Med 3. Roll Supervisor 1."

"10-4, Med 3. Supervisor 1."

Nathan turned back to the house.

"Med 3, what's your situation?" Richard said over the radio.

"Interference on scene," Nathan replied.

"Roll law enforcement."

Nathan frowned. "Law enforcement is the interference."

A pause. "10-4," Richard said.

Nathan reentered the room. Todd was waving his arm toward the patient. "—if he were in a proper frame of mind, he would give consent."

"I have no evidence that he's not in a proper frame of mind," Megan said.

The patient sat on the coffee table. Sweat dripped onto the floor. "I," he gasped, "am in a proper—frame—of mind."

Todd leered at her. "We're supposed to work together as a team. You have some kind of para-god-complex to think you can walk in here and mouth off at me."

Nathan scanned the firefighters. Most wore scowls, but the probie seemed confused.

"She's right," the probie whispered to Nathan. "And he shouldn't be talking to her like that."

"Let her handle it," Nathan muttered.

"Consent is taught the very first day of EMT school," Megan said. "I don't do anything without ongoing patient consent."

The corner of Todd's mouth twisted. "Consent," he sneered.

Megan's face paled.

He laughed. "Consent is damned near impossible to prove in court."

"We have transport refusal papers."

"Those papers are worthless." He leveled his gaze. "A lot of dirty secrets can come out in court, and after all of that, it still comes down to he-said-she-said."

Megan tipped her head to her mic. "Dispatch, Med 3, for the record, primary Paramedic Megan Henderson is advising Officer Todd Henderson that she does not have consent from the patient for treatment at this time." She raised her wrist. "0946, by my watch. Copy?"

"10-4, Med 3, duly noted in the record. 0946."

Megan straightened her shoulders. "Now it's a she-said-everyone-heard-and-its-in-

the-legal-record situation."

Todd pursed his lips and narrowed his eyes.

The patient moaned. His head rocked back and forth.

"So you're just going to leave and let him keel over?" Todd said.

"No."

"What the hell are you doing then?"

Megan walked to Nathan's side, turned back to the patient, and folded her arms. Under her breath, she said, "In five, four, three," her words slowed, "two ... one ..."

The patient dropped onto the carpet, unconscious.

Implied consent.

"Nathan, please get the stretcher," Megan said and

knelt next to the patient. "Sir?" she called and rubbed her knuckles into his sternum. "Wake up, sir. You passed out."

The patient groaned. "Okay—I want—to go—to the hospital."

"Absolutely, sir. The stretcher's coming."

Nathan retrieved the stretcher and watched Todd slink to his car. When Nathan returned, Megan settled the patient, and they returned to the ambulance. He and Megan slid the patient into the back as sirens roared up the street, and Supervisor 1 skidded to a halt.

"Why is it always you two?" Richard exclaimed.

Megan shrugged. "Someone has to make you earn your pay."

"At least there's only one more month of it. You'd better have had a damn good reason for broadcasting that shenanigan over the entire county."

"I did," she said and climbed into the back.

Fire Engine 4 drove away as Nathan slammed the ambulance doors behind Megan.

"Start talking," Richard said.

Nathan explained what had happened on scene between Todd and Megan. He measured Richard's reaction.

Richard rubbed his chin. "Is this because they're splitting up?"

"You'd have to ask him. Or Megan."

"I don't like working her in this zone, but the system said to move Med 3 to Zone 4, so that's what I had to do, or else I'd have to explain my reasoning to the upper echelons. And I didn't think Meg wanted her divorce dragged out in front of everyone."

"I think she appreciates that," said Nathan.

"I'll have a talk with the captain. Todd'll probably get

written up, but I don't know if it'll help or not. It may just ramp things up even more."

"Todd needs to be written up. It can't be avoided because of personal problems."

"I don't know," Richard mumbled. "He's a piece of work. No telling what he'll do if he thinks Meg had him written up. I don't get it. He used to be a great guy. But now ... Shit, anyone can see he's gone crooked and is hyped up on something most of the time. Son of a bitch can't walk straight."

"Why don't they test him?"

"They have," Richard said. "At least three times that I know of. But they didn't find anything. Not drugs, not ETOH, not anything. So that's as far as it went. Unless they find something solid, he's untouchable."

Nathan furrowed his brow. "Something solid. You mean other than his unacceptable behavior on the job."

"Everyone's hoping he'll straighten out on his own." Richard shrugged. "He's in the brotherhood."

"But she's a sister!"

Richard sighed. "You know that doesn't carry as much weight with some."

"And with you?"

"I'd go to bat for her if I had evidence of anything."

Nathan kicked a dandelion on the driveway.

"Do you know something you need to tell me?" Richard asked, folding his arms.

Nathan looked at the ambulance. "No."

"Then you keep an eye on her for me, okay?"

"Damn right, I will."

The ambulance door opened, and Megan stuck her head out. "Can you two finish your heart-to-heart over candlelight tonight? I've pushed an amp of D50, but he still refuses to eat. I'd like to get him to the ER before he changes his mind about transport."

200 BLOCK JENIN STREET
JULY 17, 2013. 9:00 PM

Megan flipped on the blinker and waited for traffic to clear.

"Did you ever apply to college?" Nathan asked.

"I filled out the application and the financial aid information. It's all packed up in an envelope, waiting in my car until I get the guts to drop it off."

"What do you want to study?"

She turned the ambulance into Fire Station 4 and hoped he wouldn't laugh. "I think I want to be a nurse practitioner."

"Why not a doctor?"

"I'm not smart en—"

Tones blared.

"Med 3, be en route to 45 Selviville Road, 45 Selviville Road. Burns."

"10-4," Megan said, relieved to not have to stay at Station 4. She pulled a U-turn in the station parking area and flipped on the lights and sirens. It was growing dark, and the street lights blinked on, too.

Nathan laughed. "Did you do that?"

"Heck, yeah. Give me a minute, and I'll turn the stars on, too."

"Now what were you saying about not becoming a doctor?" he asked. "And don't start this crap about you not being smart enough."

She shrugged. "I just like the nursing philosophy better, I guess. And the paramedic-to-RN bridge program is cheaper and easier to swing around a work schedule than pre-med. Maybe I could even work as a flight nurse."

"Seems like you've thought it out."

Megan warmed with his approval. "Yeah, but it's hard to do it, you know?"

"If you take the first step, the next one will be easier."

"I guess." She saw a wooden sign with '45' written on it. "Is this it?"

"Looks like it," he said.

Megan turned onto the narrow dirt road and switched off the siren. There was no need to addle their brains with sound when there was no one on the road with them. The lights reflected off the trees.

A college-age young man waved his arms at the end of another driveway. Megan rolled down the window. "Did you call an ambulance?"

"Yeah, a guy's hurt at the bonfire up there. He's messed up pretty bad."

"Where should I go?"

"Drive around past that fence. You'll see the fire beyond that bank of trees."

"Thanks."

Megan drove around and saw the fire in the distance. There were many cars in a makeshift parking area and large banners painted with Greek letters. College students milled around. Nathan got out, and Megan went to get the stretcher. The sound of a car made her look over her shoulder, and she watched as Todd's police car turned into the drive. Her mouth went dry.

Not again. I can't deal with him again. I can't.

Paralyzing terror built within her. She clung to the rail of the stretcher, gasping, trembling. She did not see the ambulance door, the stretcher, or Nathan at her side, only soggy Cheerios, milk soaking into the carpet, the jarring pain of her head hitting the floor.

"Megan," Nathan called from far away. "Megan!"

She blinked.

Nathan had her by the shoulders. "Look at me! We need to get out there."

Megan shook her head.

"He's here," Nathan said, "but you have to keep going. There's a kid out there who needs a medic, and I need your help. What's your one good thing?"

"I don't know!"

"Name it!"

Megan searched his face. "You."

His eyes softened. "I'm here. And I'm not going to let anything happen to you. Now grab that stretcher, and let's load and go."

Megan pushed the stretcher release bar and slid the stretcher out. Nathan tossed on the sterile sheet packet and grabbed the jump kit. They walked through the nervous college students, who parted like the Red Sea.

Agonized, animalistic screams reached her ears. The sweet smell of charred flesh singed her nose. On the ground lay a young man in what had been a striped, polyester clown costume. Now it was charred black and melted into bubbles of skin.

"What happened?" Nathan asked, opening a bottle of water and pouring it on the man's lower abdomen. The water hissed and steamed. He opened another.

"He was just fooling around. He jumped over the fire, but it flared up. We did that stop, drop, and roll thing. Like kindergarten."

"That's right," Nathan said. He knelt by the man, whose screams had faded into moans. Strings of spittle dripped from the patient's mouth. "We're going to get you on the ambulance and get you something for pain."

Megan estimated what percentage of the man's body was burned.

Nine, nine, eighteen, one, nine. 46% covered in second-degree burns, 4.5% third-degree.

"He needs to fly," she said.

Nathan nodded as he poured more water.

Megan tipped her head to her mic. "Dispatch, Med 3, requesting Life Flight."

"Negative, Med 3. Life Flight is out of service."

"Scratch that," Nathan grumbled.

They wrapped the patient in the sterile sheets and lifted the stretcher. The screams burst forth anew. Megan closed her eyes at the horrific sound. Quickly, they moved through the crowd and slid the stretcher into the back of the ambulance.

"Megan!" Todd called.

She glanced back and saw him pushing his way through the crowd.

Megan reached up to Nathan. He grasped her hand and pulled her into the back of the ambulance, closing the door behind her and slamming his fist down on the locks.

Megan climbed over him to the head of the stretcher. She shone a flashlight into the patient's mouth and nose. "I don't see any airway involvement." The patient moaned and whimpered. She slipped a non-rebreather mask over his face while Nathan gingerly searched for a vein in which to place an IV.

"I can't find anything I want to try and hit," he said as she turned on the heart monitor and started the blood pressure cuff.

"Switch with me," she said.

Leaning over the stretcher, Megan tied the tourniquet around the patient's left arm. Though she could not see any veins, she felt the familiar giving sensation under her fingers. She prepared the area and held traction, piercing the skin and advancing the catheter.

"Nice," Nathan said, unlocking the med box.

Taping the IV in place, Megan attached the tubing and opened the line. She glanced out the back window. "Todd's going back toward the people."

Nathan pushed the pain medication. "We're ready to go. Light it up on the way back."

As Megan climbed into the driver's seat and pulled out onto the highway, lights and sirens blaring. Her breathing returned to normal, and her stomach stopped churning. Todd hadn't tried to get into the ambulance. He hadn't even knocked. He seemed to be acting rationally. Maybe he did only want to talk.

Chapter Ten

806 BRIARTON LANE
JULY 18, 2013. 8:00 PM

Megan sat on a low stool in her garage apartment, painting a bookshelf and listening to her iPod play Katy Perry in her left ear. She found it satisfying to watch the brush slide smoothly along the grain, covering and beautifying the tired finish. She leaned back and admired her work.

Her phone vibrated on the kitchen table, and she looked between the phone and brush.

It can wait. Whoever it is, they can wait.

She dipped her brush and continued. The reminder buzz rattled again.

Fine. Fine.

Megan set the brush on the paint can lid and wiped her hands on a rag.

One missed text.
NATHAN THOMPSON: You left the cave rescue book at Station 1. I have it.
MEGAN HENDERSON: Thx
NATHAN THOMPSON: Want me to drop it by?

Megan bit her lip.

MEGAN HENDERSON: Sure.
NATHAN THOMPSON: Are you busy? I
have a movie we can watch.

Megan's stomach flip-flopped.

MEGAN HENDERSON: Ok
NATHAN THOMPSON: I'll be there in 15.
MEGAN HENDERSON: Ok

Megan dropped her phone on the table and, with her hand on her forehead, surveyed her messy apartment. The bookshelf sat half-painted on a drop cloth next to the two end tables she had already finished. Dirty dishes mounded in the sink. Clothes were scattered about the daybed that doubled as a couch. Tiny paint drops flecked her arms. He couldn't see it like this.

Megan scurried around, gathering clothes, both clean and dirty. She shoved them into a laundry basket and chucked the basket in a corner, tossing her EMS jacket on top. She threw the comforter over the bed, arranged the pillows, and drowned the dishes in a sinkful of soapy water. She brushed her teeth and scrubbed her arms until the paint peeled off. Glancing at herself in the mirror, she gasped. Her hair escaped in tufts from her messy bun and straggled at the sides of her face. Her jean shorts and green paisley peasant top were splotched in paint.

Maybe there's time to change.
She heard a knock.
Maybe not.

Megan's heart hammered in her chest as she opened the door.

Nathan smiled, leaning on the doorframe. "Hey. I brought your book."

"Thanks," she said as he handed it to her along with a DVD case. "What's this?"

"Our movie."

"*How to Train Your Dragon*'?"

"Yeah. It came out while I was deployed, and Sam insists I have to see it," Nathan said. "These are for you, too." He stood straight and brought from behind his back a dozen red roses.

Megan stared. "For me?—I—they're beautiful!" She gathered the flowers into her arms and pressed her face to the petals, inhaling the sweet scent. "I'll put them in water. Um, come in," she said, opening the door wider. She felt bedraggled as she noted his perfectly pressed black pants and neat gray shirt. His aftershave whispered in the air.

She couldn't remember if she had put on deodorant.

"This is it," she said, gesturing to the apartment. "It's just one room. But it suits me, and I like it."

"You got your curtains up," he said.

Megan glanced at the panels at the front windows and the lace valance over the kitchen sink. "Yep." She slid around him and hopped over the dropcloth. The cellophane around the roses crinkled as she set them on the table.

"Lace curtains are amazing," Nathan said, stepping over the cloth.

Her hands paused in her unwrapping of the flowers. "They're what?"

"Amazing," he said, pulling out a chair and settling himself. "There weren't any women in my platoon. Only men. Everything was male, and it was monotonous. I missed women." He laughed. "I mean, of course, I missed women, but I missed lace curtains, and nail polish, and those little poofy hair things." He pointed to her head. "Like that."

"Scrunchies?"

"Yeah. I missed being around femininity. I appreciate it now."

Megan searched through the cabinets. "I don't have anything to put these in. Really, anything."

"Hmm," Nathan said, walking to the cabinets and glancing at the contents. He opened the dorm fridge. "Well, there's an orange juice carton."

"With juice in it."

"Thirsty?"

Megan laughed. "Pour some into these," she said, taking down four glasses.

Nathan filled all four glasses and drank the last bit straight from the carton. "Now we can rinse this out and cut off the top. Instant vase."

"I saw that done once on *Mr. Rogers*, but I think it involved macaroni and glitter."

He filled the carton with water and shook it. "Just don't eat the paste."

Megan slid two of the glasses into the fridge as Nathan constructed his makeshift rose holder.

"There you go," he said, pouring the packet of preservative into the water and fluffing the flowers into place.

Megan handed him a glass. "If you ever give up EMS, you could go into flower arranging."

"Cheers," he said and clinked his glass against hers.

Megan drank her juice, blinking at the distasteful

interplay of oranges and mint toothpaste. She looked up at Nathan and realized he was studying her. He took her glass and placed it next to his on the counter. Cupping her face in his hands, he kissed her, his motions slow and relaxed, undriven by pain or the paranoia of being discovered. She reached to his shoulders and rested her fingers on his collar as his palms warmed her back.

The kiss faded. Megan stepped away, breathless and amazed. She felt as though she had kissed him, the real Nathan, for the first time.

He smiled. "Are you ready for our movie?"

Her eyes fell to the bubbly sink. Guilt pricked her conscious.

"I should really wash the dishes first,"

"You wash. I'll rinse."

Megan scrubbed the plates and handed them to Nathan. He rinsed and set them in the rack.

"Why are we doing this now?" he asked.

She paused, the water running over her hands. "Because ..." Her voice faded with realization. She turned off the faucet. "Because Todd hates dirty dishes being left in the sink. I thought you felt the same."

"You assumed."

She nodded and searched for silverware in the dishwater.

Nathan reached into the water and hooked his little finger around hers. "I do like things a particular way, it's true."

She smiled, thinking of his dusted room.

"I guess you noticed that," he said. She nodded. "But remember," he continued, "I live with Sam Mayfield, and I know where you put your 4x4 wrappers. If someone else's messiness really bothered me, I would have shriveled up a long time ago. I don't care about the dirty dishes. I care about you."

Nathan squeezed her hand and turned the water back on. Megan passed him the spoons and warmed with his acceptance. She could let her guard down.

They made quick work of the dishes. Megan drained the sink and dried her hands on a towel. Nathan stood silently behind her. She watched his reflection in the bubbles on the edge of the drain. Her heart beat faster. He placed his hands on her hips, sliding them beneath her shirt to the bare skin of her stomach. She closed her eyes, lips parted. Fear rushed through her, sweat prickling her skin.

I want this. Why am I so nervous?

He pulled her tightly against him. Her knees trembled.

"Stop!" she cried.

Immediately, Nathan released her, holding his hands out in front of her on either side, where she could see them, his fingers splayed.

"What's wrong?" he asked.

She turned around and searched his face, looking for anger or frustration and finding neither. "I don't know," she said. "I just—I needed to know if you'd stop if I asked you to."

Nathan sighed. "Megan, I want to touch you, but only if you want it. I have no expectations, and I will always stop the moment you want me to."

"But there's a point of no return, there's—"

"No. There's not. And whoever told you that is a liar. Just tell me to stop, or squeeze my arm, or tap my shoulder, and I'll stop. I'm not in a hurry, and I will never hurt you."

Megan sank onto his chest. He held her and kissed the

deepened, and he leaned on her, his weight pressing her down. Tension built; she flinched. The more she tried to calm herself, the more anxious she felt.

Nathan lifted his hands. Gently, he pulled her back against his chest and rested his head on hers. With his hand under her shirt on her bare stomach, he held her. His arms were strong and warm. Megan finally relaxed into his embrace. As she drifted toward sleep, she wondered what he thought of her. His words had been patient, but were they true?

Nathan's phone alarm buzzed. Megan blinked awake and shook his shoulder.

"Hm?" he mumbled.

"Your phone."

Nathan sat up on his elbow and shut off the alarm. He back onto the bed and pulled her to him, nuzzling her

"What time is it?" she asked.

"0430."

"Retton County?"

"Yeah, I need to go home and change. I'm going to be

"You didn't bring a uniform with you?"

"m not that presumptuous," he said, sitting up and g for his prosthetic. "You're working tonight?"

ran her fingers across his back. "Yes."

ten here now," he said, ducking away from her you start doing all that, and I'll just have to call in."

an giggled and kissed his cheek. "So call in."

net her eyes and smiled. "No. But I'll be thinking u the whole time." He stood and pulled his shirt don't see you in passing in Retton, I'll see you at tomorrow."

top of her head.

"Now," he said. "Are you ready for the movie, or do you need to wash the windows or something?"

Megan grinned and went to put the DVD in the player. "Sorry, I don't have a couch. You can move the pillows however you like."

Nathan sat on the daybed. "I should take my leg off. Would it bother you?"

"Whatever you need," she said as she clicked through the menu choices. He unzipped the inseam of his pants to the knee and took off his prosthetic. She sat on the bed next to him.

"This is Berk…" the movie began.

"Can I put my arm around you?" Nathan asked.

Megan hated that he felt the need to ask, yet the reassurance lent her the security she craved. She nodded and scooted next to him, and he wrapped his left arm around her shoulders. As she watched the movie, Megan ran her fingertips back and forth along his bicep. She tucked them under the edge of his sleeve and felt a roughness to his skin. Shifting to face him, she pushed back his sleeve. A large chunk of his deltoid was gone. Several other small pits surrounded it.

"What happened?"

"Shrapnel," he said, touching the pit.

"Are there more?"

He nodded. "I can show you."

Megan blushed. Nathan hunched his shoulders and pulled his shirt off, leaning back so she could see the pitting and scars that stretched in a swath across the left side of his body. For a moment, though, she simply enjoyed his musculature. His many hours in the pool had left their mark. Her eyes were drawn to a tattoo in Arabic script on the right side of his chest.

Nathan cleared his throat.

Her eyes flew to his. "You distracted me," she said. "What were we talking about?"

"Shrapnel."

She moved her hand over the scarring. "Did they get it all out?"

"Yeah, there's nothing left in there."

She traced her finger over the script. "What does it say?"

"*Kafir*. Infidel."

Megan snuggled her back against his bare side, and he draped his arm over her. A comfortable evening, pleasant company; she was happy. She rubbed her cheek on his shoulder, enjoying everything about him.

Megan tried to watch the movie, but her thoughts refused to sit still. She wondered if he would kiss her again. Or more.

Will he stay the night?

She glanced up at him, but he was intently watching the dragons. She kissed his arm. He looked down at her and smiled but then returned his gaze to the TV. She knew he would focus on those silly dragons until the movie was over. At work, he was never deterred from his tasks. She supposed his downtime was no different.

"Check that out!" Nathan said as the movie came to close, and he saw Hiccup's prosthetic leg. "What do you think? Should I go Viking? I wonder if the VA would pay for that."

Megan smiled as a rush of affection filled her. She climbed over him, straddled his lap, and kissed him passionately. His eyebrows lifted in surprise, but his hands gripped her hips. She broke the kiss and leaned her

forehead against his.

"You've distracted me," he said. "What were we talking about?"

"The VA?"

"Hell, no. I'm not talking about the VA right now."

He kissed her again, his hands moving slowly body. He shifted to the side and leaned her down bed.

Megan's head touched the comforter.

Cheerios. Milk. Pain radiating through her.

Megan cried out. Nathan lifted himself up to the side. She trembled, every muscle qua welled up, and she covered her face with her escaped the corner of her eye.

Oh, God, what's wrong with me? everything.

"May I hold you?" he whispered.

She nodded. He put his arm around away the tear.

"I don't understand!" she said. "I w can't I—"

"Shh," he said, brushing a hair a "What was the trigger?"

"The back of my head touching th

"Now we know. We'll know for n

"I'm sorry," she said, laying her

"Megan, look at me."

She reluctantly complied.

"None of this is your fault," past it. It just means we'll ne winked and traced his finger closed her eyes as he kissed he breast, smoothing the fabr

Megan closed the door behind him and watched through the glass as he walked down the stairs. She suspected Emily would be calling soon, wanting to know all about the owner of the mysterious truck that had been parked outside her garage overnight.

Megan let the curtain fall and walked to the kitchen table and the orange juice roses. Waking up in Nathan's arms had felt amazing, but her fears had ruined their evening. She was both thrilled and ashamed. In spite of her troubles, he had been gentle and calm, just as he always was. His patience overwhelmed her, and she wanted to grow into the strong, confident woman he encouraged her to be. He brought out the best in her.

She touched one of the petals. She knew his struggles and quirks, but in her eyes, they paled in comparison to his courage, his strength, and his honor. She didn't know how long she had been in love with him, but she wanted it to last forever.

EMS STATION 1
JULY 20, 2013. 7:40 AM

Nathan parked his truck in his usual space in the parking garage. Megan was leaning against a pillar, and the sight of her quickened his pulse.

He grinned and opened the door. "Couldn't wait two minutes to see me inside, huh?"

She tossed her hair and lifted her nose in the air as she walked to the passenger side and climbed in. "This is business, not pleasure."

He closed his door again, frowning. "What do you mean?"

She held out an envelope. "There," she said. "That's all

the money I owe you."

He exhaled with relief and laughed. "I don't want it back." He pushed the envelope away. "Don't you need it?"

"No, you have to take it." She grabbed his hand and stuffed the envelope into it. "I don't want money issues between us, especially not that much. Money complicates everything. If I had thought it meant anything but the utmost propriety, I wouldn't have taken it."

"But you didn't have to pay it back so quickly. Are you sure you don't need it?"

Megan nodded. "I'm sure. I need to know this has nothing to do with money." She smiled. "Besides, now I'm debt-free and completely on my own two—" She closed her eyes and pressed her fingers to her forehead.

"Feet." He chuckled. "And how does that feel?"

"Amazing."

He winked at her and locked the money in the glove compartment. "Now come here, and let me kiss you."

Megan leaned toward him, and he kissed her, brushing his fingers through her ponytail. He wished they were back on her daybed, but the rules were set. No PDA. He anticipated a tension-filled shift as frustrating as it was exhilarating.

She bumped her nose against his. "We need to be careful. Someone will see."

He kissed her lower lip. "We're not on the clock."

"We should be," she said, leaning away and opening the door. "Besides, I don't want to disgrace my uniform." She climbed out.

"I'm never going to live that down, am I?" he called.

They clocked in together. Richard eyed them suspiciously, and Megan blushed. When Richard's lip twitched, Nathan knew she was right. They needed to be more careful; otherwise, disclosure paperwork would be forthcoming. He sighed and followed her to the locker room.

FIRE STATION 6
JULY 20, 2013. 8:30 PM

Nathan unbuckled his seatbelt as Megan pulled the truck into the Station 6 driveway. Martin waved his arms, and she rolled down the window. The humidity spilled into the cab and felt sticky on Nathan's skin. He preferred drier climates than Barrington and grunted at the sensation.

Martin, with a toothy grin, leaned on the door. "Don't park in the driveway, Doll. We're going to play basketball before it gets any darker."

"At least it's not so hot now," she said.

"It's still a sauna," Martin said, "and now that you're here, it just got a lot hotter."

Megan laughed. "Go away, Martin."

She parked on the grass. Nathan grabbed his bag and walked around the side of the ambulance.

"Actually, I need to talk to you both," Martin said.

Nathan frowned. It sounded like serious business. He wondered if someone had reported them.

Megan leaned on the truck. "Oh? What about?"

Her tone was stilted. Nathan exchanged a glance with her.

Martin shoved his hands into his pockets.

"We've received a donation to the high-angle rescue team for new equipment and such."

Nathan crossed his arms, mildly surprised and moderately suspicious.

"A donation?" Megan said, squinting. "From whom?"

Martin shook his head and stared at the ground. "I guess someone you two helped out. The EMS director said it should be allocated to the high-angle team because you both work on it, and we always need equipment."

"How much are we talking?" asked Nathan.

"About $2,000."

Megan's jaw dropped. "Are you serious?"

Martin nodded. "I want you to pick out a harness."

"No way!" she said. "We can get cave training and—"

"It has to be used on equipment," Martin said.

"Why?"

He shrugged. "Budget allocations."

Nathan understood Megan's response—cave training would be a good team investment, and he knew she was partial to it. Martin's restrictions seemed odd, though, and he wanted the rest of the story.

Megan listed things on her fingers. "Then we can get a new basket, and brake bars, and ascenders! We'll be able to speed climb—"

"We can get everything, Doll, but I'm getting you a new harness first. You can speed climb all you want, but if that old harness breaks, you're going to be in a world of hurt." He fiddled with his phone and held it out to her. "I was thinking about this one."

Megan looked at the screen. Nathan moved to look over her shoulder.

She burst into laughter. "A Special Ops harness? That's way too much for my use. I'd be laughed off scene." She tapped the screen. "Look, it's got a holster attachment point. What the heck would I use that for? D50? Just a basic harness would be fine. And we need more people trained, not more equipment."

Martin rubbed the back of his neck. "I don't make that choice, Doll. You brought in this money, and you're going to get the most benefit."

"What about Nathan?" she asked.

"My harness is practically new," Nathan said, pleased she had thought of him.

Megan swiped the screen, flipping through catalog pages. "Oh, look! Dog harnesses! Can we get a K9? Is that equipment?" She grinned.

Martin chuckled. "I'm not getting you a dog."

"Aw, you're no fun. I've always wanted a dog." She swiped again. "This harness has a fall arrest indicator."

Martin pointed to the screen. "Look at that one. It has quick release catches for easy on and off. And a buckle that won't open under load."

Nathan leaned closer as she read the specs. It was a harness he had looked at before, and it would work well for her.

"I think you should get it," Nathan said.

Megan tilted her head. "It's a really nice harness."

"That settles it," Martin said. "One rescue harness, a new basket, some ascenders and brake bars. If you think of anything else, let me know, but I'm going to place this order pretty quickly before they decide to appropriate the money somewhere else. It'll probably take years for the county to process the purchase order."

"This is wild. Who would give that much money?" Megan mused.

Martin shrugged.

"Oh, well," she said. "Was that all?"

Martin wiggled his mustache. "I can come up with something else for you and me to do."

Megan rolled her eyes and walked into the bay.

Nathan folded his arms, standing shoulder to shoulder with Martin. "Who's the money from?"

"John Marsh's office," said Martin.

"The senator?"

"Yep."

Nathan nodded.

Martin nodded.

Nathan sighed. Dirty politics made sense. Marsh's involvement in illicit drugs could make or break the election. If Megan filed battery charges, it would look even worse. The senator's office had obviously searched both his and Megan's connections and found the most effective way to keep them both quiet without direct intervention.

"Does Marsh realize there are rules that keep us from saying anything about patient care?" Nathan asked.

"Probably. But I think he also realizes that once it got out that he was a drunk cocaine addict who groped pretty paramedics, those rules would be irrelevant."

Nathan rubbed his chin. "I wouldn't tell Megan where the money came from, if I were you. She'd throw it back in his face."

"You notice I didn't."

"Wise move."

"Let's play!" a firefighter called.

"Nathan, we need one more," Martin said.

Though Nathan had not played basketball since moving from Texas, he enjoyed it, and his height gave him a natural advantage.

"Sure," he said, hoping Megan would come back out and watch.

Martin, Robert, and Nathan against three other firefighters. They moved warily around the half court, sizing each other up. Nathan detected suspicion and saw a few glances at his leg. As Martin explained the rules, Nathan rocked back and forth on his boots.

Game on.

The other team started with the ball. A redheaded firefighter dribbled and bounced a pass to a tall guy with a beard. Martin darted forward and stole the ball, dribbling down to the line and back to the goal again. As the ginger waved his arms, Martin pivoted and passed the ball to Robert, who banked a layup off the backboard and through the hoop. High fives around.

Megan walked back across the parking lot. She leaned against the wall, talking to Carrie and tying knots with her Prusik cord. Nathan straightened his shoulders and put a jaunt in his step.

Time to shine.

The bearded guy threw a bad shot. Nathan raced in and took the ball. He spun to pass to Martin. Martin dribbled back to the line and passed to Robert, who passed back to Nathan. Ginger was in his face. Nathan faked right, made a fast break, and took a jump shot. High fives again.

The next shot went to the other team. 2-1.

Martin took the ball out and turned. He tossed to Nathan, who wove a defensive shuffle and stretched for a long-distance jumper. The ball bounced on the hoop and dropped in.

Ginger scowled at Nathan. "Great shot, but you traveled."

"Naw, man," said Martin.

Nathan shook his head. "Whatever. Let's play."

Ginger took the ball to the line. Nathan stole it back. Beard blocked the lane, shoving Nathan's shoulder. Nathan dodged around him and collided with Robert, staggering back, his arms wheeling. And fell.

His heart crashed as he hit the concrete. Megan would have The Look.

Her conversation with Carrie stopped abruptly, and she met his eyes. There was no Look of pity. Rather, one brow lifted slightly in simple anticipation. She expected him to get moving.

Martin held out his hand. Nathan took it, climbed up, and slapped the ball away from Beard. A fast break. Ginger blocked the ball.

Tones.

"Med 3, be en route to 45 Eastern Road, 45 Eastern Road. Seizure."

"10-4," Megan said as Nathan caught his breath.

Megan climbed into the driver's seat and turned over the engine as Nathan jogged around.

"That game got you really sweaty," she said, throwing him a towel from behind the seat.

He buckled his seatbelt and wiped his face and neck. "You were standing there holding up the wall, and you're sweaty." He rubbed the ache in his residual limb and hoped he hadn't injured himself.

Megan tossed her ponytail. "I beg your pardon, sir! I do not sweat."

"Your shirt begs to differ," he said.

"Am I disgracing it?" she said in tone that drove his heart rate higher.

He leaned over and tugged at her shirt where it tucked into her belt. "I would need to examine it first."

She slapped his hand. "I'm driving! Stay over there!" she giggled.

They pulled up at a small house. The porch light was on, but Nathan didn't see anyone around. Megan got the jump kit as he put his gloves on, and they walked to the house.

Nathan knocked. "Paramedics!"

"I've been here before," she whispered. "It was a seizure thing then, too."

A plump woman answered the door. "Gerald!" she called over her shoulder. "The ambulance drivers are here to take Adam to the hospital!"

Nathan pressed his lips together as he stepped into the dank closeness of a living room without air conditioning. "Where is Adam?"

She pointed to the floor. "He right there."

"Can you tell me what happened?"

"Same thing that always do. You get him to the hospital."

Nathan walked around the couch and found a teenager. He was semiconscious, clearly postictal. Nathan knelt next to him, blinking at the strong smell of warm urine on unwashed jeans.

"I'll get the stretcher," Megan said.

Nathan nodded. "Adam? Can you hear me?"

Adam moaned and tried to sit up.

"Just hang tight," Nathan said. "We're going to put you on a stretcher." He wrapped the blood pressure cuff around the boy's arm.

Megan returned, and Nathan helped maneuver Adam onto the stretcher. He went through the motions, almost without thinking and only half-listening to Megan.

"Where are his medicines?" she asked the woman.

The woman bustled away and returned with an orange pill bottle.

Megan held it up. "It's empty. How long has he been off his meds?"

"They don't work," the woman said. "He's having

seizures."

"He has to take it for it to work," Megan said, and Nathan noticed her voice had hardened.

"He don't have no more."

Megan turned the bottle sideways. "It says here he has two refills. Did you call the pharmacy?"

"If it worked, I wouldn't have to do all that."

Nathan knew Megan was about to lose her last shred of composure. He watched her slowly wet her lips.

"This medication has to be taken every day, or the seizures will come back," Megan said. "If you don't get him his medicine, then we'll just have to keep taking him to the hospital."

The woman held up her finger and moved her head sideways. "That's your job. You need to do it! Get your ass in that ambulance and take my child to the hospital!"

Megan turned on her heel, her ponytail sweeping behind her. Nathan met her flashing eyes and thanked his lucky stars that the ire he saw there was not leveled at him. He handled the remaining details as Megan stood to the side with her arms crossed and her boot turned out.

They deposited the patient at the emergency room and drove down to Station 1 to restock. Megan still pouted in icy silence. "Don't let that lady get to you," Nathan said. "Frequent flyers aren't worth the trouble of getting upset."

"I know," she said. "It's just irritating sometimes to work so hard on keeping current and advancing and improving quality of care to be considered a glorified taxi driver."

"She'd sing a different tune if she were having a heart attack or were in a car wreck."

"I guess."

He pulled the ambulance into the bay and cut the

engine. "I reek of basketball and whatever was in that house," he said, lifting the edge of his shirt to his nose. "I need to change my shirt before we go."

"I'll restock."

"Thanks."

As it was nearing midnight, the station was nearly deserted. The medics of Med 1 were tucked away in the duty room. The dispatcher sat quietly reading at her console. Nathan went to the locker room and washed up. His leg ached. He wondered again whether he had injured himself playing basketball and sat to check his prosthetic. Everything seemed in order. Just the same old nerves acting up. He clicked everything back into place and went to find Megan.

Nathan glanced through the supply room window as he passed. A flash of red uniform brought him to a skidding halt, and he stepped back to the door and peered through the glass insert.

The cords of Megan's white earbuds contrasted against her shirt and hair. Her head moved slightly with the beat as she pulled down paper packages of supplies. Her motions stilled.

A pause in the music?

Her movements restarted with more strength in her shoulders. She reached to a higher shelf, the other arm lifted in motion with the music in her ears and the silence in his own. He stared, fascinated, as she curved her body. Her eyes were closed. She danced, and turned, in a world of her own, mouthing the words of the song.

... fire, fire fire, and there is a fire, fire, fire ...

He knew the song. His lips moved with hers; his hand opened the door. With two steps, he was behind her and gently pulled the ear buds from her ears. She started and turned around. Draping the cords about her neck, he wound his arm to her back pocket and withdrew the iPod. He winked at her bemused expression and turned up the volume as high as it would go. The music was tinny coming from the ear buds, but it was loud enough for them both to hear.

... when we first started out, heard the sound, heard the song ...

Nathan took her hands and moved them in time, small steps, small movements. Megan's eyes lit up as she understood. He lifted her arm, and she moved underneath. When she turned back to him, it was with a smile.

Their eyes met as both waited for the hook. When the beat hit, they bobbed their heads together, Megan springing slightly on her toes. Their hands touched and released as they moved closer and backed away, his shoulders dipping, her hair brushing over her face. He turned her again, placing his hand on her waist to guide her. A flush crept up her neck as she warmed to his touch.

The music softened in a bridge, unable to sustain their movements. Megan stepped back, her breath quieting, though she did not turn away. Her eyes shone. But Nathan wasn't finished. He took her hands again in his and pulled her toward him, the music building and taking control.

Lifting up our hands, turning to the sky, sky, sky ...

He raised her hands, lifting their arms, moving together. He basked in her figure, savored her delicacy. Every beat, hearts in time, breath in sync. Her eyes shone. As the music faded, he ran his thumb across her cheek. He loved her.

FIRE STATION 4
JULY 21, 2013. 1:00 AM

A steady tone reported from the radio. "The National Weather Service in Barrington has issued a severe thunderstorm watch for Washington County, Retton County, Selvy County, Barrington County, Clark County, Carter County, until five a.m., Eastern Daylight Savings Ti —"

Nathan climbed out of the ambulance and shouldered his bag. Though the night was warm, he saw Megan look up at the dark roofline of her dreaded Station 4 and shiver.

"Hey," he said. She turned back. "Everything's going to be fine."

She put on a brave smile. "I'm going to get some ice water from the kitchen. Want anything?"

"No, thanks."

Megan walked on ahead. Nathan stood by the truck in the illuminated parking lot and watched the pine trees sway in the wind. He didn't need the National Weather Service; his leg had ached all day. It would rain soon.

Searing pain shot through his residual limb. It contracted his core, blinded his eyes, and buzzed in his ears. He stumbled and grappled for the side of the truck. His bag fell as he gasped through the stabbing sensation. Just as suddenly, it was gone.

Nathan leaned back against the truck, breathless.

Fuck.

Wary he would set off more pain, Nathan picked up his bag. He let himself into the dark station. Light from the kitchen shone across the common room floor.

"I think everyone's asleep upstairs," Megan whispered, ice cup in hand. "The EMS room is down that hall on the left." She turned back to the sink and began filling her cup.

Nathan found the room and turned on the overhead light. There was no lamp. There were no tables, chairs, or anything else, except a tattered couch and a trash can by the door.

I guess I'll sleep in the common room.

Pain seized him. As bile rose in his throat, he pounded his leg on the floor, trying to interrupt the nerve impulse. Groaning, he dropped to the couch. Blackness ringed his vision. He fumbled with the zipper at his inseam and clawed off the prosthetic. He struck the offending nerves with his palm repeatedly, then fell back, laying across the cushions, gasping, squeezing his eyes shut, and gritting his teeth.

A blessed coolness spread across his forehead. The pain slunk into the shadows. Megan's hand, cooled by her cup of ice water, rested on his brow as she knelt by the couch.

"What can I do?" she whispered. "There's morphine on the truck."

"You said yourself that's against the rules," he said, his voice rough, his energy drained.

"I don't care about rules right now."

Nathan pushed himself up on the cushion. "It wouldn't help anyway. It's just the storm."

"What do you usually use?"

"Whiskey."

"You rub it on?"

Nathan raised an eyebrow.

Megan's worried expression faded with realization. "I'm an idiot."

He chuckled. "I love you."

She smiled, ducking her chin.

He took her hand. "I mean that."

"I love you," she said.

Megan climbed up on the couch, and Nathan laid his head on her lap. She ran her fingers over his hair as the rain fell.

FIRE STATION 4
JULY 21, 2013. 2:30 AM

Tones blared. Nathan jolted awake.

"Med 3, be en route to mile marker 7 Highway 42, mile marker 7, Highway 42. Signal 4."

Megan cleared her throat. "10-4."

Nathan scrambled to reattach his prosthetic. "I'm coming."

As Megan stood and stretched, the intercom screeched.

"Engine 4, Rescue 4, be en route to mile marker 7 Highway 42, mile marker 7 Highway 42. Signal 4."

Boots pounded down the stairs above them as Nathan fit the pin in the socket. "You drive. I'll be there in a minute."

"You'll do anything to steal a call," she said with a wink.

"You can still have the call!"

Megan had her rain gear on and the engine running when he hopped into the passenger side and slammed the door. "Let's go!"

The fire trucks had preceded them, so Megan drove at her own pace, rain beating against the windshield. Nathan glanced at his watch. 0235.

Nothing good happens after two o'clock in the morning.

He retrieved his rain gear from his bag and unbuckled his seatbelt. Pulling on the pants and jacket, he cinched the ankle strings and tied them as tightly as he could.

The fire truck's lights pierced the darkness.

"I know this area," Megan said. "I bet … Yep. Look." She pointed at a lake. "That drainage pond only fills when it storms like this. It's usually 12 to 15 inches deep all the way across. I've already pulled two people out of here."

"These things always come in threes."

After Megan parked the ambulance, Nathan climbed out. The rain beat down and ran into his eyes, so he reached back into the truck and grabbed his baseball hat. Megan walked to his side.

A four-door car rested in the pond. The fire truck's sidelights revealed its crumpled front end. Supervisor 1 rolled up as two firefighters slogged their way out to it.

Megan sighed. "They'll need four to carry the board. Let's go."

Nathan caught her arm. "You remember when I told you I'd let you know if there was something I couldn't do? I can't go out there."

Megan smirked, incredulous. "You're a swimmer. It's like this deep," she said, estimating with her hands.

"With a different foot, I could. If I go out there, I'll lose my foot, or I'll rust like the Tin Man. I left my oil can in my other pants."

Megan grinned. "No problem. There are plenty of firefighters to help carry. And that means I steal the call back."

"You've got it," he said with a wink.

Nathan stood on the shoulder while Megan sloshed out to the car. The rain slackened; only a drizzle continued to fall. He folded his arms and watched as she contacted the patient and the firefighters determined the car's stability.

A police car drove up on scene and parked in front of the fire truck. Todd stalked toward him.

Shit. This just keeps getting better.

"Thompson!" Todd bellowed. "What the hell were you thinking, having me written up?"

Nathan continued to watch Megan, not obliging Todd by acknowledging his presence.

"Look at me, Gimp! Quit staring at her ass!"

Nathan flicked his eyes to Todd's red face.

Todd stepped closer. "You're fucking with the wrong person. You cross me again, and I'll—"

Richard walked up the road. "Back off, Todd!"

Todd sneered. He slammed his shoulder into Nathan's and walked a few paces past him. Nathan slid his jaw forward but determined to keep his focus on Megan. She had secured the patient on the backboard, and she and another firefighter were supporting the weight. "We need a fourth out here," a firefighter called over the radio.

"10-4," Richard answered. "I take it you can't go?"

Nathan shook his head.

Todd laughed. "That's the lamest shit I've ever seen. That's fucking priceless! You can't do your damn job, and now we've got to cover it. Do the taxpayers realize they're in danger from a paramedic who isn't up to snuff?"

Nathan knew Todd was trying to rile him, and he tried to dismiss it. Even so, his blood pressure shot up and pounded in his ears. His confidence weakened. He had sent Megan to do his job. He had put her in harm's way because he was unable to do it himself. He questioned his skills, his ability, and whether his service was appropriate. He hated his limb loss. He hated himself.

I don't deserve to work here. And I don't deserve her.

"Go get the backboard, Todd," Richard commanded. "Nathan, get the stretcher."

Nathan nodded and strode to the back of the ambulance as Todd waded out in the water. Nathan slung the stretcher out of the truck. The wheels slammed into the bumper, and the stretcher clattered to the asphalt in protest. Grinding his teeth, he pushed the stretcher over to where Richard stood.

Megan, Todd, and two firefighters hobbled away from the car, the water churning around their legs. They were halfway to the road.

"I'll switch the heater on in the box and warm it up," Richard said, turning away.

Out in the water, Todd stuck out his boot and caught Megan's leg. She splashed down onto her knees, the weight swinging her off balance until her shoulders dipped under the water. The firefighters shouted, and the backboard teetered downward. They quickly recovered, and Megan regained her footing, water pouring as if from a downspout from inside her rain gear.

Nathan charged to the water's edge. "Fucking bastard!"

Richard ran back, carrying a blanket. "What?"

"He tripped her!" Nathan yelled. "Todd tripped her!"

The team arrived at the edge and moved the backboard onto the stretcher.

Richard shoved the blanket at Nathan. "I'll get the patient. Take care of her."

Eyeing Todd, who was walking toward his police car, Nathan jogged to Megan and unfolded the blanket. Her hair was plastered to her head, and the red and blue lights flashed over her face. She stripped off her rain gear. Her uniform was dripping wet.

He wrapped the blanket around her shoulders. "Are you okay?"

"Cold," she said. "Did Richard see?"

Nathan looked back at the ambulance. "No."

Megan shivered. He rubbed her arms vigorously, the wool blanket scratching at his palms.

Richard called from the ambulance. "Nathan! Come on!"

"Come into the back," Nathan said. "Richard has the heat on. It'll be warm."

"In a minute," she said. "I think I pulled a muscle or something. I need to stretch a bit."

"Okay."

Nathan bounded up the side steps into the ambulance, leaving the door open.

Richard was taking the patient's blood pressure. "Megan okay?"

"Yeah, just a pulled muscle."

"She can file a report on him, but it will probably be based on her word alone. Your statement won't add much weight to it, I'm afraid."

Nathan did not reply as he continued examining the patient for injuries.

Todd's voice carried to the truck. "Meg!"

Nathan's hands froze. He stared at Richard and listened.

A mumble of voices.

"Stop!" Megan yelled. "Let go!"

Nathan hurtled out of the ambulance and sprinted down the shoulder. His prosthetic slipped on the wet grass, and he tumbled down the small embankment toward the water. Swearing, he jumped up and continued on.

The blanket she had held lay discarded on the ground. Nathan leaped over it.

Firefighters shouted as Todd and Megan struggled. Megan tore herself from Todd's grip. Todd raised his arm, a narrow, black cylinder in his hand. He swung, and Nathan heard the *shing* of the expandable baton as it lengthened. The metal rod struck Megan's thigh. She screamed, and her screams consumed Nathan. He heard nothing else, saw only the sound. Bones broke beneath his fist, and blood covered his hand. His body slowed, heavy, weighted, held back with red, blue, flashing lights.

"Dispatch, Supervisor 1! Man down times two! I've got man down times two!"

"10-4, Supervisor 1, man down times two. Sending two units, implementing system status, critical level coverage."

Nathan slowly realized Richard was gripping one of his arms, and a firefighter, the other. Todd lay unconscious and bloody.

Richard pointed at the probationary firefighter. "Go to the ambulance and tend the patient!"

The probie touched his chest. "Me?"

"You're a goddamn EMT! Go use it!"

On the ground, Megan sobbed, holding her thigh.

Nathan shook off the men and crouched at her side. "Megan!" He pulled off his gloves and ran his hands over her head and palpated her cheekbones. "Did he hit you? What hurts?" His fingers walked her collarbones.

Her jaw quivered as she gasped with pain. "Just—my—leg."

"Do you think it's broken?" he said, rolling his hands on her abdomen.

"I don't—know."

Nathan pressed her hip bones. "Richard, get me the traction splint, the rigid splints, and a backboard."

Megan groaned. "Don't you put me—on a damn backboard!"

"It's just to make transfer easier," he said as he palpated her arm.

Richard hurried back to the truck as Nathan climbed over her and withdrew his shears. He cut the side of her cargo pants. A large welt had already formed on her thigh, but there was no change in leg length. He sliced the laces of her boot and removed it from her foot, along with her sopping wet sock. Her pedal pulse beat rapidly under his fingers.

Nathan touched her thigh.

She cried out, arching her back. "You're not—doing this right!"

"If your femur's broken, it's going to hurt no matter what I do."

She lifted her head from the asphalt. "Is it displaced?"

"Would you please be the patient, and let me be the medic?"

Sirens sounded in the distance. Police cars and ambulances roared onto the scene as Richard dropped the splints and backboard beside them.

"Rigid splint," Nathan said.

Nathan and Richard worked together to splint her leg. Richard reached for the backboard, but Nathan shook his head. He checked Megan's pulse again as the paramedics from Med 1 and Med 5 ran up.

"God! What happened?"

Richard sat back on his heels. "Med 1 take over Megan." He pointed at Todd. "And Med 5 get that son of a bitch."

Nathan clasped Megan's hand as the Med 1 team lifted her onto the stretcher.

Richard grabbed Nathan's arm. "We need to go. I need you to drive the original patient to the hospital."

"But Megan—"

"Megan's in good hands."

"She's my partner!"

"Right now," Richard said, "she's a patient, and you have your own patient already. Now let's go!"

Med 1 lifted the stretcher.

Nathan squeezed Megan's hand. "I'll wait for you there."

"Okay," she said, her jaw still quivering.

"You remember what I said. Before the call."

She smiled weakly. "Yeah."

Nathan nodded and walked toward the Med 3 ambulance.

"Thompson?"

Nathan turned around as a police officer approached.

"I need to ask you a few questions."

Chapter Eleven

SACRED HEART EMERGENCY DEPARTMENT
JULY 21, 2013. 4:00 AM

Nathan swiped his ID and hurried into the emergency room. Bright and busy, no one seemed to notice his arrival. He looked up at the patient tracking screen and read the names and ER room numbers.

Henderson, Todd. 8.

Henderson, Megan. 14.

Jogging down the hall, he found room eight empty, devoid of a bed. The floor was littered with trash.

He continued past it to room 14. The bed was empty; the sheets, skewed. A drained saline IV bag hung from a stand, the tubing wrapped up over the bar.

Sam walked toward him. "She's not here. She left about 15 minutes ago."

"It's not broken then."

"No." Sam glanced over his shoulder. "Come back to radiology. I'll show you."

They walked through the darkened halls to Sam's alcove. Sam touched the computer screen. "You're not seeing this, by the way. It seems confidentiality means nothing to me."

"She's my patient."

Sam laughed. "Yeah, we just won't think too hard about that." He pointed at the film. "Femur, hip socket. You can see there's no damage. What you can't see is a lateral nerve that runs along here." He traced down the outside of the thigh. "An impact there causes a parasympathetic reaction. It would drop anyone, which is why cops carry those things. I imagine it would feel similar to those phantom pains you get sometimes, just with a baseball-sized welt at the end."

"But no damage."

Sam cleared the screen. "No. They gave her some fluids, and she walked out."

Nathan stared at the radiology home screen. The cursor flashed, ready for the next patient's ID.

Why didn't she wait for me?

"Did she say where she was going?" Nathan asked.

Sam shrugged. "No. Her apartment, I guess. You look like shit."

"Thanks. I'm going home."

"Aren't you on shift?"

Nathan rubbed the back of his neck. "Let's just say I have the rest of the day off."

"Whatever, man. Get some rest. I'm working a double until three p.m."

8735 PETERSON AVENUE, APARTMENT 218
JULY 21, 2013. 5:00 AM

Nathan had showered, but he wasn't tired. He had wandered through the kitchen, but he wasn't hungry. Put on his prosthetic but didn't want to leave. He dropped into his recliner but left the TV off. He had no interest in the score of the Braves vs. White Sox game. The light from the parking lot filtered through the blinds and cast stripes across the clock face. 0503. 0504. 0505.

He clenched and relaxed his fist, grimacing at the soreness. He had known. He had turned his back on an enemy, let his guard down. Negligence. His lack of vigilance had left her vulnerable.

'I'm here. And I won't let anything happen to you.'

He had promised, and he had failed.

If I hadn't fallen, I could have been there in time. I could have stopped him. Fucking leg!

The clock swam before him. Guilt blurred his vision. He sank forward, his face in his hands.

He opened his eyes.

Something had awakened him.

0545.

A soft knock.

The deadbolt clicked as he opened the door. Megan stood before him, the glow of the porch light casting an apricot hue on her pink sundress. His eyes roved over her. He was starving, parched, and she, brimming with relief, hope, and expectancy, offered an oasis of absolution and rest.

He extended his hand. She turned out her ankle, wrinkling the doormat in a flicker of nervous hesitation, the retracting hollows at her collarbones deepening in shadow. She placed her hand on his palm, and he led her inside.

They clung to each other in the darkness. Megan kissed his chin and entwined her hands around his neck. Their lips touched. He had never wanted anything as powerfully as he wanted her. He kissed her, one kiss melting into another, feeling her shiver beneath his hands. She was completeness; she was finality.

When the door of his room had been locked and the lamp cast a warm glow, Megan pulled the pink ponytail holder from her hair. Nathan ran his fingers through her smooth brown curls and trailed kisses down her neck to the fullness of her breasts. He held her waist and knelt, resting his head on her stomach. She stroked the hair at the back of his neck, and he brushed his cheek against her cotton skirt, feeling the softness of her abdomen underneath.

Megan stepped back to lean down and kiss his forehead. "I love you."

Nathan pulled her hips back to him. He ran his hands down the smoothness of her calves. She moved closer to his touch, bending her leg against him. He looked up at her. Her eyes were closed, and her expression, calm, as her breath responded to him. Her skirt fell in airy folds across his forearm as he caressed her thigh. She made a small sound, and he looked up again. She met his eyes, and he saw her desire with its edge of uncertainty. Wrapping his arms firmly around her hips, he held her, waited for her. He meant to take his time.

A moment later, he felt her fingers slip inside his collar. He needed to feel her hands on his shoulders and to hold her against him with nothing between them. Standing, he pulled off his shirt. She stepped close again, pulling on his pants pockets. He lifted an eyebrow with a roguish smirk, and she giggled before bashfully hiding her face against him. Her long hair feathered across his chest, and he smoothed the tendrils, gathering them on his palm and twisting them out of the way as he carefully unzipped her dress. It slid to the floor, pooling at her feet, revealing the black satin of her lingerie.

His eyes skimmed over her. The exquisite feminine

creature before him was worth all of the wait and frustration of the last few months. Only the bruise on her thigh marred her figure, and he saw nothing but ethereal perfection in the impish spirit that ensnared his soul.

A blush crept into her cheeks that made his heart race. He gauged his breathing carefully; she was making self-control increasingly difficult, but he relished the challenge that edged his senses further and higher. He tucked his finger under her bra strap and slipped it from her shoulder as he watched the throbbing pulse at her neck. Her skin bare, he ran two fingers across her shoulder, and down her arm to where the strap hung. She tipped her head to the side and leaned heavily against him. His touch slipped over satin, and their kisses intensified.

He took her hand and stepped to the bed, pulling her down beside him. He unfastened her sandals and dropped them to the floor before removing his prosthetic.

Nathan took Megan's hand and kissed it. "I love you." He covered her mouth with his before she could answer, and she replied by deepening the kiss and wrapping her arms tightly around his neck.

He pulled away. Her forehead furrowed with confusion.

Once more, Nathan took her hands in his. "May I?" he whispered.

He held her gaze. She nodded. Slowly, Nathan threaded his fingers deeply into her hair. Megan closed her eyes. Her breathing slowed. He held her head and neck, firmly, gently, securely, and leaned her back on the bed with all of the comfort and reassurance he could muster. He felt the comforter's cool smoothness on his hands as he spared her the sensation. He slowly released her, and she opened her eyes. He saw no fear, felt no tremble, save that summoned by his touch.

Megan placed her hands on his face and drew him down. Their bodies pressed together. Passion without force. Acceptance without pity. As the sky lightened, he rebuilt her trust, and she restored to him the perfect wholeness he had sought for so long.

8735 PETERSON AVENUE, APARTMENT 218
JULY 21, 2013. 10:30 AM

Nathan opened his eyes and blinked twice before believing she was real. Megan's hair spread over his pillow and down the smoothness of her back. Her bare shoulder rose and fell with her even breathing, her hips hidden by the sheets. He reached his hand to her hair and lightly traced the indentation of her spine.

Megan inhaled into wakefulness. She lifted her head then nestled once more on the pillow. Nathan slid his hand over her waist and pulled her back against his chest, sliding his arm under her head and kissing her neck.

"Good morning," he murmured, covering her shoulder in kisses.

"Tones?"

He chuckled. "No tones. No place to be." He let his breath fall over her ear. "I love you."

"I love you, too," Megan whispered, snuggling against him. She cast an abrupt glance over her shoulder. "Sam's not home, is he?" She tugged the sheet up under her arms.

"No, he's working a double until three." Nathan wrapped his arm around her and held her tightly. "Relax." He nuzzled his nose in her hair, breathing the peach fragrance. He kissed her ear. "Besides, other than Retton County, I don't really have a job to go to right now."

"What do you mean?" Megan rolled over so suddenly that her head bumped his nose. Stars burst before his eyes.

"Oh, I'm sorry!" she said.

Nathan sniffed and blinked away tears. He pinched the bridge of his nose. "It's okay." He sniffed again. "I've been suspended without pay, pending the investigation. But I don't care."

"I care. What did Richard say?"

"He doesn't think anything will come of it," he said, leaning on his elbow. "Both he and the probie were about to do the same thing. It'll be declared defensive. I'm not worried. The cop arrested Todd, not me."

"Arrested! But I didn't press charges."

"You didn't have to," Nathan said. "It was a domestic dispute, so they filed charges on behalf of the state. There are enough witnesses to corroborate what happened."

"What did they charge him with?"

"Aggravated assault and battery with a dangerous weapon. There may be other charges, too, but that was the main one. It'll all have to go before the Grand Jury."

Megan sank into the pillow and covered her face with her hands. "I don't want to go to court. It'll be a nightmare. You heard what he said. If we go to court, he's going to drag everything into the open."

"You've done nothing wrong." He brushed her hands off her cheeks. "The more they drag out, the worse it is for Todd."

"And the more humiliating it is for me."

He met her eyes. "Your dignity doesn't come from him."

Megan reached for him, and he lay back and pulled her close. She pressed her face against his chest. "I want to stay right here forever."

Nathan kissed the top of her head. "I'd like that." He held her and rubbed her shoulder.

Megan wrapped her leg around his residual limb. He tensed, waiting for her reaction to his skin, to the absence. But as she draped her arm over his chest and nestled her head into the hollow of his shoulder, he realized she thought nothing of it. He saw that she loved him, not as a medic, or an amputee, or a soldier, but as all and none. She loved him as a man.

Nathan shifted to his side. He met her eyes, saw her smile. He could live on that smile. He brushed his lips against hers, craving her mouth, and kissed her, deeply, his hands moving across her skin, seeking her curves, searching her contours. She closed her eyes. Her breath, moist on his neck, quickened as she pressed herself to him, soft and warm.

Her touch traced embers across his chest. He reveled in the tension, matching her intensity. His palm smoothed over her belly, to her back, to her thigh. She arched against him, and he covered her, her heat igniting into fire. Her body beneath his, entwined with him, her hand twisting the sheet until with a gasping shiver, she clung to him, and he fell to her embrace, damp with sweat, dropping his brow to his fist on the pillow, heavy and consumed.

Nathan's breath slowed. He kissed her forehead and nuzzled her hair, gathering her into his arms. Megan placed her hand on his face, and he cherished the light in her eyes. She curled up next to him, still and peaceful. He brushed his fingers through her hair, rubbing the strands, and watched her sleep as a sunbeam crept across the wall.

Nathan's stomach growled. He slipped away from her to the side of the bed and dressed. His belt clinked as he tucked in his shirt.

"Where are you going?" she asked.

"I'm hungry. I thought you might want some breakfast."

Megan sat up wrapped in the sheet, her hair mussy. "That would be nice. My bag is in the car."

"Oh?"

"I'm more presumptuous than you are."

He dropped back onto the bed and scooped her into his arms. "You just go ahead presume all you want to."

"Will you go get it for me?"

He held her away from him. "See, now the real truth comes out. You just want me around to do your bidding."

Megan grinned. "Well, yeah."

"Is there anything else you require, m'lady?"

"No," she said, laughing. He winked and kissed her before leaving the room.

Nathan walked to her car and found her bag next to her phone on the passenger seat. A manila envelope lay on the floorboard, addressed to the local college's admissions office. He picked up the packet and returned inside, setting it on the kitchen counter.

Megan had dressed and was sitting on the bed, fastening her sandals. The filmy skirt had fallen back and revealed the entire line of her thigh.

"Damn, you're beautiful," he said, dropping the bag by the bed.

Her eyes brightened. She hopped up and turned from side to side. "Do you like my dress?" The skirt ruffled about her knees.

"I think I'd need to take it off you to really get a good look at it." He lifted the hem.

She giggled and pulled away from him.

"I know what we can do today," he said.

Megan found her hairbrush. "Oh?"

"We can stop by the college and submit your paperwork. And the Braves and White Sox game comes on at two."

She nodded. "Okay. Have you seen my ponytail holder? I can't find it."

Nathan glanced around at the floor. "No, I haven't."

Her shoulders slumped. "Oh! It's my favorite."

"Don't worry. It'll turn up. Here's your phone. You have six missed calls."

Megan tapped the screen. "One's from Emily. One's from Richard. The rest are from the hospital, but I don't recognize the extension."

She tapped again and held it to her ear. "Yes, this is Megan Henderson ... I received a call from this number."

Nathan walked to the kitchen in courtesy and began searching for the frying pan.

Megan entered a moment later. "That was Dr. Anderson's office. He's a neurosurgeon. He needs to meet with me as soon as possible."

"Why?"

"I don't know. Something about Todd. I didn't understand what he was talking about."

SACRED HEART PROFESSIONAL OFFICE SUITE
JULY 21, 2013. 12:30 PM

Megan knocked on the doorframe. "Dr. Anderson?"

A thin man with salt and pepper hair looked up from his work. "Mrs. Henderson, come in."

Megan cringed as she stepped into the spacious office. She certainly didn't feel like Mrs. Henderson.

He gestured to a wingback chair. "Have a seat. Please."

She swallowed and sat down, crossing her ankles and clasping her hands at her knees.

"Your husband's injuries were serious. We ran a CT-scan to assess the exact nature of the injuries and determine the best course of treatment. Several bones in his face were broken, and surgery was advised to reconstruct those areas. A rather simple reconstruction, really."

Megan nodded.

"But the CT-scan also revealed something else, and I sent him immediately for an MRI. It seems your husband had a benign, slow-growing tumor—a ganglioglioma—growing in his temporal lobe near his amygdala. This type of tumor causes memory loss, balance issues, and emotional regulation difficulties, particularly rage attacks, that would increase slowly over time."

Megan's lips parted. "What?" she whispered.

"Your husband had a tumor that had been affecting—controlling—his behavior."

Megan's arms tingled, and her mind raced. "A tumor? How can a tumor control behavior?"

"It's like when you get hungry, and you snap at people. You're irritable and cross because your body doesn't have what it needs. This tumor is like that but ramped up on high octane and a thousand times more powerful. These cases often exhibit suicide attempts, violent outbursts, the need for restraints," he looked over the top of his glasses, "physical abuse of family members. Behavior along the lines of what he exhibited yesterday."

"Is he going to die?"

"Die?" He chuckled. "No! It was benign. It won't spread, and it is very easily treated. When we took him for reconstructive surgery, I went up through the nose and resected the tumor. It's already gone." He smiled and lifted his hands. "And I have more good news! Usually, in these cases, there is an immediate return of the patient's normal personality. When the anesthesia wears off, you should have your husband back with a normal, happy demeanor, just like before he got sick."

"Will he remember anything?"

Dr. Anderson pressed his lips together. "Yes, he'll remember everything, just like you do after you've eaten. There is memory ... and regret."

"He really had no control over his actions?"

"To what extent do we control our own actions, and how much does biology control? I can't answer that. It's better left to psychologists and philosophers. But just as no one questions the role of hunger in determining behavior, I do know without question that a patient's behavior is drastically altered when such a tumor is present and returns to baseline when it is removed." He leaned forward on his desk. "The surgery went very well. I expect him to wake up within the hour and go home in a couple days."

"Days!" she cried. "He just had brain surgery!"

"We can do amazing things now. A simple resection like this is really very easy. The broken facial bones will give him more trouble. You can see him now if you like," he said, standing.

Megan's eyes darted about the room. "No, not yet." She stood. "I need a moment."

"Of course. Just go to post-anesthesia care when you're ready. The nurses will let you in."

"Thank you," she said, shaking his hand. She walked from the room, her knees weak and quaking. The hallway blurred before her. Pushing through the fog, she pressed the elevator button, but she was compelled to move, to keep moving, both knowing and not knowing her destination. She stumbled to the stairwell, the elevator opening with a *bing* behind her as she entered the echoing, concrete hall. Her sandals slapped the treads, her gasping breath rebounding off the walls as she descended.

She hurried through the hallways, brushing past people, ignoring both greetings and stares. She clung to the doorframe of a darkened alcove lit only by a single light box.

"Show me," she begged.

Sam nodded. Retrieving a file from the back room, he flipped on the remaining light boxes and shoved four films under the rails. Each film was covered with pictures of brain slices.

"Each frame moves progressively lower through the skull," he said. He pointed to a frame. "You can see the tumor here, and it becomes more visible through all of these, receding here." He pointed again. "The temporal lobe is here, and the amygdala is here."

Megan studied each frame. She gripped the back of her neck as her eyes moved box to box. Undeniable. With an agonized moan, she dropped her hands to her sides and walked away.

"Megan!" Sam called, but she did not turn back.

Megan did not need the nurses to grant her access to the post-anesthesia care unit. Her fingers fumbled with her ID, her ER clearance granting her passage. She pushed through the double doors and walked to the picture window. The PACU theater was divided into separate patient care areas by curtains, each visible from the window. She scanned from left to right and froze.

Todd lay in the third bed. Tubes ran from his arms and connected to IV pumps. Air pumped into sectioned leggings that kneaded the blood in his extremities and prevented clots. His body was covered in a blue hospital gown, and more tubes snaked to racks under the bed. His face was red, and his nose and cheeks were swollen and puffy. His blond hair lay tussled on the pillow.

Their eyes met. Megan covered her mouth with her hand. The small wrinkles around his eyes softened, and he lifted his fingers slightly. A strangled sob escaped her lips.

She backed away. Fled again to the echoes. Pressed against concrete. Slid to the shadows, dark and hard. Memory, a nebulous form returning, solidifying, tangible, touchable, unmistakable, unavoidable, undeniable. She cried out under the weight of conviction.

I knew it wasn't him. In the beginning. I knew. I was going to help him. I was.

She had concentrated on her pain, her fear, her loss, and never realized it was he who had been suffering. She had failed to see, to understand, the puppet master that had pulled the strings and controlled him. Now the surgeon had cut the strings, and her husband lay crumpled and broken on the stage. Never the cause. Always a lackey. A tool. A pawn.

But no more. Todd as he'd been. His gentle hands, his sweet kiss, his kind words, his loving touch. Again, the man she had loved. To whom she had given her hand and her word. She belonged at his side. Once more, once again. 'Til death do they part.

Yet Nathan.

Her love, her life, her comfort, her strength. A kiss, a grin, a twisted sheet. She'd seen him, loved him, made her choice, waited in line at the register with no barcode found. Non-algorithmic, non-quantifiable, completely subjective confusion in her brain; a white-coated shrug clutching him away, tossing him to the restocking shelf, escorting her to the door. Desire, means, no way to obtain. Her heart torn from her body, bleeding, curling, guarding. And she sank to her side. The concrete cold against her face, sapping life from within. Tip the king.

Check mate.

CAITLYN ARMISTEAD

Chapter Twelve

8735 PETERSON AVENUE, APARTMENT 218
JULY 21, 2013. 5:45 PM

Nathan tossed aside the TV remote. The Braves had lost again. There was nothing on TV and nothing he wanted to stream. He had cleaned the kitchen and the bathroom. He had vacuumed and dusted and paced a path on the carpet.

"Hi! This is Megan. I'm probably on a call right now, so leave a—" He hit the end button.

The door opened, and he stood.

Sam walked in. "You didn't come to the gym."

"No, I'm waiting on Megan. She slept here last night," he said with a significant glance, "but she got a phone call from the hospital. She said she'd be back, but now it's almost time for her shift in Retton County. I don't know where she is."

Sam slowly set down his gym bag. "There's something I need to tell you."

"What?"

Sam explained the tumor.

Nathan blinked, incredulous. "That doctor said all of his abuse was caused by a tumor?"

Sam nodded.

"Like hell it was," said Nathan.

"Megan was really upset."

Nathan sighed. "I'll talk to her. She'll be okay."

"If you say so," Sam said. "I'm going to eat something. I have that tabletop game tonight, and I need to leave in about ten minutes. I'll probably be back by eleven unless we go to the pub or something."

"Sure."

Sam went into the kitchen, and Nathan stared at his phone. He selected the Retton County EMS office and pressed send.

"Retton County EMS."

"This is Nathan. Who is this?"

"Hey, man! It's Jimmy. I heard what happened in Barrington. That's unbelievable."

"Yeah. Let me talk to Megan, okay?"

"She's not here, man. She called in about an hour ago. I guess last night was too much for her."

Nathan frowned. "Oh. Um, okay. Thanks."

"Sure, man, no problem."

Nathan pressed end as Sam walked into the room with a sandwich and picked up the TV remote. "She's not at work," said Nathan.

Sam stopped chewing. "Where is she?" he asked, his mouth full of sandwich.

Nathan walked to the door. "I don't know, but I'm going to find her."

806 BRIARTON LANE
JULY 21, 2013. 7:45 PM

"I don't know where she is," Emily said. "Where have you looked?"

Nathan sighed with frustration and helplessness. "Sacred Heart. Station 1. Station 6. The ER. Post 4. Todd's house. Coffee shop. Everywhere."

"Wow, I don't know. I would have said to look at your place." The baby in her arms fretted. "Sometimes she goes out hiking alone."

"Where would she go?"

"I haven't been out with her in so long," she bounced the baby, "for obvious reasons." She raised the pitched of her voice and cooed to her baby. "Yes, obviously."

'I think it's my favorite place in the world—'
'I don't hike. Isn't that obvious?'
'It's not obvious to me.'

Nathan stepped off the porch. "Thanks, Emily. I have an idea."

"Good luck finding her. I hope she's okay."

Nathan drove out Highway 42. He turned into the entrance of Sunset Mountain State Park and followed the signs around to the trailhead. At the sight of Megan's car in the dirt parking area, tension left his shoulders.

Four trails split from the trailhead. The one with red, diamond-shaped blazes led to Buzzard Cliff. White-, blue-, and green-blazed trails led in three other directions. He pulled a small hydration pack from behind the seat and shoved his glove compartment first aid kit into one of the outside pockets. He locked his truck and shouldered his pack. With an extra step to check his prosthetic, he walked to the white blaze and hiked up the trail.

SUNSET MOUNTAIN STATE PARK
JULY 21, 2013. 9:00 PM

Megan sat atop a rocky outcropping. Her boots dangled over the side. She had changed into running shorts and hit the trail, pushing the miles behind her and wishing she could do the same with her life. The steep mountains, nubby green with summer leaves, formed a bowl, and she stared across the valley at the sheer, treeless face of Buzzard Cliff. The sky was a deep red, and while the evening cicadas sang to her, the mosquitoes chewed her arms.

She held a sprig of green, unopened goldenrod and slowly rolled it back and forth in her fingers. She picked it apart, carefully forcing the buds open, willing it to bloom out of its time.

A rattle of pebbles made her turn around. Nathan climbed onto the rock and sat down beside her.

She stared out at Buzzard Cliff. "You don't hike."

"I manage when I need to."

She looked back at the edge he had just scaled. "How did you climb up here?"

"Are we back to this again? I'll tell you if I find something I can't do," he said. "I did have trouble finding you."

"I didn't want to be found."

"Even by me?"

She turned away.

They sat in silence. A vulture wheeled and turned in the air above, catching the eddies and currents. Dread's icy fingers gripped her heart.

"Sam told me about the tumor," Nathan said, brushing her hair away from her shoulder. "Come on. Let's go back to my place, and we'll talk." He caressed her arm.

She shook her head and pulled away. "I can't do that."

"Okay, then we'll watch a movie or something."

"No, I can't go to your place."

"Sam has some game thing tonight. He won't be—"

She held up her palm. "You're not listening again. I won't go to your place."

Nathan frowned. "Why not?"

A tear formed and fell. "I won't cheat on my husband."

A shadow passed over Nathan's face. "He's not your husband. You're divorcing him."

"The doctor said—"

"Damn the doctor! Todd's a monster!"

"But we all have monsters. We're all capable of horrible things. We all have inner demons. All of us. Look me in the eye, and tell me you don't."

Nathan stared at the mountain, which shone red in the sunset.

"Dr. Anderson said he'll be just like he was before," she said. "How can I turn away from that?"

"You don't know that it's true. You don't know what he'll be like. It shouldn't matter at this point anyway."

"But it does matter. Todd and I were together for years. Good years! Doesn't that lay claim to anything?"

"You're suddenly in love with a memory?"

Tears streamed down her cheeks. "That memory is real again."

"But what about us? What about what we have?"

"I don't know!" She sank her fingers into her hair. "I don't know what to think. I'm confused!"

"I can see that," he said, reaching for her.

She shied away. "No. I should never have—we should never have—"

"You regret what we have together?"

"No!" she cried. "I don't know! The time wasn't right. It wasn't right!"

"You said you loved me."

"I do," Megan sobbed, pressing her fists to her forehead.

"Then it doesn't matter what happened before. You have me now."

"But I can't! If I leave him, how can you ever really trust that I wouldn't do the same to you?"

"Because I won't beat the shit out of you!"

"That wasn't him!" She shook her head. "What if you were in his place?"

"Don't compare me to him."

"Would you want me to keep my word? Would you want me to be loyal?" She looked up at him through her tears. "I have to honor my promises. I have to keep my word. If I want to be trusted, then I have to be trustworthy."

"You have a panic attack if you're in the same place as him. There is no way in hell you can have a functioning marriage."

"I owe it to him to try!"

"You owe him shit!"

"Then I owe it to myself."

"You owe it to yourself to walk away."

"How can I walk away from my marriage? It's a part of me. I can't just lose a part of me! Don't you understand?"

"Don't I?" Nathan said, pulling himself up on his knees. "Damn it, Megan! I understand better than you do! You had a good thing with Todd, maybe a great thing. But you've got to end it." He reached his hands to her face. "He beat you. He raped you. If you go back to him, I know he'll kill you. For your own sake, Megan, walk away." He kissed her forehead. "I love you. You mean everything in the world to me. Megan, please don't leave me."

She searched Nathan's face, his pleading eyes, his worried brow, and looked away. "I love you, too," she whispered and climbed down to the trail below.

8735 PETERSON AVENUE, APARTMENT 218
JULY 21, 2013. 11:30 PM

Nathan sat once more in his suede chair in the dark. His ears strained to hear a knock on the door. After more than an hour, he forced himself to admit it would never come. He mindlessly wandered through the apartment, going room to room with no purpose and little awareness. As he walked into the kitchen, he bumped his prosthetic against the wall and laughed ruefully, maniacally, that he had no toe to stub.

Megan's college application lay on the counter, and the envelope crinkled as he picked it up. Nathan realized he knew very little about her, at least of the kind of information that would be on those forms. For a fleeting moment, he considered opening the envelope, but he thought better of it and went into Sam's room instead.

Nathan brushed potato chip crumbs from the chair at Sam's desk and sat in front of the desktop computer. He clicked over to Megan's Facebook profile and clicked back in time as far as he could. Megan Lorry Henderson. Some of the very first pictures were of her high school graduation. She grinned cheesily into the camera in her cap and gown and held up her diploma. Her timeline then skipped to a volunteer fire department picnic. There were several pictures of her high-angle rescue certification class along with the note: *with Giles Martin.* Martin and Megan back to back, grinning at the camera.

The next picture showed only her hand graced with a simple engagement ring. To read her comments, though, one would have thought she was wearing four carats' worth of diamonds.

That summer was full of wedding planning—he scrolled quickly through those—but occasionally there were pictures of Megan and a newborn.

Jellybean.

Nathan slowed his scrolling. Life Event: Married Todd Henderson. Megan dressed in an elegant white gown. Megan smiling up at a younger version of Todd. It suddenly seemed real.

Nathan leaned his elbows on the desk and rubbed his temples.

He returned to scrolling. First day of EMT school. Extrication class. Emergency Vehicle Operators Course. Graduation. Began work as EMT with Barrington County Non-Emergency Transfer Service. Nathan could imagine Martin making some double entendre about his Doll. Hiking in the mountains. First day of paramedic school. Paramedic graduation. Began work as a paramedic with Barrington County Emergency Medical Services. But then the updates slowed. Not as many pictures. Not as many jokes and funny stories. And then nothing. People posted their birthday greetings to her, but there was no response. No more pictures. No more updates. Almost as if she had lost access to her profile. Or died.

The chair squeaked as Nathan leaned back. He wondered why no one had noticed. He wondered how she had been able to conceal the abuse for so long. But he knew how. He had watched her. She had been defensive and bitter, arrogant and yet overly cautious. He had seen through the act, but only because he, like Emily, had been with her in such close proximity.

Life had thrown Megan into darkness. He had found her in the shadows and not recognized how very dark they were to her. He was no longer surprised she would seize Dr. Anderson's faint glimmer of hope.

8735 PETERSON AVENUE, APARTMENT 218
JULY 22, 2013. 1:00 AM

Nathan sat at the bar in the kitchen. He heard the front door open and close, and Sam shuffled in.

"Did you find Megan?" Sam asked.

"Yeah."

Sam eyed the whiskey bottle. "Phantom pain?"

"No."

"Are you drunk?"

Nathan considered. "Yep."

"You shouldn't drink alone."

"Then get a fucking glass."

Sam did so and sat down next to him. He threw back a shot and grimaced. "So where was she? Is she okay?"

"She was out hiking. Getting away. From me, apparently. She left me. And don't say I told you so."

"I wouldn't, man. You're being defensive."

"The last time a girl left me, I got blown up, so yeah, I might be a little defensive." Nathan drained his glass. "Megan would rather be with an abusive jackass than a circus freak like me."

"That's why she left? Because of your leg?"

Nathan rotated the shot glass, each facet clattering against the counter top.

"What did she say?" Sam asked.

"I don't know."

"Were you listening?"

Nathan raised his voice. "Why do you two always assume I don't listen? She said she owed him."

"Why is that?"

"Hell if I know! She said she wouldn't cheat on her husband, that they had had good times, that she had to honor her promise."

"You're faulting her for being loyal?"

Nathan slammed his fist down. "I'm faulting him for tearing her apart!" He picked up his glass again. "She's supposed to be loyal to me, not to him."

"She's had a really big shock," Sam said, his voice quiet. "She's confused. Confused people do strange things."

"He destroyed her. I'll be damned if I'm going to sit by and watch him do it again."

"I think you're going to have to."

Nathan narrowed his eyes. "Why?"

"Because that's what she chose to do, and if you love her, you have to let her make her own choices. You don't have to agree, but you do have to allow. You have to let her go."

"But you said yourself she's confused. She can't make that decision."

"You have to trust that she's going to do what's right for her."

Nathan shook his head. "She's scared of him. That's the only reason she's going back. She's just doing what he wants because she's fucking terrified of him."

"She may be scared," Sam said, "but I don't think that's why she's going back. I don't think she wants to go back, and I don't think she loves him. At least not in a way that will last."

"She admits she doesn't love him!"

"Then she's doing it for different reasons. Reasons that have nothing to do with your leg. Not all of the shit in your life came from that IED. Right, wrong, strange, or stupid, she has a principle she's trying to uphold. And even you have to admit that it takes courage to uphold a principle when you're terrified." He leaned back in his chair and shrugged. "That or she's batshit crazy."

"I'm the one who's crazy. I love her. I've got to be with her, or I'll lose my fucking mind." He pushed away from the bar. "I'm going to bed."

Nathan locked his bedroom door and dropped to the bed, laying back and staring at the ceiling. Alcohol buzzed his brain; his brain buzzed his missing leg. He spread his arms out, feeling the surface of the bed. She had just been there. A whisper of peaches. He seized his pillow and breathed her in. A suffocating ache maligned his heart until the pillowcase was damp with tears.

He threw the pillow aside and sat on the edge of the bed, staring at his boots, drunk and heartbroken. He was tired. Bone-weary tired of the never-ending fight. Nothing to hope for, nothing to sustain him. A black beret with a blue flash taunted him from the recesses of his mind. Black and blue. Another had gone before him. Had surrendered. Had stopped. Had escaped from the pain and the hurt and the loss. The trail was already blazed, only the following remained.

Nathan opened the top dresser drawer and took from within a polished wooden case. He placed the case on the bed and opened it. On a field of blue velvet lay a pistol and two sets of dog tags.

He lifted the first chain and rested the oval tags on his palm.

THOMPSON
NATHANIEL B.
987-25-1235
A POS
CHRISTIAN

He draped the chain and tags onto the comforter next to the case and lifted the second chain. The tags were scuffed and bent.

LOWELL
ENOCH S.
982-89-4845
O POS
JEWISH

Nathan laid the second chain next to the first.

A blood-soaked hijab. A mangled body. Nothing had been left. Only relentless memories to add to other relentless memories. Anger, hatred, pain on pain that never abated, never slackened, never released.

The Beretta was always loaded. One in the chamber. Always in the case, in case. A trump card controlling even his deepest pain by controlling his existence.

Nathan knelt by the bed, finality in, at hand. Just one action, considered with dispassionate separation. Walking to the diving platform, standing over the lane, bracing for the watery cold. It was only cold, merely cold. Disconcerting, though, that the depths remained unseen and unseeable. He stared, lost in the coldness, his eyes unfocused, looking past to the carpet.

Just under the edge of the footboard lay her pink ponytail holder.

He picked it up. Her favorite, and he must return it. An

uncompleted obligation. A sigh of resignation, perhaps relief, and a strange disappointment. He returned the pistol to the case.

Nathan placed the tags on the velvet. Closed the case, secured the latch.

He walked into the hall and knocked on the doorframe of Sam's bedroom. Sam looked up from his computer.

Nathan held out the case. "Hang on to this for me."

Sam's brow furrowed. "Uh, sure. You okay?"

Nathan rubbed his thumb over the pink band in his hand, stretching it around his fingers.

One good thing.

He looked back at Sam. "Yeah. I'm okay."

Nathan returned to his room and dialed a number on his phone.

"Safe Call Now," a voice said. "This is Cara."

"I need to talk to someone."

802 WILLOWMERE DRIVE
JULY 25, 2013. 10:30 AM

Megan gripped her car's steering wheel and stared at the house. The grass was in need of mowing. Weeds threatened her flowers. Her heart pounded. She tried to swallow, but her mouth was too dry.

I can't do this.

She reached for the ignition, to back away, to leave. She turned the key.

No. I will do this.

Megan jerked the keys back. Her breath came in ragged spurts; tears stung her eyes. She pressed her lips between her teeth and inhaled slowly, seizing her breath and calming it.

She walked up the pathway and onto the porch, her tennis shoes quiet on the boards. Her fingers brushed the cold metal knob, but she hesitated, not knowing if she should knock. She'd never knocked before, but it didn't seem like her house anymore.

It must be my house again. This is my home.

Megan opened the door. There were no lights on in the house. The curtains were drawn. Todd was sitting on the couch in the dark.

He rubbed his hands on his knees. "I didn't think you'd come."

Megan closed the door behind her. In the dim light, she studied his face. It was bruised and swollen. Two black stitches protruded at his left nostril just above his lip. His blue eyes were clear.

"I'm here," she said.

Todd stood and walked toward her.

Muscles contracted. "Stop," she said and held up her trembling palm. "Just stay back. For now."

He stayed in place and nodded. "I'm sorry, Sunshine. I hate myself for what I did to you. I wish I could go back in time and stop myself, do something—anything—to keep what I did to you from happening. I see it over and over in my mind. I don't know how I can ever make it up to you."

"You didn't know what you were doing."

"But I did. I saw it. I knew."

"You couldn't control it."

"I don't think so. I don't know." He shook his head. "I just wish I could make it all go away."

"It won't ever go away. We just have to move past it."

"We? Or you and I? Is there a we?"

Megan closed her eyes. "We have to start over."

"But how? I've lost my job. I've lost my benefits. I've lost all of my credentials, everything. I can't move to a new place. I don't have permission from the court to even leave the county." He sank onto the couch. "I've lost everything. Except you."

"I promised to be here."

Todd leaned back, his hands dropping weakly to the cushions. "I'm just a patient to be tended."

"I loved you. I'm here because I loved you."

"Loved. But not now. And how could you? Love is too much to ask for."

"It's not too much to hope for."

"Meg, you're naive and simplistic. You always have been." He shrugged. "But you always do what's right."

Her heart sank. "But I haven't done what's right. I ..."

Silence fell. Megan hugged herself, trying to control her trembling.

"It's Thompson," he said.

Megan closed her eyes.

"Did you sleep with him?"

She hesitated, then nodded.

"Do you love him?"

She tried to form words.

"You don't need to answer. I can see it," he said. "So leave."

"No."

"No?"

"You couldn't control what you did," she said. "I won't let you hurt me again, but I won't leave over something you were helpless against."

"But you don't love me."

"Feelings can lie. I will not leave over feelings."

"You cheated on me."

"It wasn't cheat—" She sighed. "I won't leave because of my unfaithfulness. I was wrong, and I'm here to make it right." She met his eyes through her tears. "I'm here because of what we had. Because it was taken from me, and I want it back, and I want to make everything right. And I'm willing to fight for it."

He studied her, silently.

Megan swayed.

"You need to sit down before you pass out," he said.

Megan lowered herself into a chair across the room from him. "What are you going to do for work?"

"I'll have to see if Uncle Tim will let me work in his auto body garage. I don't know who else would hire me around here. But it won't matter for long. I'll go to prison soon."

"But you won't go to prison. You had a tumor. The grand jury will see that."

"You can't hang everything on that tumor. Those charges are severe, and they aren't going away. Trust me. They'll indict. It'll go to court. I'm looking at a minimum of five years, and I wouldn't be surprised at fifteen. I'm glad you have your own income."

"I'm going to quit Retton County. I'll spend more time here."

"Can we really do this, Megan? Is it even possible?"

"It has to be."

Chapter Thirteen

EMS STATION 1
JULY 26, 2013. 7:50 AM

Megan slid her time card and heard Nathan's familiar gait. Her stomach tightened; her heart raced. He reached around her to slide his card, and she ducked under his arm, relieved that she had avoided his eyes. That she would be in a truck with him all day niggled her mind, but she walked into the bay, ignoring reality.

Nathan joined her, and they began checking supplies. They each knew the other's routines. She could anticipate every move he made, and she made certain the fewest words possible were spoken. She avoided his gaze.

The silence pressed around them as they drove to Station 6.

At a red light, Nathan leaned back in the driver's seat and tapped his fingers on the wheel. "Are you ever going to talk to me again?"

Megan studied his hand and remembered his touch on her skin. She closed her eyes, trying to shut it out. "I don't know what to say."

"You could start with 'Hi, how are you?' Maybe we could move on to 'What do you want to eat today?'"

"I'm not hungry."

"I didn't mean now. Later. You could just look at me now."

Hesitantly, she met his gaze. His eyes softened, and a faint version of the smile she loved appeared on his lips.

"There you are," he said.

A car horn beeped. They looked up to see the green light turn yellow.

Nathan pulled into the intersection. "He acts like that light will never turn green again."

They pulled into Station 6, and Megan walked to the EMS room. A paper had been taped to the door, and she pulled it down.

"Chore list from B shift," she said as Nathan approached.

He took the paper from her, his fingers casually tracing across the back of her hand. She chafed at the exhilarating tension. "All the normal stuff," he said, holding her gaze a moment too long.

Megan bit her lip and unlocked the door. The bunks weren't made. "B must have had a late call. They didn't change the sheets at the end of shift."

"Grand. Of course, they still had time to leave a chore list."

"It's not a big deal. I'll get them."

Nathan plugged in the vacuum cleaner as Megan stripped the sheets from the bottom bunk. She tossed the pile to the floor.

"How am I supposed to vacuum?" Nathan called over the hum.

"If you don't like it, go get the laundry bag from the truck."

He switched off the vacuum cleaner. "All right, I will."

Megan followed him with her eyes, stepping to the

door to keep him in view. She checked around the bay to ensure no one was present and then stared unabashedly at him. She wondered how she could ever go back to seeing him as just another medic. She tried to blot the images and sensations from her mind.

When Nathan stepped out of the ambulance, Megan turned her attention back to the bunk bed. She pulled off the last sheets, tossed them into the pile, and retrieved clean ones from the cabinet. Nathan returned and stuffed the sheets into the chartreuse laundry bag.

Megan unfolded the clean sheet and climbed up on the bottom bunk to pull it over the corner of the top mattress. Nathan's hands slid to her waist and steadied her, his warmth seeping through her shirt. His thumb brushed her back. Such a simple movement, gentle and comforting.

"We can't do this," she said.

"Do what? Keep you from falling?" He released her, and she tottered back to the floor.

"You know what I mean. I'm trying to work things out with Todd. I just—we have to forget."

"I can't forget."

Megan sighed and moved to the other side of the bed, pulling the sheet with her.

"Are you sure you want to go back to him?" he asked as she climbed up on the bunk again.

She set the sheet in place. "I'm sure," she said, covering her doubt with determination.

Nathan stepped to her side. Standing on the rail of the bottom bunk as she was, she could look him in the eye. She studied him, a powerful silence connecting them.

Nathan traced his fingers across her cheek. Megan placed her hand on his, unable to commit, unable to move away. She stepped down.

"Kiss me," she whispered. "Just once more."

He tipped her chin up and kissed her softly. She returned his gentle kiss, but as memories filled her mind, her passion grew.

Nathan broke away and held her at arm's length. "If you're going back, you can't do this."

Megan looked down. She picked up the laundry bag.

He reached to her arm. "But I will never forget."

Her lips parted, but she backed away and carried the bag to the truck.

802 WILLOWMERE DRIVE
AUGUST 2, 2013. 10:30 AM

Megan stood at her kitchen counter and bit into a doughnut. She brushed powdered sugar off the newspaper page and turned to the comics.

The front door slammed.

"Todd?" Megan called.

Todd walked into the room. "What?"

Megan smiled. "Where've you been? I've been home for two hours. I didn't know where you were."

"No man wants to come home to a greeting like that," he said, scowling. "You should at least act happy to see me instead of giving me the third degree."

Her smile faded. "Oh. I'm sorry."

Todd opened the cabinet and took down the box of Cheerios.

Megan tensed. "Please don't pour those. I don't like the sound."

"The sound? Why would a sound bother you?"

"I don't like it," she insisted. "Please."

"I'm worried about you, Babe. Maybe you should see

someone about that." He popped open the box and took a bowl from the shelf.

Megan grabbed another doughnut and walked to the living room. The clattering chased her, and she pressed her hands to her ears, powdered sugar dusting her hair. She fought back tears, but they slipped down her cheek.

Todd followed her, carrying his cereal. He switched on the overhead light. "And now the tears." He spooned a bite into his mouth. "You really are stressed out."

She took a deep breath. "It's not that." She sat on the couch and nibbled her doughnut.

Todd tilted his head back. "Oh, I get it. The tears. The doughnut. You have PMS."

Megan stared at her doughnut.

What day is it?

"I don't think so," she said. "I'm just hungry. I think I'm losing weight."

Todd stepped back and considered her. "No, if anything, you're gaining. Emotional eating. You're the one with the doughnut in your hand."

The lights turned out, and the air in the vents stopped moving.

Megan moved to the window. "Did you pay the utility bill?"

"Yeah, I paid it."

"The utility truck is driving away." She turned back to him. "I think they just turned off the electricity. You're sure you paid it?"

"Well, okay, I may not have. It slipped my mind. I'm trying so hard, Sunshine. I can't do everything right away."

Megan sighed. "All right, just call them and pay over the phone."

"It's a simple phone call, and you won't do it? Any wife

would make a little phone call. We're a team, Megan. You need to step up more."

"I—what?"

"I've made so many changes lately. It just seems like you aren't appreciating my effort."

Megan ran her fingers through her hair. "Okay, I'll make the call. I'm just tired. We ran two codes last night and neither made it."

"You value your job more than me!"

"No, I promise I don't!"

He put down his bowl and held out his hand. "Then come here."

Megan swallowed.

"I'm not going to hit you," he said. "I don't do that anymore. I've changed, remember?"

She crossed the room and took his hand.

He lead her down the hall to the bedroom. "You just come back here and take a nap." He guided her into the room and let go of her hand. "You won't be cranky once you've had some sleep."

She nodded. "I'd like that. But what about the bill?"

"I'll take care of it. I don't mind doing you a favor." He leaned on the doorframe. "I take good care of you, Sunshine. Remember that."

FIRE STATION 6
AUGUST 13, 2013. 8:30 AM

Nathan turned off the ambulance and looked over at Megan. Her elbow rested on the passenger side door, her head on her palm. She slept peacefully, unaware they had arrived. She had fallen asleep at the second stoplight before he had even entered the thoroughfare. Dark circles surrounded her eyes. Her face was drawn, her skin pale. Her pants hung lower and bunched under her belt. He wondered how Todd treated her, if he yelled at her, if he touched her, if they—

I can't think about that.

He laid his hand on her shoulder. "Megan."

She lifted her head. "Oh."

"Why don't you go inside and lie down?"

Megan nodded and climbed out.

Nathan watched her walk to the EMS room. He pulled the hose around to wash the ambulance, a lonely chore. Several firefighters walked past him, completing their own assignments, and he noted the change in their expressions. They had noticed Megan wasn't helping him. He could only hope they wouldn't say anything to a supervisor.

Nathan rocked back and forth between his foot and his prosthetic as he finished washing the truck. He was bottoming out again, and the pressure was uncomfortable. He put the cleaning supplies away and crept into the dark EMS room.

Megan lay in her bunk. Nathan watched her a moment, his eyes tracing along her body and resting on her shoulder. He remembered kissing it the morning she had left him. He would have given anything to kiss her again. Instead, he turned away.

Nathan sat in the recliner, sighing with relief as the pressure abated. He unzipped his pant leg and added yet another sock to the socket. Though it had been over two years since the IED, his residual limb was continuing to shrink and needed frequent adjustments.

I'll need another socket soon.

He stood and clicked the prosthetic back into place, leaning his weight and checking his balance.

"Are you hurting?" Megan asked, her voice heavy with sleep.

"Not now. Needed another sock." He walked to the bunk. "I'm sorry I woke you."

"It's okay," she said, propping up on her elbows. "We need to wash the truck."

"I took care of it." He brushed his knuckle on her cheek. "Go back to sleep. I'll be in the common room."

Nathan quietly closed the door behind himself.

Martin called from the fire truck. "Nathan! Come here."

Nathan walked around.

"I'd never say it to her," Martin began, "but Megan looks like death warmed over. Is she sick?"

Nathan shrugged. "I don't think so. But I never see her eat much any more. She sleeps the entire time between calls."

"She must not be sleeping at home."

"No," Nathan said. "I know how she gets when she's around Todd."

"Fuck him! That son of a bitch is wearing on me. "

Nathan raised his brow at the venom he heard.

"Megan means a great deal to me," Martin continued. "She's my sister." He paused. "No, she's more than that. She's ..." His voice trailed away as he looked around the bay. "Listen, I stay out of her business, but after Jellybean, Megan's the most important person in my life. I'd move heaven and earth to make her one small bit happier." He cleared his throat. "As much as I hate to admit it, I've never seen her as happy as when she had taken up with you."

Nathan crossed his arms over his chest. "Taken up?"

"Everyone saw it. Everyone knows you two had a thing going on and pretty serious at that. Never underestimate the rumor mill."

Nathan's lungs burned. "But she's not happy! You see how she is. And she—she won't play with me anymore. No more wit or sarcasm. All that's gone. He's killing her! I have to make her understand!"

"Hold up, now!" Martin said, raising his palm. "If there's one thing I know about Megan, it's that that woman understands exactly what she's doing."

"But she doesn't love him. And she's miserable."

Martin sighed heavily. "I know. She'd rather kill herself with honor." He shook his head. "Just let her sleep. She feels safe here. You're here. I'm here. Here, she can let her guard down. This is her home."

Tones blared.

Nathan ripped his radio from his belt. "Fuck this! Can't these damn people solve their own fucking problems?"

"Med 3, be en route to 922 Nellon Road, 922 Nellon Road. Unknown medical."

Megan's voice spoke over the radio before he could answer. "10-4, dispatch."

"Get her some coffee," said Martin.

"She won't let me get her a damn thing."

"Do it anyway."

Megan entered the bay and walked toward the ambulance. "Let's go!"

"I'll drive," he said. "Later, Martin."

They drove to a small neighborhood of modest houses. Large trees canopied over the road, shading the driveways. In front of the house where Nathan stopped, a burgundy car with out-of-state plates sat in the driveway with the driver's door open.

Megan walked toward the car. "Sir? Did you call for an ambulance?" She stifled a yawn.

An elderly man sat in the driver's seat with his feet on the driveway. "I did. But I'm not sure I need you. I just don't feel well, and I want to get to the doctor."

Nathan handed Megan a blood pressure cuff.

"What's going on?" she asked, kneeling next to him.

"Oh, I just felt a little lightheaded. A little sick. I'm a diabetic."

Megan wrote a note on her glove. "Okay, sir. Let me take your blood pressure, and then you can decide what you want to do."

Nathan walked back to the truck for a drink of water. His phone vibrated as he shook the ice in his cup.

> TERRENCE REGAN: Jst worked multiple GSW x2 patients
>
> NATHAN THOMPSON: One more big call will put us on system status.
>
> NATHAN THOMPSON: Megan will be thrilled.
>
> TERRENCE REGAN: Should been GSW x3 Lost pt
>
> NATHAN THOMPSON: Sorry, man.
>
> TERRENCE REGAN: LOST the pt. Left scene
>
> NATHAN THOMPSON: Bizarre
>
> TERRENCE REGAN: Gangbanger. got scared. not a big loss

When Nathan returned to the car, the man was signing a transport refusal form.

"I hope you feel better," Megan said, snapping the clipboard.

The man nodded. "Thank you."

They climbed back into the ambulance. Megan pulled off her gloves, reached through the little window to the back, and tossed them into the small trash can on the floor. She rubbed gelled alcohol on her hands as Nathan put the truck in gear. "Let's go get some coffee," he said.

She pulled her Prusik cord from her pocket. "I don't want any," she said, tying a figure eight.

"I want some."

She shrugged. "Okay."

Nathan pulled up at a little corner coffee shop. Megan stayed in the truck while he went inside. He ordered a coffee he didn't need and got one for her that she didn't want.

This is a complete waste of money.

He returned to the truck, holding the cups. Megan climbed over the console and opened the door for him. "I didn't want one," she said.

"They had a deal. Buy one with milk, get one with cream and sugar for regular price."

Megan rolled her eyes and buckled her seatbelt again.

He held out her coffee. "Oh, come on. If I drink both of these, I'll be running up the sides of buildings and seeing noises."

"Good grief. Hand it here." She took a sip. "It's too hot. I'll let it sit."

8000 BLOCK NORIN ROAD
AUGUST 13, 2013. 2:00 PM

Megan awoke with a start, driving down the road.
No, wait. Nathan's driving.
Releasing her panic, she calmed her breathing. She was exhausted. Her eyes ached; her body felt heavy. A

crawling feeling filled her lungs, and her back was sore. She just wanted to rest. To sleep for days. To never wake up.

She wanted to block it out.

But it returned.

The day before, Megan had left her garden and walked inside her house in search of a glass of water. Sweat had beaded on her forehead and drenched her shirt so that it clung to her skin.

Todd stood next to the kitchen counter eating a sandwich.

"The weeding's finished," she said, filling a glass and draining it.

He ate the last bite of his lunch. "Great."

Megan washed her hands and arms in the kitchen sink. "I want a few more plants to put by the steps."

"We can get those this afternoon, if you like," he said and handed her a towel.

Megan dried off, aware he was watching her. Her heart beat faster as she hung the towel on the hook.

Todd moved closer. She could feel heat from his body. He kissed her, slipping his hand along her waistband. She endured. His lips moved along her jawline, softly down her neck as he leaned his weight against her and pressed her back to the wall. Her muscles tightened, her eyes squeezed shut. She clambered for calm, her heart pounding, her breath in short gasps.

"Todd."

"Hm?" He reached to the clasp of her bra.

She pushed against his shoulders. "Todd," she said and felt resistance against her hands. He continued kissing her neck as he fumbled with the hooks.

Terror tore through her. She struck the heel of her palm against his cheek.

Todd stumbled back with a cry of pain. He held his hand over his face. "What the hell, Meg?" he yelled.

She shook her head. "Not again."

"What are you talking about?"

"I won't let you—not—let you—" she stammered, turning away,

"I was just kissing you." He rubbed her shoulders. "Come on, girl. It's been forever. Let's get—"

"I'm not ready."

He groaned, and his hands fell away from her. "I thought we were moving on."

"It'll take time," she said, turning back.

Todd crossed his arms and stared up at the kitchen cabinets. "Time."

"In time, I'll stop reliving," she sighed, "that day, and my cracked phone, and—"

He looked back at her. "Your phone? Is that what this is about?"

"I don't care about my phone," she said. "You broke my ribs and—"

"I'm sorry about that." He flipped his hair and slouched against the counter. "I was out of control. I see that."

"You betrayed my trust that day. When you raped me, I —"

Todd rose up. "What did you say?"

Megan paused. "You raped me."

"I never raped you! Sure, we were a little rough that day, but you like it rough sometimes."

"I didn't want to—"

He stepped closer. "You never told me to stop." He

pointed in her face. "You never said no!"

Megan blinked. "I—"

"I'd never rape you, Meg. Even with a damn tumor!"

"But you did!"

"I know I'm a horrible person. Yes, I hit you. But I'm not a rapist! You've always been high strung, Meg, but I can't believe you would imagine that I would do that!"

"But you did," she whispered.

Todd walked to the back door. "Then you would have filed charges." He opened the door and laughed. "It obviously didn't affect you much. You turned right around and fucked with your partner! Quit making up stories! Aren't things bad enough without you making it worse?" He had slammed the door behind himself. She had cried.

Tones screamed. Megan pressed her hands over her ears, desperately wishing the sound to stop instead of simply turning the volume knob.

"Med 3, be en route to Mile Marker 8, Highway 42, Mile Marker 8, Highway 42, signal 4."

"10-4," Nathan said. He flipped on the lights, but not the sirens.

Megan looked up.

"There's no one on the road here," he said. "I'll turn on the siren when we get up to the intersection."

Megan braced herself for the sound as they approached the intersection. Nathan only turned on one of the sirens and left it at a simple wail, a clear tone rising up and falling down. He had driven all day, and she realized that he had been driving to most of the calls over the last couple of weeks. He had let her sleep, taking on all the supply restocking, fueling and cleaning chores, and serving as primary medic on most of the calls. He had never griped, never complained. She watched cars pull over ahead of them, her eyes misting. She knew if she looked at him, she would burst into tears.

They turned onto Highway 42 and picked up speed. The miles flew by, and soon she saw fire trucks on the scene. Nathan pulled around them and parked on the side of the road. A burgundy car with out-of-state plates had crashed into another vehicle.

Megan gasped. "Oh, my God!" It was the car of the elderly man who had signed the transport refusal. Mr. Russell. Her fingers shook as she tried again to unbuckle her seatbelt. "I'm primary!" she called to Nathan as she jumped out.

Megan ran to the car. The man was conscious, his eyes sunken. Martin held the man's neck still. "What have you got?" she called as she tried to jam her hands into gloves that didn't seem to have enough finger sleeves.

"He was driving down the wrong side of the road. Doll, that's all I know. We haven't been here long." Megan grabbed the C-collar from another firefighter and wrapped it around the man's neck. They maneuvered him onto a backboard.

"He's burning up," she said. "Mr. Russell? Can you hear me?"

He made a weak rasping sound.

"Sir, squeeze my hands."

Weakness on the left side.

"Help me get him to the truck," she said to Martin.

They loaded the stretcher into the ambulance, and Megan climbed in and flipped on the monitors. "Where's Nathan?" she asked.

"He's getting the other patient."

Other patient …

She hadn't thought of the possibility of more patients. This could have been a mass casualty, and she would have been unaware of it because of her tunnel vision on Mr. Russell.

"Were there—are there any more?"

"No, Doll, just the two."

She nodded and wrapped the blood pressure cuff around the man's arm. The green line showed a normal heart rhythm, but the beat was very fast. While the cuff inflated, she hooked up a non-rebreather mask and placed it over his head; his breathing rate was elevated, but his oxygen saturation soon stabilized.

Megan reached for a bag of saline. "Sir, I'm going to start an IV."

He made noises, and she lifted his mask. "What did you say?"

"Thirsty."

"Yes, sir," she said, repositioning the mask. "We'll get you something at the hospital."

Megan tied the tourniquet and blew the vein with her first attempt at an IV. She looked at another spot, and her second attempt was successful. She drew three tubes of blood and ran the saline. As she slid a test strip into the glucometer, the blood pressure cuff deflated. 90/50.

Nathan, Richard, and the firefighters grunted and heaved another backboard into the truck. The patient, a teenage female, was placed on the jump bench, and Nathan continued her care.

The glucometer beeped. 'EX HI.'

Shit.

"Richard, we need to go. Now. Code 3. Now." She didn't wait for an answer and changed the channel on her radio. "Med Control, this is Med 3."

Nathan reached over her for oxygen tubing, his hand lingering on her back. She slid out of the way but had to reach back over him to roll the IV clamp wide open. As the ambulance began to move, she fumbled for another IV pack.

"Go ahead, Med 3."

Megan huffed with frustration, dropping the IV pack and grabbing the clipboard. Nathan picked up the pack and moved around her to start the second IV as she flipped through to the transport refusal page.

"70-year-old male presenting at 0830 with lightheadedness. Blood pressure at the time was 100/60. Patient currently received from signal 4. Conscious, GCS 13. BP 90/50, sinus tach. O2 sat 95% via non-rebreather. Glucose levels too high to measure. Pupils equal and responsive, weakness on the left side, skin tenting. One large bore saline IV on board, another in the works."

"10-4, Med 3. What was the patient's glucose level earlier today?"

Megan closed her eyes and swallowed. "There is no history of diabetes or blood sugar level noted on that particular record."

"10-4, standby."

Megan released the speaker mic and attached IV tubing to a bag of saline, handing the end to Nathan. He popped the tourniquet and hooked up the line. She ran it wide open.

"Med 3, Med Control."

"Go ahead."

"No further orders at this time."

"10-4."

Megan sat on the counter next to the monitor and punched the button for another pressure. As the cuff inflated, she propped her feet on the stretcher bar, watched Mr. Russell breathe, and listened to Nathan giving report on his own patient over the radio: everything within normal limits. She was relieved to hear it, but it did little to assuage her guilt.

I forgot he had diabetes. I never tested him. If only ...

There was nothing she could do for Mr. Russell. He would need a great deal of care at the hospital, but for now, all she could do was watch. Her eyes roamed in a circuit from the monitor, to the pulse oximeter, to the blood pressure, to his eyes, to his chest, to his fingers, back to the monitor and around again.

Nathan sat on the edge of the far end of the jump bench. She knew he was watching her, but she determined not to look at him. She continued her vigil. Yet as the minutes passed, she found she could no longer resist his eyes.

Nathan was his usual calm self. His face was impassive, and because it revealed nothing of what his internal thoughts might have been, she took liberty to project what she felt about herself. Disappointment. Disgust. Anger. She could hear his voice saying, 'You gotta be more careful!'

They finally arrived at the hospital and turned over their patients. Megan followed the nurses around the room. "He wasn't feeling well. He has a history of diabetes. He was going to go to the doctor. He—"

"We've got it, Meg. You've said all that already. You can go."

Still she remained in the doorway.

Nathan moved to her side, his arm brushing against hers. "I'm going to go down the hill to clean the truck and restock."

"I'm coming."

In the bay of EMS Station 1, they climbed into the back of the ambulance. Nathan put on a pair of gloves and began picking up the trash. Megan dropped into the captain's chair and thought over the first call again. He pressed the trash into the can and picked it up to empty it. She snatched it from his hand and dumped it out on the floor.

"The hell!" he said.

Megan dug through the trash and found her gloves from the first call, rolled up on themselves. She pulled them apart and flipped the edge over. The ink was still legible. *Hx DM.*

"There," she said, holding it up to him. "I knew. Proof."

Nathan squatted next to her and looked her in the eye. "You made a mistake. A big one. But one that is not well documented and that no one will ever notice or care about. It was important, but you didn't lie about it or cover it up. I doubt it'll even come up for quality improvement. It's over."

"If I had asked, I know he would have let me test his blood sugar. If I had done my job, that wreck never would have happened."

"You don't know that he would have let you test. He refused care and transport. Hell, he probably won't even remember that first call at all."

"But he would have—"

He rested his hand on her thigh. "No, Megan. You don't know what he would have said, and you'll never know."

"With glucose levels like that, he couldn't have made a rational decision."

"He was alert and oriented."

"Then how do we know if anyone is fit to refuse treatment?"

"We don't. We watch. We listen. We use our best judgment and trust they will do what's right for them. You're not perfect, and no one expects you to be perfect. Except you. Let yourself be human for once."

Nathan took the gloves from her and began repacking the trash into the can. "Get some hand sanitizer before you catch the plague." He climbed out of the truck to empty the trash and get supplies.

EMS STATION 1
AUGUST 13, 2013. 6:00 PM

Nathan started up the ambulance.

"Med 3, Dispatch."

"Go ahead," he said.

"Stand by at Post 2."

"10-4."

"I've never posted at 2," Megan said.

"I have. I posted there frequently when I worked Med 1. It's over on the southwest side of town. It's that little strip mall with the orange and white striped awnings—"

"Ice cream place out at the street?"

"Yeah."

"Hmm. Well, it's system status, and that's all I have to say about that."

"I doubt it," he jabbed.

Megan opened her mouth for what he was sure was going to be a snarky retort, but her shoulders dropped, and she turned away to drink her coffee and stare out the window. He slammed the truck in gear and drove to Post 2 in icy silence. They parked in a trashy parking lot behind a building shaped like a huge ice cream cone. Nathan dreaded the idea of sitting for hours in silence. Maybe Megan would fall asleep, and it wouldn't be so tense.

Tones dropped.

Thank God.

"Med 3, be en route to 424 Main Street, 424 Main Street, Golden Acres Nursing Facility, Code 1 transport."

"10-4."

They drove without lights or sirens to the nursing home and parked by the back door. Megan rubbed her lip gloss under her nose and then held the door open as Nathan wheeled in the stretcher.

She walked toward room 19. "I want to stop and see Mrs. Williams before we get the patient." Her step caught at the door, and Nathan moved to her side.

The walls were bare and smooth and freshly painted. A potted plant sat on a table next to the made up bed.

"She's gone," Megan whispered.

Nathan's heart ached for her.

She didn't need this. Today of all days.

He clasped her hand, but she pulled away and walked down the hall.

"Excuse me," she asked an orderly. "When did Mrs. Williams pass?"

"Lady, I don't know who you're talking about," the orderly said, walking away.

Megan turned to him. "No one remembers her. No one knows she even existed."

"Just because one orderly—"

"Fuck it!" she said. "Let's get the damn patient and get out of this fucking place. I'll drive." She strode to the nurses' desk.

Nathan stared after her, stunned.

He took over the patient. Megan drove them to the hospital. It seemed a silent eternity before they reached Post 2 again and pulled into a shady corner of the lot behind the ice cream cone.

Nathan put the truck in park but didn't switch it off; they had to keep the air conditioner running.

"In what they pay for fuel," Megan said, "they could just lease an apartment for another station."

"I knew you couldn't make it all day without saying something else about system status. If it'll make you feel better, I can turn it off, and we can sit outside at those tables."

"Not my fuel."

Nathan switched off the truck. "Even so." He climbed out and walked to the bench, listening intently for her to follow. When she slammed her door, he blew out the breath he had been holding. He sat on the weathered table top, resting his boots on the bench. She climbed up next to him.

"We won't be here long," he said. "They've been running us hard today."

Megan nodded and leaned her elbows on her knees.

"I guess they want to run me ragged on my last day," he said.

Megan's head snapped around. "What?"

"It's been five months. You knew this was coming."

She straightened. "I—"

"Emily will be back for your next shift."

"But—"

"Richard wants to move Terrence back to B shift, so he said he wanted to put me at Med 1."

"Can't you ask him to let you stay Med 3?"

Nathan leveled his gaze. "Why should I?"

"Because—I—we work well together."

He sighed. "That's it?"

She looked away.

"I'm not going to let him put me at Med 1," he said.

Her smile flickered. "You're not?"

"I'm resigning."

Blood drained from her face. "Why?"

"I can't keep doing this. I can't just work with you. I can't see you in passing when we clock in, and I certainly can't keep working 24 with you." He brushed a stray hair out of her face. "Megan, I love you. I'm not aiming for second place. If we can't be together, then I need to cut ties and move on. You've resigned from Retton County, and they said I could go full time. I can work there and not see you."

A tear dropped to her cheek.

Tones screeched from the radio.

"Med 3, be en route to 60432 Westry Road, 60432 Westry Road, Green Meadows Apartments, Building F. Unknown trauma."

"10-4," Nathan said and walked to the ambulance.

60432 WESTRY ROAD, GREEN MEADOWS
APARTMENTS
AUGUST 13, 2013. 8:00 PM

Nathan considered the Green Meadows Apartments. There was nothing green in sight. There was no meadow. 'Apartments' seemed a glorified term for the three-story cinder block buildings that continued on, one after another, for the entire block. Laundry hung from windows and balconies. Trash littered the ground.

Megan walked around the front of the truck to join

him.

"Where are we going?" he asked

"Building F."

"Which one is that?"

"I don't know," she said. "This isn't my zone. Thank you, system status."

Nathan noticed a new bitterness in her sarcasm.

A group of men in baggy pants and gold chains sauntered from an alley and continued on between the buildings. Nathan eyed them warily. "Get the jump kit, but leave the stretcher. We'll wait here for PD. I think Tyler's working today."

Megan retrieved the bag. "I hear sirens."

"They're on the left side over there."

"Then that must be Building F," she said, pulling the strap over her head.

"Get back in. I'll drive around."

"Why? It's right there. We'll just walk that way."

Nathan bristled. "We should stage with law enforcement."

"Seriously? Is it worth all that? The building's right there. Look." She pointed across the plaza. "There's the F. Come on." She strode up the sidewalk.

"Megan!" Nathan called. He growled in frustration.

Scanning the area, he followed her past buildings D and E. Something didn't feel right. He saw women on the upper balconies, but none on the ground floors. No children played outside, even in the shady areas. Men lounged in front of Building F, sweating, listening to pounding music from a set of speakers. The savage beat throbbed through his chest.

'You want me. You can't get through. I say what I say. You my bitch. You my bitch.'

Nathan caught her arm. "We're going back to the truck."

'You my bitch.'

He glanced up at a second-floor apartment. A woman met his eyes and then ducked behind a curtain. It hit him. In the Afghan villages, the women and children had always known. They had always hidden before an ambush.

'You my bitch.'

"Fuck! Come on!"

Nathan gripped the back of Megan's belt and swung her toward the alley, pushing her ahead of him, trying to get to the side where PD was.

She stumbled. "What are you doing?"

"Dispatch, Med 3," he said. "What's PD's exact location?"

They rounded the corner. Five men slunk down the alley, arms hanging, hands holding their pants. Nathan jerked Megan back to the front of the building where the other group of gangbangers climbed to their feet. His heart slammed against his chest. Hyperalert, aware of every sound, every movement.

Megan's radio. Nathan punched the orange button on top, and the radio sounded an ear-piercing trill. Megan jumped, and 'Emergency 20' flashed across the small screen on top. "Twenty! Twenty! Twenty!" he called to the open mic. "Med 3! Med 3! E side of Building F! E side—"

Two men broke away from the group and walked toward them, closing the distance quickly. Nathan lunged in front of Megan and backed up until she hit the wall, her shirt snagging on the bricks. He felt her face on his back, and her hands clung to his shirt.

"Let go," he muttered. Megan released him. He withdrew his knife and flicked it open, concealing it behind his back. He heard Megan inhale.

The man on the right had smoother, stronger movements.

Leader. The other is Muscle.

Both would have a weapon, and he couldn't take them both. If he were forced to strike, he determined to cut the leader first, and he would make certain it was spectacular enough to deter the other.

"Stay back!" Nathan commanded, his body tense.

The leader locked eyes. "No one called no amb'lance."

"Man, we're just going to the other side of the building," Nathan said. His core muscles clenched so tightly they hurt.

The radio squawked. "10-4, Med 3. Law enforcement, Supervisor 1, and Med 1 en route."

"I said no one called no am'blance!" Leader pulled a gun and raised his arm.

Nathan could hear his grandfather's voice in his ears, 'Boy, never take a knife to a gunfight.'

Sorry, Pop.

Radio sounds and barking approached.

Megan stepped from behind Nathan. "Tyler! Here!"

Leader aimed at her.

Nathan shoved Leader's arm. The gun fired, and Nathan slashed his knife across the Leader's wrist, feeling the give of vessels and tissue, the resistance of bone. The gun fell away, and the thug dropped to his knees. Nathan swung back to cut his throat, but he saw the spurting blood and shoved him down instead.

Police and K9 officers swarmed the area, guns drawn, teeth bared. "Get on the ground! Get on the ground!"

Nathan rounded on Muscle, but he had already hit the concrete, arms outstretched.

Gangbangers scattered into the shadows, more officers after them. Pandemonium reigned as dogs barked, radios squawked, and officers cuffed and zip-tied gang members. Nathan turned to Megan. She stood near the wall, her eyes wide.

"You okay?" he asked.

She nodded.

Tyler jammed his knee into Leader's back as blood pooled on the concrete. Nathan took the jump kit from Megan's shoulder and dropped it on the ground next to his patient before sliding on a pair of gloves. He pulled a 4x4 from the pack, wiped his knife clean, and shoved it back into his pocket before applying pressure to the cut wrist.

"Go get the stretcher," he said to Megan. He pointed to an officer standing nearby. "Are you available to go with her?"

The officer nodded, and they walked away as other officers shuttled prisoners to their patrol cars.

Tyler shifted his knee. "I was about to shoot him. Man, I was praying."

"I'm just glad you didn't shoot me," Nathan said. "There's someone down over at Building F."

"Yeah, we found him. The kid was shot earlier today by this gang," he said, nodding his head down toward the thug under him. "They didn't want you to fix what they'd shot."

Richard puffed over to Nathan. "What in bloody hell did you think you were doing? You're a medic! You don't engage!"

Nathan applied a pressure bandage on the patient's arm. "And just let him shoot us? Yeah, I don't think so." He put his stethoscope in his ears and pumped up the blood pressure cuff.

The stretcher rattled across the plaza as Megan pushed it toward them, the other officer close behind her. She dropped the stretcher down as Nathan pulled the cuff off the patient's arm.

"Why were you even over here?" Richard said. "Don't ever come into this damn place without PD!"

Nathan chewed his cheek.

"That was me," Megan said. "I was the one who entered the scene. He was just coming after me."

"I don't want to hear anymore right now," Richard said. "Get him on the stretcher."

They pulled the thug onto the stretcher, and Tyler snapped the handcuff between the patient's arm and the rail. As a group, they moved to the ambulance, and Nathan and Richard climbed in.

Richard pointed at Megan. "You. Drive."

Nathan watched her close the first door. She met his eyes only a moment. With utter dejection written on her face, she slammed the second door.

Chapter Fourteen

EMS STATION 1
AUGUST 14, 2013. 7:50 AM

Megan and Nathan sat at the large conference table in Station 1 filling out Barrington County incident forms and statements for the police reports. Megan wrote her account, pausing occasionally to watch Nathan write his own report.

Nathan dropped his pen to the table and leaned back. "I have this form memorized."

"I'm sorry," she said.

He sighed. "Why didn't you listen to me? Why did you have to go walking in there?"

She shook her head.

"And why the hell did you step out from behind me?"

"Tyler didn't see us."

He pulled his collar. "We wear red shirts! In a microsecond, he would have."

She looked down.

"Megan, you're falling apart. You're not sleeping. You're not eating. You must be down to 110 pounds—"

"120."

"No, you're not. Your personal life is taking over your professional life. You're making mistakes that endanger yourself and others. Really, I've enabled it, so it's probably a good thing that I won't be here any more."

She stared at the hazy marks on the paper.

"Look at me," he said. She blinked and met his eyes. "You need to get yourself together. Until you do, you don't need to be on the trucks."

Her anger flared but died immediately. She knew he was right. "Is that what you're writing on there?"

Nathan stacked his papers and tapped them on the table. "What do you think I should write?" He slid his chair back and left the room.

Megan put her head down on her arms. Her shoulders shook as she fought against silent sobs. Her many mistakes scrolled before her. She plagued herself with 'what if's,' considering each of the many persons she had almost killed.

I'm a danger. I shouldn't be allowed out there.

She felt a hand on her shoulder and lifted her head as Nathan knelt by her chair and placed the manila envelope on the table.

"I've been meaning to get that back to you," he said. "Along with this." The pink ponytail holder rested on his palm.

Megan saw his forgiveness and love. One last offer. She needed only to say the word. She ached for him to hold her.

No.

She was a danger to her community, to her coworkers, and most importantly, to Nathan.

No!

Megan put the band in her pocket. "Thank you." She picked up her pen and returned to writing.

Nathan's hand dropped from her shoulder, and his

fingers traced down her back. He stood and walked to the door.

Megan spun around in her chair. "I still have your cave rescue book."

"You can keep it," he said and left the room.

802 WILLOWMERE DRIVE
AUGUST 14, 2013. 8:30 AM

Megan's phone rang as she climbed out of her car. She patted down all of her pockets and dropped back to the driver's seat to look through the center console. It continued its song. She pulled her backpack into her lap and searched the pockets. The song stopped. She puffed a hair away from her face. The phone beeped, a message received. She squeezed her hand between the seat and console and finally withdrew her phone.

Megan touched the screen and listened to the message, then lowered the phone and stared out the windshield. She walked to the porch and into the house, with no hesitation at the door.

Todd sat at the table with his newspaper and coffee. Two plates of pancakes and a container of syrup sat waiting. Megan put down her bag.

Todd looked up. "Good morning, Sunshine. Hungry?"

"You made me breakfast? That's ... really sweet."

Her eye fell on a goldenrod bouquet in a blue and white vase. "I didn't know the goldenrod was in bloom yet."

He turned a page of the paper. "Just this week. The earliest kind."

She walked to the small side table and fingered the flowers. A little green spider ran down the stalk.

Todd touched her. She started, bumping the table. The vase smashed on the floor.

"Megan!" he shouted. "You're so damn clumsy!"

"I'm sorry!"

Todd gathered the flowers, setting them in a pile on the table.

Megan knelt and began picking up pieces of the vase. "I can glue it back together." She stacked the shards on her palm. The pile slipped, and a piece sliced her skin. "Oh!" She dropped them all to the floor as blood dribbled from her hand.

Megan watched as the blood rose from the wound and dropped to the floor. She studied it as it spread across her skin and engulfed each new hair on her arm.

"Meg, you're bleeding!"

She touched her fingertips to it, and the blood smoothed over her other hand. "I am."

He grabbed a napkin from the table. "Hold pressure or something!" He gripped her arm, shifting around to his knees.

Megan stared. The red drops on her skin, her pants, the carpet, blurred and sharpened and blurred again. "How much blood can I lose?"

"What are you talking about?"

"It's a legitimate question," she said. "I can't lose it all." She touched her bloody fingertip to her tongue. Coppery.

He shrugged. "I don't know. What, a liter? Maybe two? You're the medic."

"And it would vary. From person to person, I mean."

"I suppose. I could lose more than you."

Megan sighed. "What are we doing here? What are we really trying to do?"

Todd frowned. "You're talking out of your head."

"No," she said. "I think for the first time I'm thinking clearly. I can't do this."

"Do what?"

"Stay married to you. I'm bleeding out."

"You're talking crazy, Megan! You'll only need a Band-Aid, maybe a butterfly."

"You're holding pressure while we glue things back together that will never be the same. While I bleed out." She put her hand over his. "I'll hold pressure. I have to do this myself."

Todd crossed his arms over his chest and sat back against the wall. "I still don't get it. What are you saying?"

"My attorney called. Even though we got back together, I never stopped the divorce proceedings and now everything is ready to be finalized. She can see us tomorrow if it's uncontested."

"So this is it?"

"Yeah. This is it."

"But I made you pancakes. I picked you flowers. Your special flowers."

"This is about more than you doing something for me."

"So there's nothing I can do. You're just gonna quit."

"It's been a hard decision."

"Oh, yeah, so hard for you. You still have your job. You still have your life, and your credentials, and your friends." He sneered. "And your precious Gimpy."

She looked away.

"But if you want to give up and quit, I won't stop you," he said, holding up his palms. "Too bad your marriage is unimportant. Too bad I mean nothing to you!"

"Nothing?" she said. "You meant everything to me! And you betrayed me—"

"You're the one who cheated!"

"I lived in hell!"

"I had a fucking tumor!" he shouted.

"And I gave up everything I'd rebuilt to be there for you! But I'm just not strong enough. I can't do this. I spend my life rescuing others. I'm going to rescue myself now."

His lip curled. "You always overreact. You're not trying."

"I have tried, Todd, but you're in too deep. I know you weren't always this way. I know things used to be different. Maybe the tumor did cause all the problems. But maybe it didn't. And either way, it's gone now, and you haven't changed. You're still cruel and spiteful and manipulative. You insult me and confuse me and take advantage of me. You've chosen to stay in the habits it created. I've tried to get past the beatings and the rape—

"Damn it, Meg! We're married! I didn't rape you!"

"That! We will never be fully reconciled. Our marriage is broken. Some things can't be fixed. It's time to move on. Make the best of what's left," she said. "Even though it seems like nothing is left."

Todd moved to her side. He caressed her cheek, and his touch was gentle and soothing. She faltered, wondering if she had gone too far and made the wrong choice.

His hand encircled her neck. "You always were a selfish bitch," he murmured. "I hope you die alone."

Megan pushed his hand away. "Good bye, Todd."

FIRE STATION 6
SEPTEMBER 12, 2013. 2:30 PM

Megan walked with Emily to the EMS room as Martin

sauntered toward her. "Doll, have I got something for you!"

She caught her step and excitement flowed through her. "It's finally here?"

He grinned. "I didn't think that purchase order would ever clear."

Megan laughed and followed him to the high-angle rescue trailer. Martin pulled a harness from the shelf and handed it to her.

"It's pink!" she said. "I didn't know it came in pink."

"Doll, when you're dropping the kind of bucks we did, they'd have made it in plaid. I wanted it to match your Hello Kitty helmet."

"Look, it's got a safety buckle and a really wide waist strap."

"It'll do your taxes for you, too."

Megan cut the tag and harnessed up, adjusting all of the brand new straps to fit her.

Martin whistled. "That is one mac-daddy of a harness, Doll. Well-spent Marsh money."

Megan froze. "What?"

Blood drained from Martin's face. "I—uh—Doll—I—"

"That's where the money came from? John Marsh?"

"Well ..."

"Answer me, Giles Martin!"

Martin slumped. "Yeah, he's the one who made the donation. To you and Nathan. Primarily to you."

She spun away from him and stared across the parking lot, gaping with fury, her hands on her hips.

'Pretty shtars.'

Megan giggled. She covered her mouth and tried to squelch it, but she only laughed louder. She looked back at Martin, whose face was twitching as if he was trying to decide whether to laugh with her or maintain an apologetic expression.

"You're not angry, Doll?"

"I'm terribly angry!" she said with another laugh. She cleared her throat and frowned. "I'm outrageously offended! How dare he! This is hush-up money! This is blackmail!" She burst into laughter again. "That's the most money I've ever made in ten minutes. What does that come to? $12,000 an hour?" She laughed until tears glistened at her eyes, and Martin finally laughed with her.

Megan sighed. "If I had known earlier, I would have told you where to stuff that money ... but since it's here ... it's a really nice harness."

Martin reached his hand to the strap.

Megan leaned back. "Careful, boy, you can't afford me."

As she took off the harness, Todd's green truck pulled into the station driveway. Megan's smile faded, and her skin crawled.

Martin's eyes narrowed. "What's that son of a bitch doing here? I thought everything was final."

"It is," she said. "It has been for over a month."

Todd walked toward them, a bag in his hand. His clothes were dirty and disheveled. He smelled long unwashed, and his beard was unkempt.

"What do you want?" Martin asked, his voice low and aggressive.

Todd sneered. "Still playing with dolls?" He turned to Megan. "Would you just go ahead and let him fuck you? You two have been heavy petting for years."

Megan cheeks flushed.

Martin shoved him. "Get out of here!"

Todd recovered and laughed. "This is the last of your

stuff," he said, holding the bag out to her.

Megan tossed the harness to the trailer floor and took the bag from him.

Tones.

"Med 3, be en route to 902 Highway 42, 902 Highway 42. Allergic reaction."

Carrie leaned out of the station side door. "Martin, Chief's on the phone for you."

"10-4," Megan said into the mic as Martin walked into the station. She turned on her heel.

Todd grabbed her hand and leaned close to her ear. "I'm gonna watch you die."

Megan jerked away. "I'm not scared of you anymore." Heart pounding, she strode to the truck and climbed into the passenger's seat. In the side view mirror, she saw him standing next to the trailer, watching her, his arms crossed over his chest.

Emily hopped into the truck. "You ready? Why's Todd here? Everything okay?"

"Yeah. He's leaving." Megan flipped on the lights and sirens. "Everything's fine."

They drove out Highway 42 to a mailbox with balloons tied onto it. Turning in, they followed a long driveway, past a pole holding purple martin houses, to a mobile home in the middle of a field. A line of minivans flanked the backyard.

Emily leaned over the steering wheel. "I'm going to pull around back here."

Balloons and streamers festooned a large wooden deck and a picnic table near an above ground pool. A group of little boys in swim trunks huddled together, shepherded by a young mother. One little figure lay on the ground near the table, cradled in the arms of another mother and surrounded by three other women.

"This doesn't look good," Megan muttered as Emily stopped. "Dispatch, Med 3."

"Go ahead, Med 3."

"Send me supervisor backup."

"10-4. Supervisor unavailable. County VFD has already been toned out."

Megan retrieved the pediatric bag and drug box, pulled on gloves, and hurried to the group. The little boys were crying or standing frozen with wide eyes. A baby squalled from an infant carrier on the porch.

A woman in fashionable clothes leaned on her friend. "I didn't know!"

"What happened?" Megan said.

"He couldn't breathe!"

"It was the cookie!"

"He's choking!"

"He's not!"

"I forgot his pen! I forgot his EpiPen! He's allergic to peanuts, and he ate that cookie. And I didn't see. And I don't have his EpiPen!"

A toddler ran toward the ambulance. "Fi-tuck! Fi-tuck!" A woman ran after him and scooped him up.

Amid the jumble of women's voices, Megan knelt and pried the boy from the woman who had forgotten his EpiPen. His face was blue, his eyes slits. His body was puffy and swollen, his skin covered in raised and angry hives. She laid him on the ground. His chest did not move. She felt no air movement, no pulse, and began chest compressions with one hand as she fumbled with the airway bag with the other. Behind her, a woman sobbed.

Megan placed a bag mask on his face. "Does he have a history of anything else?"

"No, just allergies! I'm telling you, it's the peanuts in the cookie!"

"Yes, ma'am."

Megan attempted to ventilate, but no air would move into the boy. She opened his mouth and saw no food, only swollen tissue.

Emily brought the stretcher.

They lifted him to the cot. Emily rushed the stretcher toward the ambulance with Megan hanging onto the side, compressing the boy's chest, and the mother running behind.

"Ma'am, we're going to take him to Sacred Heart," Megan said, lifting the stretcher wheels as Emily slid the stretcher into the ambulance. "You'll have to follow in your own car."

She nodded. "You can make it better? You can bring him back?"

Megan climbed into the truck. "We'll try." She called the code over the radio.

With the doors closed, Megan continued compressions. "Where are the firefighters?"

Emily turned on the monitor and adjusted the settings. "I don't know." She applied the pads to his chest, and they lifted their hands and read the monitor.

"V. tach," Megan said.

Emily nodded. "Shocking on three. Two, three."

The boy's shoulders shrugged with the charge.

Megan shook her head.

"Damn," Emily muttered, restarting compressions.

A knock and the ambulance door opened. Turnout gear appeared.

"It's about time!" Emily said to the firefighter. "Lose the helmet and coat and do compressions."

"I'll drop a tube," Megan said, moving to the captain's chair.

As the firefighter took over compressions, Emily opened the intraosseous case and drilled a line.

Megan slid the laryngoscope in place and held the ET tube ready. She examined the boy's throat. "I don't see cords. Cricoid pressure, please."

"Can you slide it in without visualizing?" Emily asked, applying pressure to the boy's throat with one hand and digging through the drug box with the other.

Megan attempted to place the tube. "No, it's too swollen." She shook her head. "I still can't get it. You try."

They switched places, and Emily attempted to intubate. "I can't get it either."

"Get ready to shock again," Megan said. "V. fib. Shock on three." Emily and the firefighter lifted their hands. "I'm clear. You're clear. Two. Three." She pressed the button, and the boy shrugged.

Emily sighed. "Nothing."

"Compressions," Megan said. The firefighter complied.

"We need an airway," Emily said.

Megan climbed over her and opened the cabinet. "I'm gonna cric. He needs it. There's no reason why I shouldn't," she said, mainly to herself.

She filled a syringe with saline and swabbed the skin of the boy's throat with betadine.

"Hold compressions," Megan directed. She inserted the needle into his throat and drew back carefully on the plunger. A red tinge swirled into syringe. Her stomach lurched.

Wrong place!

Bubbles entered the chamber, and her spirits lifted. She was in the correct place. An odd taste filled her mouth;

she had bitten into her lip.

Megan removed the syringe, held the cannula in place, and attached the bag. She squeezed and felt air enter the patient. "I've got it!" she said with a smile. The bag whined. "Compressions."

"Let me do it," Emily said, moving into position. "Can you drive us?" she asked the firefighter.

"Sure thing," he said and climbed out.

The bag groaned.

Megan examined the cannula and squeezed. "Wait," she muttered.

"What?"

The airway failed again. "This bag's a joke. It's not working. Air's not leaving."

"It's supposed to work," Emily said.

"It's not. Not at all," Megan said, frustrated. She pulled the bag from the adapter. Air slowly escaped. "Oh. Well, that's something."

The ambulance began to move.

"We need another option," Emily said.

Megan continued to ventilate, pulling the bag off for each long exhalation. "There's no other option. He's too little for a surgical trach. This is it." She remained crouched over the boy, never taking her eyes off the airway.

In a moment, the ambulance was flying down the highway as Emily continued compressions. Megan convinced herself the boy was pinking up on the edges, that his cyanosis was slightly less blue. Her eyes flicked to the heart monitor. Every time they could defibrillate, they stopped the truck, shocked, and wished they could move faster.

"Where's Richard?" Megan yelled up to the firefighter.

"He's on his way," he called back, "but he was out in

the county. We're going to beat him to the ER."

Megan ducked her head to look through the window. Five minutes to go.

The ambulance backed into the ER dock. "Come on," Megan said. "One more shock."

Emily pressed the button. The green line shook in jagged peaks with the defibrillation and a new repeating rhythm formed.

Megan dropped her fingers to the boy's carotid. "He's got a pulse!"

"Hell, yeah!"

Megan and Emily hurried inside and transferred care. Megan was mildly surprised that Dr. Patterson was not the receiving physician. The doctor, one she rarely worked with, maintained a stony frown. He pointed at the cannula in the boy's neck. "What is this monstrosity?"

"It's the best I could do," Megan said.

He flicked open his laryngoscope with a video screen and finagled a tube into the boy. "No difficulty for someone with skill," he declared.

Megan laughed. She threw her gloves into the trash and left the room, listening to the lovely repeating beep on the boy's heart monitor.

Emily followed her to the nurses' desk. "His comment was uncalled for. He only got that airway because of the shit ton of epi we gave."

"I hope his day is as pleasant as he is."

When the paperwork was filed, they drove down to Station 1 and restocked the ambulance.

Sitting on the jump bench, Emily finished loading the IV bucket and leaned back on the seat. "You're different, Megan."

Megan looked up as she rolled the monitor cords and

stuck new electrodes on the end. "What do you mean?"

"You're more confident in yourself and your abilities. More aggressive in care. You never would have done a needle cric before. You would have begged me to do it. And you would have chewed that doctor up and spit him out."

"He can think what he wants." She shrugged. "I did everything I could with what I had at the time. Everyone else in that room knew he was being a jackass."

"See? More confidence, less defensiveness. He changed you."

Megan slid the cabinet closed. "Divorce is a big deal. It's been a growing process. I guess Todd is—"

"I didn't mean Todd."

Megan studied the cables and thought of orange juice and fancy knots. She reached into her pocket and touched the Prusik cord.

"Why don't you call him?" Emily asked. "Or just text."

"No, I'm not going to do that."

"But why not? You still love him, right?"

Megan nodded and sat in the captain's chair. "I have too much baggage. It's better for him if I stay away."

"Really, Megan, things are going well for you. Todd's gone, and you've started school. It's like a whole new you."

"I don't make good decisions around Nathan. He's too easy to depend on. I get lax and lose situational awareness. You heard what happened. It was a nightmare."

"So don't work together. You can still date him."

Megan shrugged. "I'm not going to force it. Right now, I'm just going to focus on being me."

"Well, don't focus so much on yourself that you give up on this. You've rejected him twice. He's not going to ask again. You may have to take initiative if you want to get him back."

Chapter 15

BARRINGTON COMMUNITY COLLEGE
NOVEMBER 5, 2013. 2:15 PM

Megan took notes on a black-topped lab table.

" ... bacterial cells that vary widely in their shape, pleomorphic cells, should not be confused with cells misshapen due to environmental stresses ..."

Her phone vibrated in her backpack. She reached for it, her short hair tipping across her face. As she tapped the screen, she swept the strands back and reclipped her barrette:

```
BARRINGTON COUNTY HIGH-ANGLE RESCUE
TEAM.   BE   EN   ROUTE   TO   SUNSET
MOUNTAIN    STATE    PARK,    NORTH
ENTRANCE. FALLEN HIKER. 5 NOV 2013.
1415. BARRINGTON COUNTY EMA BLAST
TEXT SYSTEM.
```

Her phone vibrated again.

GILES MARTIN: ropes call u in?
MEGAN LORRY: sure. in class now
GILES MARTIN: sunset mtn st prk back access
MEGAN LORRY: be there asap

Megan slid her laptop into her bag. She walked quietly past the other students, smiled apologetically at the professor's raised eyebrow, and hurried to her car, feeling the adrenaline rush and a twinge of nerves. She told herself she was nervous because her training was about to be tested. But she knew it was because of the slim chance he would be there.

Megan drove with traffic. At a red light, she reached into the back seat and pulled out a Barrington EMS t-shirt. Changing her shirt without revealing anything important was the only useful skill she had learned in high school gym class.

At the state park entrance, a Clark County firefighter directed her to the correct access road that led to the scene. She drove up the glorified fire break, bumping and jostling until she wished for a four-wheel drive vehicle with larger tires and new shocks. She found a place to park, pulled her gear from the trunk, and went in search of Martin.

SUNSET MOUNTAIN STATE PARK
NOVEMBER 5, 2013. 2:45 PM

Nathan harnessed up and wound his way through the assembled trucks and trailers, looking for incident command. Fire personnel from Retton, Clark, and Barrington counties rushed around barking orders and polishing trucks in order to look their best for the evening news program. A fallen hiker. A high-angle rescue. This would certainly be the opening story.

Nathan walked across the staging area, allowing the occasional nod to personnel he recognized but ignoring the majority. He hadn't seen her in almost three months. The physical ache had finally subsided. The work incident inquiries had resolved in his favor. He had worked with his counselor and was having fewer dissociative episodes and no suicidal ideations. He had moved on. Even Sam had said he was amazed at how well Nathan had adjusted. But as he walked through the area, his nerves were taut.

Nathan found Martin pulling gear from the rescue trailer under the watchful gaze of the Clark County Emergency Management Agency Director.

"Nathan! Good to see you!" Martin said, shaking Nathan's hand and slapping his shoulder. "We've missed your expertise at practice."

"Sorry about that, but I'd like to help however I can."

"I'll take you up on it. Jack, do you know Nathan Thompson? He's our cave technician. A real specialist."

"Nice to meet you," the director said. Nathan nodded. "Martin, that makes four, right? You, Lorry, Thomas, and Nathan, here."

"Yep. We can pack in." Martin looked to Nathan. "Clark County is up at the scene now. Everyone else is waiting near the trailhead. It'll be about a mile hike into the forest."

"Any chance of ATVs?" Nathan asked.

Martin grinned. "You've never hiked the red diamond have you?"

"Ah, no."

Martin shook his head. "There's no way anything but

foot traffic could get down there."

"One casualty?"

"Yeah. Guy just got too close to the edge. Oh, there's Gerald. Excuse me," Martin hailed a passing firefighter.

Nathan took an extra rope bag. "Who's this Lorry guy? I know I've heard the name somewhere. I can't place him, though."

"Beats me," said Jack. "Barrington guy, I think."

Nathan shrugged. "All right. I'm heading to the access road."

"Stay safe."

Nathan saw Thomas at the trailhead. "Thomas!"

"Hey, Nathan! I wondered if you'd respond," he said. "I'm glad you did." They shook hands.

"Who's this new guy—Lorry? What training does he have?"

Thomas smirked. "She's walking this way. Ask her yourself."

Nathan turned around. She was still halfway across the field, but there was no mistaking her. Every feeling he had ever had for her came rushing back. He was grateful for the distance she had yet to walk; he needed the time to master himself and think of something intelligent to say.

Megan walked close enough to lock eyes with him. The blush on her cheeks made the corners of his mouth lift. She had been pretty before; now, she was the most bewitching woman he had ever seen. A healthy weight again, no more dark circles. She had cut her hair. And if she was Megan Lorry, then she was free of Todd and single.

Unless she's seeing someone else.

His heart sank. The thought seemed logical. There was no way a gorgeous, confident woman like that would still be single. He wondered whom he'd have to challenge in order to prove himself.

She was almost in speaking distance. He prepared to greet her, his heart racing.

Martin cut between them. "Get on the trail!" he shouted, marching to the narrow break in the underbrush.

The moment shattered, Nathan forgot what to say.

"Um, after you," he said, holding his hand toward the trail.

That was cheesy.

She stepped into the shadows. "Thank you."

He followed her as she walked behind Martin and Thomas. He missed her ponytail.

"How've you been?" she asked without turning around.

"Fine."

"Still with Retton?"

"Yeah. And you're still with Barrington?" he asked.

Grinning, she looked back over her shoulder. 'Barrington EMS' was written across her back.

Moron.

"Oh. Yeah," he said. "I just got off a 36-hour shift. I was asleep when the page went out. I guess I'm still a little out of it."

"That's a great frame of mind for high-angle," she said. "I was in class. It's about the same thing."

"What class?"

"Microbiology. At the college."

Bet it's some smart-ass college guy.

"Good for you," he said as the trail begin to climb. "How are classes going?"

"Pretty well. It's exhausting, though. I feel like I'm never home, and Charlie wishes he had more time with me."

Charlie, the Smart-Ass College Guy.

"But we train together a lot," she continued. "He's trying to get on the Search and Rescue team."

Charlie, the Smart-Ass College Guy: Rescue Extraordinaire.

Nathan viciously crunched a fallen tree limb under his sound foot. "I'm sure it'll all work out." He stopped. "Are you happy with him?"

Megan turned back and thought a moment. "Yeah. He's nice to have around."

They began hiking again. "You got your new harness," Nathan said. "It's very pink."

"Martin spoils me. I think he had it custom made. And this is the first chance I've had to use it. I missed practice last month because of class—no big deal. Martin ended up cancelling practice. I can't wait to try it out."

The trail became strenuous enough to quell conversation. Megan's boot slipped, and Nathan's hands jumped to her waist. He enjoyed every moment of contact, releasing her only after he was very certain she had her footing again.

Sorry, Charlie.

He chuckled to himself over his joke as they reached the top of the ridge.

"Are you laughing because I slipped?"

"No, I was just, um—That must be where we're going." He pointed along the ridgeline to a group of Clark County firefighters.

The high-angle team hiked across the top of Buzzard Cliff. Nathan looked out at the yellow and brown blanket of leaves that covered the mountainside and the surrounding view. The horizon was hazy, and the sky had the fresh, cloudless look of late fall. A fragrant, flowery scent met him as the breeze blew. It reminded him of spring.

"Oh, no. Not him," muttered Megan.

A Clark County paramedic walked toward them along the ridge. "Hey, Megan!" Ron said. "I haven't seen you since clinicals."

"You graduated. Congratulations," she said. "Excuse me, I need to get to work." She tried to move past him.

"My offer for dinner still stands," Ron said as Martin approached.

Megan's shoulders dropped. "I'm not interested, Ron."

"She's seeing someone," Nathan said.

Megan lifted her eyebrows.

Ron squinted. "You're seeing someone?"

Megan looked at Nathan with a bemused expression. "Apparently so." She snapped on her helmet.

"All right, everyone," Martin said. "Let's get to work."

The team circled up for the briefing. Ron and the fire squirrels scampered around them, trying to look terribly busy with important, mission-critical tasks.

"Our patient is Mr. Bertand," Martin said. "He and his buddy were hiking along the ridge when he got too close to the edge and tumbled over. He is 40 feet below on a ledge, in and out of responsiveness. We need to get him in a harness and a basket and bring him to the ground, 65 feet below the ledge. A team will meet us at the bottom to pack him out. You and you," he said pointing to Nathan and Megan, "on line two. I'll be on line one with Thomas belaying—Get off my rope!" he shouted. Heads turned, and Ron stumbled back, high stepping his boots. Nathan smirked; Megan rolled her eyes. "Get moving!" Martin said.

"Do you want to go on the line?" Nathan asked.

Megan nodded. "Is that okay?"

"Sure," he said, putting on his rappelling gloves. Megan pulled off her helmet. He noticed the flowery scent again. "Did you change your shampoo?"

"Yeah, the other was too expensive. Why?"

"I liked the peaches."

Megan silently adjusted the chin strap. Nathan wondered if he had angered her.

"You'll have to finance it, then," she said, replacing her helmet.

Nathan smiled. "Send me a prospectus, and I'll consider it." She ducked her chin and walked away to ready the basket.

Hey, Charlie, mind if I cut in?

Martin sidled up to Nathan. "I didn't know Megan was seeing anyone. Who is it?"

Nathan hesitated, surprised she had managed to keep her boyfriend a secret from Martin. "Some guy named Charlie."

Martin blinked and looked at Thomas, whose shoulders shook. The two burst into loud laughter. "Charlie is her dog!" Martin said. "She's training him for the SAR team!"

Megan walked over and picked up the rope. "What's so funny?"

"Nothing," Nathan said, quickly. "It's nothing—"

"He thought Charlie was your boyfriend!" Thomas said.

Megan shook her head. "Good grief." Thomas and Martin redoubled their laughter.

Nathan cringed but found it hard to be unhappy with the situation.

Charlie, you just earned yourself an entire box of biscuits.

Martin nodded to Thomas. "You got me?"

"You're good to go. Feeding belay," said Thomas. Martin leaned back and rappelled down the side of the cliff.

Megan wound the rope around her rescue eight. "So that's why you said what you did to Ron." She flipped a carabiner in her hand and clipped the eight to her harness.

"I'm sorry," Nathan said.

"Don't think you're going to get out of it that easily," Megan said, double-checking the equipment. "You cost me a fancy dinner."

"You said you weren't interested."

She lifted her chin with an impish smile. "I was playing hard to get."

"I'll take you to dinner," he said. "Will you forgive me then?"

"I'll think about it," she said. "I'm on belay."

"Belay on. I've got you," he said and smiled to himself. *I've got you.*

Megan moved to the edge. "On rappel."

He nodded. "Rappel away."

Megan leaned back and disappeared over the edge.

BUZZARD CLIFF
NOVEMBER 5, 2013. 3:15 PM

Megan took a deep breath and focused. Below her, Martin contacted the patient. His voice murmured amid the victim's groans, and she heard Martin's rescue straps clip into place as she slowly walked down the cliff.

Megan jolted left. "Shit!"

She stopped her descent.

"What is it?" Martin asked.

She pulled at the webbing. "My thigh strap broke!"

A lurch.

Scream.

Megan's body dangled from the harness,
the waist strap caught on her chest.

"Doll!"

Megan pried her eyes open.

The ground below.

Pounding.

Fall. I'm gonna fall.

Tried to swallow. Breathe.

"What the hell's going on?" Nathan shouted.

"Shut up!" she cried.

Megan moved her leg in a slow circle, searching for the rope. When she found it, she drew her knee up, caught the rope in her hand, and wrapped it several times around her boot. Standing on the rope and holding tension with one hand, she withdrew her Prusik cord from her pocket with the other. With an adequate loop, she slid the cord around her waist and reached between her thighs to grasp the lower loop section. She made three loops, and with a smooth motion, she captured all three into a carabiner, making an impromptu Swiss seat.

"You got it, Doll. Clip in."

Megan clipped the cord to her belay line D-ring.

"I'm okay!" she called up the cliff, her voice cracking. "I'm off rappel!"

"Quit your John Wayne shit and get back on your line!" Nathan yelled.

"I can't!"

"Both of her leg straps are broken," Martin called as Megan removed the rappel line from her rescue eight. "She's hanging by the waist. Belay her to the ground."

"Can you get to her?" Nathan asked.

"No, I have the casualty."

"Belay me down!" Megan shouted.

"All right!"

Megan slowly descended the cliff face as Nathan fed the belay line. She didn't breathe until her boots met dirt. "Line two on the ground!" she yelled, unclipping from the line. She heard Martin repeat the call.

Megan collapsed onto the moldy, wet leaf litter, reveling in the earth's solidness. Her breathing quieted, and she stared up at the cliff face that towered over her. She laughed in relief, in the absence of terror, in the reprieve of death. Her overtaxed muscles protested the gales that shook her, and she rolled to her side, gasping and giggling. With a last sigh, she blessed the poison ivy next to her and the root that jabbed her side.

My hand hurts.

She lifted her arm and was amazed that her fingers, blanched white with exertion, still gripped her rescue eight. She laughed again and relaxed her hand, the heavy piece falling to the ground beside her.

Megan sat up, rested her elbows on her knees, and surveyed the forest. The trees were dark with moisture, and the sunlight broke through the withering canopy in uneven beams. Taking off her helmet, she sized up her options. She saw no trail but knew the white blazes should be down the hill and to the right. She determined to meet the transport team and direct them to the site.

I'll be covered in ticks if I don't get up.

Megan stood and unclipped the waist buckle: the safety buckle that had saved her life in a harness that had almost killed her. As she pulled off one shoulder strap and then the other, the reality of her near death rolled over her.

Her movements grew faster, stronger, until with a cry, she threw the harness to the ground and leaned on her knees, panting.

The edge of the thigh strap lay on the leaves. She picked it up and stared. The end of the strap was smooth, straight, even, except for a tuft of frayed webbing at one side. She grabbed the other strap. It, too, was straight and even with only a clump of polyester threads on the edge. The straps had been cut, but not all the way through. Cut just enough to support her weight for a few minutes on the line. Before breaking.

Who would cut my harness?

Only someone on the high-angle team would have had access to her harness and then only during practice. But the last practice had been cancelled, so the only person who would have had access to the trailer since the arrival of her harness was Martin. Megan cringed.

No, it wasn't him.

Though she saw no other possibilities, she refused to believe Martin would ever try to hurt her. He would be furious to see the straps. He would rant and rage and get to the bottom of the matter. That's the Martin she knew. The Martin she knew cared about her safety.

Megan pulled her Prusik cord free of the D-ring before lugging her harness back onto her shoulders. Snapping it in place, she rested her hand on the buckle for a brief moment of gratitude. She found her rescue eight in the leaves, looped it onto her Prusik, and shoved it into her pocket. Breaking a stick into pieces, she set a trail marker to show which way she was going. After all, the Martin she knew would have her skin if he had to call out Search and Rescue to find her.

With a last look at the cliff, Megan walked down the

hill, her helmet dangling in her hand. Her stride was quick and bounding, but her anxiety congealed within her. She replayed the event in her mind. Rappelling down the mountain, calling to Nathan—

Megan slowed her pace, a silly little smile dawning on her lips. She had not had a spare moment to think about him. Butterflies quivered in her stomach. She remembered how nervous she had been when she saw him in the field, how stupid she had felt making small talk on the trail, how her heart had pounded when he had touched her waist. And he was going to take her to dinner. She stopped.

What am I going to wear?

She looked down at her boots. They were caked with mud. Leaves stuck to her clothes, and her arms were orange with clay. She smelled of sweat and the forest and could only imagine what her hair looked like.

Anything but this.

The forest opened to a dirt trail. Megan saw a tree with a white blaze.

Almost there.

A stick snapped, and footsteps approached.

Todd walked into view.

Megan dropped her helmet. "What are you doing here?"

He smirked. "You always screw up everything." He walked toward her.

Her body went numb. "You cut my harness."

"Hell, yeah, I did. You always leave your stuff lying around. I waited until Martin was out of sight. Once it was cut, all I had to do was wait for the call."

"But you had to turn in your radio."

He held up his phone. "I still get the blast texts. I got the call the same time you did. I hiked up your favorite trail and sat in your favorite spot, ready to watch the show."

"Why? What did I ever do to you?"

"You ruined my life. If you hadn't pissed me off over and over again, none of this would have happened! None of it! This is all because you couldn't just do what you were supposed to do. You always make me lose my temper! If you hadn't made me—"

"I didn't make you do anything! You chose to act that way!"

Todd lunged at her. Megan darted back. He tackled her, forcing her to the ground. Her head on the rocks, his hands on her throat.

Not again.

"Not again!" she shrieked. She sank her teeth into his shoulder. He bellowed. She scratched at the dirt, found a rock, pounded it against him, pounding him back.

"Not again!"

She scrambled to her feet. Her hand met cord. His eyes startled wide. She swung her rescue eight, the heavy steel slamming into his head. She drew her arm back.

"Not again!"

She swung and hit. Anger, rage, pound for pound, every and all. His blood on her cord, his blood on her hands.

Megan stood over him.

"Never again."

She dropped her knee to his back and leaned to check his airway. She heard air movement and pulled his hands together as she dropped the eight from the Prusik. She wound the cord tightly around his wrists.

"I may do many things wrong, but I can tie a damn knot!"

Megan sat on the trail, her back against a tree. She rubbed her knuckle over her mouth and spat blood on the ground. She heard the chatter of radio traffic, the shuffle of feet on the path, the clink and rattle of equipment. Firefighters she didn't recognize came into view and stopped, stunned. She observed them, detached, separate. They didn't know what she knew. She would wait.

Richard pushed by them. "Let me through! Good God, Megan!" He pointed at Todd. "Did you do this?"

She spat again.

"Get a stretcher!" Richard yelled at the firefighters. "Get him out of here! And get a deputy! You three, get up to the cliff!"

The firefighters jumped into motion, their movements and voices swirling around her. Megan put her head down on her arms, seeking darkness. The sounds grew and parted, split in two, by the subtle shuffle of a slightly irregular footstep from the direction of the cliff.

Megan stood and moved to the comfort of his chest, the pressure of his arms. Nathan held her and shielded her from prying eyes and questions. The trail grew quiet, only the voices of Richard and a deputy reached her ears. Megan lifted her head. Todd was gone, and Nathan's shirt was stained with blood and tears. She tried to brush the spots away.

He placed his hand over hers. "It's all right. I had trouble finding you."

"Again? I set trail markers. Didn't you see them?"

"No, I just assumed you'd follow the white blazes."

"Did Martin get the casualty down?" she asked.

Nathan nodded. "He was on his way when I went to find you."

"That's good. He—then who belayed you?"

Nathan looked away. "I belayed myself."

"You self-belayed? All your fussing at me about John Wayne shit! And you just haul off and—"

Nathan kissed the corner of her mouth.

Megan caught her breath. "That doesn't fix anything."

He smiled. "It fixes everything."

Epilogue

BARRINGTON COUNTY JUSTICE COMPLEX
APRIL 11, 2014. 2:35 PM

"All rise!"

The courtroom echoed with a rumble of movement. Nathan stood and took Megan's hand. He tried to catch her eye, but she refused and pressed her lips into a thin line.

The white-haired judge sat and shuffled his papers. "Be seated. Has the jury reached a verdict?"

"We have, Your Honor," said the foreman.

"Will the bailiff please hand me the jury's verdict?" The bailiff complied, and tension reigned as the judge read the paper and sent it back to the foreman. "The defendant will rise."

At the front of the courtroom, Todd Henderson stood.

"On the charge of rape in the second degree, we find the defendant not guilty."

Nathan's stomach clenched as if punched. He put his arm around Megan's shoulders. Her body was stiff and tense.

"On the charge of aggravated assault with a dangerous weapon, we find the defendant not guilty."

Murmurs through the courtroom. Megan sank against him. Martin reached over and took her hand.

"On the charge of aggravated battery with a dangerous weapon, we find the defendant guilty."

The murmurs warmed.

"On the charge of tampering with public equipment, we find the defendant guilty."

Silence returned.

"On the charge of violation of conditions of bond, we find the defendant guilty.

"On the charge of simple assault, we find the defendant guilty.

"On the charge of simple battery, we find the defendant guilty."

The jury foreman paused. Nathan pressed Megan's head against his shoulder and leaned his chin on her hair. The scent of peaches wafted to his nose. He kissed the top of her head and tried to relax his jaw. His hand was a fist at his side. The key verdict.

"On the charge of attempted murder, in the first degree," read the foreman, "we find the defendant guilty."

Nathan's head tipped back, and he released his fist. Megan's arms reached around his neck as she cried. He held her tightly, relishing the freedom of finality. Martin patted his shoulder, and he nodded his thanks. Others gathered around them. Richard, Sam, Emily and Matt with Annabelle. There were medics, firefighters, police officers, deputies, and dispatchers not only from Barrington but the surrounding counties as well. Some he recognized, most he did not.

For a while, they accepted the kind words, handshakes, and hugs of their friends. Megan slipped her hand into his. He winked down at her, and she smiled, but weariness wrinkled her brow and tipped her head against his arm. He led her from the courtroom, and they walked toward the parking lot, past the plaza fountain.

Nathan stopped and withdrew his pocket change. He jingled it in his hand, searched through it very carefully, and threw it all into the water.

"What was that for?" Megan asked.

Nathan watched the water as it arced into the air and fell into the pool. "The end of an old life." He drew her close and kissed her. "The beginning of a new one together."

"It's not really new."

He grinned. "Don't knock my symbolism."

Nathan slid his hand back into his pocket to the one object that remained. He rolled the ring between his fingers and hoped the time would soon be right.

Tones dropped.

They watched the on-duty medics rush to the parking lot and leap into the ambulance. It sped away with a burst of lights and sirens.

***

CAITLYN ARMISTEAD

ACKNOWLEDGEMENTS

It takes the population of a small country to write a book. And probably a communist one at that, with overcrowding and a dissatisfied undercurrent roiling of rebellion, ready to riot at the first spark of blank page.

Throng placation requires frequent influxes of verbs, strong and active, with nouns, specific, and mandated syntactic plotting at midnight alongside an Aaron and Hur of sleep deprivation and gluten-free doughnuts with powdered sugar and not those heathen ones with cream or chocolate or jelly. To have my caffeine and drink it, too.

I need those rabble rousers. Their encouragement. Their support. Their laughter and kind words and praise. I need their goading when I'm tired. Their dissatisfaction when I'm lazy. To tell me I'm wrong when I want to be right. To pry my hands away from my face/to face/two-faced ugliness I must see.

Alan, Kimberly, Holly, and Kirsten.

There are no words to describe my gratitude for your help and, most importantly, your friendship. I know. I've looked.

Neil Brown, Eric Johnson, Charity Dawn Stephen-Whiteaker, Lauren Jinkensen, Courtney Kalista, Alice Stark, Nicole Murray, and Brandon Jagielski.

Without your life experiences and extreme skills and your willingness to share them, this book would not have been possible.

Bunny, Ben, Marshall, June, Mandy, Marianne, and Cali.

Your open ears, your hawkish eyes, your blazing red pens. For them I am grateful. And stronger. And hungry for more.